# WRAP HER IN LIGHT

# WRAP HER IN LIGHT

A Novel of Ankhesenamon

Sandra Adelson

WILLIAM MORROW AND COMPANY, INC.
New York   1981

Copyright © 1981 by Sandra Adelson

Grateful acknowledgment is made for permission to use selected poems and prayers of ancient Egypt as translated in the following sources:

*The Splendor That Was Egypt*, by Margaret A. Murray, © 1963, 1949 Elsevier/Nelson Books.

*Ancient Egyptian Religion*, copyright 1948 by Columbia University Press.

All rights reserved. No part of this book may be reproduced or utilized in any form or by any means, electronic or mechanical, including photocopying, recording or by any information storage and retrieval system, without permission in writing from the Publisher. Inquiries should be addressed to William Morrow and Company, Inc., 105 Madison Ave., New York, N. Y. 10016.

**Library of Congress Cataloging in Publication Data**

Adelson, Sandra.
    Wrap her in light.

    1. Egypt—History—To 322 B.C.—Fiction.
I. Title.
PS3551.D43W7        813'.54        80-21014
ISBN 0-688-03753-4

Printed in the United States of America

First Edition

1 2 3 4 5 6 7 8 9 10

BOOK DESIGN BY MICHAEL MAUCERI

*To the Committee—*

    Bruce for technical assistance
    Marcia for critical judgments
    Rose for translating hieroglyphs
    And, especially, Mel for all the
        above
    —and much more

*To Acknowledge:*

With gratitude the editorial consultation and assistance generously and unstintingly offered by Steve and Jo Anne Blackwelder of J&S Literary Services

# PROLOGUE 1360 B.C.

In the Valley of the Kings, where the royal dead of Egypt slept, the soft rays from the disk that brightened the eastern horizon turned the bleached cliffs pink and gold.

In the city of Thebes, the morning sun brushed the massive pillars of the temple of Amon-Ra, burnished the gilt inscriptions and brought the glazed red tiles of the streets to glowing life.

In the palace garden, beds of lotuses opened their fragrant blossoms to the sun. The warm rays moved up the palace walls, streamed into the windows and touched the sleeping body of the queen with a special brightness. As Ankhesenamon opened her eyes to meet the morning, her lips formed the words, "O living Aten, Creator of Life, stay in my heart."

She was much better now. Today she could summon the strength to rise.

Immediately servants surrounded her, brushed her lustrous black hair until it shone, outlined her eyes with kohl so that their natural blue gleamed like lapis. They rubbed her body with fragrant unguents, rouged the nipples of her breasts a rosy pink and tied her linen dress tight across her waist.

Sephy, her favorite, held out the jewelry box. "Highness, shall you choose the flowered diadem?" Her voice was low and coaxing.

The carved ivory box opened to a glitter of gold and silver. The queen reached for a tray of scarab bracelets. Suddenly her arm stopped in mid-motion. The two women saw it at the same time: his necklace. Hastily Sephy tried to replace the tray, but Ankhesenamon's hand, icy and trembling, clamped on her wrist.

"Leave us," she managed, dismissing the other servants with a quick stabbing motion. Then she stood very still, letting Sephy hold her against those warm breasts that had comforted her all her life. Finally, with a shuddering sigh, she lifted the gold necklace of Nekhbet, the vulture goddess.

"Oh, Sephy, how did we forget this? It was his favorite." Her voice was steady and she breathed gratefully. "Thank you, O merciful Aten, for not abandoning me, though I am forbidden to say your name."

She studied the pectoral in her hand. The eyes of the vulture, in black obsidian, stared boldly up at her, just as they had stared at him a few short weeks ago. How he had loved it! That was how he had finally learned to read, from the necklace the bird wore around its neck, decorated with his name, Tutankhamon. She smiled, thinking of it. What an awful student he'd been. So many times they had punished him because he didn't know his lessons. She remembered how she'd sneaked him candy or honey-drenched fruit when he had been forbidden sweets and how they'd share secretly, giggling at those they tricked. He was such a spirited, naughty boy—and such a loyal one. He had never told who brought him the treats, though they had beaten him for it.

"Place this with the Wishing Cup," she told Sephy, reluctantly pulling herself back to the present, where his body stretched lifeless and cold on its bier in the Embalmer's Tent. "I want the necklace with him in the tomb. I'll bring them both to Kuya."

"My queen," the servant reminded her fearfully, "have you forgotten? The grand vizier, Ay, waits for you. He joins you, today, for the morning meal."

"Thank you, Sephy."

Her back very straight, Ankhesenamon walked to the south courtyard. The table was set near the small pool. Ay was studying the newly flowered papyrus.

"My child, I'm glad to see you so improved." He kissed her forehead as he would an infant's and she willed herself to submit. She was not a child, though he might wish it.

"Thank you, Uncle." She would not give him his titles, would remind him they were bound by ties of blood.

"This time of mourning draws soon to a close," he went on.

She picked up the sweet shat-cake and sipped her beer. "There are fifty days left."

"Nonetheless, you must begin to think—" He saw her eyes and stopped. "I hear you're very much involved in preparations for the funeral."

"I'm posing for the goddess who'll protect him in the afterlife."

"Do you think that's wise?"

"Why not?"

"It's in the style of your father's court."

She rose. "Do you dare criticize him to me? You forget yourself, Uncle. He was Pharaoh."

Silence stretched between them. Ay's eyes narrowed dangerously.

"He almost ruined Egypt!" he charged; then more calmly: "No! No more of this. Sit down, Hesen." He used the name of her childhood, the name her mother had crooned, the name her husband had moaned with his dying breath. She sat. His glance was piercing. "You're not a fool. Don't mistake me for one."

"I don't," she returned evenly, meeting his eyes.

"Very well." He paused, then got right to the point. "I've heard Memy of Bubastis visits you later this week."

"He was my lord's close friend."

"He's also a general in the army."

"Yes." Hesen preferred it this way, things cleanly spelled out between them.

Ay was saying, "He won't come. And I'll speak to Sephy after we conclude—I'm sending her back to her family. She comes from Zehut, doesn't she?"

Sephy! Her only friend at Thebes, who had cared for her since childhood. She drew a breath but kept it under control. He wouldn't guess how shaken she felt. "You can't feel so powerful if you fear a servant." Her voice was crisp and scornful.

Ay held up his hand. "I know you very well, Hesen. For all your graces, you're willful and headstrong, and I don't want you plotting with that overbearing nurse of yours." As he spoke, his eyes raked her body, and she saw them glitter as they lingered on her breasts, visible beneath the thin folds of fabric. She sat motionless, her head high.

"I never forget," he continued, "that you hold in that graceful body many treasures, the richest of which is the crown of Egypt. Consider yourself under my protection."

"Your prisoner, you mean."

"My honored queen," he corrected. "And to see that Your Highness lacks no comfort, Tey will now be your chief servant."

"Your wife."

"She can be trusted to guarantee your well-being. Come now, Hesen, let's not disagree any longer. I'm not a cruel man, you know that. While I may have removed Sephy, I won't leave you friendless. We share an affection for one person we both trust—who has just returned to Thebes. See Senumet as often as you wish."

She lowered her eyes so he couldn't see the sudden blaze of joy. Senumet, the love of her heart. In Thebes.

He took her silence for assent. "I won't keep you any longer, Hesen. You may continue your preparations for the funeral." He strode from the courtyard.

And still she sat motionless, while inside her every nerve ending screamed. She was a prisoner. . . . And yet, it was nothing new. She'd been little more than a prisoner these past nine years. Queen though she had been, and her husband Pharaoh, and though they had bowed to her—the simple peasants of Egypt, accepting it—it had been a pageant, no more. Pharaoh had been a child. Only recently had he been able to claim her as his wife, even then needing all the arts she'd learned to guide him between her legs, to take his seed into her body, to teach him that joy was still possible. A boy . . . sweet, however badly damaged by the horrors that had made him king. And the child, her child, who might have saved them—

Suddenly pain, sharp and fierce, coursed through her, and she cried aloud . . . and drowned her cry in the marble goblet. The memories were returning—all of them—the anguish, yes, but also the love. For nine years she had not dared to think of Senumet, lest her life become unendurable. Now that she was to see him again, so many images came flooding back she could hardly bear their sweet pain.

Enough! It had taken a long time, but she'd finally learned discipline. She could command the wild clamor inside her to subside. Unsteadily she gathered her basket and got to her feet. There were still duties she owed her lord, and they would be done and done well. Nothing must deter her from this last tribute.

Servants of the royal household slipped behind her as she left the palace and stepped into the blazing day. She hated Thebes, and now she would never leave it. Thebes—city of the dark gods and their oppressive temples, their hooded priests. In her heart she knew they had not only murdered her father and her husband, but they had destroyed the fresh, bright dream that had almost changed Egypt's face.

She went to the funerary tent, hastily erected near the palace, and opened the door to the room where they were readying the articles to accompany Tutankhamon in the afterlife. The artisans clad in their half-kilts stopped their work and bowed. Kuya, the foreman, greeted her:

"Highness, we're beginning to ship the statuary across the river to the valley. They're ready for your inspection."

She studied first the black statue of Anubis, the jackal god, Guardian of the Tomb, resting on his gilt pylon. As his gold eyes ground fiercely into hers, she could sense the strength of his teeth and the tearing power of the silver claws that gripped the pedestal.

"I like that," she approved. "Anubis will destroy my lord's enemies."

"And when he wakes, Pharaoh may rest on his throne once again."

Kuya led her past the hundreds of small, meticulously carved shwabati-servants, ready to tend her husband faithfully in the afterlife, around the gleaming chariots and the alabaster canopic chest with its four luminescent stoppers, each carved in Tutankhamon's likeness. Kuya stopped in front of Pharaoh's gold throne. Since Hesen would see it only once more—on the day they sealed up his body forever—she tried to memorize it. Both of them—he and she—were sculpted on its back, clad in their silver robes and bright jewelry and crowns of office. He was lounging gracefully on a curved seat; she was oiling his shoulder with fragrant unguents; above them shone the sun disk of the Aten, sending down blessed rays that ended in loving hands, hands that held the life-symbol ankh to their nostrils. Hesen traced the golden rays of the Aten with her finger. She'd not see them again . . . ever. She pulled her finger away.

"I've two more things I want you to take." She gave Kuya the vulture pectoral and the alabaster lotus cup. "I want the necklace to be closest of all the jewelry to Pharaoh's body," she directed. "One moment more," she commanded softly. Bending her head to the marble cup in Kuya's hand, she touched her lips to her lord's name, written in ebony on the rim. " 'Tutankhamon,' " she read, " 'beloved of Amon-Ra, Lord of the Two Lands. May your ka live and may you spend millions of years sitting with your face to the North Wind, your two eyes beholding happiness.' "

She asked of Kuya, "Do you remember how he hunted in the reeds, his hand faster than the ibex?"

"We would watch you too, my queen, at his side, quick to spot the fattest duck."

Tears stung her eyes and her lips trembled. Kuya hastily looked down at the offerings she had given him and backed away. "I'll take special care of these, my lady."

She took a deep breath and motioned to the Embalmer's Room. A servant, his eyes averted, opened the door, and she stepped through. "Leave me," she commanded the workers inside. When they were gone, she permitted herself to look at the bolts of fine linen they would use to wrap his body. She lifted an end, approved the delicacy of his embroidered name. Then she frowned. The gold casings for his fingers had already been prepared, she saw, but they lacked shape. She made a mental note. She moved to the worktable, where the gold mask to be placed over his head and shoulders was being fashioned. The features were already defined; and the eyes—of darkest obsidian, outlined in lapis—burned into her own. The thin membrane of his mouth had been hammered out, and she touched it with her finger. His lips were full and tender, as in life, but cold.

"Stop it," she told herself. "You are queen."

She pulled her eyes to the funerary couch. Surfaced in gold leaf, it rose four feet high; at its feet the two fierce and snarling horses bared their ivory teeth. On it rested the body of her husband, covered with bags of linen-wrapped natron. She reached out and pulled back the thin woven cloth and looked into his face.

Mummification had already begun. The rounded flesh of his cheeks had sunk and tightened, exposing the bone structure beneath, and suddenly, although he had been dead only three weeks and had lived only twenty years, she saw the old man he would never be. Her fingers trembling, she touched the wound on his left temple. Dry now, she could see the full and terrible extent of it. Aten above her, it had almost split his head in two! Oh, had she only gone hunting with him that day, the fatal blow might never have been struck!

She sank to her knees. "Forgive me, my husband, who was my true and faithful lord. I did not betray you in word or deed all those years. And I will see," she promised fiercely, "that your spirit returns and that all earthly pleasures are yours again."

She gripped the post until her body stopped heaving and she could rise. Studying his face again, she thought: He'd know the vulture pectoral that Kuya would place around his neck, and it would comfort him when he woke. And her own face—on the statue of the Goddess Selket—would strengthen him and remind him of what they had shared.

Her own past would disappear with him into the tomb. Only she would remember. And Senumet.

Purposefully she walked from the tent to the sculptors' compound. There she covered her hair with the high linen kerchief, knotted the pleated shawl under her right breast, allowed Hani to touch her royal person, hook the gold necklace, and help her mount the pedestal. Raised aloft, a sense of her own regality filled her—she was Ankhesenamon, Queen of Egypt, taking the pose of the Goddess Selket. She stretched out her slender arms in a protective curve, turned her head toward what would be the entrance to the tomb, her eyes alert, as Selket's must eternally be, for intruders.

Hani kept up a running commentary as he chipped at the block of wood. "My lady, you'll be all gold, except for the kohl marks on your eyes . . . if you permit. Ah, your eyes are so beautiful, your features so perfectly fashioned. . . . Turn your head a little . . . so. Oh, the line of your neck! A marvel! If you will, I must stop a moment to absorb."

He was in love with her, of course. They all were. She had grown accustomed to it. Really, it had nothing to do with her—it was simply that she looked like her mother, Queen Nefertiti, and there could be no greater beauty than that.

But her patience began to wear thin. "May we start again, Hani?" The stupid man was just staring at her.

"Of course, my lady, except . . . there's a feeling missing—a certain tension. I want to capture you at the moment before movement begins."

Did he understand nothing of what this was costing her? "I don't know what you're talking about," she snapped.

"Really, My Lady Hesen, how you've changed." The voice came from behind her. "You always knew everyone's heart."

Only her long years of rule kept her from running across the room. Her heart leaped, would choke her, it seemed, yet she heard her own composed voice returning, "Can it be my friend—almost brother—from the past? Can it be Senumet?" Her head turned slightly, but she was alabaster. She thought she must faint.

"My lady!" Hani interrupted urgently. "Like that! The line—the line! I must capture it!"

He worked frenziedly, while her body trembled with the effort of holding back, a torment in which time lost meaning. But when, finally, he was through and she was free to move, she held the pose a moment longer. *I will know,* she thought, *the moment I see his eyes. Help me, O living Aten, to be strong if he is lost to me.*

She turned.

Oh, he was older. There were bitter lines at his mouth, and his forehead was creased. Had she done that to him? But his eyes, more knowing than in the past—hard, almost—were filled now with love . . . for her.

They walked through the palace garden, for once blessedly free of servants, side by side, not touching. The very air between them sparked dangerously. If his hand should brush against hers, Hesen felt certain, she would burst into flame. Her heart was so full she didn't know where to begin.

"How goes it with you, Senumet?" she said at last, inadequately. "They don't speak of you to me."

"I'm now chief ambassador to your uncle, Ay."

"You're a very important man."

He turned to look at her, and the darkness of his eyes smoldered. "Not important enough to have my heart's desire."

"Once you had a girl in Thebes. Are you married now?"

He laughed. Oh, it was a sound she had never thought to hear again. For a moment, her heart sang.

"I remember," he smiled, "that you told me once what terrible things would happen to me, were I to wed."

Her answering smile triumphed over her composure. "Oh, Senumet, how can I pass myself off as your wise sovereign if you recall these intemperate, awful things of me?"

"I've thought of you as nothing less than exactly that long before you even dreamed of being queen," he answered seriously.

She drew a sharp, trembling breath. She could say nothing.

"I had thought," he said finally, "there would be someone you'd particularly ask for."

She hesitated. When she spoke, her voice was so low he could hardly hear her. "The child, Senumet—you have knowledge of her?"

"She does well. She looks like you."

"That won't help her."

"She has your spirit."

"Does she remember me?"

"Stop punishing yourself. You had no choice."

They continued in silence, Hesen following blindly where he led. Suddenly she realized they had walked out of the garden and were heading toward an overgrown path. Her pulse raced. "The magic place," she breathed. "I haven't been here for so long—I couldn't bear to come without you."

She rushed forward, heedless of the untended tangle of growth, picking her way quickly along the half-forgotten, familiar length, brushing away vines, striking at branches that caught in her hair, climbing over fallen tree trunks with a strength she had not known she possessed. Senumet followed close behind, making sure that if she stumbled he'd be there to catch her. And finally, there it was: an abandoned structure out of Egypt's long history.

It might, in the distant past, have been a temple to an ancient god . . . or a plaything for noble children. Not so many years ago, as these things went, it had been a trysting place for lovers—two careless young lovers, who couldn't know how things would turn out. The building had been a ruin even then, almost eighteen years ago, and the intervening time had not been kind to it. It was roofless now, only the walls remained, and in spots they were crumbling. The light inside was dappled green and gold, sunlight filtered through the leaves of the sweet-smelling acacia trees. The sky overhead had the look of blue enamel.

She saw fresh reeds on the floor. "Senumet, you were here. You made it ready." The pulse in her throat pounded.

"My always-love"—his eyes devoured her—"your image has been shining in my heart all these years."

"Beloved—this room is so filled with our love. Voices from the past surround me. Dearest, I am light-headed with longing."

She loosened her gown, and it settled, bodiless, to the ground. Her breasts shimmered in the dancing light. His fingers trembling, he pressed her length, breast to thigh, against him and lowered her to the fragrant reeds.

"Now I know you again," she whispered into his shoulder, feeling that dearly loved body straining against her own. His sex, hard and demanding, pressed against her belly, and he knew just where to touch her so that fire blazed along her limbs.

She was conscious only of his fingers as they relearned the curve of her breasts, the line of her thighs, the warm, moist landscape beyond, and her body responded instantly with remembered and reborn passion. She held his head in her hands, felt his hair silken and fine through her graceful fingers. When she felt she could endure no more, she became aware that his mouth was moving over her neck to her ears and cheeks, her mouth. And then the weight of him was above her, full length, almost upon her hovering in exquisite yearning, savoring the last long moment before ecstasy.

He was huge now with his need of her, and she guided him between her thighs. Her arms, overtoned with gold, circled him; she gave herself up to sensations she had never thought to feel again. As their passion crested, tears of pure joy ran down her face. The waves of love grew calmer, inundating like the flood of the Nile.

He made her face him. Their eyes locked and she didn't attempt to hide her tears.

"What is it, beloved?"

"The one wish I can never have granted—to see for a lifetime the face of my true lord."

He smoothed her blue-shadowed hair. "How was it for you these past nine years?"

"He was becoming Pharaoh." She saw her own pain reflected in his face.

"Was he ever happy?" Senumet could never forget the poor, lost boy whose crown kept slipping over his forehead.

"I did everything I could." She hesitated, then said quickly, "We were man and wife at the end."

Seeing the question in her eyes, he touched her cheek affectionately. "I can only hope he knew some joy. I loved him too."

She sighed. "How long do we have together?"

"Today and two months more."

"Until the funeral," she said without emotion.

"Yes."

"Ay sent you to spy on me." There was no point in pretense. That had never been their way.

"He still trusts me, you know."

"We did that well, at least," she said grimly, thinking of all that had failed.

He kissed her—like her, half-believing that their wish for eternity could make it so. "We'll be left alone for these two months," he pleaded.

"In all their lives, many people don't have as much." She smiled at him bravely.

They sat silently, twined about each other. At last, he let himself say, "We must talk of this. Do you know what he wants?"

"Of course. He must marry me to be Pharaoh."

He sighed. What had he hoped she would say? She was a realist by necessity, as was he, and together they had expended the energies of their lives attempting to thwart the ambition of Ay.

"Senumet, do you still have affection for him?"

"I will always be his debtor."

"Pharaoh was murdered."

"I know."

"Then you know that Ay ordered it—or even did it himself." She saw the muscles in his jaw clench before she concluded: "I won't wed him."

He gripped her hands. "You must not think of taking your own life. I will not have you doomed to everlasting darkness."

"My love," she said, moved. "But there are some choices still. In the Kingdom of the Hittites, Shubbiluliuma rules. I will ask him to send me his son to marry. I will make *him* king."

"You wish me to send that message?" Senumet's face was cold.

"Whom else can I ask?"

"It will be giving power to a foreign prince."

"Ay's hands are stained with the blood of my father, of my husband, of Smenkhare. Besides, he would never let me replace Tey as chief wife. Once king, he'll have me killed without a second thought. You know he will."

"So, once again, I must give you to another man."

She didn't answer, touched him with a hand as soft as the new-blown lotus.

"How do you wish the message phrased?"

"Tell him my husband is dead. Tell him I know he has grown sons. Tell him to send me his son for my husband, and Shubbiluliuma's son shall be king over Egypt."

"Come." He pulled her to her feet. "Make yourself beautiful for me. We'll dine alone together."

"My love, I've always asked too much of you. But every night, when I sleep and can no longer control my thoughts, I return to you alone. Truly, I've slept in your arms all these years."

He straightened her dress, removed a blossom that had caught in her hair. "Do you still pray to the Aten?"

"I could never lie to you. Although it is forbidden, the Aten is still my god."

"Then pray as you never have before that the sun be stopped in its path for two months. So may we know each other with love so full and endless it will last a lifetime."

Together, but separate, they made their way out of the magic place back up the path to the palace.

# BOOK I

# THEBES: 1378-1377 B.C.

# I

Nut, Goddess of Night, stretched her golden body across the heavens and expelled the orange globe she had swallowed at sunset. Morning officially began.

Ay stood at the rail as the barge sliced its way through the glasslike waters of the Nile. He could hear the alarms of the ibis as oxen crashed into the fields, and he saw small groups of women, water jugs carefully balanced on their heads, climbing up the steep banks.

The barge rounded a familiar bend in the river's meandering course. Ay knew it well. For twenty years and more, since he had been elevated to grand vizier, he had made this trip. Every year, in an inevitable, unending rhythm stretching eons back into the past, Pharaoh's emissaries had sailed in just this way during the months of the Inundation . . . upriver to collect the delicately veined marble from the quarries at Aswan; past the roaring cataracts into Nubia, where they loaded glittering golden nuggets; then back to Egypt's forty-two nomes. There each headman brought tribute, gratefully thanking the living god for a good flood and for the emerging layer of black, fertile mud. It would mean feast where there might have been famine, and wealth and power—and a mighty Egypt, its long arms extending deep into Punt, casting its shadow over the Great Green, stretching past dense forests of Lebanese cedars and beyond, even into the spice fields of Asia.

Ay turned his sharp glance back to the long line following his ship, barges that were laden with offerings to Pharaoh. He sighed. It was different this year, worrisomely different. The old Pharaoh he could deal with. Lazy and dissolute, Amenophis III was content to be worshiped as a living god and to accept the wealth pouring into Egypt from foreign dominions. He was too comfortable and too smart to ask how his nobles and priests distributed the riches. It was enough for him that his coffers were full. But this year there was a new king to consider as well. Amenophis III had raised his son to co-Pharaoh, and now they'd rule together. That had been Queen Tiya's doing, Ay knew, and blamed his sister bitterly for that strange, thin-lipped son of hers who now sat on the throne next to his father and cast his scholar's eyes on the priests of Amon-Ra. Besides, there was the new queen to worry about—Nefertiti of Mitanni, whose beautiful, foreign eyes had known different gods, whose Mitannian courtiers still laughed behind gilded nails at the feasts and festivals to Egypt's animal deities. Did the queen laugh too?

"My lord?"

Ay glanced at the slave, who was holding out a silver tray, offering flat, sharp morning bread and dark Theban beer. He took a long drink and restrained a grimace. He was not young anymore, and his body rebelled at the spiced, heavy food he was given on these trips. He thought longingly of the milk-softened biscuit Tey would have brought him. Tey . . . after all these years and all those women, she was still chief wife and wife of his heart. His one sorrow was that none of her children had survived, although she was a healthy woman with the wide stomach and strong thighs of a good breeder.

Even there his sister Tiya had gained on him. Take that son of hers that was now co-Pharaoh, big-breasted, feminine and soft—ridiculous! Nonetheless, this parody of a man had managed to thrust his puny, half-hidden sex into his impossibly beautiful wife often enough to have spawned five strapping girls. Indeed, Nefertiti had been big to bursting with another, even as Ay had left.

"Amon-Ra, Great Father," he prayed, "heed your child, Ay, priest at Heliopolis. Give Nefertiti a girl, O Ra, lest with a son for Horus to shine through, she laugh in your face."

His heart hurt too for his dear Tey, serving as royal nurse when her own womb was barren. He was anxious to return to Memphis, to ease her burden a little. He could have been back sooner, would have left the last stop to his deputy, were it not so essential that he himself be the one to come to Thebes. He had seen them all on this trip, the most powerful nobles and priests in the land. He had warned them, as they divided Egypt's treasures, of the new king and his strange, dangerous beliefs. But the last stop was the most important of all. Thebes was the stronghold of Amon-Ra; and Tushratta, chief priest, commanded the richest temple in Egypt.

Ay watched thoughtfully as the low, clustered buildings of Thebes began to glide past, whitewashed under the blazing sun. Feluccas with striped sails circled the barge, and Ay saw that the streets were thronged with people, their broad, jeweled collars flashing in the day's brightness, their fine linen gowns and kilts rippling with their movements. And on the dock, waiting, the priests of Amon-Ra, who had brought the god to greet him.

It took six priests to support the great solar barque on their shoulders. On it rose a pyramid of whitest sandstone, and at the very top, the Sun Disk, the living body of the god, blazed with light. The priests supporting it were highly trained. They knew just how to shift their burden to catch the sun's light so that the disk would shine with varying intensities—so that God would speak.

"Ra acknowledges his faithful son." Tushratta, chief priest, helped Ay rise and grasped his shoulders in welcome. "Accompany us to the temple, where Amon-Ra will accept your gifts . . . and where we can be private," he murmured in a lower tone.

They walked in a stately procession to the Great Temple. People bowed as the barque passed, averted their faces from the god's touch. After the ceremonies and the feeding of the god, Tushratta took Ay to his residence overlooking the sacred lake. Without his crown and scepter, Tushratta looked frail. Ay put the thought aside, knowing the priest's influence was as yet undiminished. He spread his hands on his thighs in a gesture familiar to all who knew him, signaling there were secrets he wished to share.

"I saved Thebes for my last stop, old friend, when there'd be time to visit."

Tushratta leaned forward earnestly. "I've been very anxious for your arrival. Amenophis IV has been co-Pharaoh for a year now and we've heard very little. We need to know what he's like."

"Very careful," Ay answered dryly.

The priest looked puzzled. "Of what?"

"Everything. He's not an easy man to understand." Ay chose his words with care. "There are signs, however, that trouble me. The court's too filled with foreigners that he's brought in." That would disturb Tushratta. Tributes from abroad he liked but the presence of corrupting foreign officials had always bothered him. "Most of them from Mitanni," Ay concluded darkly.

"Nefertiti's birthplace." Tushratta had made the connection.

"Where they worship an abstract, sexless god," Ay added pointedly. Actually he was also probing for information. Had word of this Aten cult penetrated to Thebes? How widespread was it? He had to know.

"It's interesting you bring that up," Tushratta said with some reluctance. "There's been a little trouble here. Nothing much, but it might portend ill. Some boys despoiled a statue of Amon, painted a strange symbol on his face." He carefully unrolled a parchment scroll and spread it on the ebony stool. "This is a copy of it."

Ay studied it thoughtfully. A gold disk was represented on the paper, with a dark, hooded cobra in the center of the southern half. Radiating from the disk were rays that ended in hands. He knew now how to proceed.

"There are secret societies in Memphis that use this as their symbol," he began.

"What does it mean?"

He rerolled the papyrus, looked directly at the old priest. "It's the symbol of the cult of the Aten."

Tushratta rocked back in disbelief. "The Aten!" he exclaimed. "But that's ridiculous. The Aten's an old Egyptian god, incorporated ages ago into Amon-Ra."

"They think it's a new god—and they've certainly given it a new twist." Ay held up his hand. "Hear me out, Tushratta. These societies speak of the Aten as a sole god, the only god, displacing all the hundreds of deities worshiped all over Egypt."

"Even Amon-Ra?" It was almost a whisper.

"Even Amon-Ra." Ay's voice rang out. Yes, he could count on Tushratta. If his god was threatened, he would be fierce in its defense.

The priest had closed his eyes. It was some moments before he asked, "Does Amenophis IV believe in this Aten?"

"I'm not sure. But I don't trust him. Or his wife." Ay paused, then decided he would not hold back with Tushratta. "Or the old queen, my sister."

The priest's eyes opened wide. "What can we do?"

Ay had him now. "At this point, nothing. Right now, my wife is royal nurse to Nefertiti's children. We'll know anything that's afoot as soon as it's spoken of."

Tushratta nodded. "Do we also know whom we can count on, should trouble come?"

Ay smiled, grasped the old man's hand warmly. "I knew you'd ask that, my friend. That's really why I saved Thebes for last. I've spoken with the most powerful nobles in the land, and with many of the headmen. We have influential friends who are worried too: One god for all Egyptians, and the peasants will forget the service they owe to their local lords. And the army fears a poet-king unconcerned with the needs of the empire."

"So. You're telling me all sorts of alliances are possible."

Ay nodded. "I think at present we need only be alert and watch. My calves are fat, my harvest rich. I'm not about to lose my estates."

Tushratta drew a deep, relieved breath. "Be assured that the priesthood of Amon will follow where you lead."

Ay shot him a sharp glance but decided, No, Tushratta didn't yet suspect. He was simply responding to the threat to his own power that had been raised.

In fact, however, Ay had something else in mind as well. Ever since his sister had risen to be queen, the thought had nagged at him: Could her brother not rise beyond her?

Senumet walked rapidly down to the banks of the Nile where his freshly washed tunic was drying in the morning sun. He felt excited, vibrant. At long last the grand vizier of Egypt had come to Thebes, had finally summoned him. He sensed everything with a heightened awareness today—from the fringed, admiring looks of the girls washing clothes in the river to the pleasant squish of the fine leather sandals that were a symbol of his manhood.

He remembered the day his father presented them, when he had slipped them on feet that had never before worn shoes, recalled how the thongs had bitten cruelly into the soft flesh between his toes. . . . But he hadn't cared. He'd worn them proudly all through the ceremonies that marked the completion of his twelve years of scribes' school, begun when he was five. A year ago that had been, yet his relief that it was over was as new as yesterday. By the gods, how his back had stung from the beatings he'd been given! Some days he'd known with absolute certainty that he'd kill the next man who'd dare take a reed to him. What he hadn't known, at that triumphant moment when school and boyhood were behind him, when the future beckoned hopefully, was that in three months' time his father would be dead, his own modest dream crushed absolutely.

Well, today was a new day, and he hadn't done badly for himself, after all. Impatiently, he plucked at his tunic, hanging on a limb of the sycamore. Still wet! He stood there, tall and broad-shouldered, with a bright witty curl to his mouth, and wasn't surprised to be hailed by the girls at the shore.

"Ho, Senumet." Kyrna called him. "Since you became fourth scribe, have you gotten so grand you don't say hello anymore?"

"Not at all!" He flashed a practiced smile, pleasantly aware they'd all stopped working to listen. "As fourth scribe, now I'll say hello in four languages." As they responded with a good deal more merriment than the remark deserved, he strolled over.

"When he's first scribe to my father, he'll beat you all for laziness." A voice sounded behind him, a little shrill.

"Nephrus!" He turned. Damn the girl! Would she never give him a minute out of her sight? "My tunic's still wet," he complained. He had told her yesterday to wash it, had reminded her not to leave it for the last minute.

"Let me see it." She pulled him behind a thick clump of papyrus where they'd be out of sight, tickled his ribs in the way that had reduced him to helpless laughter a few months ago. When he didn't respond, he saw her mouth tremble uncertainly, and he let her wrestle him to the ground.

Of course this sort of thing must be stopped. But how? He had thought he was being so clever, attracting the notice of the headman's daughter—and indeed, it had been Nephrus's attention that had moved him first to the headman's staff and then to fourth scribe. He hadn't meant to hurt the girl, but what other options had there been? His father was dead. Ay, whom his father had served so faithfully, had sent no message. So he had made his own way—flattered too much, pressed kisses that meant much less than they promised. And now, sweet Isis, here she was, thrusting her ripe, bulbous breasts at him, her nipples as red and juicy as juniper berries. Well, why not?

He bit the soft whiteness of her shoulder, dug his hands into firm buttocks, not yet thickened. In a few years' time, her body would be as pendulous as her mother's. Now she was tempting, just a little plump. His tongue thrust boldly into her mouth while almost as quickly his sex rammed between her eager thighs, found easy entrance to the heat within. Hathor, Goddess of Love, she must have a water spout in there, her juices ran so freely. When he was finished and looked at her with clear, unclouded eyes—saw her panting with desire, murmuring little love words, clutching at his arm—he felt a terrible anger at himself and with it, a gnawing that must be shame.

She touched his chest timidly. "Thebes is so beautiful," she pleaded. "We have such abundance, my father likes you, soon you'll be third scribe. . . . Why do you want more?"

"Nothing happens here, Nephrus," he said impatiently. "Each day follows the next in absolutely the same way. There's a world out there where it's possible to know glory and adventure."

"Look what it got your father."

His face hardened. He turned away.

"I'm sorry, Senumet. I didn't think!" she cried.

"Because he's dead, you mean?"

"Because he was murdered in such a stupid way on such a stupid mission."

Senumet looked past her to the stark Theban hills, where the past slept, guarded by Meres-ger, Lover of Silence. He shuddered. "Don't you understand, Nephrus? Dead is here. Walking in the same footsteps, generation after generation."

With a sigh, she pulled on her dress and left him. When she returned she was carrying the tunic. "It's dry now."

She watched him put it on. "Listen, Senumet," she persisted urgently, "what makes you so sure Ay will offer you a place?"

"Why else would he send for me?"

"Don't take it. Surely you haven't forgotten I'm the eldest daughter —all my father's estates will come to me. They're all yours, Senumet, if you stay!"

He couldn't look at her. "You've been wonderful to me, Nephrus," he managed. "Just give me a little time. Let me know what the world is—" He broke off, swallowed the rest: Don't make me say I don't love you.

"I'll see you don't forget me," she said furiously, her face red. She lunged forward and sank her teeth in his neck, then sprinted up the bank out of his angry reach.

Women. He shrugged, holding a lotus leaf to his neck as he walked up the hill to the Kenbet. He wasn't sorry at all. He would not find his answers, his life, in her body—or in any woman's, for that matter. He needed more, and she'd have to accept it. That was how it was.

But when at last he stood before Ay, he was no longer sure, suddenly, that he had read his future right. Why should this powerful man waste a minute on him? He had never experienced anyone like Ay before, whose very carriage, whose physical presence, seemed to exude greatness.

"I couldn't travel through Thebes," the grand vizier told him, "without seeing the son of my faithful Ipy. I hear good reports of you, Senumet. Rahmose, headman of Thebes, has told me how much he likes you and what plans he has for you."

Senumet felt his stomach knot painfully. The little bitch! She meant to keep him here, no matter how.

"I learned the importance of hard work from my father, my lord," he answered carefully. Let Ay remember his father's dedication. Surely that was worth something.

Ay smiled. His gold earring, of a delicacy and meticulous craftsmanship like none Senumet had ever seen before, flashed as he moved his head. "It was a routine message your father was taking to Ashuruballit of Assyria when he was set upon by Bedouins and killed. I want you to know that his murderers were caught and have been punished."

"Thank you, my lord."

"I must tell you how I loved your father. I trusted him above all others."

A tremor shot through Senumet. The alternatives of his life, having taken shape, held him precariously balanced on their fulcrum. If this man left without him, he saw with terrible clarity, the rest of his life would be ashes. He took a desperate leap.

"It was my father's only desire to serve you faithfully. I wish to be like him."

"What are you telling me, Senumet?"

Those eyes had the power to pierce his very skull and see what was written there. He would never be able to lie to this man. "With my father's death, there's a vacancy in your staff. If it's still open, I would wish that it be given me. I'd serve you with all my soul."

Ay raised his brow. "Indeed?" he said. "And what of Rahmose? Don't you owe your service to him? You've advanced over others who've worked far longer than you."

Senumet felt his cheeks grow hot. "I'll always be sensible of what I owe him. I have always done the best I could for him. He'll tell you that."

"He already has."

But still no encouragement! "Please, my lord." The words burst out of him. "All my life my father spoke of you, hoped one day you'd offer me a place. And I've prepared for it, schooled myself for it. I've studied the tongues of Syria and Babylonia and I can read their writing. The whole world calls to me. It's not enough to compute tax assessments here at Thebes or figure land allowances. I want to share in Egypt's great works."

Ay sat in silence for some time. Finally, "If I granted your wish," he said thoughtfully, "is that all you would ask of me?"

Amon be gracious, what should he do? Had Ay been informed that his father had not left money enough for private burial or for inscribing his name in the Book of the Dead? A son owed his father something, and Ay could not like it if he forgot his duty. "No, my lord. There is one more thing. My father wished only to serve you. He never thought the gods were to cut the threads of his life so soon. His name is written nowhere. His ka will never wake, will wander homeless for eternity."

"His body is in the catacombs of Thebes?"

"Yes."

"If you were given a choice—proper burial for your father and his name spelled out in the Book, or a place for you in my court—which would you choose?"

Senumet's knees trembled. What should he say? Visions of Memphis, great center of Egypt, alternately blazed and grew dim. But wait a minute . . . think, he admonished himself. That was a strange question for Ay to pose. Would he be of any use to Ay if he betrayed his father, forgot the ka's need? He took a deep breath. "The burial, my lord."

"And so"—Ay grasped his shoulders—"with that single choice you have won both. Your loyalty runs deep, my son. I know you'll remember what you owe to me."

Joy bubbled through Senumet like a fresh, cold spring. "Thank you, my lord."

"Tomorrow we'll go to the temple at Karnak. Tushratta, the chief priest, will himself inscribe your father's name in the Book of the Dead. I'll arrange for private burial. Bring your possessions with you. We sail for Memphis when we finish."

"Yes, my lord. And . . . and I vow you'll never regret your generosity. I'll serve you faithfully all the days of my life."

Ay laughed. "Go, Senumet. Make your farewells. Tomorrow your new life begins." He waved a gesture of dismissal, his well-cared-for hands glittering with gold and jewel-studded rings.

Senumet burst out of the council room. Unable to contain himself, he bounded through the fields, leaped over a fat cow lazily chewing the sweet, new grass and whooped with sheer happiness. He would even make it up with Nephrus . . . although—Mother Isis forgive him—right now he couldn't even remember her face.

# II

As the barge progressed down the river to Memphis, each day was bathed in gold. Senumet loved the rhythm of shipboard—the white sail that caught the morning breeze, the songs of the rowers who took over when the wind died, the polishing, the fishing. He was beginning to know Ay too, and to appreciate his mentor's far-ranging mind.

"You'll be assigned to Bek, the chief scribe," Ay told him finally, "where your merit will speak for you. It's possible to rise in favor there."

"So, I won't be working directly for you . . ." he tried to keep the disappointment out of his voice.

"We must know your talents—and your limits—first," Ay said. But he added kindly, "It will be a short apprenticeship, I'm sure. Come, Senumet, we feast with date wine tonight. Tomorrow we arrive."

Senumet sensed a rising excitement at the evening meal, a quickening of what had been a leisurely pace; and gradually he became aware that even the air was different here—he could smell the open, fresh breezes coming off the Great Green. Long after Ay and the other officials had retired to their tents on upper deck, he lay sleepless on his pallet, listening to the snores and grunts of the rest of the crew, stretched out, as he was, on lower deck, under a star-studded sky. He both hoped and feared. "Let me be worthy, O Gracious Lord," he silently prayed. "When you rise over the eastern horizon, know your servant Senumet and accept this gift of his willing heart. Test me, O Amon-Ra." Light bathed him before he finally slept.

Suddenly Ay was bending over him and shaking his shoulder, already up and dressed. Senumet felt his face redden when he realized that the deck was empty and he was the only one not yet up.

"Look," Ay directed, pointing to three huge shapes that gleamed in the western sky.

"The Great Pyramids," Senumet breathed, staring as they loomed larger with the barge's approach. As the sun ascended, their polished sides and sharp peaks of finest electrum became mirrors of white light.

"Those early Pharaohs"—he gasped in wonder—"were they truly mortal?"

"I expect so, Senumet. As mortal and as fallible . . ." He stopped. "Use your head, my boy. Don't be swayed by pomp and brilliance. Look beneath."

Senumet nodded, but his eyes were on the pyramids.

At Memphis, the air was assaulted with shouts and noises, such a clamor as he had never heard before. He found his patron near the landing ramp, raising his hand in greeting at two men in a golden chariot.

"We'll part here, Senumet. Go to the royal residence. I'll speak with Bek immediately and he'll have a place ready."

The landing ramp was not yet in place, but Ay leaped easily down, swung himself into the chariot and was gone in a cloud of dust and flashing bridles.

From the deck, Senumet stared at the throngs. So many people, such noise—and dirt. People seemed unconcerned that their legs were spattered with mud or that it ringed their tunics. But this wonder was soon superseded. He gawked. The women! No lips could naturally be so red or color so bright. Their bare breasts, too, they painted red or—incredibly—black. And their hair—crimped and curled and piled so outrageously high it looked to topple them. So many in the boisterous mob were not Egyptian. He stared at the tall, dark Nubians with their fierce eyes; the squat Cretans and—in the name of the Great God, what were those? Veiled and yellow, their trousers ballooning as they walked, they had slitted, menacing eyes.

Eventually he heard a familiar tune. A small band of acrobats and jugglers, clearing a space, were performing to the lilting rhythms of stringed rebabs. Charmed, he watched as red balls bounced in the air . . . until his attention was drawn to a girl leading a small boy through the crowd to a space at the edge of the cleared area. Senumet stared at her. She was lithe and slim, with a grace that set her apart. Once she looked in his direction and he stared into fringed eyes that even at this distance gleamed blue.

Then the juggler faltered. A red ball dropped and bounced into the crowd. The boy pulled free, raced after the ball and slid on the wet street. Senumet laughed as the child struggled to regain his balance in a wild parody of a clumsy acrobat, then fell—Senumet's breath caught—and was lost to sight. The milling crowd closed around the spot where the boy had been. Mother Isis! Such a small boy could be trampled under the feet of that mob. Senumet gripped the rail.

"Tutu!" the girl cried, shoving her way through the crowd. She stopped, spun around desperately. She couldn't find him. "Tutu," she shouted again, an edge of panic in her voice.

Jolted into motion, Senumet sprang from the barge and dashed into the street toward the spot where the boy had fallen. People moved aside to allow him passage, but in the center of the throng a laden donkey blocked his path. He slapped its rump impatiently. The animal screamed. Plunging forward, it crashed into a chicken pen, and suddenly feathers, brays and squawks filled the air. In an instant the donkey's owner and the vendor were exchanging rich curses, passersby were taking sides, and the shouts of angry men were mingling with the clamor of frightened animals.

The crowd flocked to the disturbance, clearing the street. And there, face down on the pavement, was the child. Senumet raced over and picked him up. Amon be praised, he was just shaken, not badly hurt at all. He looked a mess, though. Blood from a cut on his head mixed with the mud that streaked his face and robe.

The child rubbed his eye, saw that his hand came away red, and howled with fright. His cry brought the girl, eyes sparking blue fire, to their side. Senumet carefully stood the boy on his feet, but he sat down in the mud, whimpering. "Tutu!" the girl said sharply. "You are so bad . . . I'll never take you anywhere again. And you'll be punished for this!"

"Hesen," he hiccuped, "I'm bleeding. . . ."

"You'll be bleeding more before I'm finished with you."

His wails increased. The girl frowned with irritation. "Tutu, you sound like a peasant when you cry."

The boy stopped in mid-howl and stood up, sniffling. She took a scarf of fine cloth out of her basket and wiped his face and legs. Senumet had never seen material of such delicacy before. "I'm glad he's not badly hurt," he said when she was finished.

The girl looked up and smiled. He almost gasped, she was so beautiful. "I want to thank you," she said. "And you must know—I enjoyed your rescue so much. Look, I have a souvenir." She held up a chicken feather and together they burst into laughter.

"See, Tutu?" Clearly, she was no longer angry; without a second thought the girl and Tutu had slipped into what must be their usual comfortable way with each other. "You must learn to make quick decisions. Never shrink from action." She turned to Senumet. "He's very rich, you see, so he must learn how to run estates and control men wisely."

"It's too bad of you to teach me now, Hesen, when I'm hungry."

"Come"—Senumet took the boy's hand boldly—"let me buy him candy."

"You may buy me some, too." She smiled, and took his other arm.

Spirits racing, Senumet bought three rolled cones of honey-drenched fruit. They walked along companionably. Senumet watched as people stared at her.

Hesen turned her bright glance at him. "You're new to Memphis, aren't you?"

"I'm to join the royal household," he said with a touch of pride. "I'm a scribe"

"Oh, my!" She looked pleasantly impressed. "You're one of the men who makes those wonderful letters."

Tutu scowled. "Hard to read."

"Only stupid boys, who don't study, find them so," she retorted.

"Girls study," he informed her stolidly, "because they're good for nothing else."

She made a face. "What great things fill your day? Measuring that puny thing between your legs? Fighting?"

"Boys protect the empire," he tried.

"The empire belongs to girls. We control the purse."

Tutu sighed. It was always hard to argue with her. He popped a date into his mouth.

"Have you ever seen the royal family?" Senumet asked, glad for the chance to change the subject.

"Everyone in Memphis has. Shall I tell you about them?"

The pyramids loomed afresh in his mind, immense, powerful. He remembered the royal family were gods on earth. "Perhaps you shouldn't . . . dare."

She laughed. "Not at all. Let's start with the old Pharaoh. We have two now, you know. Amenophis III, the old Pharaoh, is so fat they roll him into the great hall for meals. And his breath smells so bad that he just opens his mouth and his enemies die."

"Hesen!" People seemed so easy here, Senumet used her name without thinking. "You shouldn't talk that way."

"Why not? It's true, isn't it, Tutu?"

He nodded in agreement. "And the old queen is black as night and just as scary."

"Not that the new Pharaoh looks any better," Hesen continued relentlessly. "He's tall, but he's flabby, has hips like a water horse, and is no warrior. Besides, he studies so much his eyes are quite sunk into his head."

"But his eyes are kind and he's nice," protested Tutu.

"Perhaps," she allowed. "Anyway, his queen, Nefertiti, is the most beautiful woman in the world."

"She smells good too," said the boy.

"Well, I'm glad there's one of them you approve of," Senumet ventured.

"Oh, the daughters are all right. There was a new one born last month. Six in all."

"The third princess is bad," Tutu judged, licking his fingers.

Hesen frowned at him. "She's the smartest!"

"But she's very wild."

"True."

They grew silent, considering. "You forgot the princes," Tutu realized suddenly, "and they're very nice."

"Spoiled and nasty," she said definitively.

Senumet laughed. "Shall I truly know them when I see them?"

"Of course."

"I'd like you to know me as well. I'm Senumet of Thebes." He bowed.

"You are truly welcome to Memphis, Senumet," she said graciously. "If you promise not to laugh, I'll introduce you to Tutu here."

"Why should I laugh?"

"Because he's my uncle."

The boy drew himself up to his full height. "But she never listens to me," he confided.

"I'll listen to you now," she promised, pointing to two frowning figures converging on them.

Tutu instantly burst into tears. "It wasn't my fault," he sobbed, running over to the man and woman. "She made me come."

"Brave Tutu," Hesen said scornfully. "And did you bring the chains, Senedjm?" she called to the fiercely scowling man.

"That's enough, my lady. You're not permitted here alone."

She shrugged, flipped back her shining hair and walked toward them without haste. Tutu, who had been scooped up by the woman who must be his nurse, now glared triumphantly at Hesen from his perch between ample breasts. Hesen shrugged contemptuously.

She was very fine, Senumet thought, watching the little procession until it faded from sight. Willful and reckless . . . but very fine. He kept hoping she'd turn back and wave. Never mind. Perhaps he'd see her again. Meanwhile he must locate Bek.

Once past the docks, Memphis made sense—except that it was so green. He was used to Thebes and its desolate, encroaching desert, everywhere visible, constantly fought. And the houses! Richly decorated and painted, they shone like jewels, and the tall jacaranda trees waved like feathers over their rooftops.

The royal residence itself was really a large cluster of buildings, almost a small city, surrounded by a tall fence in the shape of upstanding gold-headed spears that flashed as the sun touched them. Senumet showed a sentry the seal ring Ay had given him.

"Proceed, please, to the scribes' barracks—the easternmost group of buildings." He opened the gate.

Senumet entered and fell in love. The buildings were bright red and the decorative reliefs were outlined in gilt. The courtyard pools had rich mosaic floors and the papyrus blooming in small clusters were all the same height. The gardens were incredibly lush, overflowing with displays of bright flowers, dotted here and there with exotic birds, whose haunting songs filled the air. He arrived at the barracks totally bedazzled, uncertain about what to do next. There was no one in sight. He took a deep breath and knocked on the wooden door. When opened, he found himself looking into the merry face of a little round man with a bald head, a potbelly and the longest, most graceful fingers Senumet had ever seen.

"You must be Senumet." The man embraced him warmly. "I'm Bek. As you probably know, your father was my friend. His son is truly welcome." He grasped Senumet's hand and smiled warmly. "Come, I'll show you your new home myself. First, your bunk."

They entered the easternmost barrack. It was wonderfully cool inside. In front of each shuttered window stood a bed and a large chest, each skillfully decorated with the name of the occupant, painted in elegant hieroglyphs. Bek stopped before a bare chest.

"This will be yours, Senumet, as soon as you inscribe your name. Mind, it must be beautiful. Now, let me show you the rest."

Taking his arm, Bek led him through the complex. It was arranged like a large triangle, Senumet realized, and he had entered at its apex. He tried to memorize the location of the buildings as Bek explained them—the offices, where even now the other scribes were working, the line of barracks, the stables, the kitchens. At the beginning the order seemed logical enough, but it was not long before his feet were dragging with fatigue and he felt dizzy.

"There are the royal apartments." Bek pointed to a colonnade of limestone pillars in the shape of bound reeds which surrounded the tallest, most elaborately gilded buildings in the complex. Directly behind the columns were formal beds of bright flowers and neatly pruned small trees. As Senumet heard the soft fall of water, he realized there were fountains inside as well.

"The apartments are closed, of course," Bek remarked, "but you can get some idea of what they look like from the great hall where the whole court dines."

He waved at the sentry standing smartly at attention outside the longest of the buildings and they went in.

Was he to eat here? Senumet marveled, his senses overcome. The room was so imposing and austere he felt he would not be able to lift a morsel to his mouth. Aloof, perfect nobles were painted on the walls, their postures formal and stiff. Even the evening lotuses that rose on the pillars were closed—as if it was too cool here for them to open.

Noticing his expression, Bek laughed. "Perhaps it's all a little too much at once. You'll get used to it, my boy," he promised. "Some day you'll even think the royal family needs something more impressive."

More was unimaginable. "The royal family eats here, too?" Senumet asked. And if so, was it possible he'd know them, as the girl this morning had said?

"Oh, yes. They're in residence now, celebrating the royal birth. You'll see them tonight. And now, Senumet, I'll let you return to your bunk. I know you must be tired."

Gratefully Senumet returned to the barracks, glad they were still empty. He put away his belongings in the bare chest and lay on the pallet, certain sleep would overcome him. But he had to inscribe his name, and it must be artistic and clever, like all the others. He pictured scores of possible hieroglyphic variations of his name. Suddenly he sat up. He had it! Oh, it would be splendid. Very carefully he unwrapped the polished wooden box—his scribe's kit, a present from his father when he had traveled once to Byblos. The box was shaped like a mallard and its wings were wondrously formed. By pressing its neck, a spring released, and the wings spread apart to reveal, inside, his brushes and paints, styluses and inks.

As he chose a stylus, the strangeness and confusion of the day temporarily vanished in the joy of bringing his vision to life. He had a good, steady hand and the eye of an artist. He worked deftly and surely. When he finished, hours later, he realized he was dizzy with fatigue. But his design was beautiful. He knew he hadn't shamed himself or his father. Before he put the kit away, he cleaned the materials carefully and rewrapped them. Only then did he permit himself to lie down. He was asleep instantly.

"Sen-u-met."

His eyes jerked open. A group of young men was standing near his bed, appraising his workmanship.

"I like your line. It's very crisp."

"The bird's eye is alive."

"You've caught the curve of Horus."

Senumet's smile grew wide. He was home—in the company of those who understood.

"Welcome, Senumet." Ka-Aper, whose bunk adjoined his, was the spokesman. "You'll get to know all of us soon enough. We must dress for dinner now. The royal family will be there, you know."

Senumet laughed. "I am dressed," he confessed.

"We have a kilt for you, Senumet. You appear to have the lean flanks that will show it off." Ka-Aper opened his chest, produced the article.

Senumet tied it on while the scribes watched. Ka-Aper, looking at him critically, decided, "It sits well, my friend. And I have something that will complement it nicely." He held out a broad neckpiece of carnelian and lapis, and Senumet saw they were all wearing ornaments. The room flashed as armbands, rings and collars were adjusted.

"No, thanks," he said, embarrassed.

"Come, now. It's nothing. You must understand, Senumet—we get gifts from patrons who have private work for us." Ka-Aper winked. "Love notes, meetings, sometimes a little political intrigue. You'll see. We know everything that happens here." His smile was conspiratorial, and Senumet allowed him to fasten on the neckpiece, after which Ka-Aper slipped a wide jasper armband almost to his shoulder. "Come, we're ready now."

They strolled to the great hall. Senumet was pleased he could remember just where it was. He was getting used to palace life already. Almost casually he stepped inside . . . and was struck dumb. He had thought he knew what to expect, but—sweet Isis—he had been wrong. He had been awed before; now he would have been sure he was in the middle of an incredible dream, except that he knew he could never have imagined such glory.

The hall was festooned with flowers. Lotus in huge alabaster and carnelian vases spread their perfume, heady and sweet, and his senses reeled. Ebony and gold torches blazed, bringing to warm, stirring life those painted nobles he had thought austere. The pillars, not evening lotus at all—how could he have thought it?—were twined with curling, leafy vines. In the flickering orange glow, they were morning buds, just at the point of bursting into bloom. Everywhere the flaming torchlight rebounded from a thousand mirrors—gold and stone-studded earrings, flashing collars, gold-flecked and painted eyes. The women, elegant in their close-fitting gowns, were all beautiful; the men were no less splendid, their jewelry just as glittering, their eyes no less skillfully made up.

Senumet sat with the scribes, accepted the cup of wine and the succulent meat that were brought by young women slaves, their bodies naked except for a small cloth between their legs, their breasts lightly rouged and perfumed. As he reached across a silver tray for a glazed fig, his fingers brushed a serving girl's nipple. It hardened instantly; he pulled his hand back as if burned and was afraid to meet her glance.

Ka-Aper touched his arm. "Stand up and bow," he whispered. "The royal family enters."

The court rose to their feet, stood with lowered heads. The only sounds were the crackle of meat turning on spits and the snap of flaming torches. Unable to keep himself from looking, Senumet surreptitiously raised his head a little and saw the old Pharaoh being helped into the hall. He was astonished. He stared at an aged man, obviously incapable of walking unaided, grossly obese. In his puffed and bloated face the eyes, two dark beads, were almost lost in folds of fat. Dimpled and hanging flesh bulged over the bracelets adorning his arms, and the fingers stroking the curled beard were thick and stubby. Senumet stifled a laugh. Really, it was just as Hesen had said.

He saw next the small dark woman walking behind Pharaoh, her face almost obscured. With her enormous Hamhemet crown, topped by bundles of jasper papyrus and gold sun disks, she was hard put to keep her balance and moved in quick, awkward bursts. That must be Queen Tiya, the old Pharaoh's wife. She was very slim, maybe a third of Pharaoh's size. Struck by a sudden vision of the king taking his pleasure with her, he almost whooped out loud with laughter. He could understand why the old woman was so lined and bitter-looking.

There was a sudden stir in the court, and Ka-Aper gripped his arm. "Nefertiti's coming. For the first time since the child was born."

Senumet wondered what the fuss was about—didn't they see her all the time?—until she entered the room and time stopped.

"Bow, you fool," Ka-Aper muttered, tugging at his arm.

Realizing he was standing transfixed, Senumet lowered the line of his spine, but not his eyes. He couldn't stop looking. Her hair was swept up in a simple, high crown that left her face in a sharp relief of pure beauty: planes of incredible delicacy, arching brows over long almond eyes, a perfectly straight nose, full lips that expressed at the same time sensuality, a remarkable purity, and—in a small dimple at one corner—suppressed laughter. In all that glittering room, Nefertiti's face was the most magnificent ornament of all, and she knew it. She wore no jewelry, making simplicity of dress an arrogance . . . because no one could look anywhere but at her.

As she drew nearer, Senumet's heart began to beat painfully in his chest. He had seen that face before! No, not Nefertiti's—a face not quite so beautiful, less sophisticated, but with an unmistakable resemblance. Sweet Isis! he breathed, trying not to think what a simpleton he must have seemed, what it must mean for his future. Light-headed, he concentrated on the man stroking the queen's back and holding her hand. Double crown . . . beard of Pharonic power strapped to the chin, like the beard grotesquely tied to the old man's bloated neck . . . of course—this was the new Pharaoh, Amenophis IV. Just as she had, with impish accuracy, described him—odd; not fat, but strangely misshapen—thighs big and feminine, breasts hanging, stomach distended. But when Senumet saw his face, he knew that he couldn't laugh at Amenophis IV. It was a powerful, sensitive face, with the most intense, feeling eyes Senumet had ever seen. This man, he felt sure, would understand everything.

The two men sat on a double throne; the women on low stools next to them. "Why don't we sit now?" Senumet whispered to Ka-Aper, hoping the procession had ended.

"The royal children are coming."

There was a sudden shout outside, then a small red object was bouncing in, followed by a small boy, who dashed after it and slid to an abrupt halt before the courtier who had caught it. The boy bobbed up and down, trying to grab the ball. Senumet's mouth tightened. He knew that ball, that boy. He could even see the bruise on his forehead. "Who is that child?" he asked Ka-Aper.

"Prince Tutankhaten, the old Pharaoh's son. And that's his brother, Prince Smenkhare, who won't give him the ball."

His son! Senumet nearly choked. All hope that she might be a minor relative faded. His hands closed into hard fists and a pulse pounded in his head. He remembered her scent, her easy laughter, her soft hand on his arm . . . and watched fervidly as three of the new king's six daughters entered the hall elegantly gowned, properly regal.

He knew her right away. She shone in the same way her mother did. There seemed to be a kind of light around her, and her simplest gesture made her sisters look stolid and graceless. He felt his face stiffen as he leaned to Ka-Aper and pointed again.

"Princess Ankhesenpaaten, third daughter of the new Pharaoh."

Horus help him, what a fool he had been trying to impress her with the fact that he was joining the royal household. How important, she'd agreed. Are you new to Memphis, she had asked. What an idiot! How she must have laughed! She leaned forward now and said something to the man who had claimed her at the dock. Senumet stared as he walked across the room—toward himself? No, to Bek. What sport had she in mind?

The man returned to the royal tables, spoke to her again, pointed. Her gaze followed his direction, and suddenly, with a bright smile, she was looking right into Senumet's eyes. His face burning, trembling with rage, he stood abruptly, overturned his stool and almost ran out of the great hall.

He lay on his pallet, so out of breath his chest hurt; closed his eyes. Ultimately, he heard the others return, but wanting no questions from them he kept the rise and fall of his chest regular and steady. There was joking, the sounds of undressing, some horseplay and gradually silence. Darkness hid his shame.

Someone touched his arm. He looked into the face of her servant and sat bolt upright.

"Be still," Senedjm whispered. "Come with me. You have a visitor."

"I don't think—" Senumet began.

"You are ordered," the man cut him off sharply, and Senumet followed him into the garden.

She was waiting near the clusters of lotuses, their blossoms closed now against the cool evening air. She was still wearing the elaborate court dress and jewelry and the heavy kohl marks that made her so remote.

"Oh, Senumet"—her smile flashed brightened the night sky—"I was so worried you wouldn't come."

She was royalty. He had no right even to look into her face. "I was ordered, my lady," he murmured, his mind intercutting a confused picture of her arm on his.

"Oh, no, please don't do that. Tell him he mustn't, Senedjm. Tell him I'm not so high. Only the third princess—practically not in the succession at all."

"What do you want me to do?" Senumet asked flatly.

"Talk to me the way you did this afternoon."

"So you can laugh at me some more?"

She drew back as if he had slapped her. "Oh, no, you don't understand. Tell him, Senedjm. I'd never do that! He doesn't know that I'm very kind. Senedjm, you are standing there like a poor, dumb dolt. Speak."

Senumet couldn't help it; he burst out laughing. She looked startled for a minute, then laughed with him. "You must know that never before had a man talked to me as just a pretty girl or bought me candy. I wasn't laughing at you. I was laughing because I was happy."

"You looked happy, my lady."

"If you must say my lady, at least say My Lady Hesen."

He looked at Senedjm, who nodded.

"Very well, My Lady Hesen."

She smiled contentedly. "I've spoken to my father. You see, Tutu is stupid and needs much help if he's ever to learn to read. Tutu promised he'd study very hard if you were to teach him. And my father agreed."

Once again he looked at Senedjm, who allowed, "It is true."
Her father—the Pharaoh. . . .
"So when you finish your training," she continued, "you'll be sent for. Say you're pleased."
"Of course I am, My Lady . . . Hesen."
Her smile fairly blazed. "I'm so glad." She pressed his hand quickly and left, Senedjm following close behind. Again she seemed bathed in that special radiance.

He returned to his pallet and lay taut in the darkness, heavy with the sleep of his new compeers. As he listened to their heavy breathing, syncopated by the thumping in the cavity of his chest, he realized he was in peril. He should refuse the commission, for this rush of pure joy at her touch could do no good. And just as surely, he was aware that he could not follow his own advice, could not forgo his chance to be with her. . . .

Therein lay the danger—that his heart would always leap up whenever she was near.

# III

Senumet filled his cupped hands with scented water and rinsed his freshly shaved face, careful not to wince at the stinging pain. Balancing his mirror against the blue faience bowl, he dipped his brush into the kohl jar and outlined his eyes with deft strokes. He felt a secret pleasure as he caught the flash of his gold scarab armband. He had come here with nothing; and now, four short months later, his ornaments were richer, more finely wrought than the most senior scribe's.

"Senumet." Ka-Aper thrust his feet into the leather thongs and hastily tied his kilt. "Will you give me your stylus? I didn't have time to make a fresh one."

"Take two." Senumet handed him the finely tipped pens. "I'm cutting more this morning."

"Bet you'll have company," Narni said archly—and when the nearby scribes laughed, "I'll be happy to get lost in the reeds for you, my good man, if I can get lost in those blue eyes too."

Senumet's back stiffened.

"You could never do it," Ka-Aper interjected lightly. "You can't even find your way around Memphis, and you want to teach the princess geography?"

Senumet detained him as the scribes moved out of the barracks to begin their morning's work. "Thank you, my friend. There have been many awkward moments that were made easier by your kindness."

Ka-Aper hesitated. "Your thanks give me leave to speak. Be careful, Senumet. You've attracted too much notice. Royal favor, in this court especially, is very risky."

He left Senumet to finish his preparations alone. Shortly after, Senumet stepped into the sun-drenched day and felt his pulse quicken. Narni had been right, of course. He was not going to cut the reeds alone.

As he passed the royal residence, a robed figure hailed him—Ay. It had been months, Senumet realized, since their last meeting. A warm smile brightened his face.

"My lord, how good to see you."

Ay matched his steps to Senumet's. "Is that truly said, my son?"

"You can't doubt it!"

"No? Actually, Senumet, I have wondered from time to time where your affections are now."

Senumet stopped and looked earnestly into the grand vizier's eyes. "I did not request my present post. I've asked only one thing—to have a place on your staff."

"Well, then," Ay said without hesitation, "I'm leaving today for Thebes. The queen is fully recovered and the babe is doing well. The royal family wishes to open the court there. What if I asked you to join me?"

Senumet suppressed a sharp stab of regret. "I'll ask leave of the Pharaoh."

Ay laughed. "Not so hasty, my son. Right now you can serve us best where you are."

"How?"

"I understand that Prince Tutu may learn to read his name at long last."

"I despair of much more than that, my lord."

"His brother, Smenkhare, it is also reported, may yet be taught to figure acreage and yields."

"When related to his estates, his interest is engaged."

"You understand your duties well." Ay squinted at him. "And the princess?"

"She's a quick student," Senumet replied a little too officiously.

"Of course." Ay paused for a moment. "You must know, Senumet, that the new Pharaoh is very different from his father."

"I know that he's a scholar," Senumet answered uncomfortably. He hadn't often had audience with Amenophis IV, but once the king had consulted him about a sacred text and they had spent a pleasant hour reviewing the ancient writings. Senumet had been amazed at the sensitivity and care of his translations.

"Yes," Ay agreed. "I myself am most interested in his religious leanings. And in his priestly visitors."

"I have no knowledge of that." Senumet caught back a sigh of relief and was aware, suddenly, that his hands were wet.

"When you do become privy to such things, I wish to be informed."

"Yes, my lord." Amon help him to avoid that day.

"And don't let youth and beauty blind you, my son."

"No, my lord."

Ay circled his shoulder affectionately. "Enough for today, Senumet. I think beauty comes to you now across the field."

Ay stayed long enough to acknowledge Hesen's greeting. Grasping Senumet's hand warmly, he was finally gone.

Senumet and Hesen walked down to the banks of the Nile. Hesen, a little ahead of him, carelessly crushed the small flowers under her feet; watching her, he tensed—ordinarily she would hesitate to pick a lotus and cut short its natural life.

"What's the matter?" he asked.

She stopped, turned to look at him. "I just don't understand you, Senumet," she frowned. "I have told you and told you how vicious Ay is, and still you love him."

He hated these conversations. Didn't she realize he dare not discuss the grand vizier so freely? Besides, he owed everything to Ay. "He's been kind to me. And my father served him happily all his life."

"He's an evil, scheming man," Hesen persisted darkly, "and would willfully harm my parents."

"Hesen, what are you saying? As chief priest to Amon, he's moral leader of all the citizens of Memphis."

She sighed and grew silent and avoided meeting his eyes as he found a shaded spot under a sycamore tree and gathered reeds for shaping.

"So," he said lightly, hoping to lift her mood, "Princess Hesen has taken it into her head to be a scribe's assistant and cut his pens."

"I've broken enough." She smiled faintly.

He chose a reed for each of them. "We do it like this." He demonstrated, slicing at a fine angle.

She took the knife from him, made a cut, and the stem broke in half. "Well, I ruined it!" she exclaimed.

"Here"—he covered her hand with his—"let me show you."

Mistake! he knew immediately—he shouldn't have touched her.

Her fingers moved under his, soft and pliant, and sparks shot up his arm.

"There, that's much better!" But in fact the reed was as unevenly cut.

"Oh, yes, I see now how it's done." She didn't even look at it.

He pulled his hands away and bent over another stem. He had four of them finished before he realized her hands were lying in her lap.

"I didn't mean to silence you," he said. "Is there something in particular Ay has done? What was troubling you?"

She shut her eyes. "He wishes us to return to Thebes."

Thebes. Senumet thought of the silent valley across the river . . . the Land of the Dead. "But you'll bring the court with you—and its gaiety and life."

Her lower lip curled in the pout he had come to recognize. The third daughter of the king had a quick, impatient temper. "What do I care for that? We'll be returning to the stronghold of the dark priests of Amon-Ra."

"Twice today you've spoken critically of Amon. Remember, he's a god of thunder, too."

"Will he strike me down?" she demanded and sprang lightly to her feet. She raised her slim arms to heaven. "Hear, O Ra, if you truly dwell in the sky and can hear me, I snap my fingers at you. Destroy me now, if you dare."

"Hesen!" He was shocked, of course. But his primary thought was that she must be gotten out of the sight and hearing of those who would come at any moment to the dock. Even Pharaoh's daughter could not blaspheme freely.

"And do you really think," he said scornfully, "that you need show Amon where you are by standing in the sun? If he wished to injure you, he could find you in the shade."

She took a deep, shaky, breath, and the stiffness left her body.

"Oh, Senumet, only you dare show me how absurd I can be."

"I just don't understand why you're so angry."

She sat down beside him again, picked at a reed. After a moment, she said without looking at him, "I just thought that when you came to know them, they'd replace the false gods in your heart."

It was dangerous territory they were entering now. He didn't want to hear any more. But she was so trusting and so intemperate, she might speak to anyone, even those who would harm her. Better she tell him, where it would die. "Know whom?"

"The king, my father, and his beloved royal mistress, my mother. Instead you are loyal to Ay and his dark gods."

"One loyalty needn't cancel another."

"But it does . . . must! Can't you see that?" Her voice was rising. She was getting agitated again. He had heard it whispered that the two Pharaohs didn't agree, but he had ignored such talk, and now here he was, listening to what might be his death.

"Quietly, my lady, and calmly, explain it to me."

"All right." She pulled him into the sun. "You know that the gods of Egypt live in the darkness of their temples, which none may enter. They are jealous and vengeful and angry. They are not my gods—are not gods at all. For me there is only one deity. The Aten. The Sun Disk. I want you to know him."

Senumet whirled around. "Just a minute. I hear something."

He saw a bright party approaching the dock, where a white-sailed felucca had just glided into mooring.

"Oh, that's just Smenkhare and my sister Meritaten," she said, dismissing them.

"Prince Smenkhare is the son of Amenophis III. Be still until they pass."

"And I am the daughter of Amenophis IV. I shan't be still. Kneel with me."

They dropped to their knees in the sweet-smelling morning grass. He could hear the royal party approach—the arrogant laugh of the prince, the stilted tones of Meritaten, who took her position as heiress so seriously.

"Raise your face to the Aten and let it bless you."

He did as she bid him, hoping that would silence her.

"No, no—like this." Taking his face in her hands, she tilted it to the sun. "Know the Aten, Senumet. Its rays are touching you. They end in hands that stroke your face with warmth. Do you feel them?"

His cheeks burned where her fingers rested. She was so close he could feel the rise and fall of her chest. His senses swam.

"Yes!" It came out a strangled cry.

"Listen to my father's hymn. Let it wash over you as the Aten caresses your body:

> '*Beautiful is thine arising*
> *O Living Sun beside whom there is none else*
> *Who strengthens the eyes with thine rays*
> *Who hast created all that exists.*

*Thou risest in the Horizon of Heaven
To give life to all that thou hast made.'* "

Senumet touched her hair with trembling fingers, and the world tipped and spun around him, its only fixed points the melting blue of her eyes. As if from a great distance, he heard Smenkhare's voice raised in a question. The prince had heard something.

" 'Thy works are hidden from the face of man, O sole God,' " Hesen continued with dramatic fervor.

He had to stop her. She mustn't be discovered worshiping an heretical god. He could think of just one way to silence her effectively. Reaching out, he cupped her face in his hands and lowered his head until their lips met. At first she was startled and tried to pull back, but he worked his mouth over hers until her lips opened. Then her arms were encircling his neck; her body, alive and warm, was curving against him . . . and he felt a shuddering desire such as he had never imagined was possible.

Somehow, he pulled away. Her eyes were wide and lustrous; her lips, still parted, quivered with passion. There was no sound except the screech of an ibis overhead. At least, he thought, they'd escaped notice.

Suddenly she scrambled to her feet with a sound like a whimper, turned and ran up the riverbank. Senumet waited a few minutes until he was calm. Then he gathered the pens he had fashioned and proceeded slowly to the lecture room. Tutu would be waiting. Smenkhare should be there as well, but Senumet did not expect to see that young prince. Like his father, Smenkhare rarely let duty interfere with pleasure.

Nefertiti held the child at her breast, encouraged the little one to feed by gently stroking her cheek. Pharaoh's seed was not strong. Not a lusty babe and even smaller than the others, this would be the last child to pull at her nipples, to suck the milk of Mitanni kings, the queen thought. She leaned forward and brushed the soft forehead with her lips, Ah, poor mite, her face was wet with the effort of even those weak strivings. Nefertiti motioned for the chief nurse.

Tey dabbed at the child's face, her mouth pursed in disapproval. "My Queen, only the long years my husband Ay and I have served you give me the right to scold. It's not seemly for you to suckle the child."

"My loyal friend," Nefertiti soothed. She had learned long ago to ignore Tey. She knew very well that Tey had been placed here to spy on her, but that was an old story, and Nefertiti was used to being careful. It was bred into her bones.

She sighed. If only her third daughter had a little more caution in her nature. She worried about Hesen—bright, willful, loving, the finest of the royal children . . . how unexpectedly had the fierce blood of the Mitannis mingled with the Egyptians' brilliance and warmth! The others, compliant and dull, were perfect for the roles Amenophis had in mind, for the marriages he would arrange. But as to Hesen—Nefertiti's lips curled in the half-smile that charmed the courtiers—who knew? Perhaps in the brave, new world Pharaoh dreamed of, years in the future, there'd be a place for Hesen. Well, her children were still babes, all of them, a long way yet from ambition and lust and passions. Nefertiti sank back on the pillows, dreamily enjoying the soft lips at her breast, the little mewings of content.

Suddenly the door burst open and a wild-eyed Hesen raced in. Two guards hurried after her.

"Majesty, I couldn't—" the Nubian began.

Nefertiti sat up. "It's all right," she assured them. "You may go. Control yourself, Hesen," she said in the same soft tone.

As usual, the inflection was enough to check the girl's headlong dash. She stood in the center of her mother's apartments, her chest heaving, her face reddening with the effort of holding herself still.

Stunned, Nefertiti was thinking that she must have neglected looking at Hesen lately. Aten above her, those breasts were not a child's, and that reed-slim waist, the smooth curve of those hips would drive the nobles mad—perhaps already had. Why, the child was beautiful! She felt something stir in her chest, an emotion she had never felt before, had not expected from herself. Heaven help her, it must be what they called envy. She motioned for Tey. "The babe is wet," she declared.

As Tey took the infant away, the queen cleared the room of servants. She knew her daughter's repugnance for diplomacy. Aten only knew what Hesen would blurt out. Besides, Nefertiti needed a few minutes to understand her own heart.

*And so*, she thought, *here I am, a woman who for years has believed herself temperate above all others, when I'm foolish and vain as those I mock.*

She was uncomfortably aware of the tight band under her breasts.

Thinking it a new fashion, her court had copied it, but Nefertiti had bound herself to keep her breasts from sagging. While her bosom was still white, it was no longer firm, and her nipples were stretched and rubbery. She studied the upstanding buds on her daughter's chest, their round, firm fruit thrusting them importantly forward, and a little crease appeared in a corner of her mouth. Beneath her own diaphanous gown the queen could just make out the ugly blue stretch marks on her stomach. And if her face was still beautiful—it was; she studied it with care each morning—it would not be so forever. Inevitably—and then? She would still be queen. She could live with loss of beauty. She was a mother. She could rejoice in a daughter's fairness. She held out her arms.

A cry broke from Hesen's throat as she flung herself at her mother, buried her face in that welcoming lap and sobbed without restraint. Nefertiti stroked the blue-black tangle of hair, waited until the muffled storm subsided.

"So." She lifted her daughter's head, looked searchingly into her young, unhappy face. "You're fourteen and just becoming a woman . . . and a very lovely one. What can be so dreadful?"

"I'm not a child. You just said that"—Hesen drew herself up—"and yet you speak to me as one."

Nefertiti raised a beautiful, arched brow. "Then what is it?"

"Everything." Her lips trembled, but Hesen looked directly at her mother and kept her voice steady. "I don't want to go back to Thebes. Pharaoh was so dispirited and unhappy there, where the priests of Amon are so much more powerful and looked so darkly at him. Yet lately Ay has been strutting importantly. . . . I hate him," she finished intemperately.

"Do you?" The queen's voice was cool, although she felt a flutter of fear. How much had the child absorbed of what was going on? "Why do you hate Ay?"

An adult in the company of another, Hesen said shortly, "You know he's no friend to Aten."

"Yes."

"And there is no other god. We have believed in no other, worshiped no other since Pharaoh first took him into his heart four years ago."

Nefertiti shivered, at the same time wondering that this should disturb her. Of course they worshiped Aten. It was Pharaoh's will, and the children accepted what they were told and behaved accordingly. But Hesen's declaration of faith was something altogether different. The others were game pieces to be moved about at will. Only this one, the queen mused, of all her children, had a spirit that matched her own, and she saw, as clearly, that this fierce, lovely passion must be stamped out. An old, long-forgotten ache twisted her face briefly. Looking out of Hesen's eyes was a young Mitannian princess she scarcely remembered anymore . . . a girl who, many years ago, had been sent unwillingly into Egypt with death in her heart, who painfully and slowly had learned about duty and prudence and restraint. Hesen must learn about them too, the sooner the better.

"I'm glad you're so certain about issues that have puzzled scholars for ages," she said equably. "Please tell us so we may all free ourselves from error."

"Senumet says—" Hesen began.

"Senumet!" Nefertiti cut her off sharply. "A simple peasant!"

"He's the royal tutor." Hesen's face was white.

"He may be a traitor, and you with him!"

The girl jumped to her feet. "How can you say that, Mother? He's completely loyal. He won't even let me speak badly of Ay."

"Truly?" Nefertiti's eyes blazed and her voice shook with fury. "And how is it you dare discuss court officials with a creature who is no more than clay under your feet? Are you a common slut, that you must seek the company of servants?"

Hesen could hardly speak. "He's an educated man," she managed.

"An educated man!" the queen mimicked. "Child, child, don't confuse the flattery of lackeys with intelligence. You're so puffed up with yourself, you make it easy for them to laugh at you. Senumet educated, indeed! Hesen! Senumet is nothing."

The girl trembled with each word as if she were being struck.

"Go to your quarters," Nefertiti ordered. "And consider: Ignorance is best masked by absolute silence. Try to understand restraint if you're capable of thought."

As Hesen stood dumbly, unable to move at all, Nefertiti's heart ached. She was being cruel, but Ay must not find out the extent of Pharaoh's devotion to Aten. They could all be destroyed if she were allowed her tongue. "Go," she commanded again. "And remain there until you're summoned."

Her eyes bright with tears, Hesen stumbled out of the queen's apartments. Nefertiti could not watch her. It would pass, she told herself, and meanwhile Hesen would stay in her rooms and cry, giving them a few days to be free from worry about what damage she might do . . . during which time she herself must find out about Senumet. What had the child told him. How far had it gone? How could he be stopped?

When she rang for her servants, she realized, suddenly, that she was shaking, too. She must rest a few minutes, letting them minister to her until she felt calm again. She relaxed as they hovered around her, replacing the rings and armbands, cleaning her breasts with the sharp, cool unguents, rerouging the nipples. By the time she studied her face in the silver mirror, she was herself again.

"The kohl line is smudged," she observed. "Use the malachite shadow and sprinkle it with gold dust." She watched her eyes sparkle with new life as the bright flecks of gold were applied to her lids.

A short while later, calm and refreshed, she walked to the west courtyard where Senedjm was waiting, as summoned. He lowered his head and kept it bowed as they spoke; having been raised in the old ways, he dared not look freely on the face of a living god. Amused by the form of his homage, Nefertiti was nonetheless grateful for his absolute loyalty to Pharaoh, which he had proven with twenty years of devoted service.

"You've been guarding Princess Ankhesenpaaten," she began. "I want to know how she spends her free time."

"The princess has been very studious."

"Do not mince words with me," the queen said sharply. "Answer without evasions."

She could see that his clasped hands trembled. "She has been with Senumet, the tutor," he admitted.

"Has been?" Nefertiti's eyes flashed. "Do you mean they lie together?"

"No. No." Senedjm answered quickly. "Merely spend time in each other's company—reading, painting. The princess writes beautifully now."

"I see. And periodically they talk?"

Senedjm hesitated. He preferred to deal with Amenophis IV in such matters. He was never sure whether the queen expected him to listen or whether it was a sacrilege to have done so. He heard a sharp hiss of breath. She was getting impatient.

"Forgive me, Highness," he plunged ahead. "It is the princess, mostly, who talks. She speaks of the royal family without flattery and of the Aten and how she worships it."

"Does she mention Ay?"

His face reddened. "Yes."

"With affection and respect?"

"No."

"Tell me now of Senumet himself. Has he friends among the scribes?"

"They like him very much. He's bright, willing, very congenial."

"Do they know of the princess's favor?"

"Yes."

"Do they tease him about it?"

"Highness, please," Senedjm stuttered uncomfortably.

"Continue," she said implacably. "When they jibe at him, how does he respond? Does he talk of her?"

"Never, my lady," he replied firmly. "Not one word has he said of her or of what she has told him. Not to the scribes. Not to Ay, though he has asked."

"One more thing, Senedjm. Where is Pharaoh now?"

"In the library."

"You may go now."

He bowed and left gratefully.

Nefertiti walked thoughtfully to the library. Senedjm had given her much to consider. While his father lived, Pharaoh's position was not so secure that it couldn't be challenged, and should his devotion to Aten be published, the pressure on the old Pharaoh to disenthrone his son and raise up another, Smenkhare, would be tremendous. Obese, decrepit Amenophis III—who still had such flashes of his old power that Tiya couldn't control him. Worse, they would soon be traveling to the stronghold of their enemies where their every gesture would be studied, where Hesen's revelations could undo them in a moment.

And it seemed Hesen's carelessness could already have made Pharaoh, his queen mother, his queen wife and his daughters all hostages to a scribe.

# IV

Nefertiti climbed gracefully down the steps to the library.

Roof panels angled the sun so there was no glare, only soft light. On the stone walls, painted nobility and royalty walked sedately in gilded gardens, amused themselves with board games, wrote wistful love poems as Thoth, god of scribes and of wisdom presided from the south end of the room—an ibis head with its bright bird's eye, its pointed, sharp beak above a man's powerful torso: Thoth who when the sun vanished had come forth to dispel the darkness with his mind's light.

Amenophis IV and Queen Tiya were engaged in the board game of jackals and hounds, oblivious to everything but the play. Studying them, Nefertiti was conscious that she would never understand this little brown woman, not even of noble lineage, whom Amenophis III had elevated to chief wife, who no longer bothered masking her hard-driving force with charm. But the charm must have been there once—and it must have been considerable. Nefertiti crossed the floor to where they sat.

Tiya looked up. As usual her smile did not reach those black, stabbing eyes that in one lifetime had seen everything.

Nefertiti placed a hand on her husband's shoulder, forestalling his getting up. He gazed at her as he always did—if it please Aten, always would—with total adoration. Yet his appearance troubled her. By this time she was used to the increasingly flaccid tone of his muscles, but she couldn't help worrying about what those changes meant. He had never enjoyed robust health or certainty of strength. And there were lines of strain about his mouth; his left eye twitched nervously. He returned the pressure of her hand, stroked her arm, encircled her waist.

Tiya's mouth tightened. "Are you sure, my dear, you're quite ready to be so active?"

Nefertiti's musical laugh rang out. "The babe is almost ready to walk. Very soon we will return to Thebes."

"Yes." Pharaoh picked up an alabaster jackal and fingered it. "I think it will be a difficult move. Not for you, beloved," he added hastily, feeling her start of protest, "but for the court. There will be greater strains at Thebes, more obvious differences between my father and me."

"I wonder, my dear daughter," Tiya purred, "if your Mitannis should accompany us." Her black eyes glinted.

Nefertiti met their gaze coolly. The bitch! All these years Tiya had been trying to banish her daughter-in-law's people from court. How she wanted Nefertiti isolated, a trespasser in a foreign land! But it no longer mattered. Now Nefertiti had been in Egypt too long; moreover, while she had Pharaoh's love, she was untouchable. Actually, at this point in time, Tiya's proposal made sense. Her countrymen ridiculed the strange-faced gods of Egypt. That wouldn't do at Thebes—not at this critical time.

"Your point is well taken. My people will remain here," she acquiesced. Tiya's eyes narrowed suspiciously. Suddenly Nefertiti was glad Tiya was here—and was surprised at herself. For years she had resented the special closeness between mother and son that permitted her husband and Tiya to know each other's mind without speech. But times and conditions change. Yes, Tiya, she returned silently, we are allies, temporarily—but the final battle between us for Pharaoh has not been fought.

"I wish to consult with you both," Nefertiti ventured, "about a problem with Hesen."

Tiya frowned. "That child needs a firmer hand."

Amenophis smiled, as he always did when his favorite was named. "No, Mother. My third daughter has but an abundance of life and joy and spirit, like Neferu-Neferu Nefertiti, my beloved." His hand, warm and tender, moved in loving circles on his wife's back.

"You're blind to her wildness, my son, simply because she looks like her mother."

"For that reason alone, she would be the child of my heart."

"Nonetheless, dearest," Nefertiti insisted, "Hesen's been most indiscreet. Are you aware that she's developed a friendship with the scribe, Senumet, who was brought here by Ay?"

"How was this permitted?" Tiya's sinewy body was suddenly taut with alarm.

Pharaoh looked to his wife. "How careless has she been?"

"Senumet knows of our devotion to the Aten and our distaste for Ay."

"Has he reported that information to Ay?"

"I ascertain he has not. . . . As yet."

Tiya exhaled her relief in sharp sibilance, but still she sat rigid, like a field mouse suspecting the presence of a cobra. "He must not be allowed to confer with Ay."

"It would be dangerous for us," Nefertiti agreed.

"Nothing must be traced to me," Tiya persisted, more pointedly.

Nefertiti understood perfectly. Ay being Tiya's brother, the queen of Amenophis III must come under no suspicion of the deed both women contemplated and deemed exigent. Of what worth was a scribe? Threats so immediate must be rooted out, they assented silently. "I shall take measures . . ." Nefertiti said, as she casually straightened Pharaoh's many rings.

Suddenly, Amenophis removed his hand from his wife's grasp. "I can scarcely believe what I hear!"

"What have you heard, my son," Tiya asked, surprised.

"I hear your thoughts, and in both of you they are shameful!" In the silence that closed in after his words, his eyes seemed to penetrate shadowy corners of their minds. "Every creature on Aten's green earth is part of His loving spirit. How is it you dare even think to abolish one?"

Tiya shut the board with a loud snap. "That scribe can destroy you."

"If I murder, cheat and dissemble, I am no better than my father! I would despise myself as I despise him."

"Your father would cut you down without a backward glance, if you threatened him."

"Exactly. And if I must become him to win, I would rather lose." Amenophis IV raised his hand. The cobra ring of power snaked up his index finger, its obsidian eyes flashing black fire. "I understand you act out of love for me. But no good can be born of evil. Put such thoughts aside. I myself will speak with this Senumet."

"Yes, my son."

"Yes, my husband."

The two women spoke in concert, but as they bent their heads obediently, their eyes met in secret understanding: They'd not disobey him . . . there were other ways. They'd watch Senumet, be strict with Hesen. For Pharaoh must be fine, must walk with *maat*. And when he needed protection, they'd see that he got it, his two women. The love that made them rivals united them in his service.

On the day the boats finally left for Thebes, the sun was as gloriously bright as ever. It irritated Hesen: no matter how bleak life was, the world was always golden—each day that carried them closer to that rigid city was just as beautiful as the day that had passed. Today, as always, the sails sparkled, the water glistened. Only the curtains sheltering the royal apartments hung limply.

"Enough," Hesen complained, pushing at the ostrich-feather fan. "How can you just sit there, Meritaten, with your stupid list?"

Meritaten didn't raise her head. "An heiress can't think merely of pleasure," she murmured archly.

Hesen sniffed. "Try talking duty to Smenkhare, if Pharaoh lets him marry you and proclaims him heir."

Meritaten pursed her lips but didn't answer.

"But perhaps," Hesen went on, painting her heels a rosy pink, "in that dutiful heart, you do not dare to dream of his broad chest and muscled thighs?"

The scroll of papyrus rolled off Meritaten's lap. "Don't be jealous, Sister. One day you too will have a friendship that won't fade."

Hesen's eyes flashed. "And what is that supposed to mean?"

Meritaten picked up the scroll. "People have noticed that the scribe you made so much of seems no longer to have time for you."

"He's busy with important work," Hesen said through tight lips. "He's not lifting the skirt of every slave or getting drunk like your prince!"

"Stop it!" cried a small voice. "Please, my sisters—no more." The frail girl who was huddled on the couch watched them with frightened eyes.

"Oh, Meket." Hesen reached for her, held the light, shivering body. "Don't be upset. Nobody's angry. It's my fault; and I apologize. I'm sorry, Meritaten. There, Meket." She kissed her sister's fair hair. "Please don't start coughing."

Meketaten tried. But already the tightness in her chest was pushing up into her throat and out, racking her body with deep, barking coughs. Servants grabbed the foul-smelling potion standing nearby and forced her to swallow. Hesen wet a piece of linen with cool rose water and bathed her forehead, spoke little love words. Finally the coughing subsided and the small body fell back into the cushions.

Meritaten stood, closed the papyrus roll and brushed off her skirt. "The queen our mother must be informed of Meket's attack. You know how arguments affect our sister." She swept through the curtained passage.

"Queen Fly!" Hesen spat. "That's her future. Buzzing and stinging."

"Oh, Hesen." Meket was smiling. Her hand brushed Hesen's cheek. "How I love you! Of us all, you're the one with the spirit to be heiress. How sad that Meritaten's first and I'm second in line—"

"Dear Meket, you're the finest of us all. It's right that I'm only third. If I were queen, I'd banish everyone to Nubia."

Meket laughed. "Don't stay with me anymore now—you'll only be scolded. Escape before our mother comes to see how I do."

"Are you sure you feel well enough?" Hesen watched her anxiously.

"Quite sure." Meket waved her sister off. Not until the curtains had closed behind Hesen did she allow her hand to fall weakly on the pillows, her eyes to close. . . .

Hesen climbed easily to the top deck, where the oars were regularly oiled and left to dry, where she had a view of the Nile's bright blue ribbon winding through Egypt's length and of the entire royal barge—its rowers pulling in perfect unity, its gaily canopied royal apartments, the far-off games of the children. Leaning on the rail, she let the tears spill out and run down her cheeks. The scene with Meritaten had been her fault. She had known that even as she pursued it.

Aten's light made the waters flash silver and warmed her body, but her heart was cold. The closer they came to Thebes, the more Ay strutted. Now he was in daily conference with the old Pharaoh, who seemed increasingly to depend on him. Meanwhile her father's face grew longer and leaner, and even she, his darling, couldn't coax a smile from him. And since the scene over Senumet, her mother had remained cool and strict.

There was a jubilant shout from a lower deck. Tutu had gotten his bird! Hesen watched as Horemheb, loyal soldier, saluted him smartly, and handed him the next boomerang. Tutu dropped into his hunting crouch, tense and watchful. Horemheb picked up the crossbow, took aim, pulled the stick back, and released. The wooden arrow, shaped like a gliding mallard yet even more beautiful than its living counterpart, soared upward. Tutu hurled the boomerang, but the weapon sailed right past the decoy and curved back, landing on the deck at his feet. The boy snatched it up and threw it into the river. It appeared that all the royal children needed discipline; Hesen sighed, but her frown faded as she saw that Horemheb did not intend to let this pass. His bearing correct and military, he was scolding Tutu. She liked Horemheb. If he was no less stupid than soldiers generally, he was also patient and good-tempered and seemed less puffed up than the others with his rank and uniform and peasant good looks. And now, Tutu, his head hanging, looked properly ashamed. Well, one of them at least was not lost to remorse. Horemheb offered Tutu another boomerang, and the lesson resumed.

Her mind drifted to her own lessons with Senumet . . .

She clambered swiftly down to the work deck, careful to skirt the royal apartments and skim silently past the priests' corner, the canopied throne room and the servants' quarters, where her own Sephy waited to be called. Since scholarly lessons had been suspended aboard ship, Senumet had joined the other scribes, and it was toward their quarters she made her way. Ordinarily she would not walk through this part of the ship, where all the work was done that made life abovedeck so pleasant. Here all was bustle and noise, and wonderful scents arose and mingled—the oils, the unguents, the polish, the beer sloshing in clay vessels, and over all, the pungent marvel of honey-drenched shat-cakes. Workers looked at her curiously, then quickly bowed, averting their eyes from one who had the look of the Living God.

Hesen carried herself with the easy majesty that was so a part of her she was unaware of it. Even the uncertain breath she took as she approached the scribes' bureau went unnoticed by those whose business it was to study her.

Bek looked startled when she swept in, but he hurried to her side. "My lady?"

"Pharaoh wishes a text translated," she began.

He raised a quizzical eyebrow. "If I may have it?"

"He wishes that a scribe accompany me to his presence."

"Of course," Bek nodded. "Ka-Aper, take charge here. I'll return—"

"Oh, no," she cut him off firmly. "Pharaoh would not want to interrupt your work here. He thought another might be spared . . . perhaps Senumet?" Hesen had spoken in her usual clear tones; now she felt the sudden silence into which they had fallen. Her glance touched everyone in the room, and she saw half-smiles and bold looks before the glances were lowered and hands resumed their work.

Senumet quickly crossed the room to where she stood.

"Come with me," she ordered. Silently they proceeded out of the bureau.

They were alone at last . . . and still he did not speak. As they began their climb to her secret place, she tripped, would have fallen, but his hand was there. At the top she turned to face him—and found words wouldn't come. His eyes burned hers with an expression that made her tremble.

"There is no text," he said finally.

"No," she managed and stood mute, like Tutu.

"If Pharaoh has no need of me, then, I'll return to my duties, my lady." He bowed and would have left.

"No." Incredibly her eyes filled with tears and she reached out, gripped his arm. The muscles under her fingers hardened. She couldn't move.

"Hesen!" It sounded almost like a groan.

She fell against him, pressing herself to his bare chest. Against his will, his arms embraced her. He buried his face in her fragrant hair and they stood, motionless, outside of time as the barge sliced onward to Thebes through the heavy waters. Finally he released her and stepped back.

"Oh, Senumet," she breathed, "I've been so unhappy these past few weeks. What made you so remote?"

"As you know, we can't continue like this."

"I know nothing of the sort. My father has his harem; my grandfather as well. I only want you."

The muscles in his jaw tightened. "That's foolishness. I don't expect you to sound like a child."

She frowned. "What is being a princess if I can't have what I want?"

"There's no question of choice. Our roles were assigned at birth, as was our future."

"So you retreat, recalling the friendship that you had no right to offer in the first place," she said accusingly.

"Yes." His hand gripped the rail, the knuckles whitened. "We are scribe and princess, nothing more. And obviously the lessons should be terminated, too, since it would be very hard to maintain a proper distance."

She had noticed his knuckles, saw the pulse throb in his temple, finally understood her power. "But you love me," she said, her voice steady.

He laughed, a painful sound of cynical disdain. "What difference? Our separate worlds touched briefly—but now they spin apart."

She frowned. Something didn't make sense. "There is no problem. Nobody minded our friendship. Nothing occurred until—it had to be after the day you . . . kissed me," she said a little breathlessly. She remembered the scene that followed with her mother; remembered as well that in her careless, wild indulgence that afternoon, she had spoken of Senumet. "The queen spoke with you," she said flatly.

"No, Hesen, not the queen."

"Who, then?"

"Pharaoh."

"My father?" Her hand flew to her mouth.

"Yes, it had reached even his ears."

"Aten help me," she breathed. If her father commanded it, she had no recourse. He was supreme.

"But you may know always there's someone wishes your happiness."

"That's silly sentiment, badly said and unworthy of you," she snapped. "Even Hathor, dumb cow goddess, could do better."

His laughter surprised them both. "You're a strange mixture, Hesen. Right now, there are only flashes of the woman you will someday be. I would have wished to know her," he finished in a tone that brooked no response.

Hesen realized dully an emptiness had opened inside her that she had never felt before, would soon recognize as loss.

"At least, let the lessons continue," she cried out in a small voice. She was aware she was pleading, she who had never beseeched anything of anyone in her life, whose willing servants always anticipated her requests and satisfied her every desire. His eyes were remote—would they ever again look at her free of constraint?

"If Pharaoh so commands." He bowed and left her.

And now, when she leaned on the rail, she knew the first full and bitter taste of despair.

# V

Nefertiti dressed for the landing at Thebes. She lowered the high crown of Amenophis' own design on her head. It was a lighter, softer version of his own, but just different enough to have a distinctly non-Egyptian look. She supposed it was capriciously foolish to wear it here—they were suspicious enough of her—but some perverse instinct made her accentuate her foreignness. Even her speech was reassuming the accent she'd discarded years ago. They had never accepted her as queen, these provincial, arrogant, recalcitrant priests of Amon. So. She would make their homage even harder for them by reminding them she was alien.

Entering her husband's apartments, she caught him in an unguarded moment. His hands, hanging loosely over the chair posts, had an almost helpless look, and his face had fallen into despondent lines. She ached for him, thinking he deserved better, yet very little that really mattered to him had ever gone right. And oddly, at bottom, was the fact that although he might talk of how vulgar and how hateful his father was, he could not bear that Amenophis despised him. He knew very well that what his father wanted of a first son was a man like Smenkhare, a companion in drunkenness and gross lechery. And no matter what Amenophis IV was—no matter how hard he studied, how concerned with Egypt he was, how sensitive to its needs—he could never be that and so could never win Pharaoh's approbation—and love. Even though his mother had forced the king to accept him as heir, the whole court knew Pharaoh still laughed at him.

"My lord," she called, and watched his whole face lift with love of her. What joy, that expression. It was becoming her only fixed point in a dangerously shifting world. And love was the last thing she'd expected! Brought to Egypt as a bride to his father, she had thought she'd spend the rest of her life as a minor wife in a harem, to be used and ignored at his will. When she had first come—Aten forgive her—she had laughed at Pharaoh's son with the rest of the court; had been amused to watch him stutter and stumble around her, his face flaming with inarticulate admiration. But when she had realized he planned to ask Pharaoh for her, himself—she drew in her breath, remembering how she had seized on that wild hope and deliberately set out to dazzle him still more. And how, after a while, when he was finally able to speak to her, she had discovered a force she must respect in him, a power that still surprised her.

They had done very well together all these years, she reflected, only . . . he had given her so much, she wanted to return love for love; but it had come out, always, only gratitude. She hoped he would never guess. Love had happened to her only once, in Mitanni, and that memory had dimmed a long time ago. She had discovered that being wife to the heir was a position with so many compensations she could truthfully say she was happy. And as the years passed, she even found something to believe in again. Having never been able to love the cow-, bird- or snake-headed gods of Egypt, occasionally she had longed for the golden arms of Savriti, whom she had worshipped in Mitanni . . . until she found she could adore Aten. And since Aten could shine only through Amenophis her husband, she was coming to love Amenophis, too. Like a young girl, she thought. They just had to wait until Amenophis his father died. Then they would create a new world together.

"Come." He smiled, and took her arm. "Pharaoh wishes to speak with us before docking."

Amenophis III sat on his throne, his bulk covered by a voluminous purple caftan, stitched with silver thread that sparkled in the morning light. Tiya reclined on pillows near him.

A shadow fleetingly crossed Nefertiti's face. Tiya sat at his feet only when he was feeling better. Looking at him searchingly, she saw that his face was much less swollen, and realized that the foul oozing mass on his gums must have burst. It was too bad, really, that his health had improved on the way to Thebes . . .

"You are looking well this morning, Majesty," Amenophis IV greeted him.

"Amon be praised!" his father declared.

Nefertiti's eyes darted to her husband, noted the tightening of his mouth.

"Ay has prayed for me and I owe Amon much for my recovery." His Highness's beady eyes fixed on his son. "And in gratitude to Amon I'm going to raise the temple's tax levy. That was what I summoned you for. I want you to know before I tell the priests." His fat rippled as he settled back grandly.

"If the peasants go hungry as a result—since there'll be less food— there may be trouble from that quarter," his son suggested shrewdly, knowing how his father feared unrest. "Also, have you considered that because there'll be less grain available to ship to the colonies, the Hittites may be able to make inroads?"

"The inundation will be particularly good this year," Pharaoh answered coldly. "It will be no sacrifice to give the priests a larger share. All those who love me must agree."

"But why, Father?" Amenophis IV persisted. "It will just concentrate more power in their hands."

"Their hands are our hands. They are Egypt."

"Not true. Pharaoh holds the vision of what Egypt can be. Pharaoh molds the priests to his will."

"That way will tear the country apart."

"If, in pursuit of truth, those who live in darkness are shaken, so be it!"

Amenophis III spat. "All you moralistic fools make me sick. Together with *maat*, you'll destroy everything. Know merely what I intend and rally your support. Go now. You tire me!" He waved his son off.

Nefertiti put a soft, warning hand on her husband's arm and gently urged him away. She saw his eyes were filled with naked fury.

She didn't know how much longer she'd be able to restrain him— but she was certain the time left to them of a rancorous if peaceful truce with Amenophis III was drawing desperately short.

Four royal chariots waited at the dock. The horses stamped the sandy ground impatiently and tossed their heads. Wadjit-eyed blinders gave them the look of the god, and their ostrich plumes waved in the morning breeze. Hesen and her two older sisters were lifted into a chariot. As the driver cracked his whip, they took their place, third in the line of chariots, after the old Pharaoh and his queen and their own parents. Behind them came the two princes. Smenkhare had dismissed the driver and taken the reins himself; already his horses were out of line.

Hesen was glad her sisters were quiet during the ride to the great temple of Karnak. She took no pleasure from her lacy princess-crown of forget-me-nots, from her pink-gold pectoral, from the fact that her gown in diamonds of blue and green molded seductively to her body and was receiving many looks of warm interest. In truth, she had felt nothing since her last meeting with Senumet, who must now be somewhere in back, in the wooden carriages reserved for the court.

The horses, drawn sharply right, carried the procession along the avenue flanked by the double rows of stone rams, through the massive third pylon. They stopped at the bright electrum doors of the temple where Tushratta, chief priest, headed the welcoming officials.

Hesen watched as both Pharaohs alighted and bowed before the mighty god-place of Amon. She knew how her father must feel, and her heart ached for him.

When the doors of the temple swung open to admit them, Ay, Tushratta, and the two Pharaohs disappeared inside. Nobody else had ever entered the dark sanctuary. In the brief moment the doors parted, Hessen saw flashes of color from glowing braziers and the glitter of jewels.

The welcoming officials remained attentive, their robes rippling in the soft morning breeze, as a young woman, ripe and brilliantly adorned, came forward to tug at the sleeve of the senior official. She was overdressed, Hesen noted, but there was an animal attraction about the girl—an openness suggesting earthy delights that Hesen could sense even at this distance.

"Who is that?" she asked her charioteer.

He followed her gaze, said without hesitating, "Nephrus, my lady, daughter to Rahmose, headman of Thebes."

Hesen observed Nephrus's progress, lost her briefly in the crowd, spied her again as she pushed her way determinedly to the rear of the procession. Suddenly the stillness of the solemn greeting of the god was pierced by her cry of delight as she threw her arms around a startled young man. Eyes turned in the crowd, and Hesen reeled as if struck. Senumet. Nephrus and Senumet.

"You see"—Meritaten was always awake to opportunity—"he has the tastes of a peasant, after all."

Meket's hand stole consolingly into Hesen's.

Hesen hardly noticed. She was concentrating on controlling the ragged breaths that threatened to become hysteria. Her only thought was to cover her humiliation. Of the rest of the ceremony she saw nothing.

At the palace afterward, Hesen escaped from the bustle of arrival and took herself to the royal gardens. But their orderly beauty compounded her misery.

Smenkhare landed at her feet. "So, dear daughter of the king, you too are lost to claims of duty."

"Where did you come from?" she demanded, wrinkling her nose at his breath, which was redolent of black wine.

"My home in the heavens," he intoned.

She looked up into the dense green of the sycamore. "You've a tree house."

"And too bad for you, royal infant, since you lack the skill to ascend."

"Nonsense!" She hiked up her skirt. He gaped, but she swung herself off the ground, careless of the expanse of thigh revealed. Straining, she drew herself up through the branches. Above, a green canopy shielded a small wooden platform and she wiggled onto it. Smenkhare had followed her up the tree. Lowering himself onto the boards, he rolled over to lie beside her, ran his fingers up and down her arm. She moved away.

"Can't go far," he mocked, and she realized she was at the edge. "Here," he offered, "try this for courage."

She took the bottle of black wine and raised it to her mouth. Courage she didn't want; blankness would do. Just for a while to blot out the image of another girl in Senumet's arms. She took a long drink. Fire ran down her throat.

"Feels good, doesn't it?" Perspiration dotted Smenkhare's upper lip, his tongue moistened his mouth, and he leaned into her. "Have more."

Recklessly she took another long sip. No fire now, just a spreading warmth. She kicked off her sandals and watched them disappear through the foliage. "I'm free!" she told the prince, wiggling her toes, accepting the bottle from him again. They passed it back and forth. The first time she felt his hand exploring her waist she slapped it away. But after a while she let him hold her because she wasn't sure exactly where the platform ended, and her legs were feeling strangely heavy and vague, a little difficult to control. Just a hand to steady her—that was all; she wouldn't let him move it up or down. After a few minutes, his fingers slipped along her thigh.

"No! Stop it!" she commanded, but her words sounded thick even to her own ears and her mouth was very dry. He had to help her lift the bottle—odd that it should be so much harder to handle now when it was lighter. A little of the wine dripped down her chin. She giggled and let him lick it off her face. "Thank you," she said in that strange slurred voice.

"Always ready to serve you," he vowed, raising the bottle to his own lips. He shook it, puzzled, and realizing it was empty, sent it crashing through the leaves.

His face was close to hers. She realized it was hard to make him out. His image separated into two Smenkhares and she couldn't seem to merge them. She jerked back a little when his mouth touched her neck, but he held her firmly, and his wet lips continued to press against the hollow where her pulse fluttered.

*Why not?* she thought recklessly. Who needed Senumet with his "couldn't do this," "wouldn't do that"? Who was Senumet, anyway? There were princes who liked her! Almost angrily she threw her arms around Smenkhare and raised her face to his. He ground his lips over hers and tried to thrust his tongue inside her mouth. Oh, not like that! She tried to turn aside, but she was pinned under his weight. Her hands beat at his chest. He pulled her close, crushing her hands against his body, forced her teeth apart with the insistent pressure of his mouth on hers. She felt his harsh breath in her throat. Suddenly a hand was shoving itself between her legs. Fingers thrust into her private hair. She was frightened now, half-smothered and dizzy. The world tilted and spun; his tongue was choking her. He released her suddenly and her head snapped back. His hand pulled free one white breast, his head lowered to it, and he sucked noisily. Desperately, sobs tearing out of her, she twisted away with a strong push. The platform lurched. It tore loose from the thin anchoring ropes, and they crashed through the branches.

Her head swimming, the first thing Hesen was aware of was a heavy weight. Smenkhare had fallen on top of her and, incredibly, his mouth was clamped over hers again.

Suddenly a frenzied little body leaped on Smenkhare and was all over him, pummeling him with small fists, kicking him with sandaled toes. "Leave her. Get off her. I'll kill you." Tutu was sobbing. Smenkhare swiped at him carelessly and knocked him down. He was up in an instant, ready for battle.

All at once Hesen could breathe. The weight was gone. She turned her head and saw that Smenkhare was sprawled on the ground and Tutu was standing beside her, staring worshipfully at some tall, blurred figure on the periphery of her vision. She struggled to focus . . . made out Horemheb, his pectoral of service shining on his chest.

Smenkhare struggled to his feet, rubbing his jaw. "How did you dare touch Pharaoh's son?" he demanded angrily.

"Forgive me, Highness," Horemheb said contritely. His eyes were unrepentant. "Your . . . uh . . . back was to me and I didn't recognize you. I thought the princess was being attacked."

Smenkhare looked at Hesen, still sprawled as he had left her, her dress pulled up over her thighs.

"We fell out of the tree," he found himself explaining, although princes of the realm explained nothing. "I won't report you this time, but take care in the future."

"Yes, Majesty. Thank you, Majesty." Horemheb bowed respectfully, and still his eyes didn't leave Smenkhare's face.

"And you"—the prince brushed himself off, scowled at Tutu—"best not attack your superiors again. Others will not be so kind." He turned on his heel and, although he swayed and stumbled, made an exhibition of marching smartly away.

"One day, Horemheb," Tutu promised, "I'll make you Master of the Horse. Hesen, why are you just lying there? He's gone now."

Cautiously, Hesen eased herself up on her elbows. The world swam around her, and a bitter taste threatened to rise into her mouth.

"Close your eyes, my lady," Horemheb advised. The smell of black wine was very strong. "Forgive me, but you'll feel better in the shade."

Strong arms scooped her up effortlessly, deposited her against the offending sycamore in its cool shadow. She swallowed carefully and opened her eyes. Aten be praised. The world was again fixed in space.

"Thank you, Horemheb. I hope you won't have any trouble over this."

"Trouble? Oh, no, my lady. Everyone knows I'm just a simple soldier. Unquestionably loyal."

"To whom?" she asked curiously. In this court, allegiances were strangely twisted.

"Why, to me, of course," Tutu proclaimed.

"To you first, my comrade-in-arms." Horemheb smiled. "And also to Smenkhare and the old Pharaoh. Even to your father, my lady."

"Even? Why do you say 'even'?" she demanded.

"No reason, my lady," he stammered. "I'm no good with words. My specialty is arms. Forgive me, my lady."

Hesen closed her eyes. The sickness she felt was more than black wine.

"Stay with her, Tutu," Horemheb ordered, glad of an excuse to be off. "I'll call a servant."

Finally back in her apartments, she was sick in the basin Sephy held out, tears and sweat and sour vomit staining the scented sheets. Her dress was removed and when Sephy examined it, she clucked disgustedly and threw it away. Her limbs were bathed and soothing unguents applied to the bruises. Her hair was washed. Finally, her hair damp and curling and perfumed, her body free of all traces of dirt and dissipation, she lay back on soft pillows.

"All right, my lady"—Sephy's no-nonsense accents cut through her torpor—"tell me the truth."

"I climbed a tree and fell," she said woodenly.

"This to me?" Sephy persisted. "You who could climb a pyramid and not stub your toe?"

"I fell out of a tree," she repeated.

"Where you happened to pause to drink half a bottle of black wine."

"Oh, Sephy," she cried. "I'm so unhappy."

Relenting, the servant sat down beside her, and Hesen, sobbing, buried her face in the plump, yielding shoulder.

"No, my darling, don't cry." Sephy stroked the damp head, the heaving back. She had had the foresight to send the others away when she first saw her lady's condition. She trusted no one in the household to know Hesen's thoughts. "It's all the fault of that young man."

Hesen sat up, her eyes startled.

"Can you fool Sephy? Do I understand my baby?"

"What do you mean?"

The maid removed the traces of tears. "Not for nothing, my lady, do I spend every waking minute in your service, attentive to your slightest frown."

Hesen kissed her lovingly. "You are my own dearest."

"I saw your face when that cheap slut hugged Senumet. You were persuaded she had been his love all along, that he must have been playing with you, laughing at how easy you were."

"Yes," Hesen admitted dejectedly.

"None of that is true. That snit would do anything to have him look at her just once the way he always looks at you."

"How do you know this?"

"Her servants sought me out after the ceremonies. They wished to hear of you."

"What did they say?"

"First, I want to know what use you will make of this."

"It would ease my spirit," Hesen answered honestly. "I can be nothing but a shameless, worthless thing if he has merely used me."

"Let me speak plainly," Sephy said severely. "The way you've been acting is improper. It demeans you, tarnishes your family's honor. You behave sometimes like those women who sell themselves to men."

Hesen was shocked. "How can you say that? I am an unmarried girl—to lie with a man is a sinful act. You cannot suppose that—"

"I say the juices run sweet and hot through your body and you may be careless of the distant future."

"Sephy," she said earnestly, "I have not forgotten all your teachings and my mother's."

"Let's see how you remember." Sephy's voice took on the sing-song pattern of years past: "Thou must not trespass against the gods or the dead."

"Or the crocodile may rob me of all my potent charms," Hesen responded, as she had in the schoolroom.

"Thou must not covet what is withheld from thee."

"Or water may burst into flame as I drink." Hesen shuddered. She hated this catechism of sin and punishment.

"Thou must not bring false witness against any man."

"Or the lion will rip away my name." Were they to name all forty-two sins?

"Thou must not"—Sephy stressed each word—"lie with any man save thy wedded lord."

"Or the foes of the air may withdraw breath from my nostrils." Hesen's voice was almost a whisper. Her stomach muscles knotted painfully.

Sephy looked at her steadily. When she spoke again, her words were quiet but intense.

"I ask you, third daughter to the king, model to your sisters, have you lain with any man?"

"I have not," she whispered.

"And will not."

Hesen hesitated, but the strength of those lessons was too great. "And will not," she agreed unhappily.

Sephy stood up. "All right," she said. "That girl you saw would have given him anything to have kept him here. She would have made her father move him to first scribe, would have promised him all her estates, if he would only marry her."

"And he refused." Suddenly Hesen was aware that the room was warm with sunlight. Oh, yes, she could understand how a girl might love him. She could even feel pity for someone whose charms left him unmoved.

"So now you know," Sephy said doubtfully, watching Hesen's eyes sparkle. "He did love you. And now it's all over."

Hesen made an absent, reassuring reply, not realizing her lips were curving upward in reflection of her thoughts. All over, indeed! To find out her passion was returned, then to consider it ended? Of course not! That made no sense at all!

# VI

Once again Senumet walked with Nephrus along the riverbank. He felt separated from his old life by a gulf wider than the broad, rippling girth of the Nile he had just sailed.

"You've changed," Nephrus said hesitantly. "I can't find the old Senumet in your face."

"Happily, the old Nephrus is still there," he replied, thinking of the gusto with which she had greeted him.

"Yes, Senumet, I have no shame where you're concerned. Each day that you've been gone has been sunless."

"I've missed you too," he said guiltily, even as he rejected guilt. They'd had their time and it was ended.

"I deserve more than the meaningless compliments of a courtier." Angrily.

"But that is what I am, Nephrus!"

"My father said court life would bore you. He said that when you came to know royalty, you'd appreciate us more."

"I hope I've never failed to show gratitude to you or your father."

"I don't want gratitude, Senumet!"

"Nephrus," he begged, "let it stay as it is. You'll always have my friendship."

"While that one with the pale eyes and small breasts has only to beckon and you fly."

He stopped. "What are you talking about?"

"Those of us who care about you have had reports of the goings on at Memphis. We know how shameless your princess has been." She spat.

His eyes were ice. "It does not become you to pry into affairs that are not your concern."

"Once you were very eager for me to involve myself in your affairs!"

"That account was paid in full. And in currency of your own choosing, as I recall it."

"Your favors go where rewards are highest." Her nail furiously struck his gold armband. "Did you pay for your latest in the same coin?"

"Not at all," he said, unruffled. "There's no thought of debt or remuneration where there's regard on both sides."

Her hand flew to her mouth. Her hurt was palpable. "My father will be interested to know how you insult me."

"I'm sorry if I've given offense." He felt as if he were walking at the edge of a precipice. She was watching him, waiting; even the weakest apology would be excuse enough for her to forgive him. He wouldn't give it. Silence grew between them until her face flamed with the shame of it. Finally she spun away from him and ran down the path.

Senumet sighed. To have insulted the headman's daughter, and that headman his former patron, almost as influential as Ay. Senumet knew how dangerous it was to incur the displeasure of the powerful. Why then had he risked it? Had love made him soft? It could not be denied, he thought, that Hesen played a part, but even had Hesen never existed, he could not have cared for Nephrus. And being certain of this, surely his honesty, however painful, was in Nephrus's own best interests. Now that she knew how things really were, and could see that neither time nor distance would change them, she could finally begin her life.

In forcing Nephrus to free herself from her love of him, Senumet only hoped he had not impaired the promise of his future.

Ay waited impatiently for the banquet to begin. There had been no time after the ceremonies this morning to meet with Tushratta and Rahmose. If circumstances continued as they were going, his plans might come to fruition even sooner than he had hoped. If this were Memphis, he would already have met with the priests in his private villa, but at Thebes he stayed at the palace, where he had too many official duties for a private audience to go unremarked.

Tey finally arrived at their apartments. "I'll hurry and dress," she said a little breathlessly. "The babe fussed and it took some time to settle her. I think the queen's milk turns sour with her temper."

"What's troubling Nefertiti?" Ay questioned.

"She's still angry at Hesen, and the two of them are too much in each other's company since the queen is determined to confine her. But it's more than that. The royal women are always in low spirits at Thebes. And this year Amenophis the father is, if anything, happier to be here than ever."

"I'm wondering about Hesen. It started at Memphis," Ay reflected. "You were never able to find out what that was about." He asked, although he was sure he knew. . . .

Tey stretched out her arms and her handmaidens removed her rings and bracelets. When she stepped out of her dress, they wrapped her in a fleecy cloth. She waved them away and Ay could hear the sounds of her bath as the room filled with the scent of rose water. "You could never induce Sephy to talk," he mused.

"I think, my husband," Tey replied, "that one day it might be wise to ship Sephy home. Her allegiance is too unshakable."

Ay nodded and saluted his wife affectionately before leaving her to her bath. That bit of advice he'd remember. Meanwhile he speculated about Hesen and the queen. He had decided that Nefertiti's anger was the result of the girl's indiscretions with Senumet. A matter of little enough consequence. They might have lain together, true, but that didn't interest Ay; in any event, Hesen hadn't revealed anything important. Senumet was too young and inexperienced to have been able to conceal any sort of weighty information from the skillful questioners Ay had planted among the scribes.

He strolled into the front courtyard, where alabaster lanterns were already lit and slaves waited at the palace gates to guide the chariots and horses to their evening's stable. In the deepening dusk, Ay could already make out moving pinpoints of light. The lesser nobility, afraid to be late. Ay smiled wryly. It was still light enough to see quite well, yet these earlycomers were so proud of their affluence they could never bring themselves to dispense with their runners. Probably they would have slaves running alongside holding aloft burning torches to light the way even if they rode in brightest morning. Ay shook his head and turned to reenter the palace before they arrived—it would be inappropriate for the grand vizier to greet them. Some time later, when he returned to the courtyard with Tey on his arm, darkness had descended, but by now the road was ablaze with burning lights. He enjoyed this moment, the sparkle like a string of jewels against the clear black night, and hesitated briefly, savoring the quiet of this pageantry in contrast to what he knew the banquet hall would present. Then he led Tey over the threshold.

Ay was so used to these lavish displays—the profusions of flowers, the stacked tables—he had stopped taking note of them years ago. At Thebes, however, there was one charming addition that still delighted Ay. The elegantly carved chairs were grouped around a large interior pool in which tiered alabaster lights had been designed to float back and forth, in the course of their slow journey igniting sparks on gold bracelets and lapis earrings, catching the glitter of painted eyes. Tall alabaster lanterns were spaced along the pool's edge, encircled with beds of lotus. Sprays of water arced into the pool from the mouths of limestone lions crouching at its four corners.

Ay led his wife to a seat with the other court ladies. Tonight men and women were seated on opposite sides of the pool. As Ay took his own place, even his jaded eyes lightened at the slim and elegant look of the ladies, their legs tucked neatly beneath their chairs, their gowns curving with the lines of their well-kept bodies. Ay sipped the strong wine. Eventually Rahmose and Tushratta arrived and took places at either side of him. Greeting them, Ay relaxed. There would be time to talk. Let the festivities begin.

During the meal, the three of them watched as other guests stuffed themselves and drank deeply of the flowing wine. In all that room only Ay, Rahmose and Tushratta ate lightly—and one other, the new Pharaoh.

"He doesn't eat," Tushratta whispered. "His mouth curls with hate when he looks at his father."

Rahmose had noticed too. "Is there a reason why Amenophis IV should be particularly discontent?"

"Forgive me," Ay apologized. "I should have sent a messenger. Amenophis III decreed this morning that we may increase the tax levy for each village by one deben of silver."

Rahmose looked thoughtful, and his shrewd little eyes narrowed calculatingly. "That's a very significant addition," he announced finally.

"Two things are even more significant," Tushratta added, taking care that his words might reach their ears only. "First, we owe thanks to Ay, who convinced Pharaoh that Amon interceded in his behalf and cured him."

"That will be reflected in your portion, of course," Rahmose promised. As headman, he collected taxes and tributes from the peasants and nobility alike, and even though the priests and Pharaoh sent their own agents, it was always possible for a clever headman to alter the totals in his own favor—a power of which Ay was very aware.

"That's very thoughtful of you, my friend," he said, "but I won't accept it. It's enough to know we have common cause."

Rahmose inclined his head. "Only one thing worries me. What happens when Pharaoh sickens again?"

Ay laughed heartily. He clapped the headman's arm affectionately. "When the pustule again forms, I'll try to convince Pharaoh there's a poison in the royal house that must be purged. That man will believe anything he's told, so long as he's not told he must stop indulging himself."

Indeed, even now, Amenophis III's face shone with grease almost to his puffy eyes. His teeth tore into a leg of crisp duck, and bits of it clung to his lips. Glass after glass of wine washed the food down, and his voice thundered above all others. While one hand gripped a pomegranate, the other fondled a serving girl. Ay's glance flicked to his sister; Tiya was wisely averting her eyes. But when Pharaoh bit the breasts of the Nubian slave who was offering him dates, Ay could see the effort it took for his sister to remain indifferent.

Rahmose was the first to look away. "You said two things were more significant," he reminded Tushratta. "What's the other?"

"That we use our time here before the inundation to drive the wedge between father and son even deeper."

"Yes," Rahmose nodded. "How may we do that?"

Ay liked the way they looked to him for the next step—as he would make sure they'd turn to him after Amenophis died. First, however, he must remove the legitimate heir. "I'm thinking about a public ceremony," he said slowly, "with all of Thebes as witness. I want Amenophis III to command his son to honor any god but Aten."

"Does Pharaoh know of his son's devotion to Aten?" Rahmose asked doubtfully.

Tushratta laughed and took Ay's arm. "There's no doubt in my mind that the old king has been kept informed."

"I believe you can reasonably suppose that," Ay smiled.

"Then I've a very good idea," Rahmose suggested. "We're heading into the time of inundation. We'll have the Festival of Osiris."

"Excellent!" Ay saw the possibilities immediately.

It had sometimes occurred to him that if he had to choose a single focal point for the community's year, he would pick the Festival of Osiris. The story moved everyone: Osiris, the murdered, dismembered king of Egypt—whose wife, Isis, had ranged the length and breadth of Egypt until she located the forty-two mutilated parts of his body. Having reanimated the parts briefly with the breath of love, she had conceived the boy Horus, who ultimately avenged his father's murder. Now Osiris ruled in the Underworld, as he would forever, but the promise of his resurrection was felt each year in the new growth after the inundation. Yes, even Amenophis IV, Pharaoh though he might be, must acknowledge Osiris—or he'd be torn apart by an outraged populace. Nothing would ever be permitted to endanger the inundation.

Rahmose said hesitantly, "I want to discuss something of a personal nature with both of you that has some bearing on the festival."

Suddenly trumpets blared. Ay held up his hand. "The entertainment starts. Later we'll continue." He leaned back to allow a servant to heap his plate with glazed fruit, flat bread, and crisp, roasted pigeon. As the dancers from Amenophis III's own harem pirouetted in, Ay relaxed and munched contentedly on a date. These were the choicest and most graceful of Pharaoh's wives. Their breasts were bare and gilded, the gold flecks glittering with each movement. They wore short white skirts stretched tight across their buttocks and barely covering their dark, curling pubic hair. Their eyes were silvered, their hair parted into two braids, each swinging with the weight of a gold disk. They danced in precise unison, this line of wives, the flashing disks accentuating the rhythm clapped out by two musicians. Finally the women eased down until they rested on their knees and leaned back until their heads touched the floor between their toes. Thus bent, their bodies rose and fell, rose and fell, in a parody of copulation, while the bushes between their legs pushed out of their confines. Ay wet his lips and clapped noisily.

They were followed by wild naked acrobats who tumbled and somersaulted in and out among the stone lions and finally leaped, rolling through the air, dangerously across the pool, to gasps from the spectators. Then musicians and singers displayed their talents; the last of these, by tradition, was the famous blind harpist, who always stirred to tears those sober enough to hear his mournful chords. As usual at this point in the banquet, some of the more gluttonous guests had to be carried out. Two women were emptying their stomachs into faience basins, and a number of men had fallen off their chairs.

Rahmose said, "About my own problem—my eldest, Nephrus, has given me no peace this past year. She's developed a passion for your protégé, Senumet."

"That boy's done very well for himself."

"Too well," Rahmose returned with an edge of bitterness. "The sulks and bad temper I've had to endure would drive the blessed Isis mad. To make matters worse, Nephrus had some fight with the fellow since you've returned and has been crying and storming ever since."

Ay's mouth twitched. Was he now to settle romantic disputes? "How may I help you, Rahmose?"

"Well, Senumet is a good man, as you know. He's not what I would have chosen for Nephrus only because I thought to unite this nome to Ombos by having Nephrus marry that headman's son. Fah! What's the use? I can't bear this infernal carrying on. I've decided to let her marry Senumet."

"That's very generous," Ay remarked sincerely. "On his own, Senumet could never have hoped for such honor. And don't worry, Rahmose. He'll earn distinction in my service. None shall say Nephrus has lowered herself." That was easily done. And Ay was fond of Senumet. The boy handled himself with grace and intelligence. He'd enjoy having him close to hand.

"Thank you, my friend, but you don't entirely understand." Rahmose hesitated, obviously unhappy with having to explain further. "Nephrus has learned the boy is involved with Princess Ankhesenpaaten."

Ay shrugged. "What's 'involved'? A little dalliance—which, in fact, might be useful to us, since she's loose of tongue."

"There's more," Rahmose persisted. "Nephrus claims Senumet refused her own advances. She's convinced he's in love with the princess."

"Does that make sense to you? Really, my friend, I begin to think your daughter has a bridle on you. Senumet's a realist—I might say 'opportunist'—just like the rest of us. He's a smart boy, has always done what he has to do to assure his position."

"Still," the headman urged, "I'd like you to talk to him . . . get him to apologize and agree to a betrothal."

Ay looked at his friend and shook his head.

"All of Thebes fears you," he said finally, unable to resist the impulse.

"But not Nephrus," Rahmose agreed ruefully. "And another

thing. Tushratta, during the festival, you must appoint Senumet the scribe who paints Osiris. If my daughter is to marry him, at least let's give him some prominence."

Tushratta nodded while Ay assured Rahmose, "More than that, I'll speak to Tiya. She'll see to it that the princess keeps away from him entirely until he's safely betrothed to Nephrus. But afterward, if you don't mind, I'd like to maintain that connection between Senumet and the princess. It will give us access to information about Amenophis IV; Hesen's his favorite." Ay spoke with sincere accents, but his mind raced. He'd agree with anything Rahmose asked, of course; he needed the headman's support. But Ay wanted that connection with the princess too—a connection that might be more difficult to maintain were Senumet actually married. Well, there was a great distance between a betrothal and a wedding.

"So be it. Nephrus will have to accept it. Just let me get her betrothed."

"The sooner he gets her seeded the better," Ay suggested. "Nothing like breeding to settle them."

"No doubt Nephrus has thought of that already. With that girl, even breeding will be an ordeal," Rahmose said with conviction. "Thank Amon, of all my children only Nephrus is like her mother."

And all three relaxed in laughter.

Hesen's confinement hadn't ended with their removal to Thebes. She was even more closely watched now than before. Even so, and although she saw Senumet in occasional glimpses, for some strange reason she did not feel dispirited. There was a certainty in her heart she didn't examine. Her time would come. She didn't know how it would happen or even what her optimism meant, but a song lilted inside her, and for the first time she could wait without impatience.

She was surprised when her grandmother asked to meet with her. She was the least loved granddaughter, a fact of life she'd accepted years ago. She even understood why. Her mother and Tiya had never been able to mask their hostility perfectly, and Hesen realized some of the antagonism spilled over to herself simply because she so resembled Nefertiti. It was not difficult to understand, Hesen thought, repressing a smile as she watched Tiya walk briskly toward her. Next to Nefertiti, who would look at that bitter, nasty face?

"Highness." She bowed and kissed her grandmother's ring.

"You're looking well, child," Tiya allowed. "I see you've taken my advice and protected your face from the sun."

"I can take no credit for that. I've been confined to my rooms. Your summons is the only reason I've been allowed to walk in the garden today."

Tiya frowned. "You're too old for that kind of punishment."

Hesen thought so too, but she'd never criticize her mother.

Tiya motioned her to a seat. Without preamble, she declared, "You're willful and careless," in that brisk, assured way of hers that made Hesen want to shake her. "The grand vizier, my brother, has spoken to me about you."

"Ay? But I have nothing to do with him!" Hesen protested.

"You've had too much to do with that scribe he brought to court!"

Hesen's mouth tightened stubbornly. "He was my tutor."

"You shared more than lessons with him!" Tiya snapped. "And since you never stop to think, I suppose you have not observed how your notice has hurt him."

"How can that be?" The cry had forced itself through Hesen's lips before she could restrain it.

"He has angered the headman of Thebes."

"More likely the headman's daughter!"

Tiya shot her a contemptuous glance. "You foolish child—think! What is Senumet? Little more than a peasant, totally dependent on the goodwill of his superiors. Are you prepared to offer him advancement?"

"You know I cannot." Hesen hesitated; it occurred to her to ask, "Is Ay very angry at him?" She didn't understand why he should be, but she realized with a sudden sharp clarity the very real power Tiya and Ay held. They couldn't touch her, but Senumet could be crushed.

"My brother has spoken of sending him to a post on the frontier," Tiya declared.

"What do you want me to do?" There must be something, Hesen thought with some impatience, or she wouldn't have been summoned this afternoon.

"Keep away from him," Tiya said flatly. "He's going to be betrothed to the headman's daughter. Any further hint of scandal and he'll be exiled."

"I won't see him or speak to him again," Hesen promised, and she stopped listening. Finally Tiya tired of her lecture, and Hesen was left alone. She sprang up and walked rapidly back and forth along the path, her head pounding. If only she were older and more experienced—if only she had someone to confide in—perhaps she could figure it out! It had almost sounded as if Tiya worried about Senumet's welfare—but that was ridiculous! Then why speak that way? Insight flashed: because Tiya had been aware that Hesen would respond to those arguments in particular. Still, what was Tiya's motive? Maybe it didn't matter. They wanted him married, and she herself was somehow involved, and all kinds of political considerations were a part of it. All right. She smiled to herself. She had been waiting for a sign—well, here it was: her release, so to speak, from the forty-two sins she must guard against. She was above those commands. They dared try to end her friendship with Senumet. They lacked the power to do it! She was going to seek him out. She was going to lie with him! Her chin jutted defiantly, and she was half aware she looked much as Nefertiti must have appeared when that lady boarded the ship for Egypt, rebellion in her heart.

Senumet was desperately unhappy. After the Festival of Osiris, he was going to be betrothed. Ay had spelled it out very plainly: the royal family was angry over Hesen's involvement with him, and unless it ended quickly, in a way that assured suspicion would die as well, Hesen could be sent out of the country.

Having no choice, Senumet had seen Nephrus, apologized half-heartedly, and sealed his doom. The reconciliation had been so easy he was sick over it. He didn't know how he was going to bear the rest of his life. The only mercy was that Ay was retaining him in his service—and thanks be to Amon, he would not have to marry until the emergence. He would sail with Ay during the months after the inundation. In the meantime he could keep himself so busy helping to prepare for the flood that he would have little time to see his betrothed.

Seldom had a man been so eager for duties. Senumet made arrangements to mark and secure household goods and animals against the coming flood and to prepare food stores for those who would remain. With the other scribes, he checked the tax assessments to guarantee their accuracy, making sure all boundary lines were listed so there could be no disputes when the time came to build again. In addition to all this, Senumet spent every spare hour trying to prepare himself for the festival, studying that god's figure in all the ancient texts he could discover. As festivaltime approached, he felt the glory of Osiris's resurrection enter his heart.

The night of the festival was cool and sweet-smelling, with spices carried lightly on air up from the south. The citizens of Thebes had been gathering since well before sunset. They were an incredibly silent mass, exhaling and inhaling almost with one breath. Tonight the god would come, would promise them life for another year.

Senumet stood apart for his meeting with the god. He had bathed in the Sacred Lake and slept alone the past two nights, isolated in a private cubicle, so the spirit of the god could approach him. His eyes were painted but, although his hair was oiled, his head was bare. He wore a simple loincloth and no ornaments. He would meet Osiris unadorned, as Khnum had made him, and Osiris would see into his heart. Shivers of anticipation ran through his body and his hands hung powerless. "Osiris the reborn, give me your strength," he prayed.

On the cleared field the priests unfurled a white linen cloth that lifted under their hands like a banner, then settled slowly to the ground. They drove golden spikes into it, anchoring it firmly. On it the god would appear.

The king's daughters, wearing simple white dresses, circled the cloth, shaking their delicate, shining sistrums. Their silvery sounds mingled with the piercingly sweet notes of flutes, calling to the god, enticing him to appear. As Hesen passed Senumet, their eyes met and held. She nodded, almost imperceptibly, understanding: Somehow they'd meet.

The beat of snare drums began, at first faintly, gradually growing louder as the newly dedicated young priests came into view. Their instruments were strapped to their bare shoulders, and they marched like soldiers to the flashes of gold made by their rounded hammers as they struck the drumhead. Behind them walked Amenophis the father and Amenophis the son, also wearing only loincloths, lacking even the double crowns. From gold bands across their foreheads rose the cobra-uraeus, black and hooded, its red jasper eyes gleaming. Their feet were bare; the drums called the pace as they marched side by side. Amenophis the son was very pale, and his feet faltered in and out of the rhythm. Senumet's eyes caught Hesen staring at her father, a worried frown creasing her brow.

But Senumet had no time to think of Hesen now. As the drums beat faster and harder, the pounding entered him and he could feel the ground tremble under his feet. The god was awake. When both Pharaohs stopped at either end of the linen cloth, he grabbed the bowl of color held by a slave, and dipping his stylus into the green pigment he planted one foot on the sacred banner. Now the drums thundered and the ground quaked. Senumet touched the brush to the cloth. Suddenly all sound ceased, and the very air seemed to die. For a moment he thought his heart had stopped. Then his arm was gripped by a powerful, unseen force. He drew the first line of the White Crown. It shimmered magically. A profound sigh ran through the crowd and the drumbeats began again. They gave him strength, and he painted with an inspiration that was more than his own. In one continuous line, Osiris emerged. Freed from the Underworld, the god seemed to breathe power, his brow lofty, his hands strong and sure as they grasped the crook and flail of majesty. His outline glowed green with promise. The line finished, Senumet stood back as the spikes were removed and the cloth was held aloft for the people to view the god. They fell to their knees, chanting, "Blessed be Osiris, who gives us life."

The cloth was refastened to the ground. Slaves gathered around, each holding a marble pot, and approached to spread the rich alluvial Nile mud carefully within Osiris's outline. Each Pharaoh was handed grain in gold vessels shaped like sheaves of barley. Majestically Amenophis the father sprinkled grain carefully over the body of the god. "Hail, Osiris," he intoned, "who issues from the earth to keep Egypt alive."

As if with one motion the crowd turned to Amenophis the son. The hand of the younger Pharaoh shook so badly he must grip the vessel tight against his body. He stood absolutely still. The drumbeats ran together into a single urgent summons. Nefertiti stepped out of the crowd so he could see her. As her eyes burned into his, Amenophis managed to throw some grain sloppily onto the figure.

"He who maketh grain, brings emmer into being," Pharaoh said tonelessly.

"Generations of his children jubilate for him, greet him as King of Gods," Amenophis the father thundered robustly as he threw the grain.

The crowd turned to his son. Sweat ran down Amenophis' body in ugly rivulets and his eyes were closed. "Come forth, O King. Fill Upper and Lower Egypt," he choked, the words pulled out of him in short, heavy bursts. The grain spilled, the vessel fell unheeded to the ground. A low threatening murmur ran through the crowd. Unaware, Pharaoh stepped on the dish. The edge cut into his foot.

Seeing the red print stamped on the cloth, Senumet thought—with a leap of fear—Amon protect him! They'd think the god had hurt Pharaoh. They'd tear him to pieces!

Recklessly, in three swift steps Senumet covered the distance, fell on the bloody print and pretended to kiss the ground Pharaoh had trod. No one stopped him: his was the hand that had called forth the god. Senumet froze to the spot. Only let this end!

Amenophis III, his body glistening with sweat, scattered the remaining grain. "Hail, Osiris," he roared, "King of Gods." He fell to his knees, touched his forehead to the hem of the linen, heavy now with Osiris's body.

Amenophis IV stood rigid and unmoving. The ugly murmur became a low rumble, like distant thunder.

"The drums," Ay hissed. "Start the drums."

The steady beats began. "O-si-ris," Ay whispered, and the crowd took it up. "O-si-ris. O-si-ris," they chanted, their eyes fixed on Pharaoh the younger. A trembling began in his body. His eyes were wet. Suddenly a man stepped forward, then another. Senumet held his breath, willed Pharaoh to speak.

His knees gave way and he sank to the ground. "Hail, Osiris," he whispered. Still the drums beat, the chant continued. "Hail, Osiris." Tears streamed down his face and his mouth twitched. "King of Gods."

Across the body of the god, his glance met his father's. They remained thus, staring at each other, their eyes glittering with light from the burning torches, their mouths tight with hate.

But it was over, Senumet exulted. Thank Amon, it was over! He got up quickly, crossed swiftly to where Hesen was standing and eased in beside her. "Steady!"

"I'm all right. I'm all right!" she repeated.

"Where can we meet?" There were too many eyes here. Even now, they were noticed.

"The East Gate." She moved away.

He let the crowd close in front of him, turned sharply right, and moved to the old part of the palace. Thebes was so ancient, the entire complex had been growing for hundreds of years; its center had shifted as the additions multiplied, with the older sections often untended. It was to this most ancient part of the palace that he now made his way. The modern glazed-tile border yielded to the stone curtain-wall of bound reeds. The very air was different—stiller, more mysterious, more pungent from the rich, neglected undergrowth. His eyes strained. Then, to the side, a slim white form slipped from behind a tree and he recognized her lithe figure.

"Come," she said, led him into a copse of trees, over dead vines and brambles along an obscured path visible only to Hesen's eyes. They stopped at a crumbling ruin.

"We played here as children." Her voice was hushed as if she were praying. They stepped inside. Moonlight beaming through vines and the rafters and pillars of the ruin glanced off her hair, her face. He hadn't seen her in weeks; soon they would be separated for months after the Inundation, then perhaps forever. She mustn't hear it from anyone else. "There's something—"

"I've got to—" she began at the same time.

They stopped. If they remained silent, they'd drown in each other's eyes. She was the first to speak.

"You'll be betrothed," she said flatly.

"I wanted to tell you myself." As if that could matter, he thought bleakly.

"I've not come here tonight to talk. A man should have a memorable betrothal." She stepped toward him.

"Hesen." He backed away. "I won't let you—"

"For God's sake, you stupid man," she said softly, her eyes bright, "it's me coming to you, my tunic loose at the shoulders." Her dress fell away. Her body, touched by the light of Shu, had a golden pearl glow, and her breasts were pink-tipped and trembling. She clasped her hands over them, and stood with lowered eyes, lashes fluttering on pale cheeks.

Aten help her, she thought wildly as an unexpected coldness fanned out, touched every part of her, and she stood frozen. Oh, she had wanted so much to offer herself freely, and she had planned it that way. But she had had no way of knowing how she would feel, standing naked before him. The arms covering her breasts shivered. If her life had depended on it, she couldn't look at his face.

A powerful tenderness gripped Senumet as he watched his bold, sweet love, and he was weak with longing. It should be easy to refuse her gift—she hadn't the strength to insist—and if he could, they'd be safe. But he knew in the same breath that he would not turn away, crushing that trusting, warm spirit. No! He'd take her gently and tenderly, with a generosity to match her own.

"Beloved"—his voice was choked with love—"let me look at you." He lowered her arms, and when they hung limply at her sides, he raised her head. Her eyes were wet, and he wiped away the moisture on cheeks still covered by the light down of youth.

"You bring me a gift," he whispered huskily, "richer than all Pharaoh's gold."

Trustfully, she raised her face to his. He lowered his head until their lips met. She stood stiff, yet, and unresponsive, but he worked his mouth over hers until her lips parted and he tasted the salt of her tears. Her breath, moist and sweet, mingled with his and their tongues met.

Hesen felt warmth slowly returning to her body, in tingling waves that left her limp as they washed over her. Her hands rose, caressed his back, that seemed to burn under her fingers.

He lowered her to the marble floor of the ancient temple, explored her curving wonder, tasted her—sweeter than honey. She felt him, warm, smooth, hard, between her legs. Her body arced to receive him; her hands stroked his body, as far as she could reach, memorizing the feel of his thighs. Slowly he moved, very slowly . . . never forgetting, not even in the rising tide of his desire, that this was her first time. Sweet Hathor, Mother of Desire, make it good for her. No pain for her.

She surprised him as she always would, his hot, sweet love. All her fears forgotten, she was ready for him. He moved with deliberate slowness deeper, ever more sweetly, then as passion's own rhythm carried him past his own effort upward and outward, faster. . . . And she was there with him, impelled and impelling, until he couldn't tell where he ended and she began. Straining, breathless, they were gloriously together, still, at the moment of completion. Her body moved in convulsive spasms and she moaned. Or was that he? Or both? He buried his face in her neck. Finally, with a shuddering sigh, he withdrew and they lay side by side.

"Why, beloved?" he asked.

"Terrible things are in the wind. You saw their beginning tonight, as I did." She pressed her mouth against his shoulder, his neck. "This is for all the nights that can never be ours. This is to please us both, while we still can."

"So this is good-bye." He could see the tears on her cheeks.

"Oh, no. We'll have this again, whenever and wherever we can, married or no, Senumet, until the end of our days."

"You are my always love," he told her.

When she returned to her apartments, she didn't hide her face. Sephy would see her exactly as she was. If Sephy wished to wail, let her cry. It was done.

And nothing had ever pleased Hesen more.

# VII

In the mountains of Punt, so many miles to the south that the distance had never been reckoned, the pale winter sun brightened, scattering its jewels carelessly across snow-covered heights. Blocks of ice, pierced by the warming rays, broke free, crashed forward in clouds of powdery whiteness. Rivulets of newly condensed water ran down mountainsides, widened into streams, sliced into the cliffs, poured into cold, dark lakes.

Next, the rains came, gently at first, then in hard sheets beating steadily for days that lengthened into weeks. The water softened crisp snow into slush, flattened great leafy bushes, drenched the ground until it could absorb no more. Puddles ran into greater puddles and overflowed into swollen lakes. The lakes, engorged and turbulent, poured over their banks, the unbounded water no longer some minor lake or stream. The surge had become the White Nile, foaming and dangerous, ready for its big run.

At Khartum, 1,350 miles away from the sea, the white water was joined by the Blue Nile rushing out of the east, from the mountains of Abyssinia, freighted with rich loam.

Double now in size, the flood rolled forward with unimaginable power. One hundred and forty miles below the union of the two Niles, the river splashed into the tableland of Nubian sandstone. There its tortuous course between desert cliffs doubled it back upon itself, so that sometimes it must flow due south before it wound north again, making its track a vast, forced S. In six different places the pushing current crashed against outcroppings of stubborn rock. Year after year the Nile had spent its fury on those stones without eroding them, and this year too they stood unscathed. Hurtling onward, the river smashed against the final barrier at Elephantine. Once past this rough granite shoulder, it would be able to race freely through Egypt proper, on an unobstructed course across the eastern plains of the Sahara to the delta and the sea at its northern end. The going would be swift and violent, accelerated by the natural underground trench cut into the riverbed that ran the length of the country and was lined by smooth, black, alluvial deposits.

At Thebes they awaited the cataclysm. Every day, tense and expectant, they watched as Rahmose was rowed to the Nilometer to get a reading. But they could see for themselves. Higher and higher the Nile rose. Soon it would burst over the steep banks here at Thebes. They were ready for it. Huge basins were set to catch the overflow and store it until it could be released in the fields when needed. Bins had been built in the desert for food to keep those remaining until the emergence. Household animals moved restlessly in safe, shaded pens, branded by their owners, to be claimed in three months' time. The desert was bright, too, with Theban tents, a fair distance from last year's watermark. Families, soon to be separated, clung together, danced wildly, drank too much, were freer with each other in this communal intimacy than ever before. From their tents, they could see the freshly painted feluccas moored in neat rows, waiting for the flood waters to make the land a lake.

They all had their assignments, the men of Thebes. Some were to go to Memphis, others to Hieropolis, some to the Fayum; a number had been directed to the marble quarries at Aswan, where they would work on Pharaoh's mighty projects. And if their women daily climbed the high platforms, deep in the desert, that commanded a view of the river, it was not for first sight of the crashing waters. They sought a last look at loved homes, gardens coaxed out of the desert, hand-tiled entryways. They did not mourn. *Never mind*, they told themselves. *We'll build again, make it even better*. But their faces clouded as they watched the bright eyes of their men, eager for coming adventures.

It was sighted as it roared into Syene, first stop after the cataract at Elephantine. The waters at Thebes responded immediately. Dark and muddy, they covered the dock area with a thin, wet laver. Hardy children refused to leave the platforms, demanded their meals be brought to them, sat sweat-drenched but heedless of the blazing sun. They wanted a good viewing place.

"It comes!" Horns blared the signal. The citizens of Thebes raced to the platforms, scrambled up the steep steps and ladders, and stood —a silent, fearful mass, exposed under a desert sky. All eyes stared intently past the arid sands, the ribbon of green . . . to the churning river.

Tushratta stood on the highest platform. He raised his arms.

"Welcome Hapy, God of all Life."

Brass cymbals flashed as fifty priests struck them in unison, underlining his words.

> "*Hapy makest the Nile to preserve His people.*
> *Lord of us all,*
> *He hath set a Nile in Heaven,*
> *That it may fall for us,*
> *Making floods upon the mountains*
> *Like the Great Sea*
> *Watering our fields, granting us Life.*
> *Praise Hapy. Praise him. Praise.*"

With one motion the citizens of Thebes turned toward the river, arms raised in homage. Then they heard it—a faint rumble, barely discernible, drowned out by the alarms of a flock of ibis overhead. It grew to thunder, the ground trembled, the platform shook. Louder and louder it roared, until voices could no longer be distinguished. People gripped each other's arms. It was here!

A huge, churning wall of water, higher even than the first pylon, crashed upon their land. Small acacia trees were ripped up and carried along, spinning crazily. Mud-brick huts were leveled; reclaimed docks were swept away; roads were smashed to pieces; hard-won fields churned. They gasped as the waters struck the third pylon, crashed, even, into the bright electrum doors of the temple, pushed deeper into the city, hit the thick walls of the empty palace, rose over its gaily painted walls and coated its bright mosaic floor with thick black mud. Then the flood leveled out and was still. The water glistened where the city had been, its flat surface broken occasionally by a broad lotus capital or etched pillar or tall sycamore. Every year, stretching back to the beginning of time, they must rebuild on the verdant strip of land hugging the river—the only habitable land in all Egypt. They rebuilt thankfully, grateful for the black soil that meant life.

A joyous cry pierced the silence, and another; then the air rang with shouting. People embraced with wild abandon. Feast it would be this year, not famine. Blessed be Hapy, God of the Nile. The inundation was good.

Again the crash of the cymbals reverberated, bounced off the spreading waters and echoed even more strongly than before. Almost as one, the Thebans turned to the gilded, canopied platform set apart from the rough, hastily erected stands on which they had waited.

The royal family, crowns of office glittering, stretched out their hands to bless the entire population, who fell to their knees—gratefully, adoring the strength that each year could call forth the Nile God. The royal family stood like statues of themselves, down to the smallest child, and accepted the homage of their people. In this glorious rebirth, personal differences were put aside. They were all part of the god.

Only Nefertiti hung back, didn't stretch out her hands with the others. She turned her face northward to stare at the rushing waters tearing down through Egypt's plains until its force would finally pour into the Great Green.

Nefertiti sighed. Ever since that wretched ceremony, Pharaoh had withdrawn. Distant and cold, he hadn't come to her for three weeks. Now, in that crush of royal children, his father and mother, the grand vizier and headman, she slipped unobtrusively closer, pressed her firm warm thigh against his. He moved away. In her first shock of response, Nefertiti read indifference in the deep creases on his face. Without him, there was nothing. And the queen shivered in blazing heat.

Everything seemed to be slipping away. Even her daughters! She had never before been uncertain of her own children's love. But Meritaten had changed. After the festival, Meritaten had spent more time with Tey than with her own mother. Even now, she stood next to Ay's wife. And Meket worried her. She had barely returned to the palace after the Ceremony of Osiris before her body was racked by the most violent spasms Nefertiti had ever seen. For three days and three nights the coughing raged, and Meket couldn't eat or talk, was just able to breathe in raw, rasping gulps. Slowly the seizure had come to an end, but still Meket was weak and listless. Even now, weeks later, she was barely strong enough to stand unaided. Nefertiti saw that only Hesen's arm, strong and willing, was keeping Meket upright. And the child was so pale she looked almost transparent. And Hesen—never once since the quarrel had she tried to speak to her mother. Nefertiti thought dully, *There's such a radiance about Hesen these days. She's found something; she doesn't need me anymore.*

Suddenly the queen was filled with a consuming urgency to be free of all this, to be gone from Thebes—an impulse so strong she couldn't keep still. She strode restlessly back and forth on the platform, pretending to study the inundation. Aten be praised, they would leave soon. Suddenly she made up her mind. She had been planning to take Meket, but she'd include Hesen too. When they were off on Pharaoh's barge, just the four of them, for three months, sailing the Nile under the king's brilliant cartouche, collecting tribute—surely, then Meket would be cured, Hesen would confide in her mother again, and Pharaoh would be restored to himself. Perhaps her husband had forgotten the ways she could restore him.

The days that followed nearly drove her mad with the restricted movements life in the royal desert pavilions dictated. Despite her desperation to be gone, the family of Amenophis IV was scheduled to be the last to leave. First, the old Pharaoh and Smenkhare sailed. Tiya had refused to join them because there had been bitter words between the king and queen about their son. Nefertiti thought Tiya foolish to rage so; on the other hand, in three months' time, the men's tempers would have cooled too. As she observed the female slaves Amenophis III had included, the laden vessels of date wine, Nefertiti's mouth curled. No doubt he'd forget, in the riotous months ahead, that he even had a queen, or a son who had displeased him. Tey had also refused to go with Ay and the scribes he had chosen, a flare-up that might have had something to do with Tashray, Ay's concubine, who would soon come to term. Ay had produced other children over the years with other concubines, of course. But Tashray's lineage included a slave who had had a child by Pharaoh— and that child had been Tashray's grandmother. Even those few precious drops of royal blood made this breeding different to Ay. His pride in that swelling body did not go unnoticed by his wife.

Nefertiti, watching it all, had had enough of the jealousies and plots and squabblings of the court And still they could not set forth. Clay vessels broke on the royal barge; the wine had to be restocked. A crack was discovered in the tiller. When they were finally called aboard, the boat's motion, her own relief were dizzying. Half afraid she would wake from the dream, she stood at the rail, scarcely daring to breathe as the barge swung upriver.

At last, as Thebes faded to a distant glimmer, the knot in her chest loosened. It did not even disturb her that Pharaoh had gone directly to his tent. Already she could feel her cheeks glow, and she knew her eyes were sparkling. She heard a soft step behind her.

"Highness?" Hesen's voice was hesitant.

Nefertiti almost smiled. Already the new intimacy she desired was beginning. "See to Meket," the queen suggested gently. "You're the only one she responds to."

"I already have." Hesen replied as quietly.

Nefertiti appraised her daughter—no longer to receive orders, but a woman who knew what needed doing and did it. . . . "You've changed, Hesen." The words came without thinking from the queen's new awareness. There was a certainty about Hesen now, and the reserve that went with it. A thought struck Nefertiti. "Have you become truly a woman?"

The girl met her mother's eyes unflinchingly. "Yes."

*Fool!* Nefertiti told herself sharply. How had she failed to recognize Hesen's glow? Was she so old her own youth had completely faded—and her first love? Her eyes softened. Senumet. It must have been Senumet. He possessed a powerful maleness about him even the queen sensed. He would know just how to take Hesen so that her body flamed and how to be gentle to bond them in a way passion alone could never do.

Well, why not? Hesen would know little enough the rest of her life about love given and freely returned. Only how, Nefertiti wondered, had they managed to meet—spied on and watched and closely attended as they were? Of course Nefertiti would have prevented it had she been informed, and her servants would answer for their laxness! And the relationship must be severed. If that young man was half as resourceful and intelligent as reports painted him, he could use Hesen's love against Pharaoh himself. That he had not done so yet was no proof against the future.

"You'll not see him again," she began, but her voice was not severe. "Almost, my daughter, I am glad you know what love is. The memory will sustain you through all the bleak years that are your heritage. You will learn love is not everything and there are real compensations to duty." Her voice thickened. "Once I knew love, too. In Mitanni." Unable to say more, she pretended to study the cliffs lining the riverbank.

Nefertiti felt a light touch on her arm and heard Hesen's voice, breathless and tentative. "Mother, I understand so much more now. I think of you as a princess, younger even than I am now, coming from Mitanni and leaving everything behind. And being cheerful and giving. Your spirit blesses me, Mother."

Nefertiti's eyes were suddenly moist. "I never imagined that across the gulf of years I'd experience those moments again with my own daughter." She warmed with an expansion of love for her third daughter, the only one of her five children who would ever really know her.

Hesen sank to her knees. "I only pray that someday I may have your strength and your grace."

The queen touched Hesen's head. "It comes of suffering, freely accepted."

"I know—I mean, I'm learning there are all kinds of terrible possibilities."

"Are you talking about the court?"

"I'm afraid for my father. I've never seen him so unhappy or so at odds with Pharaoh."

"I won't lie to you," Nefertiti said slowly. Hesen had spoken candidly, with intelligence tempered by love. She deserved the truth. "I fear a permanent rift between them."

Hesen rose to her feet. "What will that mean . . . for us?"

Nefertiti brushed her daughter's cheek with a light kiss. "I don't know. It waits at the end of this journey. All we can do, my darling, is grow close and strengthen ourselves for what lies ahead."

"And try to ease Pharaoh's burden," Hesen murmured from the warmth of her mother's embrace. She hadn't realized how much she had missed the queen's favor. She felt as if a great wound were beginning to heal.

Hesen's calm persisted during the next few days, a contentment augmented by the rhythm of the Nile, the slowness of the hours, the increasing closeness with her mother. She was cheered, too, that Meket seemed stronger and brighter than she had in months. She was able to sit; color returned to her cheeks. Sometimes she would even join Hesen on deck.

"You're beginning to look like my sister again," Hesen said, her arm supporting Meket's steps.

Meket held Hesen's arm tightly. Blue veins bulged in her hand; her wrist was so frail it looked like a tender shoot a breeze might snap. "Life gathers in you, my dearest, even as its sap drains from me."

"Rouse yourself," Hesen demanded. "Life is sweet and rich."

Meket turned huge, dark eyes on her sister. "Not for me."

"Then make it so."

"There are things I can't bear," Meket whispered. "Love."

Suddenly images came flooding back to Hesen—his hand on her breast, mouths clinging, body on body. For her, love made all the rest endurable.

"Our parents talk of royal marriages," Meket went on, her mouth prim. "Hesen, have you looked at our new sister? I think of our parents, creating that little thing—I see their bodies—" She shuddered. "Let them order me to a husband. I won't do it." Her voice rose. "I can't!"

"No, no, little sister. It's not like that at all. It's very beautiful." She'd let Meket know, wanting only to banish her sister's fears.

Meket's eyes widened.

"And it's wonderful. Two people becoming part of each other, completely knowing each other."

"Hesen!" Meket's face was so white it looked transparent. "You let a man put his sex into you!"

"Animals mate with perfect ease, and like theirs, our bodies are designed for it."

"Aten protect us! It was that scribe!"

"Listen to me, Meket!" Hesen gripped her shoulders, tried to infuse some of her own warmth into the thin body. "Care about someone. What I've felt you can feel too. Let life in."

Meket's eyes gleamed with tears. She flung her arms around her sister. "Don't go away from me," she begged. "I can't go with you!"

Hesen said nothing, but as the days passed, she watched her sister, and a terrible fear entered her heart.

The boat approached the fifth nome in the village of Ombos. The white sails of the first feluccas billowed a greeting long before the welcoming officials were sighted. The wind was brisk; Pharaoh's cartouche, brilliantly green and taut, shone over the waters. As the feluccas drew closer, Amenophis IV sat on his throne, his hands gripping its lion-headed posts, his face remote. Nefertiti, standing at his side, saw that beads of perspiration stood out on his forehead, although the day was cool. Under the heavy kohl line and malachite shadow, her eyes were watchful.

On the royal barge a shout went up: "They're here!" Horemheb, in charge of the royal guard, ordered the ladders lowered to the smaller boats; then the headman and his party were helped to mount. In the delegation were priests who carried a small statue of Seth, god of Upper Egypt, whom they worshiped above all others. Carved out of wood, Seth's long ears and donkey face were almost laughable. It was a rude image, poorly executed. Then why did Pharaoh's face become so pale and his hands tremble? Nefertiti moved closer. When she touched his arm, she was aware it was unpleasantly damp; a tremor rippled through it.

The priests approached Pharaoh's throne, placed the statue of Seth at his feet in homage.

Amenophis IV pulled himself to his feet, covered his eyes with a shaking hand.

"Beloved," the queen urged. Understanding suddenly that he was drowning in some private darkness, she locked her hands in his and faced him. She knew he couldn't remember what he was to perform.

"To remember this harvest," she whispered.

"Torememberthisharvest," he repeated woodenly. His words ran together.

"—in the year two of the coregency . . ."

"—intheyeartwoofthecoregency . . ."

"—accept Egypt's gifts."

"—acceptEgypt'sgifts." Pharaoh swayed. Nefertiti knew that only the force flowing between their linked hands kept him upright. Aware with equal certainty that he would never be able to distribute the gifts and that she couldn't leave him, she cast desperately about.

Hesen materialized at her side, her eyes frightened but courageous.

"The gifts," Nefertiti commanded under her breath. "Distribute the gifts."

Slim and straight, Hesen summoned a slave with an imperious gesture that seemed, as she executed it, utterly familiar. She would later remember that she had seen the queen use it. She took a scarab ring, like the one her father wore, from the tray the slave offered. With a dazzling smile, she handed it to the first official. "Accept Pharaoh's gift," she said sweetly, "from his daughter's hand."

As she walked among them, flattering them with looks from blue eyes as intense as the Blue Nile at midday, the hand that dispersed the rings was as cold as the frozen waters of the Underworld and a terrible void was opening in her heart. Whatever was going to happen had begun! Afterward, taking her place next to the queen, she didn't know Pharaoh anymore. She had the terrifying sensation he wasn't there.

The men of Ombos looked uncertain. Finally the priests replaced the statue of Seth on his solar barque. "The Lord of Upper Egypt thanks Amenophis, son of Amenophis, son of Thutmosis the Mighty. Seth will shine on your jubilee and bring you glory."

Amazingly, in that moment, the sun disappeared behind a cloud and shadow darkened the deck. "O Aten, my father," Pharaoh moaned, "do not hide yourself from your loyal son!" Pulling his hand away from Nefertiti, he lurched forward and crashed through the stunned assembly. He stumbled through the curtains into the royal tent. Shocked silence momentarily stopped the villagers' mouths. Nefertiti knew she had to act quickly before they came to their senses.

Her voice rang loud and clear. "Men of Ombos, know Pharaoh's heart is too full for speech. Know he blesses you and honors Seth, your god." She bowed before the image, ordering the entire royal party to their knees.

Goodwill, even laughter, flowed back into the day. The sun shone again. Temporarily, it seemed, the men of Ombos had forgotten in the smiles of the queen and her daughter the strange behavior of the king. With Hesen at her side, Nefertiti completed the rituals, thankful for the strength in her daughter that she could depend upon. Life was taking Hesen in hand to test her spirit, the queen thought, with sadness at its inevitability. And knowing her own trials were not yet over—nor Pharaoh's—Nefertiti lifted her head in the brave gesture with which the fierce kings of Mitanni had grasped spears and joined battle.

At evening, Nefertiti no longer could wait for her lord to come to her. The stars glinted brightly overhead. The waters slapped lightly at the barge as it glided toward the next village. The guards outside Pharaoh's quarters bowed. "Majesty," they murmured, opening the curtains for the queen.

"Leave us," she commanded the servants within.

The thin sheet-gold poles of the king's canopy glowed in the soft evening light. The fine linen hangings did not stir in the heavy air. Behind them, she could make out Pharaoh's unmoving bulk on his ebony-and-gold bed. She pulled back the netting. Pharaoh's face was as white as the limestone cliffs. His eyes were closed. The light of an oil lamp flickered shadows across his body. *Aten help me*, she prayed silently.

"Beloved!" Fearfully she took his cold, unresponsive hand in both of hers. He let out a shuddering sigh. Grateful tears sprang to her eyes. At least he knew her. His hand touched her face. "Dearest," he whispered, "forgive."

"Too long you have been absent from me, husband," she said in a clear, normal voice. "I've waited for weeks now."

"Neferu-Neferu, my soul hungered for you. But how could I ask you to share my burden? I've known all these years . . . you didn't love me."

Oh, he mustn't believe that. If he should falter, she would be lost as well. Suddenly, she was filled with a radiant certainty. This man was Aten. Only through him could the god shine. She could worship him. The longed-for love entered her heart. "I adore you," she said huskily. "You are Aten. Command me. Together we will lift whatever burden is too great for you alone."

"Oh, my dearest!" His voice was hoarse with longing. "I had given up hope of ever hearing that!"

"Then trust me," she pleaded. "Let me share what troubles you."

"For a long time now," he began—his hands reached out and gripped hers—"the Aten has been first in my heart."

"And in mine."

"I could offer prayers to the other gods of Egypt not because I accepted them, but because I didn't want to offend those who truly believed in their holiness."

"You are ever gracious, beloved."

"I can't do it any longer," he almost cried out. "I've seen my father humiliate Tiya. I've watched while he grew more gross and indulgent and corrupt. And then he offered more taxes to the priests of Amon, and forced me publicly to honor Osiris and name him king of gods."

"I felt pain for your sufferings, beloved."

"Aten entered my heart the next day, bade me name no other god. He is sole god, over Egypt and the world."

She hesitated. "I thought you were going to wait until you ruled alone."

"Because of the danger!" he scoffed. "As if the All-Powerful cares for personal safety. He is supreme. And He has spoken."

"What shall we do?" she whispered.

"Today I could not honor Seth. I will not honor Hathor tomorrow."

"What will happen at Thebes?"

"I cannot tell. Only I will name no other god but Aten."

"Nor shall I." Her voice shook, but emotion rose in her; she felt its peace flooding her soul. "What they will, they must do to us both."

"Be very sure, Nefertiti." He looked deep into her eyes. "The future is clouded and uncertain. This choice breaks with all the known past. We cannot tell what will lie ahead."

She raised Pharaoh's hand to her lips. "You fill my entire being, beloved. Aten fills my soul. What need I fear?"

His eyes still gleaming with the god's own light, he drew her toward him. She let her gown fall open, held his head against her breasts, soft and fragrant with perfume.

"I could forget there is any other world but this," he breathed, his mouth at her nipple.

Six children had she held thus; six small heads had taken comfort in just that spot. She rocked him, murmured little love words. His breath, moist and warm, deepened; his mouth fell away from her breast. He slept. She held him through much of the night, though her own body ached with his weight. The sky was just lightening when he woke.

"I've not had such peace in weeks," he told her. The light of the god had receded. They were man and woman again.

She nodded toward the curtains. "Look," she said almost shyly, "it's day. A new day."

"Then let in the sun," he smiled. And with the joy of it, his voice rose: "Open wide the curtains. For this little time we stand straight and walk with *maat*."

# VIII

When Pharaoh's barge raised oars and dropped sail at villages farther along the Nile, neither Pharaoh nor Nefertiti would appear to accept tribute and homage from officials and patron gods. Hesen greeted the headsmen and priests with Horemheb's help.

At first, on the day after Ombos, she feared that her parents kept to Pharaoh's pavilion because there might be some sickness Pharaoh wished to hide. But when she saw her parents together, her uncertainties vanished. Both were in blazing health. Happiness shone from Pharaoh, and Nefertiti's eyes worshiped her husband. Like the Aten, their joy radiated throughout the ship, and in its light all were more generous to one another. Even Meket bloomed, gaining weight and strength. Happy endings seemed possible, and so compelling was the illusion that Hesen resolutely put transience out of mind. When her eyes saw steep banks reappear, she stoutly maintained the flood waters were as high as ever. Yet the barge betrayed her, finally turning in the river for the return to Thebes.

That night, as a servant prepared Hesen for sleep, Nefertiti swept into her tent. The queen was serene as she sat by Hesen's cosmetic table and amused herself with the wooden cat, eyes of lapis, a red ribbon around its neck. Yet the aura around her was so grave that Hesen felt dread.

The servant dismissed, the queen began, "Three months ago, I wouldn't be here talking to you. But now I trust you—and to prepare yourself, you must know. Your father and I will never name another god but Aten."

A thrill pierced Hesen. Really, she had known it since the first day they hid their faces from headsmen. Suddenly she envisioned Ay, a murderous, charging bull, and Tushratta and an army of shaven disciples, fiercely howling for blood. "What will the priests of Amon do?" she whispered.

Nefertiti raised a slender white hand. "We will see," she said simply, and swept from the tent.

Hesen heard in her words a knell. She spent a nearly sleepless night praying for the faith and equanimity of her parents—or at least the strength to assume it.

Each day more of the land emerged. From the barge they could see lotuses and papyrus pushing up to obscure the black and shining soil. They passed the docks of villages, festooned with early jacaranda and roses. Workers perched high on temple pillars scrubbed at layers of mud and looked up to salute Pharaoh and the royal family as they glided past. Hearing the call of cattle, plaintive and deep, they knew the animals had been released from their pens and were working the land again. Flashes of fire dotted the banks from ovens where the mud-brick tiles for new huts were being glazed.

*Life renews itself*, thought Hesen, but her fear sapped at the beauty. At Thebes the body of Osiris would be covered now with green seedlings, neatly tended, watered reverently every day, but shielded from view by painted screens that opened only to Ra—until the Feast of Osiris, after their own return. A sob tore from Hesen and she muffled it with her fist.

Arriving at Thebes late at night, they dropped anchor and waited like a brooding crocodile on the black river. In the morning, determined that no one would discover how she felt, Hesen dressed very carefully for their landing. She drew the kohl line darker than she had ever worn it before, filled in shadow until her eyes sparkled with blue light, and chose a flashing gold collar.

They were the last ship to return, and all Thebes turned out to welcome them. The city shone, gleaming and new, the streets flashing red-and-green-tiled pavements. Bright signs proclaimed the newly opened shops; market stalls were stacked high with tempting delicacies. The pillars of Karnak, huge and round, bore freshened gilt letters on clean red sandstone, and Thutmosis' obelisk, electrum-tipped, blazed in the bright sun.

Amenophis III, carried to the docks on a litter, was more monstrously obese than ever—even his caftan bulged over his bulk. At his side, Tiya scanned the ship, excited and eager, for a sight of her son.

In the throngs on the docks, Hesen saw Senumet immediately, as she had known she would. Most of the scribes were small and slight and a little bent from squinting over tablets. In contrast, Senumet was tall and broad; and even at this distance Hesen thought she could see his flashing, appreciative eye, his smile that couldn't help challenging even as it warmly flattered. He was bronzed and dark from those three months with Ay. His chest muscles were firm, and the mat of curling hair, bleached by the sun, shone with each breath. Little shivers ran up Hesen's body. Moments passed before she even noticed Nephrus, clinging possessively to his arm, looking riper than ever. Hesen pulled her eyes away.

Pharaoh and the queen, hand in hand, walked down the landing ramp, radiance so awesome that the crowd fell back. When it was Hesen's turn to be lifted into her chariot, her head involuntarily turned, her eyes searching for Senumet. And he was there. Across the distance of the milling crowd, their eyes caught and held, speaking worlds.

At the palace, Sephy clucked disapproval of Hesen's sun-darkened complexion. Creaming Hesen's face and rouging her palms, Sephy ordered her followed by a sunshade whenever she ventured outside into Aten's rays. The nurse, however, praised Hesen's slimness and her upstanding breasts, fuller than when she'd left Thebes. She had missed Sephy's chatter, she realized. After a few days, however, Sephy grew strangely quiet. Her mouth looked permanently tucked in. "Have you a burr under your tongue, Sephy?" Hesen asked and demanded to know what bothered her. "They talk," was all Sephy would say.

Hesen had no need for explanations. Pharaoh's actions on the barge were whispered by the crew, and the tales circulated.

Hesen was with Nefertiti when Tiya came to them. Immediately Hesen knew Tiya was unsettled by wagging tongues.

"I'd like a word with you, Daughter." The angular old woman's eyes burned at Hesen, and Hesen made a movement to rise. She was forestalled by Nefertiti's hand on her arm. The hand was surprisingly cold, and Hesen understood her mother dreaded this conference.

"The princess and I have no secrets," Nefertiti said easily.

"I hear strange stories," Tiya grated, "of what happened on your ship."

"Pharaoh has found peace."

"And how has he done that?"

Lightning quick: "He will acknowledge no other god save Aten."

"And you permitted it?" Tiya cried in disbelief. "While his father lives? What are you thinking of?"

"Of his ka and of mine." Nefertiti's eyes shone with light. "Pharaoh and I will stand with *maat*. Together. Whenever he decides."

"So," Tiya hissed, "you think you've won, don't you? You'd destroy him to vanquish me!"

Nefertiti sprang to her feet. "You dare to speak so to me?"

"Daughter, wait!" Tiya put up her hand, tried to temper her high, quavering pitch into a placating tone. "Forgive me. Let's not quarrel. But think, Daughter! One god for all Egypt? Not in all our long history has it ever been so, nor will it be while Pharaoh, my son's father, lives. And the people will not give up the old gods easily. Time is needed to prepare Egypt for a single deity, and time is needed to weaken the hold of the priests on Egypt. If he defies his father and the old gods, he pulls down doom upon himself and you and his children. Perhaps if I spoke to him, urged him to wait?"

"You may try," Nefertiti said without emotion, her face unrelenting.

And Tiya left them without another word.

Even as she adored her mother, Hesen felt pity for Tiya. In the days that followed, Hesen watched her grandmother approach her son. When she spoke, he bent his head courteously, but Hesen could see he did not hear his mother. His attention was absorbed always by his inner light. And by his wife.

Having failed to move her son, Tiya directed her desperate efforts at her husband. The two of them had been living in separate apartments since the return to Thebes, so Tiya saw Amenophis III only at public meals and must fawn and simper beguilingly like a girl in the presence of the court. She fed delicacies into that foul, oozing hole of a mouth and admired laughingly the gusto with which Amenophis fondled naked slaves. After they had eaten, Tiya would have the senet board brought to them, for Amenophis loved planning his moves to the soothing melodies of harpists; he loved the decisive clicks of the carved ivory disks on the cedar playing board; he loved winning. Tiya flattered his skill and feigned delight as she let him win.

As one of the older princesses attending the meals at court which their parents shunned, Hesen was pained by Tiya's attempts to cajole Amenophis' favor. She understood her grandmother's fear of the Festival of Osiris, her desire to avoid it at all costs. For who knew what terrible events might follow a confrontation between Pharaohs? But Hesen also understood—and that was what made Tiya's humiliation so pitiable—that her grandmother's efforts must also fail with her husband. How could she hope to persuade him to forgo the festival when he so loved debauchery, when Ay, the priests, and the people's expectation of grand celebration were aligned with Pharaoh against her?

Seven nights, and then Tiya did not join Amenophis for the evening meal. When the duck was served and Tiya's place by her husband was still empty, Hesen knew her grandmother had realized her failure.

So. The festival was inevitable. Inexorably it would be.

Not Osiris or Amon willed it, but Aten, so that his glory might be revealed to all Egypt.

Hesen believed in the power of her father's vision. Blessed be Aten, who sweetens the air in our nostrils, she prayed silently. Let come the break between my father and his father. Whatever follows, know that thy daughter is ready, O merciful Aten. I am in thy hands. Thy will be done.

Senumet felt he was standing on the threshold of a nightmare. The court abounded with frightening rumors about Amenophis IV—who had not appeared publicly since disembarking—talk of dark seizures, of madness—and of Aten. Senumet made it his business to follow the whirlwind comings and goings of Ay, and what he saw filled him with great unease: the grand vizier daily closeted with Amenophis the father, off to meetings with a grimly determined Tushratta and more ominously with Nacht, commander of the garrison. That Ay grew careless of secrecy about these meetings frightened him still more—and that Ay appeared jubilant. In the presence of nobles, courtiers and foreign ambassadors, Ay lavished attention on Smenkhare, and in the streets Smenkhare was often to be seen with Ay in his chariot or in his sedan, borne on the shoulders of neophyte priests.

When he caught glimpses of Hesen, her face was strained and small, although she was always gallantly smiling. Her smile disturbed him—he worried that in her devotion to Amenophis IV, she was naïvely eager for the approaching crisis and might impetuously call down a terrible fate on her head. In sleepless hours of the night, he tried to think of a role he might play as Ay's protégé—for anything he might do to shelter his love from the coming storm. To his despair, he could discover no way to protect her.

And through all of this, Nephrus buzzed at him like a swarm of gnats attracted in the heat by his sweat, pressing for marriage.

"There's nothing to stop us. We can be married immediately."

"You must know, Nephrus, it would be more appropriate to wait until I demanded the ceremony and urged you to agree."

She ignored him. "Tell me why we can't wed right away. I promise I'll treat you to such delights, you'll forget the feast of the god."

"I have important duties to perform."

"Don't be silly. My father will speak with Ay."

His eyes were as cold as his heart. "If my work is nothing, I am nothing. If you interfere, I'll end this betrothal."

Her face whitened, her mouth twisted with pain. She took a deep breath. "Right after the feast, our wedding—you said."

He nodded. Anger and pity and despair intermingled and boiled in his chest, and he could hardly breathe. But in that instant, he had decided: Somehow, he would cut Nephrus out of his life. This wedding would never be.

On the morning of the feast, the city ovens were in constant use. The body of Osiris, its growing grain finally exposed, was placed in the field. The huge standing frame that stretched its fabric smooth was wood, carved in an elaborate floral and feather pattern, highlighted with turquoise and quartz and carnelian. Four gold rosettes in each corner hid the junctures of the wood. The new green shoots covering Osiris' body fluttered in the gentle breeze and gave off a sweet perfume. As they bustled about it, the workers lowered their heads in grateful thanks. They surrounded Osiris with alabaster pedestal tables, so that the priests and the royal family would feast under his beneficent eye. A space was cleared for the musicians and dancers on the grass, which had been cut to a springy lightness. Clay vessels filled with the god's own black beer were placed at frequent intervals both on the royal tables and on the wooden tables that would serve the populace of Thebes, except for slaves. At last, all was in readiness.

At dusk, all of Thebes turned out for the feast. Osiris' body, lit by gold braziers, cast a huge flickering shadow over the entire field. The tables were stacked high with ten different kinds of meat, five kinds of crisp, spiced poultry, sixteen different breads; one table bore only loaves of crushed lotus. Cheese and fruit were heaped, and shat-cakes, fried in honey, rose in tempting pyramids. The people of Thebes were summoned to fill their plates. As they approached the tables, all citizens must pass the royal pavilion where huge ostrich fans kept night insects away from the living gods and their families. The moving lines of Thebans bowed gratefully to Pharaoh the father and Pharaoh the son.

As the feast progressed, acrobats whirled and leaped; the music grew frenzied; the barrels of wine steadily emptied. Laughter was insistent and loud. After the long abstinence, Thebes was ready to let its passions run free for a night.

Ay, his face glowing, and Rahmose watched the royal family with shadowed eyes, in their minds the same dark thought: the break between father and son was imminent—could the fragile truce between the two Pharaohs withstand the pressures of tonight? Amenophis the father had chewed upon the cud of Ay's suggestion that the disease in the king's mouth might stem from the gods' displeasure with his son's heresy, and yesterday Pharaoh had almost taken the step of rescinding that son's position and proclaiming Smenkhare the royal heir, a realignment that would name Ay as regent. Ay eagerly hoped Pharaoh the son would be provoked by the festival to offend his father grievously. Nacht had deployed, at Ay's order, many soldiers here tonight. Yes, everything was ready for the fall of Amenophis IV.

Already Amenophis the father, Ay saw, was beastially drunk. Smenkhare was keeping pace with him. And what a loud voice the small prince Tutu had. It bellowed from the royal pavilion.

Ay turned his attention to the other royal family and could hardly suppress his contempt. All the princesses were present except the babe, but Ay's gaze was fixed on the two who wore the crowns. They looked pleased with themselves, as if the night around them was holy only where they sat, the horsefaced Pharaoh and his incongruously beautiful queen, linked arm in arm and looking as if they sublimely *believed* in their own divinity. And the third daughter, on the other side of her father, looking more like her mother every day and easily her mother's equal in arrogance, wore also an expression of superior ecstasy.

With grim satisfaction, Ay gloated. Perhaps after tonight, they would never again be so proud.

Feeling the infectious, joyous abandon of the festival, Hesen was daring to think: Maybe they could come through this night safely.

She smiled as the young men of Thebes, eyes glittering, bodies limber, wooed girls they desired in dance. Her foot tapped the rhythm. She wished she could join them.

The blatant sensuality of the dancing and the throbbing beat were also affecting Amenophis III. Tongue glistening between parted lips, drunkenly surging with desire, he hungrily watched the dancers. Finally he emitted a throaty grunt and struggled to rise. Two slaves hauled him to his feet—which physicians had warned him might break under the weight of his body. He tottered as he scanned the nearby women with a practiced eye.

Hesen felt his gaze that burned the clothes from her body. She moved closer to her father. The old Pharaoh beckoned. She averted her eyes, pretending not to see, but then a slave knelt before her, sent by the old Pharaoh to force her attention. She directed a frantic, pleading glance at her mother; the queen's face was unreadable. She wanted to appeal to her father but was afraid to spark his antagonism toward the old Pharaoh. And Tiya was nodding at her, a command to do as bidden. Repelled by the thought of being touched by the old man, she obeyed and walked to where he stood.

He put a fat, wet hand on her waist. "Come," he wheezed, "we'll join the god." He lumbered with her among the dancers.

Pharaoh's breath assaulted her with the stench of rotting flesh—her stomach turned—as he belched and incredibly began to move. Fat jiggling, he stamped to the rebabs. Sweat poured down Pharaoh's face. His labored breath rasped like grinding stone. A thin string of spittle overflowed the corner of his mouth. His fingers dug into her buttocks. He shook her so that her hair tumbled down. He ground his monstrous thighs against her.

"Please—let me go," she cried.

At the edge of the ring of spectators, just to the left of the musicians, Senumet stared in impotent anguish at the grotesque spectacle of Pharaoh molesting his granddaughter in dance. "Play something else," he ordered the conductor in desperation, "a beat Pharaoh dislikes."

"Are you mad?" the conductor shouted.

Laughing obscenely, Pharaoh shook her so that her breasts bounced vigorously. *Aten protect me!* Hesen thought. *He doesn't remember who I am!* Trying to wrench herself free, she discovered his flabbiness concealed a surprising strength, and suddenly he smashed her against his chest.

Why didn't someone from the royal pavilion stop him? Senumet wondered desperately—perhaps they couldn't see what was happening for the other dancers. How to get to her? He grabbed a girl, he'd dance her onto the green and strike Amenophis *accidentally*—divert his attention. The girl he grabbed screamed, "Beast! Hani!" A boy came to her defense and Senumet dropped him with a blow to the jaw while the girl ran away.

Pharaoh stopped dancing, the music utterly forgotten. His head was shoving between Hesen's breasts. His tongue, wet and rough, pushed under her thin gown and reached for her nipple. His hands tore at her dress, mauling the flesh of her upper thighs beneath the linen. Then his heavy hands gripped her shoulders. He was forcing her down onto the grass—before all the people of Thebes!

Senumet was almost wild—he had to stop that bloated animal. Blood roared in his ears as he saw only Hesen's terrified face in a red blaze. And he was striding forward—he would hurl Pharaoh to the ends of the world. Soldiers that he ignored ran toward him as he pushed aside dancers and headed for the king—one flashing a sword from its scabbard. But he would reach Pharaoh before the soldiers killed him.

Suddenly Amenophis IV strode from the royal pavilion, his face a mask of fury. Tiya cried impassioned pleas to Nefertiti to go after him, hold him back, but Nefertiti was a statue, her eyes fixed on her husband, unblinking and bright. Tiya turned to Smenkhare, but the prince drunkenly couldn't understand. Tiya buried her face in her hands.

Forced to her knees, Hesen struggled to prevent the bulk of her grandfather from falling on top of her and pinning her beneath him. Tears of shame and fear blinded her and streaked her face.

Senumet was suddenly aware that dancers were clearing the green —and there was Amenophis IV, reaching the old Pharaoh and Hesen before him. She was rescued! Clenching his fists, he whirled to battle the soldiers who converged on him.

"Father!" Amenophis IV's voice was like tempered metal, cold and hard; and at its cutting edge, the musicians stopped playing, the soldiers hesitated and the crowd surrounding the green fell silent.

The fingers of Amenophis IV closed like a vise over his father's upper arm. "Release the princess. She has had enough dancing."

His father's eyes flamed. "You dare to touch the living god?"

"The princess is tired."

"The Lion of Egypt does not listen to pigs!" Amenophis roared, his face purple. But he let go of Hesen and pivoted his weight like a hippo to strike at his son's restraining arm. Suddenly his eyes bulged. He grew rigid. His mouth gaped. An awesome scream tore from his throat. Like a falling colossus, he crashed forward, face down on the wet grass.

While Amenophis led a weeping Hesen back to her mother, Tushratta ran to the fallen king. Six priests sprang to Tushratta's side; hands linked, they cordoned off the prostrate Pharaoh.

Within minutes Amenophis IV returned, followed by four soldiers bearing a litter. They halted before the chain of priests standing guard. For one awful moment, Pharaoh and the priests glared at each other, unmoving and hostile; then the hands lowered, and Pharaoh strode past the priests to the fallen king.

"Bear him to the palace," he ordered.

"No!" Tushratta shouted.

Ay shoved through the priests to Tushratta's side. Amon help them, this would ruin everything. Amenophis could not die—not yet! "Careful," he warned Tushratta.

The priest shook off Ay's hand and hurled at Pharaoh's son, "You will not touch him!"

"Do you dare dispute me?" Amenophis demanded. "I am king!"

"And I am first to the god. Amon will tend him!"

Suddenly the huge prostrate body heaved. The priests bent in unison and carefully turned him over. Pharaoh's eyes rolled heavenward; nearly senseless, he moaned. A murmur of relief radiated outward through the throng; many fell to their knees. "He lives."

"Bear him away," Pharaoh the son ordered.

"Don't stop him," Ay whispered sharply. As quickly, he realized the old priest's fear—Tushratta was convinced that by giving Pharaoh to his son, he'd be sending him to certain death. Ay, however, realized that if Amenophis III were to die, it was better he die in the royal house than in the house of Amon.

"Let Amon cast out any man who touches him!" Tushratta's wrath gave his curse unexpected power. "Amon spit fire on your heads if you disobey!"

Terrified, the soldiers dropped the litter and fled from the god.

Amenophis IV loomed over Tushratta. His crown seemed to send off sparks. He pointed at the priest, his shadow-finger the length of a spear. "You and your god have not the strength to command *me!*"

"You are Pharaoh," Ay called firmly, "and you are supreme." He hoped Amenophis would remember that in this moment of crisis only Ay had remained staunch in his support. "Tushratta, you overstep."

A gurgle from the prone Pharaoh stopped them all. Pharaoh was conscious; he struggled to sit. Two priests supported him, their faces wet from lifting his weight.

"Not—dead—yet," he gasped. "Amon save me."

"Pharaoh calls the god," Tushratta shouted. "Let us pray to Amon-Ra."

"No!" Amenophis IV thundered. Afterward, everyone who had seen him would swear his face was lit by light from an unknown source.

When Pharaoh spoke, as if a cord stretched between them, Nefertiti was drawn to his side. He turned his face toward her and love flared between them with an incandescent force. She was tautly erect; her body trembled.

"Do you deny the gods of your fathers?" Tushratta cried incredulously.

Nefertiti slipped her hand into her husband's. "Now!" she breathed. "Now, beloved!"

"There is no god save Aten!" Amenophis IV was free. His voice soared. "Egypt will lift her face only to Aten." His words seemed to come directly from the god. "Aten is omnipotent, and I am his servant. As I labor for his glory, I will no longer live among you. I will found a new city and a new way of life. Free. Open. Conceived in truth."

"You are expunged from the House of Light," Tushratta roared.

"I have entered it and it is mine!" Amenophis IV flung his hands over his head. His body quivered with ecstasy. "From this day forward I will permit no one to call me by the false god's name. I am the Spirit of Aten. Akhenaten. I will be Akhenaten into eternity."

They turned, the king and queen, with one motion. The crowd drew back, opening an avenue to the royal carriage, and the pair moved forward. Their shadows were long and shimmering; they were bathed in golden light. The terrified citizens of Thebes hid their faces from they knew not what. Akhenaten, who had been Amenophis, and his queen climbed easily into the chariot and were gone in a flash of sparkling bridles.

"What will become of Egypt?" Tushratta moaned, his hands clasping and unclasping.

"Let us ensure that Egypt lives," Ay reminded him dryly, gesturing at the fallen king. Accompanied by Tiya, they bore Pharaoh away.

The noise of the crowd swelled again. As the people began to disperse, Hesen, her face shining, signaled Senumet. Then she ran—on feet so light they never touched the ground—to the magic place.

*Now I'll be with him*, her heart sang, joy bubbling out in bursts of laughter. She arrived first at the old ruin, breathless and scarcely able to contain herself until she heard a noise on the path behind her. She flung herself at the approaching figure coming through the darkest shadows of the night. She kissed his face, his brow, his chin, his neck. "Beloved, you took so long! Isn't it glorious?"

"Glorious?" Senumet whispered grimly.

"Wasn't Pharaoh wonderful? And grandfather struck down by a just god. Now my father's will shall be known all over Egypt. The Aten shall reign."

Senumet's chest tightened. She was nearly hysterical and had no idea at all of what had really occurred. "Amenophis may recover," he tried.

"Never!" she crowed. "Aten will keep him powerless and weak. Truth shall shine on Egypt."

He turned her in his arms and directed her toward the looming complex of Karnak, dark and massive. "The old gods are not vanquished yet," he said severely. "Go slowly, Hesen. Your enemies are powerful and treacherous. Tell no one of your thoughts, my love."

He tried to embrace her more closely to comfort her, but furiously she flailed against him and broke free. "You have spoiled this night for me—how could you?" she cried. And she whirled and ran from the ruin along the path, disappearing into the darkness.

Senumet waited, hoping she'd return. Finally he made his way back to the barracks of the scribes.

Someone had to show her the sober truth, but what a fool he had been to rush into it.

In the palace, the old king lay on his bed. Incense burned in hanging censers and its smoke hung heavy and sweet about him. Physicians placed healing amulets on Pharaoh's chest. Tushratta and the priests sent up waves of prayers and incantations in a constant vigil while Pharaoh drifted in and out of some private world, muttering unintelligibly and recognizing no one around him.

A muscle twitched in Ay's cheek as he damned that mindless, lecherous, gluttonous mountain of flesh for the ruin of his well-laid strategy. Might the searing flames of the Underworld consume him! Now the son could not be challenged—his claim was too strong. But Ay was not yet defeated. There was nothing to be gained here, however. He offered Tiya his sympathy and turned on his heel.

Ay went to proclaim his loyalty to Akhenaten.

At dawn, Nefertiti, her eyes shadowed by the long night, entered Amenophis' bedchamber. Tiya sat by the bed. Tushratta and the priests still intoned prayers. The smoke of the incense rasped her throat. She touched Tiya's arm—just as Amenophis opened his eyes and fixed them on his wife.

"Arm . . . can't move . . . arm," he whimpered. The words were slurred by the droop of his mouth at the left side. At the left corner, too, his eye was pulled down.

Tushratta hurried to his side. "Amon saved you from death, yet death had already touched your left arm."

"Son . . . touched . . . arm . . ."

"No, beloved!" Tiya cried in alarm and warned the priest with a quelling look.

Pharaoh's fingers plucked at the coverlet, and Tiya stroked his hand until his breathing deepened and he was again asleep.

Having held her silence, Nefertiti bent to Tiya's ear. "You must rest, too," and she helped Tiya to her feet. "You'll be called when Pharaoh wakes."

Nefertiti took the old woman to Pharaoh's audience chamber and sat her in an ebony chair. After sending servants for beer and cakes, she pointed to the closed doors of Pharaoh's apartments and said, "Ay has been with my husband for hours and is still with him."

"That snake," Tiya muttered.

"Pharaoh has named him vizier both to him and to his father."

"And you did not protest?"

"He professes his wishes to understand the Aten, and he'll serve both Pharaohs equally. After all, without Akhenaten's favor, his power has no future. And he can be useful."

"A priest of Amon for all these years? You are a fool," Tiya declared. At seeing Nefertiti's icy expression, she blurted, "Oh, Daughter, no quarrels. Tell me you do not seriously intend to leave. Tell me you will stay at Thebes."

"Already Akhenaten has ordered a fleet of barges."

"No!"

Nefertiti's face turned radiant. She had known the old and the frightened would not dare to follow their dream. "We will go where the god directs Pharaoh. Where Aten bids us rest, there Pharaoh will name his city."

"May Aten protect you for a passel of fools!" Tiya covered her eyes. "Whom will Pharaoh take?"

"His children." The queen paused. "And Tutu and Smenkhare. He feels great concern for their moral growth."

"Amenophis won't be able to stop him," Tiya said in resignation. "He will be many months recovering, if at all. I've seen that frozen death before."

"And he will take Horemheb as general."

Tiya approved. "A good choice. Horemheb has no politics. Which scribes?"

"Bek. Pharaoh has appointed him Chief Sculptor and Master of the Works."

Tiya nodded. "Bek has always lusted after position. He'll obey who has the most to offer. In the same way, if Ay suggests Senumet, you should accept him in your court."

Nefertiti's eyebrow arched. "Just a few months ago, we feared him —with reason. I trust him even less now." On the barge, away from Thebes, Hesen's indiscretion seemed unimportant. But in the swirl of events, Nefertiti saw things differently.

"You're wrong," Tiya declared. "I've been watching him. He's smart and he's quick. No one makes a fool of him. He's got a way that commands respect, and people are willing to follow him. And he'll be loyal. When he could have exposed us he did not. Ay favors him. If I'm right, Ay will rely on him more and more."

Nefertiti considered. Finally she nodded agreement. She was not so foolish that she would refuse to listen to Tiya when the old woman made sense. A spy in Ay's camp could be quite useful. "So," she said, "you accept our departure."

"Have I a choice?" Tiya's mouth was a tight line of determination. "I'll stay here and watch the priests, try to protect us from their plots. Amenophis my husband will never rule again with the same power, of that I'm sure."

The two women grew silent. Suddenly a sob tore out of Tiya's throat. Impulsively, she took Nefertiti in her arms and clasped her hand. "Take care of my son," she pleaded. "Help him to be wise."

"He is all my life," Nefertiti said simply, accepting the embrace.

"I believe you," Tiya sighed. "He is both our lives."

Queens of Egypt, they waited for the studded doors to open and the man who filled both their souls to emerge.

# IX

Nefertiti greeted the new day with a sense of purpose and fulfillment she had never known before. Time stretched ahead of her, rich and glowing with promise. She had just studied her image, making an adjustment to her wig, sparkling with gold tubes that threaded the long curls, when Meritaten asked for an audience.

She was surprised. Meritaten, compliant and accepting, rarely had anything to say. And the queen was more surprised when she saw her first daughter. The girl was disheveled, without makeup, still in her nightrobe. She failed to greet her mother with the courtesy that was her habit.

Meritaten burst out, "No one will talk of anything but our leaving our home and court—all our life here—to go into the desert—into nothing!" Beside herself, the girl wailed, "Why? What need have we for another city and another temple?"

Nefertiti certainly hadn't expected dissension from this quarter—and any dissension in her own house was intolerable. "We go where Pharaoh leads," she reprimanded. "We go where we may worship the Aten freely."

"The Aten was always your god, not mine," Meritaten cried, her face flushed. "If we're to be free, I should be free to worship Mother Isis—and to live where I want to."

Nefertiti could hardly believe her ears. How could her eldest, the next queen, flesh of her flesh, be so blind? "You are heiress," she said with taut patience. "I did not expect I would have to remind you."

"When I'm queen," Meritaten lashed out, "I'll return to Thebes and crush the Aten."

Nefertiti's hand whipped out, struck her daughter's cheek with a sharp crack. The girl's head rocked back and she almost fell. There was a horrified silence. Quick tears distorted Meritaten's features. "Forgive me," she choked, reaching for her mother's hand.

Nefertiti's fingers stung from the force of her blow. "It would behoove you not to forget again," she said finally, forcing her voice to be even, "that your only freedom is to obey. Now leave me. I'll try to forget this indiscretion."

She watched her daughter stumble from the room and tried to summon up the joy of this morning. It wouldn't be easy, the way ahead. But she was committed to Pharaoh's vision, and if, to forge a new world, the fires must consume the unseeing, she would accept that too —though she might lose her own daughter in the flames.

Her mind turned to Meket, another problem. At least the girl had had no violent attack in months, and for that she must be grateful. Still, the weak chronic cough persisted and the girl was increasingly listless. Only Hesen, of all her children, did she think of with pride— and love. Hesen had the richness of spirit and inner grace to understand and feel the glory of Aten. Hesen would have an important place at her mother's side in their new world.

In the coming weeks the entire city of Thebes was galvanized with preparations for the departure. Twenty royal barges gathered at the dock. Huge linen sails were spread in the fields and an army of barefoot women swarmed over them, embroidering giant hieroglyphs representing Pharaoh's new name and enclosing them in the oval cartouche of royalty.

Temporary pens were installed near the docks where braying donkeys moved restlessly, horses pounded the ground in displeasure at confinement. Flats of sprouting seedlings were stacked near the ships, and each morning servants climbed high ladders and soaked them.

Slaves marched up twenty ramps bearing crated furniture, clothes, linens. Tools and farm implements were placed aboard. Then they hoisted up the huge vessels of sesame, flaxseed and castor oil—and the wine.

The scribe-scholar Meire, historian of the old kingdom, was appointed high priest to Aten, and he began the selection of his stewards. Bek considered and chose his scribes. For his part, Ay filled positions with men he could trust, carefully avoiding Tushratta and Rahmose. Yet he did not forget his old friends. When everything was settled, they'd meet in secret. If Amenophis lived and grew strong again—they need do nothing, at least for the present. If he died, however, they would have to move swiftly and dramatically—unleash the power of tradition that smoldered in every Egyptian's heart.

On the evening of the twenty-fifth of the month Thoth, Senumet walked along the wharves. That day the royal tents had been erected on the top deck of the barge that was to bear Pharaoh and his family. As Senumet watched potted palms, their trunks sheathed in gold, being hoisted aboard, he told himself: If you stay behind, it is your own fault. If it is within your power, do not be separated from her!

He had so little time. Tomorrow he would seek an audience with Ay, and if Ay failed him, then with Akhenaten himself. To sail on the royal barge or on one of the ships in its wake, he would declare his devotion to Pharaoh's new god-that-is-the-One-God, and if Pharaoh asked it, would thrust his drawing hand into a brazier of hot coals to prove it.

Ironically, on the next morning, the summons came.

The faint light of dawn had begun to gray the shadows in the scribes' barracks when a hand touched his shoulder, awakening him instantly from fitful sleep. The hand belonged to an acolyte of the temple of Ra, and the boy's shaven pate gleamed in the morning twilight. The priest-to-be whispered so as not to disturb the two sleeping scribes flanking Senumet on bunks not an arm's reach away.

"You are wanted by Ay. Come."

His fingers trembling, Senumet dressed himself to the songs of the crested hoopoes, perched in the mimosa trees outside the scribes' quarters, then followed the acolyte to the new apartments of Ay in the compound of the palace, next to the golden house where the royal family—and Hesen—slumbered.

The tarpaulin that gathered the dew of night had been rolled back from the open roof of Ay's bedchamber, and the servants were drawing back the flowing curtains that divided the room from the veranda. Ay was with his barber, who was patting the oil from the grand vizier's freshly scraped skull and face.

"Senumet," Ay greeted him warmly enough, "you look well, my boy." He beckoned Senumet closer until he could reach out with his thick fingers and grip Senumet's biceps, as if testing the firmness of the muscle. "I hear you are becoming expert with the sword. You bested Meruka in two out of three bouts?"

"It is true."

"Do you aspire to exchange the stylus for the blade and enter the service of Horemheb?"

Senumet grinned. "You cannot suspect that of me, my lord."

A lovely female slave, a Nubian by the look of her, appeared with a tray of lacquers for Ay's nails. Without taking his eyes from Senumet, Ay extended his right hand for a manicure and continued. "But there is nothing like the feel of a sword in a man's hand, especially when he is confident of its use and therefore unafraid."

"Much like the feel of a well-wrought stylus in a man's hand, my lord, or the controlled tongue in a man's mouth, for both can be as sharp as the blade."

Ay threw back his head and laughed. "A truth that time will never dispute!"

"I learned it at my father's knee, my lord."

"You know I'm to be grand vizier to both Pharaohs."

"Egypt will be well served, my lord."

"And you know that I'm charged with assembling a court for the young Pharaoh, henceforth to be known as Akhenaten."

"Yes, my lord." Senumet felt a thrill of hope, but he kept his face impassive.

Ay indulged in silence, and as the moments crawled by, Senumet ached with the strain between his squared shoulders, at the base of his rigid spine. Suddenly, with a gesture of his hand, Ay dismissed the slave. When they were alone, Ay asked, "Are you still loyal to Ra?"

In a single shallow breath, Senumet said, "The sign of Ra is painted on my father's tomb. He holds my father's ka in his two hands."

"Sometimes loyalties take unexpected turns." Ay's face had become unreadable. "In certain circumstances we serve best by appearing to serve another."

"So men—and gods—must understand, my lord." Again Senumet waited, certain he had made no mistake. He was convinced Ay had no intention of abandoning his fealty to Amon and the old gods— or to the power and riches such ties still commanded. He only hoped his words would assure Ay that in principle they were allies.

"How would you feel, Senumet, about joining Akhenaten's court?"

Senumet was careful to appear to give the matter consideration as he gambled, like Ay playing ends against the middle. "To bend the knee and bow the head, to touch the earth at sunrise and midday to the Aten?" he said at last.

"But your true service would be to me, and through me to Amon."

Once more Senumet hesitated. It was a serious proposition, and by agreeing too quickly he might arouse Ay's suspicion. In the interval, it occurred to him exactly what he should say. It pleased him that the words he finally spoke were true: "I'll never forget what I owe to you, my lord."

"So you are willing."

"I am willing, my lord. There is one problem, however."

"Yes?" Ay did not seem surprised.

"Nephrus, my betrothed."

"The date of the nuptials has been set . . ."

"Eight days hence." Senumet made himself look doubtful, but warmth filled his body. It was going to work! He'd be free of Nephrus, too! "May I be absolutely honest, my lord?"

Ay nodded.

"I believe I am correct in thinking that, as in the past, I may be of most service through . . . closeness . . . to the royal family?"

Ay did not withhold his answer. "Delicately phrased."

"Then—as you, my lord, are aware—any involvement must lessen, were I wed."

"The difficulty of your wedding, even the difficulty presented by your betrothal, are problems of which I have not been unaware." Ay's gaze transfixed Senumet, as if impaling a locust. "However, if you are aboard a vessel on the Nile and your betrothed remains in Thebes, how is it that you can break the jar with her? Must not the ceremony be postponed . . . indefinitely?"

"Whatever you think, my lord."

"I'll speak with Rahmose."

"Thank you, my lord."

Wordlessly, Ay dismissed Senumet, and Senumet left the chamber knowing the grand vizier was scrutinizing his retreating back.

Once before Senumet had ended a conference with Ay by running down the stairs and shouting with joy. He was older now. When he left this time, his knees trembled.

Late the next afternoon, Senumet sat in the hall of scribes, where a hundred hands were at work, employed in the voluminous business of writing—copying, translating foreign tablets, recording allotments of land, keeping accounts—through which Egypt functioned and was preserved on rolls of papyrus. To his left sat a group of young scribes, copying recent judgments by the headman of Memphis for inclusion in the body of law, a task Senumet had delegated to them. Senumet's own stylus flowed with graceful precision across the papyrus stretched over his crossed legs, translating the King of Babylon's letter from the cuneiform in which it had been written to the Egyptian hieratic.

"To Amenophis the father and son, the great Kings of Egypt," Senumet copied, "my brothers who love me and whom I love. Thou sendest my father a namkhar of pure gold but thou sendest me only a tablet of gold—and that alloyed with copper. Let my brothers send gold in great quantities—more gold to me than to my father. In my brothers' land, gold is as common as dust."

Without a moment's pause Senumet's hand framed the answer Ay had directed him to send when the letter had been translated for the grand vizier.

"To Kadashman-Bel, King of Babylon, who has increased Pharaohs' love and drawn us ten times closer than in the days of his father. The Pharaohs of Egypt beg the gods to cause this deep friendship to prosper into eternity. Inasmuch as it grieved our hearts when the shipment of gold before last was undefended against hostile tribes—know that the great god Amon forbids us enrich the Bedouin barbarians. Only secure thy borders and twenty times twenty namkhars of gold will be sent to our brother, Kadashman-Bel, King of all Babylon, whom we love."

Senumet was just about to affix the royal seal to the papyrus sheet when he heard a voice raised in caterwauling fury beyond the reed screens in the courtyard. Senumet felt his own throat go dry.

Curious scribes laid aside their styluses and peered into the courtyard.

Ka-Aper, a little pale, appeared at Senumet's shoulder. "You have a visitor," he said inadequately.

Senumet stepped outside. The descending sun left a trail of red bruises across the sky. Nephrus, black kohl streaking her face, ran at him and spat upon him. Her spittle struck his bare chest.

"You piece of dung! You leprous swine!" she wailed.

"Nephrus, please—" he tried, although his tongue stuck to his mouth. "Stop!"

"Stop? Stop?" she howled to the audience of staring scribes, and beat at her breasts. "He wants me to stop! I won't stop until his face is scarred and his lying tongue is severed!"

She attacked. Before he could defend himself, her nails, stained red with henna, flew to his face and clawed away skin and flesh. They fought until he managed to pinion her arms to her side. He felt a sticky wetness on his cheeks as she thrashed and sobbed in his imprisoning embrace.

"May your body rot! May worms eat your heart and corruption ooze from you!" With a mighty pull she wrenched free. "Look!" She spun toward the gallery of scribes. "Look what he had!" She ripped open her dress. Her breasts, white and heaving, fell out.

Like the gawking scribes, Senumet was struck speechless by the spectacle of Nephrus. Had she no shame?

She seized the material of her skirt between both hands and shredded it until she exposed the bush between her legs, curling and full. She pounded her thighs with her fists. "All this," she screamed "whenever his pole of flesh wanted! All this he had. And more!" Sobbing she collapsed to her knees.

Chagrin at his own humiliation, anger at Nephrus's self-degradation whipped through Senumet. And he was judged a peasant! She was lower than the beetle scuttling along the ground pushing its own dung. Brutally he hauled her to her feet. She struggled hysterically, but he swept her up and bore her from the courtyard, through the gate in the fence of upraised spears, down the public walk that led to the river. At least, at this time of day, the riverbank would be quiet. There she could scream herself hoarse until her throat bled. He did not feel her blows on his face and shoulders, and all the while he carried her, he kept up a running litany: "Nephrus, have done. You forget who you are. Have you no pride? Calm yourself and listen to your own voice."

Finally she was still. Gratefully, he relaxed his hold. She arched her body and tore herself out of his arm. "You think I'm finished? You think my love was a pretense, a convenience—like yours? No, Senumet, it is real. I love you. For me there is nothing else. If I can't have you, I'd rather be dead!"

She whirled around, crashed through the tall papyrus and flung herself in the Nile, her body thrashing like a great white fish. He dived in after her, reached her in five strong strokes and tried to grab her. She struck and kicked at him. Water ran in her mouth, her nose; she gagged and choked. She sank beneath the water and then broke the surface, spraying water around them. With a frightening shock, he realized she could not swim. She *was* drowning. Yes, he had wished her dead, but he could not let her die.

Filling his lungs, he submerged. Underwater he studied her flailing arms and legs until her body, again sinking, drifted downward toward him. Bubbles of air escaped her lips as she took in water, and her body grew limp, as if she were resting. Swimming quickly beneath her, he encircled her with his left arm. A strong upward push and he heaved them both to the surface, heads out of the water, to gulp at air. Her arm thrashed at his head. Without emotion, he smashed his fist, hard and sure, against her jaw. As she sagged, he cupped her chin in his hand and began to swim.

Having towed her to the shore, he delivered her, sodden and coughing, into the hands of the waiting scribes who had followed them and had waded into the river's edge. Four of them carried her away.

He returned to the barracks and bathed the scratches on his face. One, particularly deep and ugly, ran from the wing of his nose to the lobe of his ear. He lay on his pallet and closed his eyes. The other scribes returned, but they spoke in whispers among themselves, none daring to refuse his unspoken request for privacy and quiet.

In the morning the scribes were friendly enough, but there was a constraint that had never existed before. Senumet understood. Many of the witnesses to Nephrus's shame were to remain in Thebes; they wanted no part of risking Rahmose's displeasure. And what could Senumet say?

After the morning meal, he separated himself from the group and as he picked his way to the great hall alone, a robed figure hurried toward him—Hesen's servant! Suddenly he was light-headed with gladness. He hadn't allowed himself to hope for this.

Disapproval showed in every stiff line of Sephy's body. "Tonight," she snapped. Then she whirled on her heel angrily and was gone.

Dusk was just deepening the blue of the sky when he slipped to the magic place, but twilight shaded into black and the moon rose, a thin silver blade, while he watched the tangled path with a fierce intensity. He heard the soft rustle before he saw her . . . the same, yet each time more dear, more vital, so fine and fresh and delicately molded. He ached with the joy of her nearness. They hadn't spoken since the night of the feast, when she was angry.

"You musn't play with wild beasts," she greeted him, a cool finger touching his face at the point of that one raised weal.

He stiffened. He wouldn't laugh at Nephrus with her. "It isn't a joke. Don't make it one."

She scrutinized him for a moment. "I haven't forgotten how badly you acted after the feast," she said severely. "And what you told me was false and mean. Soon our glorious journey begins—every jealous and petty thought will be left behind. The world shall work beautifully and wonderfully. You were wrong!" she finished triumphantly.

He stood silent, his whole heart in his eyes. "Hesen!" It was torn out of him.

She smiled and held out her arms magnanimously. "Well, I forgive you," she pronounced.

He crushed her to his chest, buried his face in the sweet fragrance of her hair, forgot in the joy of accepting her mercy that he had done nothing wrong.

"Look how shameless I've become," she said huskily, opening his kilt.

He didn't even hear her, his blood sang so loud in his ears. He took her fiercely out of his long-suppressed need, and she matched his primitive hunger with sharp teeth and strong thighs and a driving desire of her own. Finally, they fell apart, drenched with the sweat of their struggle. Senumet, fingers still unsteady, traced the delicate line of her spine.

"So," she said, still breathless. "You will come with us."

"Yes."

A warning sprang to his lips, but he choked it back. Her reckless faith should be curbed, but he'd not risk her wrath again. Let her meet the day with hope and joy. If she were wrong, the world would cruelly rebuke her all too soon.

# X

It was the morning of the third day of the month Sobek, and the barges were ready. At the first pink beginning of day, when the cliffs in the valley were still dark shadows, the last animals were herded aboard the ships. Slaves, humming to the swish of reed brushes, swept clean pavements that had been buried under mud and pens and dung, and stands for the parting ceremonies, garlanded with lotus and roses, were moved into place. Small groups of Thebans trickled to the dock, laden with baskets and boxes and gifts. Shouts and tearful good-byes scattered a flock of early herons; and the first feluccas, packed with well-wishers vying for the best viewing spots, bobbed in the rippling waters. As the sky glowed with golden lights, flutes played by the royal musicians welcomed the day with silvery cadences. The crowds at the dock grew larger, and the stands filled with glittering, crowned officials.

They began to board—these pioneers—first the servants and farmers and artisans and their families . . . then the soldiers—Horemheb leading, browned, muscled, jeweled . . . next the scribes, Senumet among them, tall and broad, looking more soldier than scholar, his heart racing with the excitement of departure . . . and last, the nobles and officials of the new court.

The royal family were driven to the dock in gilded chariots, and as they drew to a halt, Pharaoh, wearing the double crown and newly fashioned Aten pectoral, held out his hands:

"Bright is the earth," he intoned, in a blessing of his own composing.

> "The darkness is banished,
> The two lands are in daily festivity.
> Yonder is the river, great and wide,
> Where we set out in thy adoring hands,
> O Lord of us all, O merciful Aten,
> Who leads us by thy love."

He stepped from his chariot and knelt, his face raised to his god. The populace prostrated themselves before him. On the platform, Ay and Rahmose lowered themselves too, though their eyes were cold. Tushratta would not come—Ay knew that Tiya, kneeling beside him, had noted that absence—but Tushratta could not bear to look on the face of the criminal Pharaoh, nor would the chief priest of Amon allow his presence to condone the worship of the upstart god.

Now Meire, chief priest to Aten, his crown of gold and lapis sun disks scattering sparks of new daylight, offered the departing prayer from his place next to Ay on the platform:

> "Bless thy son Akhenaten,
> Whom thou hast made wise in thy designs
> And in thy might.
> The world and its people are in his hands
> By thy decree,
> For he is thy son
> Who came forth from thy limbs,
> The King, living in truth,
> The lord of the two lands
> Who leads us—
> Our Pharaoh, son to the god—
> Whom we follow with willing hearts."

Having descended the platform, the priest led the royal children in an ordered procession to the first barge. As Hesen's foot touched the oiled wooden deck, she was filled with a sense of incredible buoyancy. She was leaving Thebes forever. She had never known before that happiness so could fill her that its pressure would actually hurt.

Now, Pharaoh and his queen—radiant with Aten's pure white light—climbed aboard. Pharaoh was led to the foremost deck, where his throne waited, emblazoned with silver ankhs. A semicircle of stiff parchment on a wooden pole protected his head from the sun.

The captain gave the signal. Immediately twenty trumpeters sounded a brassy note. Crews scurried; twenty linen sails unrolled; they were lashed to the crossbeams and turned to meet the soft morning wind. The sheets rippled musically, then the name Akhenaten, green and shimmering, billowed out on twenty surfaces and covered the harbor.

A shout rang out. Twenty royal ships drew gently away from the docks, the cheers of those lining the shore mingling with the calls of the smaller crowds on the decks. They were under way.

Pharaoh sat on his throne, unmoving, all the long Egyptian days. His meals were brought to him and he ate, thanking Aten for his bounty. Otherwise he remained silent, his eyes fixed ahead, searching the flat horizon, waiting for a signal from his god.

Hesen waited with him, certainty in her heart. It felt so right, here on the Nile, sailing into the sun, directed by the god, free and open and living in *maat*. From wherever she was on the ship, she had only to turn her head to see Pharaoh, strong and steady and loving. Meanwhile, Sephy, preoccupied with a more immediate concern, refused to leave her mistress's side, where she insisted on following Hesen's every movement with the linen shade. Annoyed, Hesen had to allow privately that she had perhaps been a little careless. In her eagerness to acknowledge Aten, after the feast, she had opened herself to him completely. Her face was now very burned, and Sephy was adamant: The sun must not bathe her any longer. Actually Hesen was not convinced that the darker color was ugly. To her way of thinking, she wore a new skin, now. If the old was coming off in great, ugly patches on her nose, she was glad to lose it. Still, if Sephy wished to run after her protecting her face with a linen shade—let her. If they were to live in tents in the desert, so be it. . . . Anything, anything, so long as her father, who was Akhenaten, would remain so confident and lighthearted and her mother would always sit at his side like a fixed star as she did now, an embodiment of love and serenity. And Senumet, the very center and focus of content . . . Senumet would be near them, with them, wherever their journey led.

The days slipped into each other and became a week. They lost the sense of an early end to their voyage. Wine flowed less freely, and talk predicted the rationing of food. Tempers flared. Meket, who had begun the journey calmly enough, was now bursting into tears for no reason and refusing to eat.

"Please, dearest," Hesen coaxed, trying to tempt her with a small piece of melon, "you must get strong so you can share in our wonderful new world."

Meket turned her head away.

"Darling, you'll see—everything is possible now."

But after a half hour of this, even Hesen's relentless enthusiasm faltered.

"Well, then," she said finally, "eat because you give me pain to see you this way."

Meket managed a small smile and accepted a morsel. Unfortunately, it was harder to watch her efforts to swallow than to have her refuse to eat at all.

Recounting this later to the queen, Hesen summed up impatiently, "But for how long can she starve herself, after all? She'll get used to it. Meritaten has calmed down."

Nefertiti smiled at her daughter. "Not everyone has your strength, Hesen," she reminded her favorite, "or your convictions. Don't mock Meritaten because she can't see the Aten, or Meket because she fears the unknown."

"Or Smenkhare for being wicked? Or Horemheb for being stupid? Or Ay for being a hypocrite?"

"So stiff-necked you are, my daughter." Nefertiti laughed. "It's not easy for people to give up beliefs of many generations. Even your scribe hasn't accepted Aten."

"But we can discuss it without anger. And besides"—Hesen smiled —"I've not given up on his conversion."

Nefertiti frowned. "I've been meaning to talk with you about that scribe."

"Yes?"

"There was some sort of incident before we left, and a great deal of gossip. I understand he was supposed to marry but did not. And that you were mentioned."

"My name was never spoken." Hesen's voice took on an edge.

As if she had not been interrupted, Nefertiti went on, "Do you plan to continue your relationship with this man?"

Hesen hesitated only the space of a breath. "I'll never do anything to embarrass Pharaoh. That I promise," she said firmly.

It was less assurance than her mother wanted, but she was reluctant to force the issue. The child was no fool and she adored Akhenaten. Nefertiti would be content with that.

The second week ended, and there was still no sign of the promised site. Eyes were fixed boldly on Pharaoh now, and an undertone of whispers became discernible, punctuated by snide laughter. Squabbles broke out more frequently, jealousies hardened, voices were raised in disputes over preferment.

While life was becoming more difficult in the close quarters, however, the worsening atmosphere had no effect on Senumet. He was, in fact, happier than he'd expected to be, and for each day that slipped away in peaceful ease, he was thankful. He preferred not to think too far ahead. If he strained his eyes and stared with great concentration, he might catch a glimpse of Hesen's shining head, but he felt no burning desire to lessen the distance between them. Glory, passion and adventure had less reality, for the moment, than the rhythm of oars, sunlight and everyday duties. And he was grateful to have been reaccepted by the two score of scribes whom Bek had selected to make the journey.

"Senumet!"

He looked up from his work to see Bek hurrying over excitedly, holding out sheets of papyrus. "I've just spoken with Pharaoh. Everything is to be changed, even our art forms. Our chisels and brushes are to tell what we truly see—we will no longer follow blindly the patterns the ancients laid down. Just look at these!"

Senumet opened the roll of papyrus, stared at the rough sketch of a nude girl, verging on womanhood. There was something about that face. Isis be blessed! They were not idealized features he looked at, wiped clean of individuality, as they had always been. This was the Princess Meketaten—full frontal view of her, not in stylized profile—just as she was in life. Frail and slender, her body had a timid look with those delicate breasts and tight thighs. Her mouth was pulled in, too, just the way she held it—fearful of passion. She had been captured in swift, sure lines. She seemed almost ready to leap off the page. The scribes had never drawn from life before.

"It's wonderful," Senumet breathed.

Fingers trembling, he flipped the other sheets. Nothing was frozen any longer. Bek had freed the wild bull jumping in the field, the coursing hound, the fleeing, frightened game. Senumet could hardly believe it. "We can paint as we see," he repeated.

"When Pharaoh says he lives in truth, he means it," Bek assured him.

"But that can't extend to our portrayals of himself," Senumet replied skeptically. How could Pharaoh permit them to show that flabby stomach, the feminine thighs, those strange full breasts, his elongated horseface, as the form of the living god?

"Even that!"

The two men stared at each other, Bek's wonderment reverberating in Senumet. "Truly," Bek said finally, "we enter a new world."

A world where anything might be possible. And Senumet's unruly heart whispered, But not all possibilities are beautiful. . . .

It had been three weeks since they set out, and they had sailed nearly three hundred miles below Thebes. Still, sunrises passed into sunsets and darkness into dawn, and Pharaoh gave no word. Now the riverbanks were high and impregnable cliffs, plunging directly into the Nile without even a hint of beach, and the voices of the skeptics multiplied.

"Where is the promised site?"

"When will Pharaoh's god answer?"

"Does the god truly speak to him?"

"Is there such a god?"

Nefertiti refused to hear them. Each day, as her husband waited, tense and expectant, she saw that the god was with him. And each night when the god slept and she held the sleeping man in her arms, she could sense the Aten's warmth, flowing through Pharaoh. Let Aten test her too—she'd not be found wanting. And on the second day of the fourth week, she felt a difference. Pharaoh leaned forward more eagerly, and his body began to quiver. Nefertiti's eyes scanned the shore. The cliffs—wasn't their line a little less forward? She gripped the rail. Soon everyone on the barge felt the growing excitement. The rowers pulled more quickly, catching its echo. Soon there could be no doubt. The cliffs were receding, as if the forbidding land were drawing back and opening to admit them.

Barely daring to breathe, Nefertiti took a place on a low stool next to the king. She could not now be seated on the throne near his. This was not a moment to be shared equally. Akhenaten was with the god.

And Pharaoh seemed to shine. His eyes were so luminous, his face so nakedly worshipful that none could see him without believing. And the miracle unfolded.

On both banks of the Nile, the rounded green-touched cliffs rolled back in a series of elevated plateaus—the last and widest, a golden beach, reaching to the river. As they glided past, hushed with awe at the extent of it, it seemed that the god had scooped out a vast circular amphitheater, broken by a curving blue enamel sea and rimmed around by peaks burnished orange. Caught in Pharaoh's dream, the people lining the rails had the same vision—it seemed so obvious: a temple on the highest plateau! The palace adjoining it! Neat, planted fields to the south where the valley was greenest! Estates and houses and shops and markets on descending slopes, and docks lining the beach. It was a jewellike gift they stared at—calling for creation.

Pharaoh was standing now, his body trembling with the strength of his dream. He raised his hand. The signal rippled through waving arms on twenty ships. Rudders were feathered, oars were locked in a simultaneous flash of bright color and the barges glided to a stop. The breeze died too, at the very moment before the sails could be furled—so they seemed to collapse at a signal from the god.

"A sign," the doubters whispered, and doubted no more.

A spontaneous cheer burst out, was carried down the line of twenty barges to where, on the last, the king was only a golden blur.

Akhenaten held his hand aloft and acknowledged their homage. Finally in a voice stronger and firmer and more passionate than he had ever used, Pharaoh spoke to his god. "Hear, O Aten, all-powerful, giver of all mercies, accept my testimony. For this place is my witness forever. Here will I make Akhet-Aten for God my Father as his house on earth. On its south, its north, its east, its west will I demark it. Never again shall I pass beyond the southern landmark of Akhet-Aten on the south nor journey farther than its northern landmark on the north. I shall raise up here temples and palaces and altars to my Father, to Aten, in whom is life forever and ever."

A ringing cheer burst forth, again rolled on and was renewed by throats that hours before had constricted in scornful laughter. Goblets overflowed with date wine, and grateful toasts were pledged to Pharaoh and his god. Hesen shouted until she was hoarse, prayed with wholehearted fervor, drank wine until she was light-headed and giggling—until the very noise of the festivities suddenly erased her smile with a sober thought: How was all this affecting poor Meket? For the past week the whispers and derisive comments and scornful laughs directed at Pharaoh had so upset Meket that a place had been made for the fragile princess below deck, where the oils and scented linens were stored. There, in a curtained space smelling of roses, Meket was tended by careful servants.

She must have heard the shouts. She must know the ships had stopped. And her servants must be here on deck—at least, all but her nurse Yuya—of that Hesen was sure. Yuya would never leave her charge, just as Sephy would never leave Hesen, were she ill. Picking up a fresh glass of wine—Meket would have some small share in the day's events—Hesen reluctantly pulled herself away and climbed below deck, shutting her eyes to hasten their adjustment to the soft, flickering light.

When she opened them, her heart lurched. There were too many people here. Why weren't they on deck? Why were there so many men? She drew in her breath sharply as she caught the flash of their pectorals. Physicians! And that smell . . . the same heavy incense had hung in the palace after Amenophis' collapse. The goblet fell from her nerveless fingers and splintered on the deck.

Yuya detached herself from the crowd of servants and approached her. Hesen could see her eyes were red-rimmed and swollen.

"My lady." She gripped Hesen's hands. "Meket has died. An easy death," she added hurriedly, as Hesen's face whitened. "She went gently to meet her god."

"Let me see her," Hesen managed, her body shaking. It wasn't true. Life could not have blown out of Meket, not now—not when there was so much to rejoice in—when the future beckoned so brightly.

Hesen moved to the closed curtains. With unsteady fingers, she pulled back the heavy cloth. The servants inside paused in their ministrations, stepped quickly aside, and Hesen looked at her sister.

Meket's body had already been arranged in the discreet posture of death. Nude, stretched absolutely straight, arms close to the sides, palms down, head back, the body lay poised for its journey into the Underworld—to be united with its ka.

Spots of flashing light danced in front of Hesen's eyes, so intently did she fix her gaze on those tiny breasts, willing them to move, as they must if her sister breathed. They were absolutely still, and Hesen noticed the thin linen band wrapped around Meket's head— to hold the chin firm so the mouth, lacking sentience to control it, would not stiffen and open unsightly.

"No!" Hensen cried in anguish, and flung herself at that still figure. It was cold. She ripped off that obscene band and rubbed her warm living hands on Meket's cheeks. Her sister's mouth gaped open and her pink tongue slipped out.

"No!" Hesen screamed again, but she knew that mouth would never again curve in a smile. Those eyes would never again see the Nile, never know joy. In an instant, excitement, dreams, shared pleasures—all could be blotted out, irrevocably ended.

Suddenly a thought struck her, knocking the breath out of her body. All of Pharaoh's plans—his wonderful projects—must be put aside. The very first construction at Akhet-Aten would be a tomb. A dark enclosed place where Pharaoh's issue would be sealed. Blackness swirled around her. Was it a sign from the god? O merciful Aten, let Pharaoh's vision flourish. Bless thy true son.

Slowly she pulled herself to her feet. Taking Yuya with her, she painfully made her way abovedeck. Her parents must be informed. She must be the one to tell them.

When there was so much to do and so many people looking to them for direction, Pharaoh and his queen could not openly mourn. Hesen had never loved or respected her parents more than when they stood in the royal chariot and rode to each boundary of Akhet-Aten, marking the sites of the fourteen stelas that would bear its name. Neither flinched when they passed the cliff hollow where Meket's tomb was being cut.

No one would find Hesen lacking in courage either. She masked her grief, managed to appear calm and resourceful during the chaotic days that followed their landing. Tents sprang up on shore, where they'd live until the palace was built; and Hesen, seeing to it that her belongings and her younger sisters' were unloaded properly and placed in some order in the tents, somehow also found time to help her parents direct the first efforts at settlement. If it was a relief at night to discard that controlled mask, Hesen was determined that no one need know it. But on the third night, after a day of incessant and conflicting demands, she collapsed, weeping, on her bed. Sephy was beside her instantly, gathering the exhausted girl into her arms.

Suddenly the curtains parted and the queen entered, her white grown billowing behind her. Hesen scrambled to a sitting position, wiping her eyes. Sephy backed out of the tent.

"So," Nefertiti said gently, "my Hesen learns life may be bitter even when it is sweetest."

Hesen managed a smile. "And the sun keeps shining even when I'd prefer darkness."

"We're less important than we think, more important than we realize," Nefertiti told her, smoothing back a tendril of her daughter's hair.

Hesen's eyes threatened to overflow again. "I don't understand."

"Have you thought, dearest, about the fact that you're now second daughter to the king, next in line after the heiress."

Pain stabbed Hesen anew. "Meritaten has always been very well." Nefertiti gasped.

Immediately, Hesen was sorry. "Forgive me," she said miserably. How could she have forgotten the queen's own grief? "I didn't think."

"That could be accepted from the third daughter to Pharaoh." Nefertiti's voice was quiet but unbending. "You're no longer that. Now you're Pharaoh's ambassador. Anything you do will be taken as representative of him."

Hesen met her eyes. "Pharaoh is all-supreme. I'll do what I must."

She was standing on the sandy hillock three weeks after the landing, watching the Nile traffic, when her eye caught a knot of movement on shore. A crowd seemed to be gathering. She leaned forward, followed their growing numbers as they ran along the beach. She strained her eyes—then she saw it. A ship that had been obscured by the other tall sails. A boat from the direction of Thebes. A black boat, flying a black flag. The feluccas glided to either side of it and gave it a clear passage. She could just make out the gilt letters on its banner. "Amenophis III."

"Hurry, Senedjm," she urged the servant, indicating the whip. The two horses pulling the chariot seemed to fly over the turf, the ostrich plumes on their heads whipping back as they galloped to the settlement.

The black ship pulled alongside the dock. Darkly dressed messengers leaped down, pushed through the excited crowds and hurried to the royal tent, set apart by four tall columns.

The news swept through the city: *Amenophis III was dead! Long life to Pharaoh, Son of Aten!*

Akhenaten and Nefertiti received the royal messengers and ordered the news of Pharaoh's death officially announced. They commanded a memorial service for the evening and directed the entire city into mourning. Inwardly the king and queen realized that a crisis was upon them—the time of the relative peace was over. They were no longer secessionists—they were Egypt. At sundown they managed to find a private moment to walk together on the empty beach.

Violet and gold shadows settled on the water, and the high, bordering cliffs, set afire with the last of the sun's rays, glowed with rosy brilliance. Nebertcher, Lord of Creation, might have seen it just this way when he fashioned the land out of inert *nenu*. But Nefertiti was blind to the beauty of the evening.

"Who shall go to Thebes for the funeral?" she asked without preamble.

Akhenaten took her hand, which trembled despite her effort to control it. "Don't be afraid, beloved. I won't return to Thebes."

But she was not satisfied. "No one must persuade you otherwise."

He walked without speaking. At last he said, "I am disappointed you continue to believe me a fool. As for Thebes, I plan to name Smenkhare heir, betroth him to our Meritaten, and send him to wrestle Ay and Tushratta's lions."

"Smenkhare should go, yes. But someone from your house must be there, too."

"We have an ambassador."

"You do not think to give them Meritaten!"

"And possibly lose heir and heiress together? Indeed, that would be a mission to remember. No, my dear queen, not Meritaten. Hesen."

"Oh, beloved—"

"No," he interrupted, "you will not tell me she is too young, too intemperate, too trusting. I have been watching our daughter. Do not underestimate Hesen. The stakes are high, but I don't think she will fail. She has the intelligence for the game of diplomacy."

"Besides," Nefertiti agreed, "there's no one else."

In the days that followed, Hesen was scheduled for so many meetings and received so many instructions her head ached. But there was one privilege. Nefertiti summoned her to tell her she had granted Senumet a private audience. In the rush of pure delight, Hesen neglected to ask the reason or even to wonder about it.

They were to meet in what would one day be the south garden. Hands tightly clasped, she waited, seated on an undecorated bench in a neatly marked sandy rectangle that in some long-distant future would be a sycamore grove.

She watched him come toward her, his purposeful strength showing itself in his stride. Her body trembled.

"Highness." He bowed formally, his face serious.

"I thought we were finished with formal charades."

"No, my lady. How can we be finished with that? Our situation is different now. You're second princess."

"I've heard that so often it makes my head ache . . . but what has been between us, Senumet—"

"Don't pretend nothing's changed. We can't risk being together. The magic place is gone."

Quick tears sprang to her eyes. "Life takes unexpected twists—you told me that. Look—we've managed to meet after all."

"Why do you think the queen granted us this time?"

"You made up a reason."

"No. I told her the truth—just as I plan to tell you."

"Another lecture!"

"A short one—just to caution you to be very careful at Thebes."

"You're too late," she said, her eyes fixed on his hands that should have reached to take hers. "At least seventeen people have told me that already."

"And I know the attention you pay to warnings! But you'll be tested at Thebes. They will bluster to frighten you and question you to confuse you, and try to force you to declare your loyalties. They are masters at the art."

"My loyalties are no secret."

"But you will not declare them."

She was surprised. "And why not? Aten is freely worshiped now. He is Pharaoh's god!"

"Life takes many twists—now I'm quoting you. It's not necessary for everything to be clear. Be evasive. Hedge every answer."

"Still, some things are true," she said impatiently. "There is only one Pharaoh, and he is Akhenaten."

"But you will be dealing with clever, ambitious men who want Pharaoh's power for themselves—and don't care what they must do to get it."

"Could you be referring to your trusted patron?"

"A word in praise of Amon would be wise," he went on doggedly.

"That's ridiculous, Amon is crushed and weak. We are in power!"

"For now," he stressed. "The future is shrouded and so as not to forfeit it, our speech should be clever rather than heartfelt."

She was disappointed in him. "The royal family speaks with *maat*," she said coldly.

"You haven't forgotten that it was the queen who granted me this time?"

Hesen had forgotten. She was shaken by the implications. "You told her about praising Amon?" Then it must be true.

"Yes."

"Oh!" A frightened cry. So all of them were agreed: it was politic that she betray her god. "Oh, Senumet, how I wish we could lie together!"

"You sound like a child." The worst thing he could do was to sympathize with her. Let her be angry at him, only let her feel strong. But the knife of his cruelty twisted in his own heart.

"You have made your point. If I must play those dreadful games—I will."

"Princess Ankhesenpaaten will be brilliant," he responded more gently. "She will play like one who has studied diplomacy for many years."

"I am in Aten's hand," she said, eyes unflinching. "He will guide me. His truth shall shine upon me and light my way."

Senumet gripped her hands, careless of who might be spying. At last he pulled himself away. The picture of her sitting there, her back straight and proud, would be engraved for all time on his soul.

# XI

Ay awaited the embassy from Akhet-Aten with eager anticipation. His plan was a long shot, but he wouldn't have another chance like this for years. If bold, decisive action would serve, Smenkhare would then be Pharaoh and Ay his trusted regent—if only Akhenaten returned to Thebes!

Pharaoh was a fool to have left. Absent when Amenophis died, he'd lost the enormous advantage physical presence would have given him in this strongest, most powerful city in Egypt. Ay, of course, had done all he could to fill the power vacuum with himself—a strategy Pharaoh had furthered himself by agreeing to Ay's advisement that Nacht retain his position as commander of the garrison at Thebes.

Oh, Ay had met often with Nacht, had filled his beefy head with the glorious titles that would accrue to him if Ay were regent, the battles Nacht would lead against cities rich with plunder. Nacht was ready to declare his support for Smenkhare. And who would stand for Pharaoh? Only an untried Horemheb and the soldiers that young man had recruited—and there was a good chance, Ay thought, that Akhenaten, foolish dreamer that he was, would not even have sense enough to bring them.

The priests of Thebes had been active too. Tushratta had directed his most trusted acolyte to scamper along the beamed roof of the temple and cover the slit that allowed the sun's rays to illuminate Amon's disk. Now, when Tushratta plunged his cleaver into the goat's neck for the morning sacrifice, Amon would not shine his acceptance. The message was clear: Amon was displeased with his children. The Thebans walked with a great unease.

If only Pharaoh came! Ay had done all he could to lull his fears. The boat he'd sent to Akhet-Aten was small. No room for soldiers. Here, it seemed to say, come back in safety. Keru-eff, the captain, carried messages from Tiya. "Heal the rift between Aten and Amon," they begged, "for Egypt's sake. Come home." Sealed with her cartouche, how was Akhenaten to guess they were forgeries? The messages she had actually sent warned her son not to venture to Thebes—but those messages had been destroyed and the couriers who carried them killed.

And in the time that elapsed before Pharaoh's ship arrived, Ay planned to play Tiya down as queen and raise up Sit-Amon, the mother of Tutu and Smenkhare, who had been Pharaoh's daughter as well as wife. Tiya would vanish like dried chaff in the wind, and his sister's decline in stature would begin with the first memorial service for Amenophis III.

Before sunrise on the morning of the year when Sirius would first be visible, all Thebes knelt at the dock, eyes on the eastern horizon. On Ay's arm, Tiya was led to a place next to Sit-Amon. No farther forward, no greater in importance. She made no protest—how could she? She knelt and lifted her eyes to the star, Pharaoh's first appearance in heaven.

To the accompaniment of the double pipes, Tushratta praised Pharaoh:

> "... *who cultivated grain and loved the harvest god,*
> *Whom the Nile greeted in every valley.*
> *None was hungry in his years; none thirsted then;*
> *Men dwelt in peace, and knowing he wrought it,*
>   *blessed his bounty.*
> *We wish him everlasting life."*

The orange rim of the sun pushed over the horizon; Sirius disappeared. But it would return. Pharaoh's light would not forsake his land.

The people shuffled to their feet. As the dock area emptied, Tiya demanded of Ay, "Why was Sit-Amon next to me?"

"Isn't she mother to Pharaoh's sons?"

"She has no right. My son is Pharaoh!"

"Yet none from the seed of Amenophis can be disregarded."

"Disregarded? For what?"

"Grief has made you too sensitive," Ay soothed. "Why not stay in your quarters tonight and rest? Sit-Amon will welcome Rib-Addi of Byblos."

"It would be rude if the queen ignored so loyal a vassal."

"He'll understand if Pharaoh's chief wife is overwhelmed by sorrow."

Tiya paled. Conflicting emotions played briefly over her face. "Perhaps you're right. Send him to me after, Brother, so I may acknowledge his message and thank him." She swept past him and was gone.

With grudging admiration, Ay thought: *Almost certainly there had been no message.* By the pretext she hoped to make him edgy. She was an opponent who would make the winning even sweeter.

All her senses sharpened, Hesen was aware of ominous undercurrents during their preparations for the journey. First, Keru-eff hovered unnecessarily around the court, always near Nefertiti when he should have been watching his crew, who were too often drunk.

"How is it that Pharaoh will not come to Thebes?" he asked each morning as if repetition would change the answer. "His mother, Queen Tiya, charged me particularly to bring him."

"As was explained," Nefertiti would begin patiently, "Pharaoh made a powerful vow to the god that even a king must honor."

"Not to be present at his father's funeral! Not to pay him respects! What will Egypt think?"

At this point Nefertiti's pitch would rise. The queen's eye would flash. "Pharaoh's heir and his daughter, Princess Ankhesenpaaten, will attend. Will you criticize Pharaoh?"

Keru-eff's whine would subside into silence.

Then Pharaoh replaced Keru-eff's small ship with the much larger royal barge, capable of holding the guard.

"The citizens of Thebes will be angry," Keru-eff told Nefertiti stiffly, "when they see all those soldiers. It will look as if Pharaoh questions their loyalty."

"They should understand, rather, that Pharaoh honors his father." Nefertiti frowned. "Now desist, Keru-eff. This eternal questioning makes me wonder if your abilities to serve Pharaoh might not have been overestimated. Would that issue bear scrutiny?"

On the day of their departure, Hesen boarded the Thebes-bound ship with a heavy heart. Her father's blessing had been reassuring, but as Akhet-Aten receded, she could not think further than: *I was chosen because I am expendable.* She did not, of course, doubt her father's love. An heiress had to be protected. At the same time, Thebes must not be lost. She felt young and untried to take on a city . . . yet victory or defeat were hers alone.

She was disturbed without being surprised when Smenkhare and Keru-eff began to seclude themselves daily for private conferences from which she was excluded. She had expected they would plot. Yet, desperate at the idea of being left solitary, she found herself with Horemheb, who alone seemed not to be conspiring against Pharaoh. Unable to accept shipboard inactivity, Horemheb had devised a constant round of drills for the guard. But when the sun was high overhead and the ship was quiet, he fussed with his weapons, and she joined him, even helped him polish his shield.

"Look, Horemheb," she said one afternoon, "how brightly the Aten shines on Pharaoh." She flashed the shield at him.

"Everything must shine equally," he said critically.

She pursed her mouth and rubbed diligently. Then she put down the pumice. "How delightful to be working like this."

Horemheb's face reddened. "Are you making fun of me, my lady?"

"Aten forgive me if I gave you that impression. No, of course not."

"Well," he explained, "I couldn't figure why you'd want to be shining my weapons."

She sighed and hesitated. "You see," she said finally, "I can be honest, too. I've never represented Pharaoh before and I'm frightened. This—and you—are helping me."

Although Horemheb was young, duties sat heavily upon him. Now, as he smiled, the years lifted and Hesen saw the big gangling boy he still was, all knees and elbows.

"I'm afraid myself," he confessed. "I've never been in sole charge of the guard before."

"You've come far in Pharaoh's service."

"Yes. I've been very lucky."

"Not lucky at all," she disagreed. "You told me your secret once. Total loyalty."

Again she had embarrassed him. "I know, today you're expected to laugh at banners and trumpets and all of that," he said, taking over the polishing of his shield.

"No. It's simply that I don't understand your loyalty. You don't even believe in Aten. . . ."

"I believe in Egypt," he said rather fiercely.

"I don't understand the difference."

"Forgive me, my lady. I'm not a courtier with pretty speeches."

"Tell me anyway."

He spread his hands on the table. They were broad and calloused and stubby, rough-looking and thick.

"You see, my lady," he began, "we're just peasants. My parents are farmers. They live in a small village that's destroyed each year by the waters."

"I didn't know." She looked at him curiously, remembering the silent crowds on the platforms staring at the flood waters—who had always been numbers and colors, a thunderous cheer—and the crowds of peasants bowing whenever she passed. She had never considered the individuals that they were, the people who mourned for lost homes and belongings. The realization brought shame. She wished now she had looked at their faces more closely.

"But look at me, my lady—I'm a peasant, and I'm in charge of the royal guards. Only in Egypt could it happen."

She smiled. "Is that patriotism speaking, or knowledge? Have you seen other places?" She had a remote memory of the map of the world in the schoolroom, but no place had ever seemed real to her outside the Nile Valley.

"I was a foot soldier," he answered. "I fought many campaigns and I've seen other peasants in other lands. They were naked and half-starved. They owned nothing, not even dreams. It would not occur to them even to think of having some land of their own to work. And then I'd come home to find my father getting fat and buying another ox or a cow. Not that a peasant has an easy life—it's work and work hard every day except at festival time. But there's enough to fill your belly and a little left over, and at the end maybe you have a son who can sit with a princess."

"Thank you for telling me. I've never thought about Egypt that way before."

Horemheb cleared his throat uncomfortably. "Look, my lady"—he picked up the pumice—"you were holding it wrong."

She studied the way he did it. "Let me try again."

They sat in companionable silence, polishing, until the shadows lengthened and the ship stirred to the evening's activities. Outwardly the night was routine, like the morning that followed it, but Hesen felt renewed. The shadows of her worries seemed less threatening in the new light Horemheb had cast, and she wholeheartedly gave herself over to viewing the world without royal blinders. She discovered that she could no longer stand at the rail, thoughtlessly drifting past the lines of people bowing on shore, could no longer accept their presence and their gesture as *homage*—a-right-and-proper-thing. Now the thin, naked boys were other Horemhebs: women were mothers who prayed for their sons; muscled arms were the power of men who knew the hardships of work but also its dream—that through honest effort all things were possible. To be princess, Hesen saw, meant more than riches, power and protocol—it was an honor and a responsibility of a magnitude she had only begun to see. She did not intend either to let it go or have it wrested from her.

**She was ready for Thebes!**

Hesen dressed carefully for the landing. Sephy paid particular attention to her face. Blue shadow was brushed on her lids and extended to her arched brows. When the blue had been flecked with gold dust, Sephy painted kohl in a sharp black line around Hesen's eyes and along her brows. Rouge, applied high on her cheekbones, made her face glow, and her lip color was brighter than she normally wore it. The result was a model of beauty so striking that Sephy herself gasped when she saw it whole.

Hesen stood straight, nude and proud, while perfumed unguents were rubbed into her body and her upstanding nipples were reddened. When each slender foot had been encircled with gold-claw anklets, Hesen held up her arms, and Sephy molded to her body a diaphanous, gilt-threaded sheath that covered one shoulder and plunged below the opposite breast, baring its pink-tipped milky whiteness. For the waist there was a gold and amethyst leopard-headed girdle, for the neck a high collar of polished lapis beads, their color exactly matching Hesen's eyes and reflecting their blazing light. Gold and lapis bracelets circled her arms; her fingers must wear a plethora of sparkling, studded rings. Two hours had passed when Sephy swept up her hair and arranged a long black wig over her head.

"Now the headdress," Hesen ordered.

Sephy's lips parted in awe. "You're magnificent—and the headdress is so heavy. There's no need to make your neck and shoulders ache. . . ."

"Thebes must be dazzled. Take it out."

Obediently, Sephy got out the inlaid ivory box and shook out the long headdress placed inside. Even in the muted light of the covered tent, it glittered brilliantly. With painstaking care, Sephy adjusted the long, flexible golden cowl over her mistress's wig, placing precisely the weight of nine hundred individual rosettes strung together on fine supports, each rosette inlaid with turquoise or carnelian or colored frit. The headdress weighed over ten pounds, but Hesen did not feel its weight—she felt its opulence.

Before the fifth hour of morning drained through the waterclock, Hesen felt the barge roll slowly, turning in the river toward the docks of Thebes, and heard the shouts of the crew answered by the dockmen on the shore. She felt the barge shiver as the hull scraped stone pilings. Footsteps trod the wood of the decks, and the clarion brass of trumpets from the shore announced the arrival of Ay, Tushratta, and Queen Tiya. Sephy darted in and out of the tent. At last she could report that the grand vizier, the chief priest, the queen, and the lesser nobility were ceremoniously assembled on the dock.

Again came the herald of many trumpets.

"Now, my lady," Sephy whispered breathlessly, and proudly opened the curtain on Thebes for her mistress to pass.

Hesen walked out of the tent with a slow measured step. She couldn't have hurried even if she wanted to—her dress was so tight. In the corner of her eye, she caught the stunned faces of the ship's crew and gauged the first effect of her glory. As she approached the two soldiers, flanking the head of the landing ramp like twin sentinels, she was bathed in sun, and she knew that she must be a golden dazzle, enveloped in a thousand lights, from the gilt of her dress and her jeweled arms to the intricate blazing cowl. Smenkhare, already with a foot on the ramp, fell back in awe and let her precede him. Horemheb moved forward and steadied her as she stepped up onto the ramp, then backed away, respectfully, bowing his head. She stood very still for a minute and let her glittering vision sink into the eyes of the hushed crowds on shore. She saw Ay in a tight group with Tushratta and Rahmose, attended by a corps of priests, before the throng. Ay's eyes were huge, his mouth hung open. Clearly he had never expected this vision of royal splendor. Near him was Tiya, white and lined, leaning heavily on a handmaiden. But as she watched Hesen, she stood a little straighter. *Yes, you see*, Hesen thought with satisfaction. *Do I look prepared to lose?* Her gaze moved to take in the soldiers of the garrison too—everywhere and armed. She drew strength from the knowledge that Horemheb was behind her and that the guard was waiting below deck, alert and ready, fully dressed for battle, waiting to be summoned.

She proceeded regally, confidently down the ramp.

They couldn't ignore her—they didn't dare. Tushratta stepped forward first and acknowledged her with a stiff nod. His embrace he saved for Smenkhare.

"Pharaoh's spirit blesses his true son," the priest intoned. "We welcome you, Prince of the Realm, Son to the God, for Pharaoh's funeral."

Hesen waited expressionless. In time Rahmose, too, bowed to her, but his eyes narrowed with hate and his lips were white with silent anger. Only after he had turned to Smenkhare did he raise his voice. "The son of Amenophis is the son of Horus. Welcome to the child of the God."

Ay had not yet spoken. Hesen saw how his chest heaved and his eyes darted to the ship, searching, hungry for the appearance of one more passenger . . . and her heart sang: He wasn't there! That craving would have to starve this time. They hadn't named him yet; they didn't want to. But they hadn't reckoned on his daughter. And now, in front of this crowded square, packed with soldiers, citizens and officials, Hesen was going to shout his name.

"Akhenaten, Pharaoh of Egypt . . ." she began. Her voice trembled and thinned. All right. She hadn't done this before. She took a deep breath. She would be heard!

"Akhenaten, Pharaoh of Egypt . . ." she tried again. Much better! Her voice rang out strong and firm. Ay's face looked almost murderous. Yes, hear, O Egypt! She would shout Pharaoh's name again and again. They would not forget it!

"*Akhenaten, Pharaoh of Egypt!* . . . honors his father with treasures for the afterlife. He wished to be with the queen"—Hesen gave Tiya her title, for they must not ignore her either—"but we mourn another loss. The Princess Meketaten has died." Unexpectedly, her breath deserted her. Conscious of controlling every muscle by will, she paused as if for effect.

"We mourn with you," Ay interjected quickly, seeing his advantage. "But we regret Pharaoh's absence. Amenophis would wish the Pharaoh of Egypt to sanctify himself at his father's bier."

Smenkhare stirred. Hesen thought quickly: *Would he speak?* But no, not yet. First he must take a swaggering step forward, raise his hands to his hips. . . . How fortunate he was too pompous to speak without posturing! "—But Pharaoh has sent his heir in his place," she rushed on. "Prince Smenkhare has been betrothed to the true heiress,

Princess Meritaten." Smenkhare turned on her a look so fierce that she was thankful for the crowd surrounding them.

Guards grouped around Smenkhare. She saw Ay signal to Nacht, and a squad of soldiers detached from the platoon at the dock and marched straight toward her. She felt a jolt of shock. Did they plan to take her prisoner?

She flung up her arm, and on the deck Horemheb raised a copper trumpet to his mouth and shattered the heavy air with his own brazen call.

The barge rumbled with the thunder of marching feet, and the guard emerged from lower deck, row upon row of bronzed shoulders, until they swarmed over the landing ramp, in precise formation, uniform and gleaming in their battle armor. The crowds behind Hesen splayed to either side of her; the soldiers formed a perfect semicircle of protection at her back, halted in unison and stood smartly at attention. With their swords glinting in the sun, finely honed and polished, their powerful bodies in prime condition, they were a bellicose masterpiece—a crack unit flamboyantly fearless of battle.

Ay watched them coldly, refusing to halt the approach of Nacht's men until the two lines of soldiers had nearly met. Impassively they stared into each other's eyes. Horemheb's men almost trembled with readiness.

Entrapped at the center, between the two lines of raised blades, Hesen held her breath. Gasps and cries expectant of blood emanated from the citizens of Thebes.

Sharply Ay jabbed retreat, and Nacht waved back his men.

Hesen inhaled deeply. The world spun around her and there was a roaring in her head. She felt herself smiling, heard her voice responding diplomatically, but her consciousness focused only on the fact that Ay's thrust, at least for the moment, had been parried. There would be no dramatic move against Akhenaten, as represented by her person.

Guards wielding spears parted the crowds before her chariot. Her driver snapped the reins. The horses pranced, waving their blue plumes above their ears, and the chariot wheels spun sand, then clattered as they rolled into the tiles of the streets.

His monumental figure rigid with fury, Ay watched her ride away. As at the Feast of Osiris, his clever stratagems had come to naught— for the second time the sands had shifted in an eyeblink and the bulwarks of his intrigue had collapsed into rubble, leaving him choking on the dust. He spat. He had almost made a cataclysmic mistake this morning. His guts twisting with rage, he had been able to see nothing but savage murder when he summoned the garrison to march at Hesen. In retrospect, his loss of control was frightening.

He had known as soon as he saw the large ship that his plans had miscarried. But even then he had not appreciated how dexterously Akhenaten had moved—to have named Smenkhare heir, to have sent the second daughter— Had Pharaoh sent Meritaten, Ay might still have prevailed . . . but Hesen—sweet Amon, how had Hesen summoned such magnificence? And then for Akhenaten to have included the guard . . . Young and untried Horemheb might be, but that boy understood command. Ay had severely underestimated Akhenaten— no fool, after all, but a true descendant of the mighty Thutmosis.

Well, a skirmish was not the war. But he tasted gall, realizing how long that war must needs be now, seeing the time until his victory stretch out like a horizonless desert to be traversed. Amon gird his loins, the future would require all the intelligence and strength he could muster. The lesson had been painful but well-learned. Now that the enemy had been measured, he would be fought on his own terms when Ay met him again; and next time Horemheb would be recruited to stand with Ay. In the meantime he must see to his own ranks— refine their gold, cast out their dross. . . .

"Nacht!" he shouted suddenly.

The commander sprang to his side. "Yes?"

Ay waved for his chariot. "About Keru-eff. I want his death by dawn tomorrow."

Henceforth, there could be but one response to failure.

In Hesen's old apartment at the palace, Sephy pulled the perspiration-wet sheath and warm jewels from her mistress's body. Lying passively in the bath, tension draining from her, Hesen was lulled by the footsteps of slaves who at regular intervals brought in hot water and as quietly departed. For an hour she was absolutely at peace.

"My lady."

Hesen opened her eyes. Sephy was bending over her.

"Queen Tiya is here."

Slaves hurriedly brought towels, Sephy slipped a white cotton gown over Hesen's head and fastened a gold filigree girdle at her waist, a girl held out to Sephy the tray lined with pots and brushes.

"No." Hesen gestured impatiently. "Don't bother with makeup. Admit the queen."

Tiya swept across the room with an appropriately regal measure to her step, but as she took Hesen's hands, her own arms trembled. Seeing her granddaughter with her hair tumbling down her back, her cheeks still pink from the bath, her eyes naked and unpainted, love that was almost a physical pain twisted in the old woman's chest.

When the servants had been dismissed, she drew Hesen to her and kissed her with uncharacteristic warmth. "Wonderful girl!"

"I did well!" Hesen smiled, ready to be praised.

"You were perfect—had your father been here, he might have been taken prisoner and Smenkhare named Pharaoh."

The words loosed evil in the room. "How did they think to dare? You are queen, and Amenophis himself proclaimed my father Pharaoh!"

"Amenophis is dead!"

Hesen stared at her grandmother in silence. Then her mouth tightened. "But my father was smarter."

"Because Hesen was brave, we've won . . . temporarily. But they'll try again," Tiya declared angrily. "And again, until we—or they—are completely destroyed."

Hesen could make no response. She did not wish to consider the inexorable course of the contest.

Reverting to gentleness, Tiya went on, "How well do you know Horemheb, my dear?"

"Horemheb?"

"I think they'll try to bribe him to switch the loyalty of the royal guard to Smenkhare."

"Then they will be disappointed. Horemheb won't do it."

"You sound very sure, but principles can be bent like a sword in the heat of a forge. And they're deviously clever."

"Well, Horemheb isn't clever at all, Horemheb is stubborn. When he gets something in his head, he's immovable—and his head is loyal to Pharaoh."

Tiya hesitated uncomfortably. "You're very beautiful, child. It would appear you could capture anyone's heart and bind him to you. You might be particularly—womanly—with him."

There was a long silence. "You'd do anything for Akhenaten."

"Yes." Implacable fervor flared in the old woman's eyes. "And *you* must be prepared to do the same."

Hesen felt a terrible coldness spread through her body.

The next few days were the most bitter Hesen had ever spent. She had never before realized how ugly and twisted the world was, how, under an infinite sky that lighted a myriad of beauties, men could lie and plot and occupy themselves so singlemindedly in the service of evil. Each day was spent listening more carefully than she had ever done before, straining to hear through the smooth, unctuous accents of Ay and Tushratta what they really planned. Only one thought sustained her: How had it happened in such a self-seeking world that she and Senumet had shared such beautiful moments? She had always felt the wonder of their love; now she realized as well how rare it was, and she was filled with humble gratitude. She regretted that she might never be able to show him how glad she was, for she doubted that they'd let her return. While her fear rose, she could not discuss it with anyone. Even Tiya was lost to her, since one or another of Ay's men was always present when she and Tiya were together.

The day of Amenophis' funeral dawned dry and cool as the burial party emerged from the palace. They proceeded to the docks, while on each side rows of peasants prostrated themselves before the gods-on-earth. The great barque bearing Amenophis' coffin was hauled to the wharf. As the heavy burden was lowered to the lead barge, the sun glinted off Nekhbet's golden wings, curving around the sarcophagus, and they seemed to flutter protectively. Slowly, the six other barges that made up the royal cortege were rowed across the Nile, to wails from the peasants lining the shore.

"Screaming asses!" Smenkhare muttered to Hesen. "My head is ready to burst."

"From your mourning party?" she whispered back.

"No—from all this healthful air."

Ay frowned at them. They shut their mouths. Hesen had never seen Ay so formidable. Dressed as a priest of Amon, his head was completely shaved, and his heavily black-rimmed eyes bored into anyone in his line of vision. The leopard skin on his bare chest moved with his breath, so that a live dangerous cat seemed to caress him.

He and the ten other priests were the first to debark and first in the procession to the tomb. The royal guard, official bearers of the coffin to its final resting place, were next. The official mourners followed; under the cover of their air-rending lamentations, Hesen, walking next to Tiya, whispered, "I want to leave this week."

"You'll be permitted to go," the queen assured her. "You were right about Horemheb. They couldn't match Pharaoh's price. And so long as the guard is loyal, they can't touch you."

"This time you'll come too."

Tiya shook her head. "Someone must know what they are plotting here."

Deep in the Valley of the Kings the colonnaded court of Deir-el Bahri had been cut into a recess in the desert wall, and the wide, several-leveled expanse of columns with their processional ramps led the eye back and up to the jagged cliffs that formed the backdrop for the temple. A savage landscape, transmuted to awe-inspiring beauty by an artist's vision. Hesen feasted her eyes. She had never before seen this funerary temple of the only woman king of Egypt—even royalty was forbidden to walk in the Valley of the Kings except, as now, for a burial of a member of Pharaoh's household. Surely her grandfather's monument could not compare, though she knew that Amenophis had specifically set out to surpass this tribute to one of his female ancestors.

Passing the file of sacred trees, their procession moved on across the stark desert landscape, following the line of the cliffs. The sharp bleached stones underfoot made walking a chore, and Tiya had to be assisted as they picked their way under the blazing sun. Loose skree that had split off from the cliffs was amassed at the base of the rock walls, and stony debris covered countless entrances to the tombs of Egypt's rulers. Hesen had to blink to clear her vision. Sand and cliffs were merging together in a white blaze that seemed to tear sight from the eyes, and the sky, equally blank, afforded no relief.

At last before them they saw the statues, enormous monoliths looming up as they approached until it seemed the carved heads must touch the blue enamel sky. Her grandfather and Tiya, carved in limestone, gazed regally over their domain. Awed, Hesen turned to look at her grandmother, whose eyes were raised to her own likeness. Was Tiya actually here, alive, or had she been transformed by the power of the dead into monumental rock?

The procession entered the path between the two statues and stopped before a solid stone wall, emblazoned with Amenophis' cartouche. The tremendous coffin was placed on its ramp. The ritual shout went forth: "Hail, Amenophis! Bless your servants. You are no longer on earth. You are in the sky with your brothers! You rushed at the sky like a heron! You kissed the sky like a falcon!"

Torches were lit and the procession followed the coffin into the tomb. The cold, damp air and the blackness after the sunlit, arid valley sent shivers down Hesen's spine and she felt suddenly breathless with the irrational fear that she had truly entered the Underworld. Light from the torches brought to flickering life the painted vultures overhead, the demons and curling snakes that Pharaoh must vanquish on his journey to everlasting life. They entered an antechamber. Here, the paintings depicted Pharaoh being greeted by the gods to whom he now belonged—Hathor, goddess of love . . . Anubis, jackal-headed guardian . . . Osiris, god of the dead. Beyond, the corridor widened into a huge, square chamber. Magic spells and golden gods animated its walls, while the nude body of Nut stretched widely across its ceiling. Under her quiet rule Pharaoh would rest forever. On each side of the room smaller chambers glowed with royal thrones, royal beds, golden chariots, chests of inlaid ivory—the stored-up treasure of a god-king, carefully prepared for Amenophis to use in the Underworld, all to be sealed with him forever.

Suddenly overwhelmed, Hesen felt physically ill. She could barely stand upright for the rest of the ceremonies. Afterward, it took an enormous act of will to force one foot mechanically after the other up through the chill of the steep tunnel, out into searing heat and emptiness for the endless walk back over the dust and pebbles. At the barge at last, she sank gratefully on the bench and closed her eyes.

"My dear niece"—Ay sat next to her—"I'm afraid this has been a little too much for you."

"I'm unused to the headdress," she said, sitting straighter. Aten protect her, she would not admit weakness to Ay.

"Tiya told me you plan to leave this week. Do you feel strong enough?"

"I *must* leave."

"Why?" he asked sharply.

Her face registered surprise. "There was no time to mourn for Meket," she said quickly. *Forgive me, my sister.*

"True. I briefly forgot." He paused decently before adding, "My wife, Tey, shall go back with you as well. She pines for the royal babe."

"My mother will be delighted to see her."

"I've given Smenkhare messages for Pharaoh. And I myself will be coming to Akhet-Aten soon. I plan to make my home at both capitals."

"It's very beautiful." She stopped. This was her chance. She could feel Senumet urging her on but the words stubbornly stuck in her throat. She would not deny Aten!

A screen seemed to snap shut behind Ay's eyes. As she stared at their impenetrable black, he started to rise. She had to stop him—

"Senumet still teaches me." The words sounded wrong to her ears, but she had his attention. "He explained how one belief shouldn't cancel another."

He looked at her with interest masking his surprise. Might this strange, willful child be of use to him one day? "Do you believe that?" he asked.

"I'll tell you honestly. Senumet has said I may trust you. I was sent because I can hold both beliefs in my heart."

Unexpectedly he put his powerful hands on her shoulders and kissed her. "It's good to know Hesen's heart is so big. I'm glad Senumet has been helpful."

As her senses reeled with repulsion and fear, she made her lips smile. She had done as Senumet bid; she had degraded herself. Her gloom persisted all the way back to Akhet-Aten. City of light.

Yet eventually the cliff receded and the vast plain unrolled as she had left it. Tents clustered on the city's slopes in vivid groups. Pillars were silhouetted against the sky. The fresh electrum coating on the huge temple doors blazed back the sun's light.

It existed. Gratitude and peace flooded Hesen's being, and tears streamed down her face. All that she wished was just to remain here forever, a dream dependent on the fragile hope that Pharaoh's vision could be strong enough to dispel the powerful forces planning, gathering, closing their circle around Akhet-Aten with a single end—to crush him.

# BOOK II

# AKHET-ATEN: 1377-1369 B.C.

# XII

During the next three years, Akhenaten, Pharaoh of Egypt, changed the face of the realm.

At the beginning, in the interests of peace and unity, he permitted the worship of all gods. But as his city neared completion, as a substantial number of headmen and other bureaucrats were replaced by his agents, and as a new priesthood to Aten was installed in all the nomes, Akhenaten was ready to move. The royal decree went out; worship of other gods was forbidden. The wealth of temples was shipped to Akhet-Aten and dispersed again to temples of the new god. At Karnak and Memphis and Heliopolis, doors were thrown open and priests, at the point of spears, banished from the precincts to live or die as they wished, save that they never again adore the old gods.

Monumental statues of Akhenaten sprang up throughout Egypt, his long, sensitive face responsive to all men. A little frightened, the peasants stared at his trunk and legs—could that deformed and sexless body insure the harvest, the resurrection, the Inundation? Osiris was gone; who would wake their ka? Who would die and spill his blood each year, so they all might flourish? And who could they consult when disputes must be settled? Those new headmen were strangers—what did they know of the history of conflicting hereditary claims? Secretly the peasants of Egypt begged forgiveness of the old gods.

Akhenaten, knowing it would take time for the old loyalties to weaken, was not unaware of the undercurrents. But there were three good inundations in the first years of sole reign; the Aten shone over the land; his city was beautiful; his children were thriving; his queen radiated a well-being that seemed more than human. For his own part, he was filled with such inner strength he knew he must prevail. Wasn't Aten the beneficent father of all men? In his light, inspired by the wondrous beauty of truth, would not all men be blessed? It was so clear to him, everyone must see it.

In the bliss of Akhet-Aten it was difficult to believe that men still fought and killed for power in the circumference of the empire. Yet from Tunip came pleas that an aggressive Aziru be stopped from attacking. "Tunip, thy city weeps," the letter accused. "Her tears flow and you send us no help." Demands poured in for troops also from Zemrida and Rib-Addi and Dor. Akhenaten would send no troops. Aten cherished life—his son could not take it. Since he had to respond in some way, he would dispatch an ambassador to gather firsthand the state of affairs. Seeking a loyal man whose intelligence and observation would be sharp, he chose Senumet. And Senumet's mission would buy time.

For Hesen, these three years had been wonderful, watching Akhet-Aten grow out of sand and dreams. With an army of artisans at his command, Bek transformed Pharaoh's vision into stone and brick and marble. With feverish speed, the city had sprung up on different parts of the vast plain—the south city with its mansions, the central city with the palace and temple and Kings-Way stretching west to the riverbank, and the north suburb with its smaller homes grouped around the city's markets and quays.

The palace was a tribute to the infinite possibilities of light. As Aten's rays moved across the sky, they touched different parts of the huge building, so that the stone inlays and glazed tiles and glass mosaics on doors and pillars and walls flashed with sparkling brilliance, replicated again and again as the sun moved to other walls and doors and pillars—and visitors marveled, becoming convinced that the Aten daily blessed individually each part of the palace.

It should have been enough for Hesen, but hungers she had suppressed gnawed at her. She felt their ache when Smenkhare and Meritaten were married, and in the first months there was a sense of the excitement of creation. In a short time, Meritaten's body swelled with new life. She miscarried, but still there had been a glorious feeling of completion, and a feeling that the child had merely been postponed. They would try again.

Only Hesen must moisten that thin, cork shield and thrust it, like the whores she had heard about in Thebes, into her secret opening where life might start. Aten blessed creation; Hesen must thwart it. At least with Senumet. She had continued their intimacy, of course.

Yet their love could never fruit. And they had very little time left. Meritaten must only assure the succession; then Hesen would be wed. Already they negotiated with the Syrian ambassador. And Senumet was making final preparations to leave on Pharaoh's mission. Who knew, when he returned, if he'd still find her here? She might be queen in a foreign city. If so, they would be forever lost to each other —and Hesen would have nothing. . . .

Recklessly, Hesen weighted the shield with a bleached white stone and consigned it to the depths of the Nile. For four nights she lay with Senumet unprotected—the way to her womb open and moist with the fluid that would hold his seed.

On the day he set sail, she would not go to the dock to see him board. How could she bid him good-bye in full view of the populace? Their farewells had been made the night before in the union of their bodies. Even now his seed, propelled forward by the explosive force of their passions, was spiraling toward her womb. Even though she sat in the garden, her back to the river, she knew the instant when his barge drew away from the dock. She could feel his physical presence receding. "O merciful Aten, creator of life," she prayed, "let this child be formed—conceived in your light, in your love, in your trust."

Over the next weeks there were changes in her body. Her breasts swelled; the nipples enlarged and darkened. There was a fullness in her stomach that became nausea at the sight or smell of food, and kneeling made her sick and dizzy. Anxiously, she looked for signs of the monthly bleeding. There were none. Life was growing in her. Why else would she be unable to retain the food she had relished all her life? The fourth week passed and her breasts grew fuller still, and blue veins traced their surface. At six weeks, again she did not bleed. Now she was certain: her body sheltered a tiny child, his and hers, sleeping under her heart. Joy flowed through her. Her days had never been sweeter. Completely absorbed in her body and its miraculous, long-awaited changes, she was aware of nothing and no one else.

Dreaming alone in the south garden one late afternoon, she was surprised out of her reverie by the sound of Sephy's footsteps.

"I want a private audience, my lady," the maid demanded, her dark face scowling.

They walked to a bench at the end of the garden, where the Nile sparkled through openings in the clustered border of blue centaurea edged with small daisies.

"You are a fool"—Sephy's tone was unrelentingly harsh—"more

stupid than the lowest trash that walk the streets of Egypt."

Hesen gasped.

"Did you think to fool me?" Sephy demanded scornfully. "I, who sort your things for washing? Twice there has been no sign of the monthly bleeding. I, who rouge your breasts and have seen them change?"

Truth was, Hesen was glad Sephy knew. She had wanted to hug the knowledge to herself just a little while longer, but it finally must be discussed. Better to share it first with Sephy. "Yes," she admitted, "I am with child."

"No one suspects," Sephy said tensely. "I could not let them whisper about you."

An unpleasant shock coursed through Hesen. She had never considered . . . had not been thinking . . . of course the servants would notice the absence of soiled linens. Not a drop of blood for two months!

Sephy was saying, "When I understood what had occurred, I took your linens and sheets to the temple after the morning sacrifice. I bribed the workman. I told them my daughter—" Her voice faltered, her hands closed into tight fists in her struggle for control. Hesen's lips drew into a tight stubborn line. She suspected Sephy was leading her where she did not wish to follow.

"I dipped your garments in the blood of the slain animals," Sephy went on, grimly. "Then I gave them to the women to be washed."

"I would rather you had saved yourself the trouble," Hesen declared in a wave of pride. "I don't intend to hide it!"

"Stop being stupid." Sephy was deadly serious. "You cannot have this child."

"*I want it!*" Hesen answered in the same determined voice.

"When you were a babe you wanted a sword and a horse and a gold collar. Now you want a child. Have you thought how pleased your mother will be? How eagerly they will accept your coupling with a peasant? Have you planned who will wed the Syrian prince when you're banished with your squawking bastard? Not one of your sisters—they're not old enough. Pharaoh's name will be a joke from Kush to Punt! And what life awaits that child for whose birth you want to sacrifice everything? A despised outcast, what place can he make? I thought you were a woman." Contempt curled her mouth. "I see you're a worse fool even than Smenkhare!"

Hesen waited until the first burst of rage subsided. "It's fortunate for you"—her voice was low and threatening—"that there are years of service to your credit. I should have you whipped for this."

"Have me whipped?" Sephy laughed. "Do it soon, then. In a few months you'll be in no position to give orders!"

Aten help her to deal patiently with fools dragging with them all the barren old ways, Hesen thought. She felt such an impatience she thought she might strike the old woman down. "It's you who mistake, Sephy!" she said as calmly as she could manage. "We no longer live in Thebes, but you carry its darkness in your heart."

Sephy made a move to speak.

"Silence!" Hesen countered sharply. "In Akhet-Aten we live in truth. Here we walk hand in hand with nature. You've heard Pharaoh. Whatever is spontaneous and natural is right."

"He didn't mean that for his second daughter!"

"He means it for himself. He means it for all of us! And how dare you call Senumet a peasant! Pharaoh has decreed all men may rise to whatever heights their talents and industry take them. It was Pharaoh who named Senumet ambassador."

Sephy wouldn't be stilled. "He'll never name him son!" And before Hesen could respond, "Ask the queen if you may couple as your heart dictates. Ask her if she'll give Egypt a common prince."

"For Aten's sake," Hesen burst out, her fingers instinctively sheltering her abdomen. "You cannot tell me that with all this freedom, I can have nothing."

"Yes!" Sephy pounced on it. "A servant—a slave—is freer than you!"

"This time you go too far. This time—"

"Go!" Sephy folded her arms, gestured angrily at the palace. "Ignore Sephy, who speaks out of love. Birth your baby—but don't come crying to me when you're banished." She spun on her heel and marched away, leaving Hesen fuming at her stout, retreating back, forced to permit her the last word, since to shout after her like a common market slut would convey that Sephy had not only won the battlefield, she had cracked the fortress as well.

Afterward Hesen could no longer bear to be touched by Sephy, knowing how she felt. She avoided looking at the maid's stricken, admonishing face. And Sephy's fingers on her face or breasts were damp and unpleasant. Every entrance Sephy made into her apartments stirred alarming recollections of Nefertiti's lectures about the responsibilities of second princess. Bewildered and fearful, Hesen could not bring herself to confront the queen with the truth that was growing within the peaceful darkness of her body.

"Well, daughter"—Nefertiti stopped Hesen after morning prayers—"I have good news. Meritaten is again with child. Negotiations have opened with Syria for your marriage."

Hesen felt a sharp pain at her mother's words. Her sister's child would be hoped for and prayed over, while Hesen's own ... She considered carefully before she spoke, though she was hopeful. Didn't the living god kiss his own children in public and personally give them food? There was nothing wrong in what she'd done. Wasn't Aten a god of love? "It would make me very unhappy to leave Egypt. I'd like you to reconsider this marriage. This land nourishes me," Hesen rushed on. "I'd be content to spend all my life in the Nile Valley."

Nefertiti's face took on that cold look Hesen hadn't seen since the days of Memphis and Thebes. "Happiness will come with acceptance of duty," she said severely. "In any case, happiness is not your lot."

"But Pharaoh commands us to live in truth." Hesen's heartbeat hammered.

"No doubt living in truth, for you, has come to mean getting what you want." Nefertiti's laugh rang out metallically. "Your position is the same as it has always been, Hesen. As are the strictures upon you."

Hesen felt physically sick. Beyond this, she realized she was past the point of reason. She could care about nothing but that secret child carried inside her, protected now and nourished. "What strictures?"

"Prudence and piety," Nefertiti answered sharply. "And obedience. *Maat* does not mean freedom."

Hesen couldn't speak. Rudely, without leave-taking, she stumbled away. Aten protect her, she'd been a fool. Her punishment would be swift and severe, even though Pharaoh loved her. And the child—her sister's babe would live in splendor, respected and bowed to, while hers— No!

She reached her apartments, far from Nefertiti. Then pure pain burst out of her.

Maidservants came running. She fell into a fit of weeping, and through it all she saw Sephy's face, solid and resigned and sad, beyond preaching or scolding, all love. The hands that stroked

Hesen's back were gentle, the breasts that cradled her head were soft and giving.

"No, no, my darling," Sephy crooned. "Don't fret. Just trust me. You'll see."

Hesen dragged through the next few days, hardly speaking at all, trying to communicate with her body, to feel, while she still could, the first faint stirrings of life. It became agony, now, to smile at Meritaten, radiant with her hopeful tidings. Only in sleep could she forget . . . sleep until she dreamed . . . dreamed of a turtle named Senumet that rose up from the Nile to walk on land, but the desert dried him, and he could not find his way back to the life-giving mud. . . .

Someone was shaking her.

Reluctantly she pulled her eyes open to Sephy's whispered complaints. "You sleep as if drugged, my lady. You must get up."

Her heart turned to stone. It was tonight.

"First"—Sephy bustled around her—"you must disguise yourself. Here, put this on." She slipped a shapeless linen caftan over Hesen's head and removed her rings. "You must cover your face." When she tied on a cloth mask, Hesen's sight, narrowed to two small slits, was clouded and unclear. "Where are we going?" she whispered.

"Later," Sephy promised, removing the sandals Hesen had put on. "Please, my lady, we must go silently. Senedjm replaces the guard at your door. No one shall enter and Senedjm will ask no questions." While she spoke, Sephy pulled Hesen through the curtains and tied a cloth over her own face. Hesen saw her feet were bare too. Standing in the shadows of the back portico, Hesen felt shame that she must be part of this.

Sephy's hand clamped on her arm. "Not a sound," she hissed, and Hesen suddenly heard the rhythmic click of sandals on the marble floor, faint at first, increasing in volume. The sentries! Drawing as far into the darkness as she could, Hesen held her breath, clasping both arms tight over her breasts to muffle the pounding of her heart. The clicks thundered in her ears. Moonlight glanced off the polished blade of a sword, and gilt armbands. Then they had passed her, and the sounds of their marching feet diminished until the far-off beat disappeared in the cacophony of night insects.

"Now!" Sephy grunted. Taking Hesen's hand, she hurried as fast and as lightly as her bulk permitted across the portico and through the garden to the back hedge, where she stopped. "Careful, my lady." She studied the dense foliage as she caught her breath. "Here."

She yanked vines aside and gestured *Come!* Hesen saw that the hedge had been thinned to make a passageway. Quick tears stung her eyes. Sephy had done all of this, and after Hesen had abused her so harshly. "Oh, Sephy . . ." she cried in a small voice.

"Not now, we've no time."

They pushed through the strong, green vines, emerging a few minutes later on the dune that sloped down to the river. The moon was high and bright. "Come." Sephy pitched over the sandhill and, stumbling off-balance, managed to scramble down its length. Hesen jumped lightly after her, the sand fine and cool beneath her feet. Panting, they ran along the beach, hugging the dune, hoping no one would notice their wavering shadows that stretched and contracted over the uneven configuration of the beach. Sprinting forward for a few more paces, Sephy turned sharply and darted into a recess in the hill. Hesen followed blindly. As she made the turn, a man materialized out of the shadows. She gasped.

Sephy slowed to a walk, stopped a safe distance from the stranger, and motioned for Hesen to stand slightly behind her.

"I have the beasts," the man said.

Sephy held up a purse. "Show them first."

The man disappeared. He was back a few minutes later, holding the bridles of two donkeys. Sephy threw him the purse. Catching it, he dropped the donkeys' bridles and scurried off into the dark. The placid animals waited. Hesen mounted one after some struggle; Sephy managed to lift her bulk onto the back of the other. Hesen's animal was willing and fast. As it fell into a sturdy trot behind its mate, Hesen emptied her mind, determined to be conscious only of the smooth muscles moving under her body. They rode north first, skirting the city, then turned left and began to climb. Eventually the sand underfoot changed to rock; still the plucky animals kept an easy balance as they threaded their way through the hills where the newly readied tombs had been cut.

A few lengths ahead, Sephy drew her donkey to a halt and dismounted. "This is the place," she said as Hesen drew up. Hesen slid off the donkey, despair making her feet suddenly too weak to stand. Sephy tethered the animals to a sycamore trunk. Beyond the tree was an awesome cliff, a high sheet of solid rock that cut off the moon, and Hesen saw that in its base one spot was darker than all the rest. Taking Hesen's arm, Sephy moved her toward the black hole.

"Wait!" Hesen pulled back. "That's a tomb!"

"And where else can this night's work be done?"

The cave sloped sharply downward. They turned right, then left—into light, a large, glowing rectangle in which torches were visible, the entrance to a large room.

The first thing Hesen saw upon entering was a stenciled outline of her parents riding in a chariot. This drawing dominated the entire south wall. Over their heads the Aten shone, but in line only—the emblem was unfinished, had not yet been chiseled out. Hesen felt warmth return to her body. Under Pharaoh's eyes, no harm could come to her. She drank in his features in the light thrown off by glowing braziers.

There was a sound behind her. She whirled around, gasped and took three quick steps backward. A lion with black, piercing eyes and shining teeth stood beside her. Then she realized—no, not a lion. Beneath the bestial head was a human form, male-shaped. But the face of the thing was menacing, terrible.

Sephy took the silver censers the thing held out and spread them around the room. Next, she heated a twig over a brazier until it glowed and inserted it into the censers, one by one. Soon a heavy scent filled the room. Hesen's head felt light.

"Woman!" The creature pointed a long finger at Sephy. "Put her on the pylon."

"That's sacred," Hesen cut him off. "It can't be touched until it holds the sarcophagus."

"Woman! What kind of daughter do you raise? Is she so brazen as to speak in the presence of Bes?"

Hesen forgot where she was in her horror at his response. "Bes?" she cried. "How dare you name Bes when only the Aten may be worshiped?"

"Quiet, fool!" Sephy warned, and shook her.

The man pulled a goblet out of the basket at his feet. "I saw the animals as I came in," he said. "The choice is mine, I trust."

"Yes," Sephy answered shortly.

"And the purse?"

Sephy reached into her caftan and pulled it out. "Not until you finish." Her eyes were onyx beads, polished and hard.

"Very well," he agreed after a long minute. Turning, he poured a red liquid into the cup. "Drink it!"

Hesen accepted the cup. "What is it?"

"Woman!" he shouted, lunging toward her.

Aten preserve her, Hesen thought, was she just to obey blindly? A cur was treated better.

"I want to know too," Sephy said stubbornly.

"It's the juice of the poppy, to loosen her. The entrance to her womb must relax." He pulled out a long copper instrument with a flat tip, almost in the shape of a spoon. "Then I can pass this through and scoop out the dirty conception." With a swift thrusting motion, he parodied in the air the action he planned to take. The metal rod gleamed wickedly in the flickering lamplight.

Hesen drained the cup, no longer caring. Let it be poison. Sephy took her hand. Hesen grasped tightly, focusing on that handclasp, the only warmth she could feel, thinking, *Bless Sephy*, who was all love. Reaching forward, she kissed Sephy impulsively and felt Sephy's mask was wet.

"Don't cry." She was confused—her own words were slurred. Trying to speak more clearly, she found she couldn't move her tongue at all. Why, her whole body was on fire. So was the room. They'd better escape . . . but first she had to rest. Sephy eased her down on the pylon. In some slow but otherwise lucid corner of her mind she sensed that it was beginning.

"Wait! Not yet!" The words came out unintelligible grunts and the room spun with the effort of speaking. Only the Aten overhead was firm. From it loving hands reached down, held the ankh to her nostrils and caressed her.

Suddenly the lion filled her field of vision, its tongue panting and red, its teeth bared.

> *"Evil spirits,"* it spoke, *"Bes demands you vanish!*
> *You snakes and monsters and curling beasts*
> *Do not interfere with this work,*
> *Return to your dark beginnings*
> *We offer you sweet scents and bloody destruction.*
> *Begone!"*

All around her now hooded monsters twined and writhed, and among them Bes watched with his awful smile. Frantically, she searched for the Aten. There! Above her! So long as she could see it, she was safe.

Someone pulled her legs apart and held them. Look at the god!

> *Thou art my comfort and my strength*
> *O Lord of all Creation.*

The tip of the metal rod pushed into her entrance, probing and cold.

*Thou drivest away the night*
*At thy dawning the earth sings.*

Pressure was almost unbearable. And now the pain began. Low in her body, becoming all at once a stab so severe it seemed her body must rip apart, subsiding, then knifing again. And all the time that rod pushed farther and farther into her, violating her, tearing her, scooping out that tiny, longed-for, living thing.

*By thee man liveth*
*My breath is thy gift*
*I am bound by thy glory*
*And thine infinite goodness.*

There was a rush of wetness on her thighs and a foul smell. Her legs were trembling with weakness, her face was damp; she was bathed in sweat-drenched cloth.

"It's over, dearest, it's over," Sephy was crooning by her face.

"The purse," the man demanded. A grunt. "The amount seems right. Now get out of here."

"She still bleeds," Sephy protested.

"It'll stop. Get her out while it's still dark."

He threw Sephy a cloth and Hesen felt that she was being cleaned. It was very hard to focus, impossible to move. She remembered her journey here. How could they return? But Sephy, with a quick motion, picked Hesen up. Trying to cling, Hesen knew that she was being carried up the long passageway out of the tomb, could hear the powerful beating of Sephy's heart and her irregular, gasping breaths. Then they were moving in an easy rhythm. Somehow they both rode one donkey and Sephy held her safe, cradled like a babe in her soft, warm arms. How Sephy found the strength to carry her back, Hesen would never know. The next thing she was aware of was the sun touching her body and the sweet scent of the fresh linen in her own bed and Sephy's anxious face watching her.

For one wild moment out of the context of time, before she felt the pad between her legs and the dull ache in her womb, she imagined all of it was a dream.

In that delusion, Hesen had almost smiled.

# XIII

For one hundred years after the fall of the twelfth dynasty, the foreign Hyksos had ruled Egypt, plunging the country into darkness. Then a Theban dynasty burst forth, aggressive and mighty. Having crushed and driven out the invaders, the Theban pharaohs of the eighteenth dynasty conquered and ruled from northern Syria to the fourth cataract of the Nile on the south, tempering power with intelligence to weld their dominions into a compact realm, the outposts of which poured wealth and splendor into Egypt at a rate never equaled again. For two hundred and thirty years the empire flourished . . . until, in the first four years of his rule, Akhenaten splintered its focus and the fragile balance was lost. The internal convulsions resulting from the banishment of the old gods weakened the bond between ruler and ruled. Order could no longer be taken for granted. Armed to defend what they no longer understood, Egypt's troops became concerned with pay rather than glory. When Pharaoh disregarded the colonies' pleas for military help, the Hittites, sensing weakness, advanced from the north, and towns crumbled under the onslaught. The Asiatic dominions toppled one by one. Initially shocked by the ease of their victories, the invaders rushed exultantly onward to the very frontier on the northeastern delta of Egypt herself. . . .

Although his commission was grave—to report the extent of the empire's weakness—Senumet was nonetheless excited. Having never been outside the boundaries of Egypt, he did not know what to expect, and for him the journey was an adventure. Water, for instance, had always been the Nile, a comprehensible flow, its movements predictable and ordered, the shore on either side never too far away. So the Great Green overwhelmed him, that water-without-bounds, an expanse so vast that even the sky curved to meet its endlessly rippling surface. Here dark clouds could change a mellow afternoon to harsh winds and beating rain; the capricious climate was disturbing to an Egyptian accustomed to days invariably blessed by sun. The people were variable as well, subject to sudden squalls of temper, their social bonds forged in orgies of bloody sacrificial worship.

At each port where Senumet's small party docked, they were greeted respectfully and ceremoniously and Senumet was treated with all the honor due Pharaoh's ambassador. On the other hand, what he was shown, what he took care to see, profoundly disturbed him. He did not have to travel far to realize that the remnants of protocol were all that was left of Egypt in the provinces. There was no empire anymore—that was the long and short of it.

King Akizzi showed him the smoldering ruins of the once-verdant Orontes Valley, devastated by the Hittites. Nothing remained of Nukhashshi except charred ruins. Ubi was gone too, its crumbling, deserted buildings home only to scuttling rodents. Wherever he was received, Senumet heard tales of threatened invasions and treachery, accompanied by desperate pleas for help. He had to return home—Pharaoh must know the true state of affairs. They had been gone less than eight months when he ordered the tour cut short.

Making a circular return, they sailed down the Gulf of Suez in the direction of Punt to gather reports from Nubia. Even in this southern stronghold there were small rebellions, less organized and effective than in Asia, but increasing in frequency.

As Senumet's party crossed the Wadi Foakhir for the journey back down the Nile, not even the prosperous look of the river valley could dispel their sense of foreboding. Senumet spent the afternoons staring at the familiar loved banks, the broad calm Nile. Would destruction and chaos also waste Egypt within? Nearing Thebes, he decided to report to Ay before continuing to Akhet-Aten.

His first sight of that city shocked him. He hadn't been back the three years since Akhenaten abandoned it. What in the name of Amon had happened?

"Sir"—the commander approached him at the deck rail—"the dock's silted up and we can't get close. You'll have to take a felucca."

Indeed, the harbor, once bustling and crowded, was empty, and reeds had overgrown the landing area. Beyond, the city itself had a shabby and untended look. Paint had flaked off many of the buildings, grass sprouted in great clumps between the tiles of the streets, and fields were ragged and sparse. Upon landing, Senumet hurried from the dock through streets that neglect had stripped, past piles of rags, broken furniture and earthenware. At the temple, the great doors were off their hinges and light streamed in onto bare altars. No god was in the sanctuary. The offering tables were empty. Two dirty, unkempt children darted in and out among the massive pillars, laughing.

Of the former glory only the palace remained and even that had changed. Most of it was closed. Only Tiya was in residence there now, and her court was small. Walking through the courtyard, Senumet was relieved to find that the flowers were still tended; he had been afraid weeds might have swallowed up this last refuge.

Ay's offices were in Nefertiti's old apartments. Ay greeted Senumet with an affectionate embrace. "You look older, my son, and very tired."

"I've seen terrible things."

"None more so, I'm sure, than your first sight of Thebes. I suppose you know that the name of Amon has been expunged even from the tombs."

"Pharaoh opened them?" Once sealed, the tombs were never to be seen by mortal man again. That was sacrilege indeed.

"Even his father's, Amenophis'."

Senumet was silent, unnerved at this evidence that melancholy, intellectual Pharaoh had been directly responsible for such savagery.

"We must talk tonight," Ay was saying. "Privately."

He met Ay at a wharf where a small rowboat was concealed. Quietly and in total darkness, Senumet's powerful arms to the oars, they pulled across the river to the Valley of Kings. Leaving the boat hidden among the reeds, they skirted the sleeping villages of grave workers and by a circuitous route made their silent way into the shrouded hills of the sacred tombs.

Finally Ay permitted himself to whisper. "You've become a true diplomat, Senumet."

"As always, my lord, I am a great cultivator of patience."

"The most serviceable of the virtues." Ay smiled. "And occasionally it is satisfied." He gestured toward a door cut into the cliff.

Senumet pulled it open. Followed by Ay, who shut the door behind them, he walked carefully down dark ramps toward a flickering light.

"We've moved the Temple of Amon here." Ay's voice echoed hollowly as they came to a cavernous room, intended originally as a tomb but unfinished. Carefully piled on all sides were riches from the Temple of Karnak.

Senumet's eyes were drawn to the gold statuette of Pharaoh, wearing the blue crown and squatting in the pose of the newly born Sun God arising from the waters of chaos on a lotus flower. There were stela with prayers picked out in lapis, alabaster lamps, ivory representations of Amon in the guise of a ram, black basalt statues of Mut, mother goddess of Thebes.

Distracted by movement toward the rear of the cavern, Senumet turned—Tushratta was there, a mere shriveled wisp of a man now, seated on an empty sarcophagus in the half-light. His right hand fluttered before him in a rhythmic tremor.

"You see, my boy, what we are come to," Tushratta quavered.

"Even so, you have salvaged a great deal." Senumet's admiration for the effort was sincere.

"We had no dearth of assistance," Tushratta said warmly. "Amon has many worshipers still. As many strong arms serve him as mouths profess loyalty to Pharaoh."

"I would have thought Rahmose was among those friends."

Ay's mouth tightened. "He's dead, Senumet."

"Dead?"

"When Pharaoh replaced all the headmen with his own agents, Rahmose became a man without a purpose. Before him, the title had been his father's and his father's father's! His body was found floating face down in the river."

According to tradition, if a man committed suicide, after his death when Thoth weighed his heart against the feather of truth, he'd be considered unworthy and his ka would not waken. Stories, of course, superstition—but the sense of irrevocable annihilation was powerful, even in Senumet. "He deserved a better death," he said inadequately.

Tushratta broke the thoughtful silence. "Several months after that his daughter Nephrus married and went with her husband to his village. There was nothing for her here. Her father's estates had all been confiscated by Pharaoh."

"So many changes," Senumet said quietly.

Tushratta cleared his throat, a deathlike rattle, but when he spoke, his voice rang with anger. "Ah, it's too much for an old man. The new officials know absolutely nothing—they can't allot the land, they don't understand the nomes; their assessments bring outcries of injustice from everyone."

"The whole empire is seething with unrest," Senumet responded. Here, at least, his news would be received with gladness—a fact that merely added another weight to his own spirits. "Pharaoh must send troops. The Hittites attack on the north and east, the Bedouins advance, and many vassals Akhenaten considers loyal have become unreliable."

"Don't report *that* to Pharaoh!" Ay said crisply. "Let him be betrayed, let him lose the empire! We'll see how long he keeps Egypt's support. We'll spread rumors here of massive losses."

"They're not rumors." Senumet's tone was flat. "Ugarit and Niy have already fallen and Byblos is vulnerable."

"We must depose Pharaoh!" Tushratta croaked fiercely. "Corrupt and mismanaged as Egypt is now, who knows but that it may fall as well. I meet this month with the priests of Amon. Oh, yes, they still tend the flame of his worship among the people, albeit in secret. They'll spread the word of the empire's losses."

Ay had been scrutinizing Senumet's face. Now he said carefully, "We're equipping a secret army. All we need is a general. I want you to sound out Horemheb. Events may have kneaded to pliancy his obstinate loyalties . . ."

Senumet nodded. It was a dangerous game he played.

"He's at Akhet-Aten now," Ay continued. "I've just returned from there." Senumet did not blink. Although he longed to ask of the royal family, he would not. Ay was testing him again—always testing. "But with or without Horemheb at my side, Pharaoh is finished!" Ay's words echoed in the hollow tombs, the amplification lending them the ring of prophecy. "This time I will not lose!"

Senumet swayed imperceptibly as he felt a terrible vise closing upon him. Ay on one side—on the other, Pharaoh.

He wondered in the next few days, while his ship was being stocked, if Tiya would speak with him. He waited in vain. She made no attempt to arrange a meeting. Observing her from a distance, he thought the old queen had worn well in the past few years. While her face had hardened slightly, her eyes were even sharper than before; clearly she missed nothing.

On the day he set sail, he stopped at the palace to take formal leave, and since Ay was momentarily occupied by a petitioner, it was Tiya who greeted Senumet formally. After a few words, without the slightest change in her tone or practiced smile, the old woman said, "Tell Pharaoh exactly what you've seen."

"Of course," he answered, without exhibiting his surprise.

"Don't lie or minimize as they've told you. And don't pretend to misunderstand me."

"No, Highness."

"I always knew you'd prove a true courtier. May you prosper in Akhet-Aten," she concluded as Ay joined them.

"I had thought," Ay said musingly, as he walked Senumet to the dock, "my sister would try to give you messages for her son."

"I imagine Her Highness questions my loyalty."

"Possible, certainly. . . ."

"She made no attempt to speak with me in privacy."

"I know that very well." Ay laughed. "Did you think I'd leave knowledge of her actions to chance?"

"I have not been away *that* long, my lord," he countered.

Thankfully he boarded the ship.

Hesen had told him once that away from Akhet-Aten, she couldn't believe it really existed. He understood, now, exactly what she'd meant—except that his sense of the magic was sharpened by his fear that Akhet-Aten was a mirage which could not exist much longer.

Illogically, the accumulated darkness in his soul lifted at first sight of Pharaoh's city. It rose from the blue enamel river like an insubstantial dream of beauty. Moving fingers of the sun danced and played on the colored stone inlays of the palace, sweeping across the glazed tiles of the temples, sparkling through the glass mosaics of its mansions. As Senumet entered its streets again, he thirstily drank in the purity of the air, the lightness with which the citizens stepped. He waved to friends from his chariot as he rode to the palace from the docks, past the markets with their noisy abundance, past the Maru-Aten with its lakes and basins, gay with painted pavements, past the temples with their airy, spacious, rooflless courts, finally clattering onto the glazed, flower-bordered tiles of the Kings-Way that led to the palace.

The palace was thronged, but in the dazzle of foreign dignitaries and Egyptian nobility, he saw her right away. She had grown much more beautiful in the past year—but in the next instant he was aware that this was a beauty of artifice. Everything was more studied, from her makeup to the complex folds of her gown to her heavy jewelry. He admired the effect, but it did not move him. Only the child inside the mask had the power to do that. For that child, he would betray anyone; would lie, steal—yes, even kill.

Their eyes met. They knew each other so well, there was need for nothing more than a slight nod. As for the separation, it simply was no more. Its distance and time had evaporated in that brief glance. Now they could wait however long they must.

Senumet gave his entire attention to Pharaoh. Akhenaten looked overburdened. The demands of kingship had furrowed crevices in his forehead, and the skin stretched tight over his cheekbones. Only his eyes were startlingly alive. As Pharaoh rose eagerly, greeted him, Senumet realized the man was ill. His body was grossly abnormal. His large, flabby abdomen, strange to see in such an ascetic, bulged over his kilt; his thighs had become so huge and round that he was forced to walk with an odd, rolling gait; and his grip, when he warmly pressed Senumet's hand, was boneless.

"Blessed be Pharaoh, son of Aten." Bowing, Senumet pressed his lips to the cartouche on Pharaoh's ring.

Akhenaten touched Senumet's head affectionately. "You were often in our thoughts and prayers. We rejoice, having you home."

Home, Senumet thought. Yes. Not just to Hesen, but to this man, too, whom he had come to love.

Nefertiti moved to Pharaoh's side. "There has been much building since you left. Before you and Pharaoh become immersed in solemn matters, you must see it all."

He bowed and thanked her. All the strength that had sapped out of Pharaoh seemed to be reposited in her; she was blazingly, indomitably vital. She turned her lovely gaze on Pharaoh. "Beloved, I've neglected my prayers today, waiting to greet Senumet. Will you be so good as to excuse me from court. I want to spend the afternoon at my temple."

"Don't tire yourself, dearest."

Senumet was touched by their love. In the foreign capitals he had seen, nowhere else did the ruling family display openly such affection.

"Go now, my friend," Akhenaten dismissed him. "Renew yourself, see your brothers. Here the hours walk with us. We will hear your report tomorrow."

"Thank you, Highness." Senumet bowed and backed away, his

eyes on the departing queen, marveling at her eternal youth and beauty.

"She must have a queue of lovers at her temple," a voice confided in his ear. "Nobody could pray so much."

Startled, Senumet turned and found Smenkhare.

"Yo, old tutor." The prince laughed.

"How goes it with you, Highness?" There was no point in being annoyed at the prince's ribald jest. Smenkhare was incapable of understanding love or loyalty. His dissipations had tarnished his face, corroding the flesh under his eyes, darkening the corners of his mouth and embittering his smile. He was becoming puffy, too, unexpected so early in a body that was solidly well-muscled.

He answered Senumet dispiritedly, "Time goes very slowly."

Senumet had only one real interest in Smenkhare. "Your wife, I hope she is well."

"Well?" A slight curl twisted Smenkhare's lips. "Hard to say. Dutiful? Absolutely. Yes, I could say of her, the Princess Meritaten is a *dutiful* woman."

"She had miscarried not too long before I left."

"That must have been the first time. Twice more has it run down her thighs. But she's more than eager to try again."

"I don't see her." Senumet looked around the throne room.

"Of course not. She's always on her couch, working herself up for another nightly try—either that or, once seeded, lying there holding her belly to retain it."

"I see," Senumet said, feeling a stab of pity for Meritaten and her joyless life.

"So, old tutor, I have more of duties than I do of pleasures, I assure you." As he spoke, Smenkhare stared as if distracted toward the courtyard. Senumet followed his gaze and spotted a slave, a beautiful boy in that limbo between youth and manhood, sullenly holding a fan of shimmering peacock feathers and awaiting a summons from anyone who felt the need of a cooling disturbance of air. The boy was from Crete, to judge from the crimped ringlets of his hair. Already his back was beginning to know its breadth, and above strong forearms his biceps were long and full. His rounded calves told Senumet the boy was a runner, sometimes used as a swift messenger, and between his well-defined thighs, his sex hung incongruously long and thick for his age. His sultry black eyes were locked with Smenkhare's, but when he noticed Senumet's attention, he fixed them on Senumet, arrogantly teasing.

So that was the course Smenkhare's unbridled desires had taken, Senumet thought sadly.

Smenkhare said smirkingly, "I'll leave you now to pursue your own diversion."

"Thank you, Highness."

"I think *she* may have refined her arts with the help of the Syrian ambassador." He walked briskly past the Cretan slave into the courtyard. Hesitating but a moment, the boy followed.

And that slime would be the next Pharaoh! Senumet blanked the thought from his mind as he made his way back along the Kings-Way to the beach and a small kiosklike temple, Hesen's Sun-Shade.

He slipped inside, preparing himself for a long wait. But he heard her soon enough, walking with friends, her bright voice lilting and laughing. Every tone had long since become part of him. She opened the front entry a few inches and calling gaily to her companions, stretched an arm blindly in. Hidden by the high walls, he gripped her hand, and they stayed . . . so . . . while the others drifted away. Suddenly she stood in the doorway, and the door was swinging shut behind her.

She stood statuesque. He had no desire but to drink in the sight of her graceful body, her shining hair rippling in the new style down her back, her matchless eyes. But something was wrong. There was a new, faint line in the corner of her mouth, and her eyes were hard.

"Do you think to read me like a love poem?" she laughed shrilly. "Lo, she comes to you, bright with her thousand treasures."

"Shall we walk in peace to the edge of old age?" he countered. "I would *we* were a love poem, and poetry is anything but peace. Yet I would be with you each unhurried day."

She touched his cheek. "Welcome back, my friend, brother, lover. I've missed you."

Twining their fingers together, he said, "I was afraid to ask for you. There was talk before I left that you were to wed."

"Thank Meritaten, whose seed runs out of her, that I did not. Strange she cannot hold a child—she's always holding her belly. And animals do it easily enough."

There was something very wrong. His Hesen had not always been so coldly unsympathetic. It pained him to hear her echo Smenkhare's callous manner. "All Egypt must rejoice when she succeeds." He offered the empty conventional response.

"Egypt should have better things to do!"

Why this anger?

She twisted away. "Tell me about your journey. What did you learn?"

They'd not leave here without her heart opening to him, but he'd follow now where she led. "The empire is lost." He sighed. "Pharaoh must fight."

"Fight? Who is equipped to fight? The royal guard doesn't carry the crossbow or sword anymore—just the boomerang."

"They can't attack with the boomerang!" Senumet protested, shocked.

She said without meeting his eyes, "They're supposed to be armed only for defense."

"The army won't consent to that for long. Nor will Egypt. What about you, Hesen?"

"Once I would have," she said deliberately. "I thought everything must be open and honest."

"No more?" He had loved that in her.

"I've discovered honesty is all deceit, which everyone calls diplomacy."

"Except your father . . ."

"Oh, I'm very confused," she cried. "Pharaoh talks about living in truth, and the queen, if possible, seems to believe even more strongly than Pharaoh. My mother is fierce, Senumet. You haven't seen it yet, but she'll do anything to strengthen Aten."

"That should please you, beloved."

"But, Senumet . . . I only followed Aten's teachings!" She stopped.

He could see how she strained for control. He gripped her shoulders hard. A terrible suspicion darted through his mind, remembering from those last days before he left, her sudden interest in children. "How did you live in truth?" he pressed.

"I drank too much black beer," she tried, but her voice shook.

"Were you with child?"

"I was with *maat*, I was with Aten. I was with—"

He shook her. "Answer me!" He had never used such a tone with her before. She sagged against him, her face a mask of pain.

"Yes," she whispered.

"Oh, my dearest!" He crushed her to him fiercely "And all alone."

Her grief, so long held in check, flooded her with all the pain she had not yet acknowledged, the awareness of immortality denied, of love trimmed clean of fruit. "I wanted it, Senumet," she sobbed into his shoulder. "We did nothing wrong. We walked in truth and loved each other and created life. And her response—the queen's—was 'that happiness was not something I could hope for.'"

He had never known he could feel such anguish, such despair at his own helplessness. He could do nothing to remove this hurt. She had dared to dream this wonderful new world belonged to her too. "But it's true, beloved," he said softly. "I tried to tell you but did not know how, yet I think you suspected . . . and I loved you for that too—that you would never accept it."

She raised a tear-streaked face. "What are you saying—never accepted what?"

He had to force himself to speak the words: "That your life was ruined the moment you were born."

Her face was remote as she considered it. Never had truth been spelled out so harshly before. Suddenly a wide smile brightened her face and her eyes shone in the old way. For a terrible moment he thought she'd gone mad.

"You are right," she said finally, almost triumphantly. "I never thought of it that way. I see it now. Every joy that I have felt, I have stolen!" Her hands moved to the fastenings of her tunic and untied them. "And in the moment after this, we'll share my stolen joy."

"Remember," he warned, "if disaster strikes the moment after that, it will be merely the way things are . . ."

She let the tunic fall. Moving into his arms, she whispered, "We'll not be bothered by the way things are." Tenderly she clasped her hands behind his back, used her strength to press her body to his. "I can guarantee it . . . for an hour or two."

But Aten granted them the day. And they were rich with the thievery of their happiness when the sun turned the sky crimson and the lavender shadows deepened into dusk.

# XIV

Senumet's bleak reports of the state of the empire assured Pharaoh that Rib-Addi's desperately urgent pleas for Egypt's troops were no exaggeration. Without Egyptian reinforcements and arms, Byblos would fall to the Hittites, and Egypt's empire would be no more. Pharaoh took counsel with himself, his god, Horemheb, and his queen, and when a strong gust of genetic memories and accusations of his warrior ancestors nearly swayed him to answer with battalions of Egypt's might, Nefertiti zealously reminded him of his god's truth and his commitment. At last, Pharaoh decreed to an uncomprehending Horemheb and a despairing Senumet that he would send only fifty of the guard under Horemheb to rescue Rib-Addi and his royal family. As Pharaoh's emissary and translator, Senumet would accompany them.

Ten days after their departure, Hesen touched the crop to her horse's flank and let out the reins. Responsive and skittish, the animal wildly tore up the beach, throwing large clumps of damp sand. Her arm taut, her hair whipping back, she lost herself in the racing motion of her chariot until she spotted a small figure. Tutu. Waving at her.

She pulled sharply on the bit and drew back. The horse slowed and nervously halted as Tutu sprinted to the chariot.

"I knew you'd remember," he hailed her. He swung aboard.

In fact, she had forgotten her promise to let him drive her chariot. She offered him the reins. The chariot lurched forward.

He came almost to her shoulders, almost a man now, tall for his age, but he'd never make a soldier—which he dreamed of and desired above all else.

When Tutu drew up the horses at last before the palace, Hesen drew a grateful breath that they were both still whole, no broken bones and mangled flesh. He was not an experienced charioteer.

"We'll do this again tomorrow," he announced. "Now let's take my spear and go fishing."

"Forgive me, Tutu, but no." She knew how empty his days were since he had not been chosen by Horemheb to join the guard that traveled to Byblos, as her own days had emptied with Senumet's departure. "I must talk with the queen."

She would make one last try. For if Nefertiti would bend, Pharaoh would send troops. It was still not too late.

Her mother was in conference with Bek. Hesen sat gracefully on cushions near them and did not like what she heard. Nefertiti criticized Bek's sketches for the tomb paintings. Her subjects' faces must be more enraptured in their adoration of herself and Pharaoh; the riches heaped upon the royal family must be more finely detailed. As Bek gathered his materials, the queen turned to her daughter.

"Your appearance is disheveled. You should have seen to yourself before entering my apartments."

Hesen made her tone apologetic. "I wanted to speak with you before you leave for your temple."

"Not the rescue party again. Let there be an end to it!"

Her posture was ingratiating. "Mother, I who so love Aten would do nothing against him, but enlighten me. I don't understand."

Nefertiti leaned back, resigned but annoyed. "We have had this discussion too many times before."

"Rib-Addi of Byblos is Pharaoh's most loyal vassal, is he not? And much of Egypt's wealth depends on Phoenician ships."

"True."

"Then how can we abandon him?"

"Because to keep the empire, Egypt would spit fire on innocent heads!"

"Don't the Hittites spit fire on the innocent?"

"As the god wills," Nefertiti said reverently.

"But foreign peoples have benefited by Egypt's dominion. Under Egypt they have lived free from fear—and there has always been an empire!"

"The immortal laughs at you. Why should Egypt save the world? Why should Egypt have an empire?"

"Think of all the people who will suffer and die by Hittite swords!" Hesen cried angrily. It was unendurable.

"Silence!" Nefertiti commanded. "You set yourself before the will of the god? What is important is that when we raise our hands to Aten, they are not stained with blood. Spend the afternoon at your temple, praying for humility!"

Hesen calmed herself. This was too important for her to be carried away by emotions. "Senumet told me how the old beliefs still cling. Egypt won't accept the loss of the empire."

"The issue is irrelevant, if one lives by Aten's light and walks with *maat*." Nefertiti stood.

"You always taught me to live by caution and restraint," Hesen ventured.

"I was in error."

Nefertiti strode from her reception room into her inner chambers. The double doors were closed by slaves afer her. The audience was over.

Looking hopelessly after her, Hesen thought once again how her mother had grown implacable during the construction of Akhet-Aten. To present an opposing opinion was to incur her stern and righteous displeasure, as if she, not Pharaoh, were the incarnate god, and her every word was spoken with the god's tongue. She listened to no music except that which the god conducted, and she pushed Pharaoh to extremes, against his better judgment. Living gods were both men and gods, Hesen considered. As men, they must live on and deal with the earth. If they abstracted themselves to gods, what then? What doom?

She worried for her mother, on whom Egypt's fate appeared to pivot. She worried for the rescue party that must sneak in and out of Byblos against an army. She worried for Senumet. She was deeply troubled for Egypt—deeply troubled for them all.

During their journey to Byblos, Senumet and Horemheb took their meals together, a little apart from the others—Horemheb because he was the commander of the guard and his position set him apart, Senumet because he was not of their corps at all. It was not long, however, before they realized this arrangement had come to be sought by them both. They discovered they shared the same love for Egypt and a scorn for barbaric peoples.

They traveled by ship so far as the Egyptian stronghold of Gaza, then overland by horse. As they passed through Berytus and met the first of the desperate refugees streaming out of Byblos, they became increasingly disturbed by what they heard. Stories of fierce attacks that couldn't be repelled because Egypt had not sent arms, shocking details of the terrible atrocities of the Hittites, the slow starvation the people of Byblos must endure. Of all the families they met, not one was intact—at least one member was missing, savagely murdered, horribly raped.

At sunset of the last day of the second week, the Egyptians reached the hills ringing Byblos and made their camp in the heavily scented forest of mighty cedars and waited for darkness to hide them. Night came swiftly here. The sky melted into the purple haze on the horizon and then turned black. Even the gold and violet of the sea lapping at Byblos's shores darkened as swiftly as if a curtain had been suddenly lowered.

Not far from their camp the guard built smoky fires in the caves that dotted the hillside and prepared their evening meal. Senumet and Horemheb leaned against fragrant tree trunks and watched the points of flickering light randomly appearing to the north and east of the beleaguered city below them. Finally Horemheb struck the trunk of a cedar in impotent rage.

"It would be so easy! Senumet, look how they expose their positions."

Senumet followed his gaze. "Can it be a trick?"

"I know it's not! Why do you think Egypt's been supreme all these years?"

"Because of our greater numbers, better arms . . ."

"Not at all. We've been supreme because we think. What these barbarians call war is a wild rushing down the mountain, shouting and waving clubs. With just two forces, each of five hundred men, we'd chop off half their strength. In the meantime, our archers would send up flaming arrows, volley after volley, so what was left of their forces would find hell raining on their heads." Horemheb paused, seeing the battle that would never be fought. "By the gods —it makes me sick! Egyptian blood has built this land. And here stand I—with fifty men and no crossbows!"

Horemheb stalked away toward the fires in the caves, where he tore two legs off a duck roasting on a spit and returned, handing one to Senumet. Setekhy followed him, carrying flagons of beer. Horemheb tore at the meat with his teeth. Finally he asked hesitantly, "Do you understand . . . Pharaoh . . . and his Aten?"

It was for Horemheb, Senumet knew, a bold question, since it implied doubt in the man and the deity he was sworn to serve. "I understand that the Aten shows Pharaoh a world that is not of human nature as we know it."

Horemheb seemed to consider this as he chewed. "Well, Pharaoh is different, I'll grant you that . . . and the royal family. I will tell you, Senumet, a few years ago I told Princess Ankhesenpaaten about my family, how proud they were of me. She commissioned a medal struck in bronze, one of its kind, bearing my likeness. She journeyed to my village—Her Highness, the Princess Ankhesenpaaten, daughter to the living god—entered a peasant's house of mud bricks, spoke with them, and placed her gift in my parents' hands."

This was the Hesen he loved, Senumet thought, with her impulsive enthusiasms that even now broke through her acquired decorum. He was proud of the generosity of her gesture.

Horemheb added softly, "My parents would die for her, Senumet."

With a tightening in his chest that was not jealousy—for of jealousy there was no need—but rather the surprise of recognition, Senumet realized that Horemheb had just revealed to him his most precious secret. This man himself would die for Hesen. This man worshiped Hesen with emotion that was nearly as intense as his own. "She is kind," Senumet said, but he knew that he must offer Horemheb more. "With Horemheb at her side, she has always felt safe."

"And with Senumet," Horemheb declared. He gazed directly at Senumet, disclosing in his eyes a knowledge he would not commit to words.

This was a moment they would not speak of again, and Senumet felt he could not let it pass without acknowledging their bond. "All other women are common, next to her," he said.

"I must place the sentinels," Horemheb announced and stood. Senumet stood with him. "In Thebes," Horemheb continued, "I watched the sword in your hand when you practiced with Meruka. If we fight here at Byblos, I would be pleased if you were by my side."

Horemheb gripped Senumet's shoulder. They were separated only by the length of Horemheb's arm. Senumet returned the gesture and felt the strength in the man's shoulder. Then Horemheb broke his hold and disappeared into the night.

Alone, Senumet stared into the inky darkness where sky and earth were divided only by the pinpoints, differing in brilliance, of the stars and the fires of the Hittites. The city of Byblos dared to show no lights. There must be strands of hope, he thought, that would weave the world of Pharaoh to the world as it was, if only he could find the clear-sighted wisdom to perceive them.

# XV

The first day after their arrival at Byblos, even before the morning sun could warm to gold the light brown stones of the palace, Senumet and Horemheb strode to the council room for their meeting with the nobles. Their shadows, distorted wavering lengths, followed them in the torchlight, which flickered in the winding corridors and illuminated the stares of the posted sentries.

They were early: The knowledge of the message they carried was reason enough to have banished sleep. As they approached the tall wooden doors of the council room, servants rushed to open them, pulling at the massive bronze handles. The room inside was dim; even the clustered torches spaced at regular intervals could brighten only small areas of the rich, dark paneling. A large cedar table dominated the room, intricately worked with Astarte's symbol. The splendor of the abstract female form, picked out in brass studs, left no doubt as to the patron deity of Byblos. The table was flanked by tall wooden chairs. Wood was everywhere in this tree-rich land: as Pharaoh's citadel wore light, Byblos's palace was heavy with the majesty of wood, from its carved steps with their ornate balustrades to its ornamental window frames—everywhere the smell of cedar mingled with the resins and oils used to enhance its rich luster. Weighted with this unfamiliar dark luxury, the two Egyptians stood tense and uncomfortable in the council room. Although Senumet could have postponed this meeting, he would not let the people of this doomed city nourish the wild false hope he had read on their faces when the small Egyptian force rode through the entrance gate. And try as he must to justify Pharaoh, he could not minimize the imminent loss of Byblos or mock the achievements of its citizens. The thick gold-brown walls of the city curved around a culture as rich and as varied as that of the Nile Valley itself. Must those crenelated towers be demolished, those precious tablets, with their records of man's strivings, be smashed?

Senumet and Horemheb had not long to wait. Almost immediately the chieftains and nobles of Byblos silently filed in. Their set faces needed no interpretation: They were as disturbed about this meeting as their guests.

Senumet frowned as he studied them. With their clothes intricately draped, brightly colored, belted with links of gold chain, the Phoenicians looked exactly like the traders they had become. What arts of war they had once known were long since forgotten. And what particularly struck Senumet today was the tribal resemblances among these leaders as they took their places one by one in front of the tall chairs, and an appreciation grew in him at this people united by blood and by their complex and harmonious culture. Yesterday in the crush of introductions, greeted as he had been by a bewildering amalgam of forms and faces, each one carrying some strain of a neighboring tribe, the people of Byblos had seemed almost savagely strange. Some were squat, some dark; some had slitted eyes, others wore crimped hair—they were foreign, indistinguishable from the barbarians who threatened them. Today, in this procession of the chieftains and nobles, he saw the men who had extended the limits of the known world. They were not prepossessing, these Phoenicians: slight, rather short, red-bearded, they carried their power in the sharpness of their identical pale blue eyes. Rib-Addi, their leader, distinguishable from the rest only by the gold circlet on his head, gestured Senumet and Horemheb to chairs to his right and left.

"What message does Akhenaten of Egypt send to us?" he demanded coldly.

Senumet stood to address the assembly. "We are sent by Akhenaten, Pharaoh of Egypt, son of Aten, Lord of the Two Lands, who places us at your disposal. We are commanded to render you and your families all possible assistance to move to Egypt, where you will be met with honor and respect."

"We are truly grateful." Rib-Addi's voice was measured. "We have learned from our sages about Egypt's gifts to the world. We have written about them using our alphabet. Yet is it not also true that even Egypt must use our alphabet to send messages to other countries? And is it not a fact that Egypt's great wealth must be transported on boats made from *our* wood? Our ships, as Pharaoh knows, have penetrated to the farthest corners of the world."

Senumet's hands closed into hard fists. "Pharaoh respects the glorious achievements of the people of Byblos."

Rib-Addi leaned forward darkly. "Respect? The measure of Pharaoh's respect can be taken from this little force he has sent. He knows, then, that our spirit is mighty though our numbers are few—and supplies fewer still."

"All your needs will be met in Egypt. And we will learn much from your teachings." Senumet's words fell into dead silence.

"Here, our women stand with us," Rib-Addi said at last. "We must have their consent. Summon Elyssa."

Nubian slaves with dark, oiled bodies tugged at the bronze knobs and pulled open the doors. Head high and proud, Rib-Addi's woman, Elyssa, swept in, followed by wives of the chieftains and nobles.

Although they struggled to mask it, the Phoenicians had been totally dependent on imported goods; thus, when trade was stopped, so ended the luxuries and many necessities, including a great deal of the foodstuffs they had depended upon. Elyssa's robe under the heavy gold necklace was worn, and her skin hung loosely on a skeletal frame. Her red, scaly eyelids were mute evidence of deprivation, both of adequate diet and of the kohl to hide that dire shortages existed. Yet her abdomen swelled with life, by its size soon to be birthed. To claim what heritage? Senumet wondered bleakly.

He extended his gaze to the line of women behind her—all were gaunt and scaly-eyed. Suddenly Senumet understood: They were purposely starving themselves—so that most of the food could go to the men, who must be strong in battle.

Rib-Addi rose to greet her, imprisoned a small hand in his huge one. "Elyssa, queen of the city and of my heart, know that the great Pharaoh offers us escape to Egypt. What say you, Elyssa . . . for the women of Byblos? Shall we accept Pharaoh's offer?"

Elyssa stared at Senumet, outrage darkening her pale eyes. "Never! We will place our bodies under the feet of the dark barbarians. Tell your Pharaoh that."

"So, Senumet of Thebes," Rib-Addi's ringing voice claimed his attention again, "regretfully we must decline your king's offer. Perhaps he will understand that we cannot abandon our women to be slaughtered, will he not? But please, tell Pharaoh also how bravely we died. Only know," he finished in fierce accents, "that Egypt's name shall be written in shame from this day forward."

His fist crashed on the table and the heavy wood vibrated. In the next instant twenty fists from the corded arms of the twenty nobles pounded their support.

The hot flames of Horus coursed through Senumet. He heard his own voice rising in a shout: "Command us, Rib-Addi of Byblos. By the gods, we will fight with you and defend your people. Under the bright light of Amon-Ra we will find a good and worthy death."

Horemheb sprang up next to him, his sword flashing silver as he held it aloft. "People of Byblos," Horemheb cried, "we pledge you our arms and our hearts. We will fight with you!"

Shouts of approval burst spontaneously from every corner of the room. Hands and feet pounded a salute. Then the entire company was on their feet, renewing the full-throated sound. Their cheers fell sweetly on the Egyptians' ears.

Rib-Addi's face shone. "Blessed be the men of the Nile, whose strength, joined with ours, shall smite the black hearts of the barbarians."

Swept along as he was by the fervor and shouting and warm fellowship, Senumet felt like a giant among giants, as if courage and will were enough. Even so, he knew ironically that what all this meant, what it would lead to, was no more—nor less—than death.

In his tent late that night, the sharp mountain air making him grateful for the fur pelts Rib-Addi had provided, Senumet lay sleepless, the memory of Hesen a tearing pain in his chest. For what quixotic impulse had he thrown away the chance to go home? Never to feel the hot sand of Egypt between his toes. Never to dip his oar in the silken waters of the Nile. And worse—much worse—never to touch again that soft velvet body he knew better than his own . . . never again to taste her mouth's nectar. Hesen! He groaned, and buried his face in the linen coverings of his pallet.

No one suspected his torment. Committing himself wholeheartedly to the grand, futile effort of saving Byblos, he was busy from dawn through half the night taking the measure of what weapons were available, deploying them sensibly, even helping to drill into a military force those effete traders, more at home with pens than swords. Though cynically he laughed—as the gods must be doing—nonetheless all the activity was productive of some unexpected practical gain. First, it gave the people of Byblos hope: The stream of refugees leaving was stemmed, and Egypt's name was no longer reviled. Foolish that he should care, but he did. Second—and Senumet's mouth twitched in private amusement—the preparations kept Horemheb occupied, and an inactive Horemheb would have been more dangerous than the advancing hordes. So they readied themselves, optimistic when sane men would despair.

Five sunsets came and went, and five uneventful dawns. Still no attack, though the campfires still burned ominously in the darkness.

On the sixth day Horemheb could stand it no longer. "I can't figure it," he burst out. As they did each evening at dusk, he and Senumet were walking the ramparts, checking the flickering lights on the hills. "I know those Hittites!" Horemheb went on. "They should have attacked."

"Do you complain?" Senumet chided him—although their enemy's passivity troubled him too. "We have a little more time to prepare."

"I've been thinking about that," Horemheb said, looking at the vast sloping plain to the west. "I told you the Hittites have no notion of military maneuvers and formation. They run down the hill waving clubs and axes, masses of them depending on their fearsome savagery and overwhelming numbers for victory. Now, look at the way Byblos is laid out."

Senumet studied the plan of the city, attempting to see it strategically, as Horemheb did. The palace was at the extreme eastern tip—its four towers actually becoming the easternmost boundary from which the crenelated ramparts which encircled the rest of Byblos extended. Behind the palace rose steep, cedar-covered hills—another barrier to attack. To the south were the relatively strong allies of Egypt whom the Hittites were not yet prepared to battle. Their only strategy was to isolate and crush their enemies—one by one. Senumet looked north to the accessible rounded peaks of the anti-Lebanon where the Hittites now camped—down which they would pour to the western plain. Treeless, grass-covered, it curved up from the natural inlet of the Great Green and the small, once-bustling harbor to the very walls of the city. Steps of the same golden-brown stone Byblos was built of, on which, in normal times, traders would carry their goods, led from the harbor to the west gate. That entrance to the city, and two others, were permanently sealed. Only the southern gate remained open, and that well-guarded, allowing the stream of refugees access to the still secure south. Clearly, the attack could come only from the western plain.

Senumet's mind locked into Horemheb's. "You mean we can force them to attack where we can make some reasonable defense?"

"It would take time, but given a few days and some manpower, we could make the entire plain an obstacle course—except for one cleared path they must use." He grinned: "What do you say, Senumet?"

Senumet admired Horemheb's zeal and energy. Silencing his own doubts, he nodded his approval. Although he scorned empty gestures, they nonetheless eased the inevitable dying.

In the next few days, Horemheb had half the population swarming into the steep eastern hills, felling huge cedars and hurling those trunks from the western ramparts, crashing them on the exterior plain. Great slabs ripped from buildings were dropped with a smash; large pieces were hauled down the hill until they rested against the tree trunks; chunks of stone littered the outside field. In a week's time, the plain was so choked with debris an advancing army could scarcely stumble across it, except for a wide path left clear between two artificial hillocks. To Senumet, it was an obvious ploy: Not even barbarians would attack through a path of a defender's choosing! But Horemheb was pleased and Senumet made himself sound more enthusiastic than he was. He didn't have to exaggerate, however, the improvement in the army. Byblos's scribblers, traders and seamen now responded with a ferocity equal to the Guards'—handled their weapons with confidence, gave every indication they'd stand firm. The men of Egypt had done all they could. The defense was ready.

Senumet continued to study the flickering pinpoints of Hittite campfires each night. On the third night after the obstacle course was finished, he sensed a difference.

"To the northeast" he asked Horemheb, "does something strike you?"

"I've been counting too. There are fewer fires. They seem to be leaving."

"Probably not for long. They must be massing to attack elsewhere."

"My thought too, but where?" Horemheb watched Senumet's face, confident that the map of the world would unroll in the scribe's mind.

"Where indeed?" Senumet considered. Cardemsh? No. Assyria? No. Babylonia? Of course not. One choice really—the nearest kingdom—the ripest, most vulnerable, lying exposed at the confluence of the Tigris and Euphrates rivers. A cold blackness gripped him.

Seeing Senumet's face darken, Horemheb urged, "Where?"

Senumet turned to him. "Mitanni!" he ground out. He watched as the same implications sobered Horemheb's face. What would Pharaoh do now that Nefertiti's birthplace was threatened? In her passionate consuming devotion to Aten, what would his queen demand? Senumet regretted more than ever that heedless burst of heroism that had impelled him to throw away his life: Hesen would have need of him now as never before, and he was powerless to reach her. He stared intently into the impenetrable depths of the sky, willed his love to know his longings, willed her to be strong.

The next afternoon, across deserts and mountains and rivers, on the golden sands of the lowest plateau at Akhet-Aten, Hesen walked with her sisters and worried about Senumet. Weeks had elapsed. His ship, laden with refugees and treasures, should have long since sailed up the Nile, but reports had trickled out of Palestine of a small Egyptian force at Rib-Addi's side.

She should have guessed the mission would not be so simple as it had first appeared. If only he could have made his speech to Rib-Addi and left—quickly—before the hosts of other issues had time to enmesh him.

She had a sudden mental image of Senumet as he had appeared before Pharaoh: tall and erect, making his impassioned plea for an army to accompany him to Byblos. Had she really believed that seeing Byblos and its endangered populace would weaken his deeply felt concerns? She had not. But—Aten help her—she had not expected to feel such pain, such a sense of permanent, irreplaceable loss. And her heart, willful and incorrigible still, pounded with hope every time a sail shimmered into view, until her eyes could make out its markings and she was cast again into despair.

She glanced at Sherit and Neferu running ahead of her, sending up a gritty wake, shouting as loudly as peasant children—and, unfortunately, as infrequently corrected. No one had time for the princesses. The queen was busy with her prayers; Pharaoh preoccupied himself with increasingly burdensome affairs of state, Meritaten was absorbed in her body; and the court, these days, had grown more lax than ever. Order and ceremony disintegrated.

Hesen sighed and hurried after the children.

A brief wail behind her brought her to a quick stop. Penre. She always forgot that youngest sister. Contritely she waited as Penre's small, fat legs—churning as fast they could—plodded determinedly after her sisters. The poor child was gasping for breath.

"There, Penre you may choose the spot for our morning meal."

Pointing gratefully to the sycamore next to her, Penre collapsed at its trunk and wiped her streaming face with her skirt. As she summoned back Neferu and Sherit, Hesen hid a smile. Poor rumpled

Penre, always a little dirty, never quite keeping up! With a graceful wave of her hand, Hesen indicated to the servants following them where the stools and the small tables were to be placed and waited patiently while grapes, figs and flat bread were set out in wicker trays and wine was poured into glass goblets. She had made it a point to take the morning meal with her sisters every few days. Realizing that bright memories of the love and warmth of her own childhood were sustaining her even now, Hesen felt a responsibility to give her sisters a share of it too.

She held up her glass and, looking into its sparkle of deep purple lights, heard the liquid call of a jaunty redstart perched in the sycamore. Although she was grown now and well past such things, nonetheless she couldn't stop herself from making a small bargain with the gods. She wouldn't look again until they finished eating, she promised, only let his ship now be rounding the quarry at Hatnub. Let it just be coming into view when next she looked. Picking up a grape, she concentrated on food that stuck in her throat, annoyed at her foolishness. He had remained at Byblos. Accept it! she demanded firmly.

She was suddenly aware that Sherit and Neferu were both staring at her with some urgency. Finally, Sherit, the oldest, licked her fingers noisily and was emboldened to speak.

"Hesen, we would like to take our meals at court, please. We don't fall asleep anymore when poetry is read."

Neferu's back was so straight she seemed suspended from a string. "We don't squirm anymore, either," she asserted.

"You just licked your fingers, Sherit," Hesen corrected, keeping her voice gentle, "Neferu, your dress is around your waist. And you were both shouting before in a most unroyal way."

Their faces fell.

"But I shall ask the queen anyway, because I know you would be very careful." She smiled as they exploded their excitement.

"My dress is exactly right," Penre burst in, "and I always stay awake all night." The curls of her youth lock were matted where she had twisted them around sticky fingers; wine had left a purple reminder on her chin.

If it were up to me only, Hesen wished in quick sympathy—but Nefertiti demanded elegance of her court, and Penre was just not up to that. "Soon, little one," she promised. "Every day you become more and more a princess."

"Baah!" The cry exploded from somewhere overhead. At the same instant a small black object flashed through the foliage of the sycamore under which they sat—and plopped in Penre's lap.

"Yee!" she screamed. "A beetle!" She started to scramble up, then stopped, rigid with fright, her eyes fixed on the shining black body only temporarily stunned. "Look," she managed, "how grown up I am!"

"Baah!" A much larger body crashed to the sand and stood on sturdy legs. It had a green nose and two huge fangs where a lower lip should have been.

"Hesen!" It was more than even a grown-up princess could be expected to bear. Penre hurtled to comfort and buried her face in her sister's lap.

"It's just Tutu being silly," Hesen said severely, stroking Penre's back. "Princes strut like kings, but they act like donkeys!"

He jumped up and down, extracted a tablet from his robe, and flashed it, tantalizingly out of reach. "I stole it from Bek. It's a message from Byblos!" He stood poised, ready to run, watching her out of bright, dark eyes.

She held out a hand that was firm and steady. "Give that to me!" Although she did not raise her voice, there was an unmistakable note of command in its soft tone.

Tutu hesitated, the beginnings of a frown beneath his brows.

"Give it to me," she repeated.

Clearly puzzled and unhappy that his ruse had failed to make her pursue him as when they had played in the past, Tutu shuffled over and placed the ostracon in Hesen's hands.

She read only a schoolboy's exercise on the slate. "Your lessons! And all wrong, as usual." Relief made her giddy. "Stand up and do that over, right now in the sand. And Aten pity you if you make a mistake."

Tutu rudely snatched the stick Penre offered. If he had got it wrong the first time, he'd get it wronger now, a thought that was written in a scowl on his face.

"Writing," Hesen dictated as Tutu scratched in the sand, "will cause man to be remembered. It is more substantial than a palace built of stone or a tomb carved from the cliffs in the west."

Suddenly they heard the soft thuds of horses' hooves. They looked up. Alone in his chariot, Pharaoh pounded down the beach toward them. Tutu happily dropped the stick and obliterated his efforts with a grubby toe. Akhenaten drew in the reins and stopped in front of his second daughter.

"I looked for you at the morning meal." His familiar deep voice held a forbidding note. "Ride with me."

She realized his eyes were glassy and he was unaware of the presence of his other daughters and Tutu, crouching, properly humble, in the sand.

"I have just received a disquieting message," Pharaoh imparted, one hand pounding the gilded guardrail. "I have need to discuss it with you."

Her lungs compressed by the leaden weight in her chest, Hesen's mouth framed the word "Byblos?" She had no breath to give it voice; he must read its sense from her lip's movement.

"Not Byblos," he said. "Mitanni."

Breathing again, she climbed into the chariot. He loosened the reins and the horses broke into a trot. His face clean of expression, he kept his eyes fixed on the river edge ahead. She had seen that frightening blankness once before. Placing a steady hand on his arm, she urged in her usual tone, "A message from Mitanni?"

Without inflection, he said, "The main Hittite force has left Byblos. It appears they'll attack Mitanni first."

For the first time in weeks, Hesen felt vitality flowing through her body . . . and was ashamed. Humbly she begged forgiveness of Aten. All his creatures must be equally valued, and it was wrong that the slaughter of her mother's people should mean less to her than the survival of one man. Then the dilemma of Pharaoh's position struck her. "Are the Mitannis able to defend themselves?" she asked abruptly. Still his eyes were distant. Inwardly she struggled again. Aten could not ask his son to relinquish every earthly love, she thought.

When he spoke, Akhenaten's response startled her by being entirely reasonable. "The Mitannis are a refined and exquisite people," he said. "They are not warriors. In the past they have defended themselves by bargaining with their enemies."

"Then it is Egypt's hope," she said flatly, "that they will do so again."

"They will be decimated by these barbarians."

So. His eyes were not clouded by unrealistic hopes. Sensing a fundamental change in him, she waited, but he did not go on. "What shall Pharaoh's response be?" she prodded at last.

"Ah, Daughter!" It was almost a groan—so bitter, so sad that Hesen's eyes spontaneously filled with tears. "Consider: Aten commands I shall not take life; but clearly, in our imperfect world, refusing to kill will not end bloodshed."

"No," she agreed. "The Hittites will attack, whatever you do."

"And if I let them have their way, as I am doing at Byblos, and they murder and loot and pillage, will my hands be clean of sin?"

*No!* her heart cried out. Bitterly she said, "Your decision for Byblos ensures that the good will be destroyed."

Still holding the reins, he placed his heavy hand on her small one. "It is too late for Byblos, but must it be too late for Mitanni? Shall I follow obediently and unquestioningly the dictates of my god?"

Excitement rose in Hesen. She could not see how he could abandon his god, his queen, his followers. The issue was too philosophical. Yet in a flash she did not care. This was unmistakably sanity, at last. Hesen spoke from the heart: "Send troops!" Certainty gave her voice power. "You do it to save lives. Aten will approve."

Pharaoh regarded her, his eyes bright with unshed tears. "Thank you, Daughter. I had wrestled to that very conclusion. I trust and am strengthened by your brave, loyal heart."

"Shall you tell her now?" No need to name *her*.

"*We* will tell her now." Pharaoh's words translated into his wrist's movement. The horses veered sharply right.

"All my being is yours to command," she pledged her father desperately. "We stand together."

# XVI

Nefertiti waited impatiently.

Not until the sun reached the exact center of the sculptor's complex—the point when its light was purest and brightest—would Bek humbly, in speeches of impossibly tedious rhetoric, request her presence. He was permitted this authority only because he was fashioning her master portrait—the bust from which all representations of her must be modeled.

"He leaves the compound," Aahmose reported, a little breathless from running with the news.

Nefertiti swept out of her apartment, her servants hurrying to keep up. "I'll meet him," she declared, "and spare myself his speeches."

Bek's face fell when he spotted the queen and her entourage: part of his daily ritual was lost. She knew how each extra moment he spent with her brought joy to his heart, but she was not placed on earth to brighten his day, or any man's.

As she sat on the cushioned stool in his workroom, her hands relaxed in her lap, Bek fussed with her blue crown, his fingers lingering beyond the sculpture's need on her neck. Were he not so brilliant an artist, she'd have him whipped!

Finally he removed the cloth from the sculpted piece and began to work. She hadn't yet seen the stone. "Today you will show it to me," she reminded him.

The morning wore on. A dull ache began high on her back from holding the same pose. She ignored it, pleased at her ability to disregard physical discomfort. She watched Bek's hands as they expertly blended colors of vegetable origins mingled with resins and oils. His eyes swiveled from her to the statue. Knowing the effect of light on her face, she surmised, from Bek's short, delicate strokes, that he added the glow illuminating her high cheekbones. The dimple in the corner of her mouth deepened with pleasure.

"Finally, it is done." Regret thickened Bek's voice as he rotated the pedestal on which the bust was placed. When it had made a half-circle, Nefertiti looked straight at—herself.

Silently she studied it. Surely that was not stone she looked at. That high blue crown under which her hair was swept must be the same stiff fabric that rested so lightly on her own head. The striped ribbon circling it, like her own, must shimmer with the very fineness of the linen. And the face itself—great Aten!—those lips must be blushing flesh . . . the eyes, fringed with lash, must any moment blink! He had captured everything: the dimple in the right corner of her mouth; the bright eyelids some called sensuous, the arching brows, the high, foreign cheekbones; the long, slim neck—and something more . . . something even her careful daily study had overlooked. He had captured *her*. His creation breathed her very soul, with its hard-won serenity and, finally, its love. Under the high double crown she looked into the eyes of a woman who, given everything, at last knew who she was. That woman awed her.

"Yes," she whispered, unconsciously responding to its challenge. Then, sensing Bek's anxiety, she turned a dazzling smile on him. "Magnificent!"

His body sagged in relief. Caught between surprise and scorn, she thought, *He could not have doubted the piece's merit!* "Thank you, my lady!"

With a nod, Nefertiti left his workroom, lifting her chin regally. She would not betray how shaken his artistry had left her—how she trembled to think that any mortal might have such insight into her soul.

In the south garden, she sat down on a curved bench near the small pool, watching tiny goldfish dart beneath its blue surface. Letting the quiet beauty of the day wash over her, she began to put things in perspective. No one else would see what she saw in that statue—except for Pharaoh. To that she had no objection. The serenity and regality of that face was partly his. When she looked up, she saw—as if her thoughts had conjured him—Akhenaten hurrying toward her, with Hesen at his side, and as quickly realized that their faces were grim.

*Byblos has fallen and all with it*, Nefertiti thought as she rose to meet them. She was glad Pharaoh had told Hesen first. Reaching for Hesen's hand, she held it in both of hers, warmly, comfortingly. "There is dreadful news," she ventured, sparing preliminaries.

Hesen's look was not at all what she had expected. Even before her daughter spoke, somehow their positions became reversed, and it was Nefertiti's hand that was now being held.

"No, Mother." Hesen's voice was a low note of pain. "They have withdrawn from Byblos."

"What then?" She turned to Pharaoh.

His arm encircled her waist with loving warmth. "Beloved, they attack Mitanni."

She felt as if she had been struck. Breath seemed to leave her body in an explosive burst. Mitanni! Before her eyes bright images overlapped: the lush green valley, flowering ziggurats, the glazed blue walls of the city; stately, fair people . . . her people . . . enveloped in their elegant white and green garments and flashing silver beads; the golden, loving arms of Savriti. She took a deep, careful breath. The south garden came into focus. The world looked as it always had—the pool was as blue, the lotus as sweet—but the world had altered. The past was severed, and without it, the present would never be the same again.

"Beloved!" Even Pharaoh's voice sounded remote—or was it that she was encapsulated and separated by her own special pain? Aware that the wound had been severe, she allowed herself to sink deeper into its numbness. Her hand lay in Hesen's like a small, dead bird.

"Beloved, your people will not perish," he was saying.

"No," she whispered. In her mind their golden spirits hovered in the sunlight and came to rest in Savriti's hands.

"We will send an army to their aid."

Her vision splintered. "Are you mad? Aten forbids the shedding of blood." Let Savriti care for her children. Nefertiti belonged to Aten.

"If I do nothing," Pharaoh said levelly, "the slaughter that will surely follow will just as truly be my fault as if my hand held a sword."

"*You must not take life,*" Nefertiti reiterated, as if she had not heard.

"Beloved, comprehend the paradox. I take life either way."

"Aten's command is clear. You must have no part in killing. If he wills it, Mitanni will fall. Even you, his son, cannot partake of

Aten's omniscience, his universal design. You dare not question him. His plan may be to test our love. You will do nothing." Her voice stung their ears like the granule-laden winds of a desert sandstorm.

"Mother," Hesen cried, horrified. "You can't realize what you're saying." Seeing irresolution flicker over Pharaoh's face, she pleaded urgently. "Send an army, Father. Don't let them be slaughtered!"

Nefertiti blazed with the strength of her faith. "I forbid it! You think you act out of love, but in your reasoning are the sounds of the weak and faithless, the blind and the erroneous! I shall summon my people now—before the false gods persuade you to stop me—I shall tell them Mitanni is doomed." She turned and strode toward the palace, her white gown rippling behind her.

"Stop her, Father!" Hesen implored. "Have soldiers restrain her—have her taken to her rooms until her senses are restored."

He stood like one transfixed. "Her eyes see clearly. Perhaps," he said dully, "I have lost the light."

Desperate to stop Nefertiti—not knowing what would move Pharaoh to action—Hesen was almost in a frenzy. "Prevent her now," she begged. "We can think about it later when everyone is calmer. Just don't let her do something that can't be reversed. Father!" she screamed. "Father, hear me!"

Still Pharaoh's eyes stared blankly. By herself then, she would drag Nefertiti back, struggle and scream though she might. She tore after her mother. Then she heard it: the first trumpet call! Its blaring, brazen cry was picked up by other trumpets until all of Akhet-Aten echoed to a brassy note. She was too late. They would come to the palace now, the Mitannis, from wherever in the city they happened to be—markets, feluccas, love beds, everywhere. Slowly Hesen made her way to the throne room. She would stand with her mother, though it break her heart.

Mitannis were streaming into the palace as Hesen mounted the dais next to her mother. "Please," she whispered desperately. She was stopped by a quelling look from her mother.

Hesen stared at the mass of elegant men and women below them—their almond eyes raised to her mother, their faces tense and watchful. The only sounds were the excited calls of the children, who, unaccustomed to the magnificence of the throne room, clearly expected a festival.

"My brothers"—firmly, clearly, Nefertiti's voice filled the huge room and carried into the courtyard, where some few Mitannis, unable to wedge into the throne room, were standing. "I must speak of misfortune. Today I shall place a heavy burden on you, to be borne all our days—" She took a deep shuddering breath, then said it all at once. "The Hittites attack. Mitanni is doomed."

A deep, horrified gasp followed her words, then wails of pain. Suddenly a man's deep voice carried over the din: "Tell us, Nefertiti of Mitanni, when do Pharaoh's troops set out? I will stand with my Egyptian brothers for my people."

"And I."

"I, too."

A wave of masculine assent rippled through the crowd. And in a flash, the hands of each man there, clenched into fists, were flung up, and the hands of the women too, who would stand with their husbands and brothers, until Hesen stared at a sea of quivering arms.

"Command us, Nefertiti of Mitanni!"

A trembling began in the pit of Hesen's stomach that she recognized as fear. They would tear the queen apart! She stepped defiantly closer to her mother. What they would do to Nefertiti they must do to her as well.

When the roar receded, the queen's voice rang out clear and high. "There will be no troops!"

Nefertiti's words took a few minutes to sink into their collective consciousness. There was a murmur. Over it rose a baritone. "Lead us to Pharaoh then, Nefertiti. Together we will persuade him."

They had not yet seen the true outline of her message.

"It is *my* decision not to send troops. It is *my* will that orders no defense to be raised. Aten forbids it, and Aten is my God."

In the stunned silence that followed, Hesen's glance caught Senedjm edging through a door at the rear. She sent up a grateful prayer. Bless Senedjm, ever loyal . . . sensing danger, rushing to summon help. Merciful Aten, she whispered, let him be in time.

Within the blink of an eye, pandemonium had broken out.

"Your brother sits on the throne—do you owe him nothing?"

"His blood calls to you!"

Nefertiti's mouth was absolutely white. "I have one allegiance now—to Aten."

"Slut!" The word bounced off the walls. The crowd took it up like a chant. "Slut . . . slut . . . slut!"

Eyes bulging, mouth curled scornfully, a huge hairy courtier with hands like ham hocks climbed onto the dais. Hesen would have stepped in front of the queen, but Nefertiti's hand thrust her back.

Working his mouth, the man expelled a forceful jet of saliva. The spittle struck Nefertiti's cheek and oozed down her chin. The shouts grew louder and angrier. Another man leaped onto the dais. Another. Daggers flashed.

Again trumpets blared, calling another unmistakable message.

Above the rising din was the thunder of horses' hooves on the tiled courtyard, the screams of those Mitannis outside through whom the animals plunged. The guard burst into the throne room—pushing with their steeds through the crowd, heedless who was crushed under their horses' thrusting feet or caught in their swords' slashing arcs. Blades found their marks; screams pierced the air; blood stained the bright mosaics. Clutching their babies, women searched for a safe corner. There was none as well-trained horses maneuvered around gilded pillars. A small child wiggled free of his mother's clasp—ran terrified, toward the courtyard. He was toppled by the milling crowd, his chest crushed by the foreleg of a rearing beast.

It was over in seconds. But if Hesen and the queen were safe, the tile floor of the throne room was stained with the blood of the Mitannis, and the bright, gay mosaics had been crushed beyond repair.

The guard herded the Mitannis from the throne room, the mob fragmenting into groups, some angry, some despairing, some carrying their wounded.

Hesen wanted to comfort the queen before the servants came to attend them. "Mother—" she began tentatively.

Nefertiti turned, her face a stone mask that barred Hesen's way. There was no room in Nefertiti's breast for softness or love; fanatic certainty had replaced them. Lifting a fold of skirt, Hesen wiped away the spittle still on her mother's face. This done, her own sight blurring with unshed tears, she left the throne room, her footsteps echoing hollowly.

She was not to see the queen again for a week. Persuaded by Pharaoh to accept a heavy guard, Nefertiti remained in her apartments. He would not punish her countrymen; nonetheless, they'd not have another opportunity near her, and they wouldn't be long at Akhet-Aten. In clipped, anguished voices they had begged Akhenaten for ships to return home. Black they'd paint the vessels, and they would carry black sails . . . to fly the red and green flag of Mitanni for the last time.

Hesen was heavily guarded, too. Standing with the queen had damned her as well in their eyes, and Pharaoh feared a crazed

Mitanni might speed her journey to the Underworld. Hesen did not protest. In truth, she was relieved to have her activities restricted. She needed time to interpret what had happened and to dim her nightmare memories of that meeting. She was thankful for Sephy's presence, for the comfort in every solid fiber of her. And Tutu. Slipping daily past the guards, the prince would triumphantly spring up—on the terrace, in her clothing chest, in her bed. And this day—"Tutu! Today you go too far!"—giggling in the room where her bath was being readied, incongruously redolent of roses.

"Look!" He was so delighted with himself she couldn't help smiling, especially when he showed her a loaf of lotus bread still warm from the ovens. "I grabbed it when they oiled the crust," he confided. He offered her a generous hunk. "Remember when I used to be punished and you brought me candy?"

She let the sweet dough melt in her mouth.

"Oh, Hesen." He sighed, surprising her with sudden melancholy. "It was easier then. I didn't have to worry."

She wouldn't laugh or minimize his concern. "What worries you, Tutu?"

"Horemheb . . . and Senumet."

She kept her tone casual, reassuring. "Right now, I'm sure they're all right."

"But"—he hesitated; his face strained with the effort of piecing it together. "I was thinking—when the Hittites have destroyed Mitanni, are they going to forget Byblos?"

Her first impulse was to lie. She rejected it. If he had the understanding and strength to ask, he should not be denied the truth. "No, they won't forget."

"Tell me, then—I've been hoping . . . do you think the Guard might already have left Byblos?"

"Each day that passes makes that more unlikely."

"Oh." Despite his efforts, his lower lip trembled.

"We can ask Aten to guide them," she offered finally.

Some of the tension left his face. "Now!" he insisted.

She took his hand and they stepped out to the terrace adjoining her quarters, knelt among the potted palms, the daisy border, and prayed silently, intent on the need that filled both their souls: *Aten, merciful father, guide them safely home.*

Three days later, the Mitannis' ships, sitting like grim black birds in the harbor, were declared seaworthy. There were no officials at the dock for parting ceremonies. Yet though Egyptians—peasants, nobility and royalty alike—were hidden indoors, hundreds of screened eyes followed the mournful procession. Flanked by armed guards, the Mitannis boarded the boats, their robes somber-colored where, a few short days ago, they would have dazzled—their faces dark instead of glowing with health and joy. In profound silence, the ships pulled into the current, then slowly and ungracefully—for the Mitannis had never been sailors—began their passage downriver.

From the terrace, Hesen watched, willing them quickly gone. Suddenly a stab of brightness dazzled her vision. Shading her eyes, she scanned the bordering hills. Aten protect her—on the crest of a small hill Nefertiti, untended, stood straight as a spear in her chariot: it was that vehicle, gilded with hammered gold, that had reflected the blinding shaft of light. As her sight cleared, Hesen realized her mother was dressed totally in black, recognizable only by her crown.

As the ships rounded the promontory, the Mitannis raised their voices in an age-old dirge, anger and grief weighting the words with damning accusation. The lament swelled, filled the hills, echoed with contrapuntal emphasis. Hesen watched her mother, half in awe. Each note, she knew, etched another line on Nefertiti's face; yet her body, rigid and unrelenting, reaffirmed her decision and accepted the judgment of her people as its price. When the last boat passed the hill on which the queen stood, the Mitannis, black blurs in identical poses on four decks, loosed a barrage of dark arrows, which rose in a strong steady line—almost straight up in the air.

Thinking that the arrows were meant for her mother, Hesen gasped. Then she realized they were aimed at the sun. She watched the straining upward flight until the shafts seemed to hang suspended in the still air. In the second before their downward plunge must begin, they burst into flames and were consumed in a blaze of orange. So, beneath Aten's sun, the Mitannis would shortly be consumed and their bright culture with them—obliterated for all time. Tears streaking her face, Hesen watched thankfully as the clumsy ships disappeared in a blue curve of the river.

Nefertiti at last pulled the reins, and her horses, flicking their heads, obediently began the tricky descent. Her hands automatically feeding instructions to the animals with her usual dexterity, Nefertiti's mind was free to examine, dispassionately and objectively, the pain, the loss, the emptiness that every nerve end dispatched to its neighbor. Today's sailing was not the end of it: Just as every man, woman, child on those boats was tied to her in special ways—kinship, a shared past, a common heritage—so each of their deaths killed a part of her.

"O Aten, my Father," she prayed, "remember only that I chose you and was true to your commands. Forget that in this moment of pain and weakness, which I abjure, my eyes are blinded by tears."

Akhet-Aten returned to a semblance of normalcy, made easier by the queen's absence from court. Nefertiti's meals were carried to her Sun-Shade, where she spent the entire day and evening. The only times she could be seen were on her solitary walks to and from her temple. After one look at her suffering face, unpainted and naked, the people of Akhet-Aten avoided the Kings-Way when they knew she would be traveling it.

There was still one final blow to be delivered. When it came three weeks later, Hesen read it on Pharaoh's face; and Nefertiti, returning to the palace that night, took one look at her husband's eyes and read it too. Crablike and halting, she stumbled back to the temple.

Dazed at the sight of her mother's pain, Hesen twisted her hands together: And Aten forgive her, all she could think was—Byblos. Is Byblos next?

Hundreds of miles upriver at Thebes, holding a scroll bearing the same message Pharaoh had read, Ay gloated triumphantly. Mitanni had not only been lost, it had been horribly raped. Its blood would permanently stain that green valley, darken the shining waters. And Byblos, to follow, would be even worse. At Byblos, Egyptian blood would flow—Egypt's richest and most valiant. Ay breathed deeply. While he regretted the inevitable loss of Senumet and Horemheb, their foolish heroism would spark the peasants' smoldering resentment into outright revolution . . . carefully fanned by Ay and the priests of Amon.

Snapping shut the papyrus with a deft motion, Ay carried it to the scribes' bureau. Ka-Aper had been an eminently satisfactory choice for chief scribe. While not so imaginative as Bek, Ka-Aper was more workmanlike, more alert to nuance, more sensible to whom he owed his position. Servants rolled up the reed screen at his approach.

With the most powerful nobles now at Akhet-Aten, there was much less private work for those scribes remaining at Thebes; many fewer gifts from wealthy patrons. Where they had once been at the center of royal activity, now they handled minor matters of an increasingly unimportant nome. Today Nofret the headman was among them, conferring with Ka-Aper. Nofret looked uneasy, Ay perceived—as well he should: His mismanagement had almost emptied the treasury of Thebes. And were he only aware of what Ay planned for him, he'd look frantic!

"Nofret, I bring grave tidings." Ay handed Ka-Aper the papyrus. "Mitanni has fallen."

Ka-Aper studied it, gave Ay a quick, searching look. "Might we discuss it further? There's a construction here that seems ambiguous."

As Ay inclined his head slightly in acknowledgement, Nofret mumbled, "Yes . . . well; that—uh . . . very grave news." Ay felt his teeth clench involuntarily. Nofret's opacity of mind continued unimpaired by experience. Fool! Did he really not understand the grand vizier would not personally deliver a message—servants' work—unless he had secrets to discuss? "You are aware, Nofret," Ay reminded him, "I leave later this week for the port city of Zoan. With the Guard still at Byblos, I don't feel I can wait for reports to reach us here."

Relief animating his face—he had forgotten Ay's trip—Nofret agreed enthusiastically. "Certainly you should get the news immediately. If there's any assistance—" Letting his words dangle, he backed uncomfortably out of the workroom.

Ay and Ka-Aper walked to the east garden, taking the scroll with them.

"It's all set, my lord. They will lay down their styluses—and their plows and their tools—two days after you set sail. The entire work force of Thebes will refuse to perform any service until they're paid."

"And the treasury is empty!" Ay gloated. "For how long are they prepared to be idle?"

"Long enough. Two months' supply of food has been diverted to our storerooms in the valley. We have Nacht's support as well. The army will not use force against us."

"Remember, you are not to negotiate with Nofret or any of Pharaoh's emissaries."

"I will deal only with Tushratta. All of Egypt shall know it was a priest of Amon who ended the first work stoppage in our history."

"There must be no hint of my involvement," Ay warned sharply.

"None, my lord." Ka-Aper bowed. Straightening, he looked over Ay's shoulder. "I'll now take my leave. Queen Tiya approaches."

Eyes narrowing slightly, Ay turned to greet her. Every time he met his sister, it was with barely concealed triumph. She knew well what the auguries were. Limping badly, her hands unsteady on the Nubian-headed cane, she haltingly advanced. With three quick strides he covered the distance between them.

"I know," she forstalled him, "Mitanni has fallen."

"And how my heart—"

She interrupted. "I crave a favor, my brother. You go to Zoan this week?"

"Yes."

Her face had an unhealthy yellow cast. Death had already entered her body, Ay thought dispassionately. It would have its way with her soon enough.

"I would like to travel with you to Akhet-Aten. My daughter needs me now."

"Of course," he concurred easily. Once he would have tried to stop her, would have feared what she—still wily and dangerous—would advise her son. No more. It was almost all played out now.

He did not pause to regret that out of their long-shared past, soon to be ended forever, there was nothing left for even a passing sorrow.

# XVII

Each night Senumet and Horemheb counted more and more campfires, until finally the entire hillside was studded with flickering lights.

Only one thing remained undone. In the unlikely event there were survivors among the Egyptians, they must be provided with some means of safe return.

A boat was placed in a small copse near the harbor. Some bread, dried fruit, leeks and beans were stored, a quantity of water, a few jugs of wine. Horemheb called his countrymen together. "After the assault, make your way to this copse." He indicated a point on the detailed map of the harbor. "Stay hidden until the moon has traversed half the sky. Give all our brothers a chance to reach the harbor. Then we will set sail." He stared at each of them in turn. He trusted them: In these past few weeks they had truly become brothers. "All signs indicate the attack will come in the morning," he concluded. "You have your assignments."

Senumet raised his right hand in benediction. "May Horus guide your blades true, my brothers, and may Amon light your way."

Senumet slept well that night—without dreams. There was nothing to hope for except a brave death and nothing to regret: in the weeks that had elapsed, he had severed one by one all the claims that had bound him to this earth. He had given up the pretense of bending his knee to Aten, and his soul was his own again. It was Thoth he called upon to judge his heart's purity.

Drums summoned him before the birds sent up the racket of their morning song. With his sword strapped to his hip and his dagger sheathed across his chest, the flanks of his horse bony and sharp against his thighs, he led his one hundred men through the south gate.

Concealed by the rubble they had piled, Senumet and his company sat silent and attentive behind the south hillock, steady hands calming their horses. On the other side waited Horemheb with an equal number of men.

When bands of brightness first lightened the horizon, Senumet became aware of a faint thunderous rumble. His heart began to race. The Hittites—surely thousands of them—pounded down the hills.

The sounds of galloping hooves grew louder. Senumet stared to his left, ready any moment for the invaders to bypass the obstacles prepared for them, convinced that they would overrun the very spot on which he stood. But, no! Blessed Amon, great of spirit, great of strength, the barbarians came exactly the way he and Horemheb had planned—and he had doubted. Excitement coursed through him. *This* day would be theirs!

Horses thundered by—hundreds of them. He could almost feel their hot breath, protected as he was only by a shallow screen of debris. His eyes scanned the horizon. There—as planned—one bright arrow in a triumphant arc.

Raising his shield, he watched a hundred shields follow his signal and flash. He waved his sword. His men shouted wildly and charged, hitting the center of the teeming Hittite lines exactly as Horemheb came down the other side.

Confusion and disarray. The Hittites had never even considered an attack. Horses screamed and reared in panic. Weapons flashed. Slashing with ferocious power, Senumet's sword knew its first taste of blood. In wonder he saw it slide through soft flesh and pull easily out from vital organs, bits of curling intestine stuck to its shaft.

"You learned well," a voice panted near him.

Sweat driping from his brow, Senumet raised his head to shout at Meruka, but they were separated by the claims of battle. The Hittites broke ranks. About half the force, desperate to escape the punishing defenders, charged forward to the walls of the city. There Rib-Addi flung at them the remaining troops. A hell of slashing blades at their heels and at their chests, the barbarians fled. Horns blared retreat. They trampled their own wounded, heading back into the dark safe hills—back to regroup, back . . . to return at daybreak.

In triumph—the sweeter for its being unexpected—the men of Byblos marched into the city to a wildly cheering populace. Garlands of daisies circling his neck, Senumet thought their joy was harder to bear than their stoic silence. There were no prospects for cheering tomorrow.

He and Horemheb did not attend the banquets—the last ceremony of a dead people—that would end in orgiastic dissipation. Instead they checked the huge vats spaced along the ramparts, making sure piles of faggots were stacked near each one, and that small fires were already banked. Precious oil had been collected from every household, and every drop in the city had been poured into those vats, together with large stones.

Before daybreak they gave the signal. Fires were stoked; flames leaped beneath the vats. The oil smoked. Finally it bubbled wickedly.

They had a plan for this day too. The Egyptians would be deployed around the palace and the east wall it bordered—Byblos's last defense. The city was designed so that one broad cobbled road led directly up the hill to the palace. Citizens of Byblos were deployed in rings on every second street crossing that road, both north and south of it, so that they would temporarily trap the Hittites. Each layer of defenders would have to be overcome before the invaders could advance. If they stood firm—and they would—the prize would cost those murdering hordes dear.

In the flush of yesterday's excitement, Senumet had not really seen the Hittites. He would make sure to look at them today. He stood on the ramparts as dawn broke to their now-familiar thunder and braced himself as wave after wave of them seethed awkwardly down the hills, points of sunlight glinting off the blades of sharp axes. Savage shouts bellowed revenge from each throat. Revenge sharpened the ferocity with which they dug heavy curled boots into their animals' flanks. With their long beards streaming over their shoulders behind them, pointed leather hats jutting forward, it seemed they would charge through the very walls of the city.

"Now!"

Ramming the boiling vats with lengths of cedar, the men on the ramparts tilted them forward. The bubbling contents poured over the walls, raining scalding death on the first wave of Hittites. The smell of sizzling flesh fouled the air. Men and beasts screamed agony.

Senumet raced his horse back to the palace to take his place with his Egyptian brothers. He knew he need not have hurried, that some time must elapse before the enemy would storm the inner circle.

Nonetheless, the scene in front of him was shocking. In battle dress, some of his men lounged on the curved steps of the palace, resting their shields carelessly against the ornate balustrades. Others sprawled, apparently half-asleep, in the shadows of four golden towers. Some, in small groups, were even betting on the direction of the wind's shift—discernible in the rippling banners carrying the bright purple and yellow flower that was Byblos's standard.

Below them came the sounds of the first clash—the ringing of metal on metal, the screams of the wounded, the crashing of boots on the cobbled road. Rising and falling in waves, the battle grew louder. One by one each ring of defenders fell, and the Hittites advanced. The first few appeared over the crest of the road shouting wildly, waving their axes over their heads. At the merest sign from Horemheb, the Egyptians sprang to attention, swords drawn. Initially Senumet's sword sang as it flashed. But more and more Hittites rushed up the hill as ring by ring the defenders were overcome. The moment came when Senumet was facing three at once—blood and matted hair and bits of flesh clinging to the blades of their axes, swinging closer—and he realized his arm was tired. It was hard to whirl the sword in the flamboyant arcs that had torn through their guard. From the right an ax hit his weapon and knocked it out of his hand. He backed away from a slashing blade. From the left, another Hittite—mouth drawn back over rotting teeth—lunged at him. Senumet twisted sharply. Managing to grab the man's unarmed hand, he bent the arm back with such force that bone cracked. But the Hittite, eyes fierce, ignoring his agony, angled the ax so his next blow would split Senumet's skull.

Ducking his own attacker, Horemheb, also swordless, buried his knife in the Hittite's back. Senumet grabbed the ax before the man hit the ground. He had no time to throw Horemheb a grateful smile before crashing the metal blade through the skull of an approaching barbarian, spattering brain and shards of bone.

Suddenly a savage cheer went up. Senumet's heart lurched. Rib-Addi had been taken. Four Hittites, their muscles bulging, dragged the king of Byblos into the palace courtyard, where they hacked at him. Hittites circled him, howling chants of death at the sight of the streaming rivulets springing from his chest.

A woman's scream rent the air. Barbarians storming the palace had found Elyssa and were dragging her out, their hands twined through her bright hair.

In a last frenzied burst Rib-Addi struggled free, crawled to reach her. An ax flashed and split his body almost in two. An arc of his blood spurted, splashing the man who had struck him. He sank, his intestines, pink and shiny, spilling out on the sand.

With a hoarse cry that was almost a sob, Horemheb lunged at Rib-Addi's murderer, a knife in each hand—heedless that his path must take him past a ring of Hittites. A swinging club smashed against his temple, spinning him around and down. The Hittite raised the club with both hands over his prone body.

Blessed Isis! Desperate to stop the Hittite, Senumet realized he couldn't move fast enough. The instant expanded. His eyes riveted on the club gripped in those powerful hands. In his own hand was a knife. Must be fast—must be accurate. *Help me, Amon,* he prayed . . . and hurled the knife. It hit Horemheb's attacker with such force he staggered several steps before collapsing. Red foam gurgled from his nostrils and mouth.

Planting himself in front of his fallen comrade, Senumet was lunging for the club when his arm exploded. His vision reddened—darkened; waves of pain rolled over him. He was hurtling through space. The ground rose up and struck him.

He opened his eyes almost immediately to the sound of boisterous laughter. Had he gone mad? When his vision cleared, he saw what they made sport of . . . and was violently ill. *Merciful father, merciful father . . .*

Her dress had been torn off, and naked and screaming, Elyssa was pinned to the ground by four Hittites, one at each limb, her white abdomen huge and heaving. A Hittite soldier took three running steps, his heavy boots leaving their imprints in the ground, and leaped on that soft, yielding belly. Senumet had never heard a human being scream the way Elyssa did. A small donkey he had seen once, its body caught by a scythe, had screamed so. Another Hittite landed on her—his boots gouged bloody tracks on her body. They pushed and jostled. A fight broke out for the chance to be next. Her screams stopped. She must have fainted, Senumet thought, hoping she was dead. But a barbarian ran his knife along her naked breast—a red stripe following its point—and she screamed again, her head thrashing violently. A huge soldier smashed on her abdomen, his boots making a deep pit in the rounded flesh. Blood and water gushed out of her, and Senumet could discern a pale mass that might have been a child between her legs. At last her body went slack. They kicked her aside.

No defender was left standing. Shouting triumphantly, the Hittites tore into the palace and the richly ornamented temple that adjoined it.

*I must have lost consciousness*, Senumet realized as the screaming agony of his arm jolted him back to awareness—to a silence so profound he thought he was dead. Cautiously he raised his head. It thudded violently, but he forced himself to hold steady. All around him bloody, battered men lay awkwardly still. Not all dead! A moan to his right—an Egyptian sprawled clumsily on the ground. His eyes opened once—Horemheb was alive! . . .

What did it matter? Senumet thought bleakly. Then he remembered. The Hittites were in the palaces and mansions, looting and raping. He had a little time before they returned to kill the wounded. Where to hide? The wall extending from the palace . . . in the recess of the stairs that led to the ramparts. Could he do it? He pulled himself to his knees.

The world tilted and spun around him . . . his right arm was useless . . . his right shoulder seemed to have disappeared entirely. With his one good hand, he tried to grip Horemheb. Now to haul him up. *Amon guide me*, he prayed—and clumsily, haltingly, on his knees, blood and dust mingling with his sweat—slowly he rolled Horemheb to the small alcove at the foot of the rampart steps. With his last reserves, he pushed his friend's body through. Not good enough: They could still be seen, but he could do no more. The edges of his vision blurred and he felt himself falling.

"Senumet!"

Faintly, he heard his name; then more insistently.

"Senumet!"

His eyes jerked open. For a minute he didn't know where he was, then he saw the face inches from his own—Horemheb, an enormous swelling on his forehead forcing one eye closed. They were lying on the ramparts, hidden by its crenelations; Horemheb must have carried him up. Raising himself with effort, Senumet could see the blaze of fires. He heard shouts, wild laughter, an occasional scream—testimony to a successful looting.

Below them the silent field was littered with prone figures. Four Hittite soldiers picked their way among the dead and wounded, prodding inert bodies with the tip of their curled boots for signs of life. A moan, the flash of a blade, a gurgle. The Hittites took no prisoners—but they did take trophies. Senumet noticed woven bags slung over their shoulders. With strokes of scimitars they hacked off the right hands of the fallen and tossed the dripping prizes into the bags.

He shut his eyes.

"Senumet!" Horemheb hissed anxiously. "Stay awake. We must make a move soon."

They waited for the sky to darken. They were lucky—tonight the moon was obscured by a heavy cloud cover; there was no pale silvery light to limn their forms. Wind began to stir. As he felt Horemheb shiver next to him, he was suddenly aware he was on fire. His head, his face, his body burned with intense heat. His brain baked. He knew what that meant: fever . . . delirium . . . a wound that sped its poison throughout his body. . . .

"Now!" Horemheb whispered and slipped Senumet's good arm over his own broad shoulder. Weakly, Senumet tried to disengage himself. Why should he hold Horemheb back? Why should they both die?

"Leave me. Save yourself."

"Stop wasting time," Horemheb grunted, hoisting Senumet on his back. Stumbling a little, he picked his way down the stairs as silently as he could and moved along the wall until they reached the south gate, from which they would make their way to the sea. No soldiers were posted there. Why should there be? The attackers inside knew they had nothing to fear. Nonetheless Horemheb moved defensively alert until he slipped through the gate. Senumet forced himself to stay conscious, determined to grip Horemheb with his one good arm to ease the burden a little. Each running step Horemheb took sent shocks of pain through him. Through a ringing in his head, he heard Horemheb pant, "We're here!"

Hands reached for him; wooden thwarts supported his back; his nose filled with the oiled fragrance of wood; the couch rocked. Something about a boat nagged at him. "How many?" he managed through cracked lips.

"Eight, now counting the two of you." It was Setekhy who answered.

From a very great distance he heard someone say, "I don't know if we can save the arm." He recognized the voice: Meruka. He was glad Meruka had escaped as well. He strained to listen.

"The arm be damned!" It was Horemheb's voice that barked, "I don't know if we can save him!"

What poor bastard did they talk about? he wondered dully, and tried to listen, but he was spinning away, and their voices faded and finally disappeared.

\* \* \*

All Egypt reeled under the impact of continuously grim tidings. Having barely absorbed Mitanni's loss, they were stunned by the work stoppage at Thebes. No wages, no work. Emboldened by Thebes' action, workers at Bubastis and Ombos joined the strike, and then at Memphis, all cities—like most of the cities and villages in Egypt—with treasuries depleted by mismanagement and Pharaoh's demands for tribute to support Akhet-Aten. Headsmen and officials appointed by Akhenaten feared for their safety, and generals and commanders refused to call out the army against the workers until the strike was beyond the scope of martial force. Egypt was falling apart, without and within. Under Ay's clandestine direction from Zoan, the network of Amon's loyal priesthood fanned the fires of anger against Pharaoh.

Even Akhet-Aten was not spared unrest. The feather and wave of Amon was painted on the dock in large, clumsy, red hieroglyphs. A deep gash obliterated the name of *Aten* from the fifth stella. By night vandals roamed the streets.

In the palace, sickness afflicted the royal family. Only a shadow of her former self, Nefertiti grew even more haggard and haunted. Pharaoh drew into silent melancholy, staring at unseen horrors, letting Bek's translation of cuneiform missives pile up unread. Frail at her arrival three weeks ago, Tiya appeared to shrink and took on the yellow hue of crushed daisies. Light was leaving Akhet-Aten.

On the twelfth day of Sothis, the news reached Egypt that Byblos had fallen. While the army grew fat at home, the Guard, Egypt's most honored soldiers, had been hacked to pieces. Violent mobs rampaged in the streets of Egypt's cities, and at Memphis stoned the priest of Aten in his temple.

When the message detailing Byblos's loss reached the court, Hesen received the news in expressionless silence. Waiting, she had come to accept his death. All this shadowed time when she had dragged through her days, she had been mourning.

That evening Tiya entered her apartment and dismissed her servants. She had been expecting this. She had known her grandmother had a purpose when she first arrived. The old queen had never attempted this trip before. That she had done so now implied she had business so momentous it could not be trusted to a slate tablet in the hands of a messenger, no matter how trusted or how expensively bought.

Tiya proceeded right to the point: "I need your help. Akhenaten's foolish dream must end . . . now, before we're all destroyed. Already the people begin to riot. It could mean open rebellion. We must move first."

"I wish you had seen Akhet-Aten when it was first built," Hesen said—tacit admission that it was finished.

Tiya had no patience for sentiment. "Will Nefertiti help?"

Hesen shook her head.

"I keep thinking it was my fault. I should never have encouraged him or exposed my own unhappiness." Tiya lashed herself bitterly—"I should have given him early to Amenophis to rear."

Hesen had a sudden perception of deep, interlocking layers; truth, hardly discernible at best, was either interspersed through all of them or there not at all. "No, Grandmother, it was a glorious vision."

Tiya looked at her shrewdly. "Enough. There is no gain in reviewing what can't be altered. Let us find Pharaoh."

Akhenaten was in the throne room: That surprised them—he had refused to use it since Nefertiti's meeting with the Mitannis, when blood had been spilled. But tonight he was on his throne, the double crown he had not worn in weeks gleaming with reflected torchlight—symbolizing the power that had come thousands of years before by the union of the Red and Black Lands, combining Upper Egypt's white miter and its serpent of royal glory with Lower Egypt's red crown—the luxuriant ostrich feather binding them both. Hesen felt a thrill of pride whenever she saw him so. He was Egypt—the majesty and the wealth and the brilliance of the Two Lands.

Smenkhare and Meritaten stood before him.

Realizing she hadn't truly looked at her sister lately, Hesen thought suddenly, *This latest pregnancy will come to term.* All the others had run down her legs before her abdomen even had a chance to swell. Smenkhare's hand on her back was more loving, gentler than Hesen had ever seen it.

"Go, now," Pharaoh ordered the prince and the heiress. "We will speak more of this in days to come."

Hesen frowned. She should be pleased that Pharaoh attended to duty—why this clutch of fear? Because his eyes were dead.

As Meritaten glided past, she flashed Hesen a gloriously happy smile, then turned her glowing eyes to Smenkhare, in close attendance next to her, his face, for once, not clouded by sullen temper.

Hesen knelt at her father's feet and kissed his ring, her eyes questioning him silently, but Tiya faced him squarely, pain and pride in her rigid spine.

"So," she said without preamble, "you have moved already, my son."

He reached out for her. Almost unwillingly she moved forward so that he could take her hand. As if at peace—one hand on Hesen's shining hair, the other gripping Tiya's fingers—Pharaoh looked at them both lovingly.

"Listen carefully," he told them, "and remember. It was all done before you came. Neither of you had a part in it. The decision is mine and mine alone; you are to feel no pain and no guilt."

Tiya sank to her knees; her eyes, bright as the decan-atar, fixed on her son.

"As terrible as the destruction outside our borders has been, I have borne it. . . . But now, when rebellion and bloodshed spread to Egypt herself—" He shook his head sadly. "A beautiful dream, the Aten and its truth . . . and it *is* truth—but not for this time. Egypt can't understand it, is not ready to accept it. And I will not have the country torn apart by civil war. Aten will reign here in Akhet-Aten, with me—that is agreed upon. In the rest of our land, Amon-Ra and all the other gods will be permitted to emerge. I do not wish to see this or rule over it; therefore, I have appointed Smenkhare co-Pharaoh. He and Meritaten will rule from Thebes. I won't demean either you, Hesen, or you, Tiya, by asking you to choose where you shall live. I know your hearts. I am nourished by your love. Take courage. Someday, in a future perhaps none of us shall see, Aten will come again. It may be He will bear another name, but He will come. One thing more. Hesen—" For the first time Pharaoh's voice faltered. "I must ask you to tell your mother. You must say—" He couldn't continue. Finally: "If you love me, go . . . now . . . without speaking."

Hesen managed to rise. Feeling as if she'd swallowed something ragged-edged and metallic, she dutifully supported Tiya as the old woman limped the length of the room. Objectively she marveled that there were no limits to pain, that it was impossible to measure agony. At least, she thought grimly, after this, nothing else could possibly increase despair.

She didn't have to tell her mother, after all: Nefertiti discovered it herself. There could be no secrets in the palace, particularly since Meritaten blazed with the joy of Pharaoh's new decree, and was not reticent.

Summoned to the queen's apartments, Hesen went with a reluctance she had never felt before in Nefertiti's presence. But she could not recognize this woman as her mother. The queen's spirit had fled weeks ago, leaving only a carapace, stooped and feverishly bitter.

"So," Nefertiti began. Even her voice was different—brittle and lifeless. "No one had the courage to tell me—not even you, Hesen."

"You don't understand, Mother. Pharaoh has—"

"Pharaoh is weak and unworthy. He lost the vision. I will not see him or live with him again."

"Mother!" The plea was tinged with fear.

"Poor Hesen!"—but Nefertiti's tone was unemotional, the comfort rote. "You must carry every burden. I shall not tell Pharaoh of my decision. *You* must."

"Please," Hesen begged, "think what this will do to him—to us all. You are his strength."

For one brief instant the old Nefertiti flashed in the queen's eyes. "Too many deaths stand between us. I sacrificed everything to Aten. Disavow Him now, and I would have to die." She covered her face.

And Hesen saw that love and understanding and respect were not enough, that the cruel sweep of events could irrevocably spin apart people who cared deeply about each other. And there was nothing she or anyone could do.

# XVIII

Heralds spread the word of the coregency throughout Akhet-Aten, and emissaries were dispatched to all the nomes. The decree stunned Egypt and, initially, increased the very unrest it was designed to allay. Amon would rise again. Would he coexist with Aten or would Aten worshipers be stripped of their wealth? To whose voice should they listen? What would they owe the new king?

Courted and bowed to, Smenkhare expanded with his new importance, even permitted Meritaten a share in the glory as she was swelling with his child. Hesen observed it all with a sorrow beyond tears. Daily, her time was spent attending Pharaoh—keeping him occupied with a succession of minor officials, anything to keep him from noticing that the court's attention had shifted to Smenkhare, anything to prevent him from deciding he must speak to Nefertiti.

Each night she went to her mother, begging reasonably, arguing passionately, but the queen was adamant. She would grant Hesen just one boon; she would wait until Meritaten and Smenkhare left for Thebes before abandoning her husband. In return, she demanded Hesen's help in preparing the north palace for her residence, and Hesen must persuade Tutu to live with her there.

"Why Tutu?" Hesen demanded, unwilling to have him separated from his friends and family.

"Tutu has a loving, warm heart," Nefertiti explained in the dry monotone that had become perpetual. "He is also of royal blood. His faith must be maintained."

The day of the sailing dawned rosy and bright as always. For the second time in two months a significant departure was taking place at Akhet-Aten without ceremonies and blessings. How could Meire, chief priest to Aten, bless the new Pharaoh's journey . . . which would end in the resurrection of Amon-Ra?

And today, directly after the ships had sailed, Nefertiti would leave the court for the north palace. Hesen found it difficult to think as Sephy dressed her. Suddenly she couldn't breathe. Whirling, she swept out on the terrace.

Tutu had just pulled his new chariot into the courtyard. It was heaped with bright painted chests. Surely Nefertiti was not leaving *now* in full view of the entire court! Was Pharaoh to be publicly humiliated?

Hesen flew back through her room and into the hall, turning a deaf ear to Sephy's protest as she hiked her gown to her knees. Running heedlessly down the twisting corridors to Nefertiti's apartments, she caught the queen just as she was sweeping out.

"Wait!" The hand that grasped her mother's arms was not gentle. "You will not leave now!"

Nefertiti looked coolly at Hesen's fingers, but made no attempt to remove them. "I would have spared him this if you had had the courage to tell him. There has been a conspiracy of silence. I will end it now!"

"It should be ended," Hesen agreed, keeping her voice firm. "I'll tell him this very day. Please go back now."

The queen's eyes burned into hers with a fierce black light. "Remove your hand!" Her voice was that low, silken tone Hesen had never been able to counter. Her fingers loosened. Angry at herself for not standing her ground, she followed her mother into the courtyard, her heart pounding. At least, she prayed, let Nefertiti be gone before Akhenaten comes. As she should have known, however, Nefertiti had chosen this time carefully: As the queen swung into the chariot, Pharaoh and his ministers entered the courtyard. He saw Nefertiti: his whole face brightened. Apparently he thought she was coming to join him. He took a joyful step toward her, the despair of weeks suddenly lifting. Nefertiti spun around. She stared intently at him with her burning black eyes, her face as cold as marble. He staggered back as if struck and would have fallen, but Senedjm was there.

Hesen ran to his side. "Father. She will return. She needs time . . ." She went on talking, not knowing what she said—just speaking in soft, low notes of love, her hand steady and warm on his arm.

Finally, with the spastic gait of a sleepwalker, Pharaoh climbed into his chariot, Senedjm on one side, Hesen on the other.

Standing next to Akhenaten, all her attention concentrated on him and his pain, she did not hear the clatter of Nefertiti's carriage, or Tutu's farewell. Before Pharaoh's own horses set in motion, she turned to send the queen a last, mute appeal; she stared at empty space.

At the docks, clusters of those who were being left behind stared belligerently at Pharaoh; he didn't see them. Hesen doubted he saw Meritaten either—resplendent in her Hemhemet crown, waving regally to the people with Smenkhare at her side.

Finally, the boats bearing the new rulers swung into the river.

Back in her rooms, Hesen allowed Sephy her way with her. She sat obediently in the cool bath, let gentle fingers rub her body with scented oils, submitted to being wrapped in soft lengths of linen. Sephy wanted to comfort her. There were some things, however, that couldn't be stroked away.

She waited until the sky darkened and the Nile flashed with purple lights; then she summoned Senedjm.

"I changed his kilt and bathed him," Senedjm reported. "He has not spoken since this afternoon."

"Stay with him." It was a stupid command: Senedjm would never leave. "Come to me again in the morning."

But even his god's light next morning did not lighten Pharaoh's darkness.

In the next few days, Hesen was busier than she had ever been, and while Pharaoh remained unresponsive, not one of her duties gave her the slightest pleasure.

Mornings she spent at Tiya's side. Her grandmother barely rose from deep slumber now. Soon she would slip entirely away, Hesen thought, and better that than watch her son fade before her eyes.

In the late morning and continuing through early afternoon, she would hurry through court duties—receive the few officials, approve mortuary designs, meet with Pharaoh's ministers to plan for the inundation. Then, she was free to spend time with her father.

They led Pharaoh—he followed their commands unprotestingly—to a bench overlooking the Nile. Sitting there, his cloudy eyes watching the river, Hesen at his side, he seemed a little easier. Although he didn't speak to her, occasionally he would press her hand, all he was capable of giving.

Evenings belonged to her sisters. Dislocated by all that had happened, they had been shocked out of their adult poses and seemed to be reverting to the squabbling, squawking infants they no longer were. Bombarded with complaints, besieged by wailings, she tried to be patient and serene, though she wanted to slap them.

Finally, exhausted by her labors, Hesen would sink into dreamless sleep—to rise unrefreshed to a world in which she must careen through the same dreadful routine again. It couldn't continue indefinitely, she knew; something must change it. How profoundly she could not know. But when she saw Senedjm's face that twenty-eighth day of the month Sothis, she knew intuitively that something had occurred which would alter the fabric of her life.

"My lady." Senedjm's voice was a high, thin plea. "This morning he just lay in his bed, his eyes open and staring. It was a long time before he heard me. He waits for you now, my lady, but—" The servant's voice choked.

"Yes?" she demanded.

"I'm frightened."

Hesen hurried to her father. As usual, he had been taken to his place overlooking the Nile, but today he looked old and shriveled sitting there, his flesh hanging in loose folds over his kilt.

"Father," she cried.

Slowly his blank, hurt eyes turned to meet hers. Struggling to respond, all he could manage was a low, moaning "Neferu."

It was torn out of him, the name of his beloved.

Sitting next to him, Hesen forced conviction into her voice. "She needs some time, Father. She'll be back."

"Neferu," Pharaoh crooned. His fingers touched her cheek gently and he smiled as if drunk.

*Aten give me strength*, Hesen prayed instinctively. He mistook her for the queen: "No, Father," she tried helplessly. "I am Hesen your daughter, who loves you."

Her voice seemed to comfort him. Raising her hand to his lips, he kissed it—lingeringly, passionately. Cherishing her hand, he resumed his study of barges and feluccas on the river—oddly, appearing more alert than he had been in days.

Hesen wondered, What terrifying darkness was his soul passing through? Pharaoh's hand holding hers was warm and living. His body yet contained his ka, and somewhere beneath the pain of what he had lost—his dream, his faith, his queen—Pharaoh was still there. She must find him and release him. His eyes continuing to appear intelligent, Pharaoh began to murmur tenderly, but Hesen could not make out the words. She responded with the old, soothing litany. Time passed.

Finally, Senedjm reappeared and guided the king back to the palace.

Mechanically, Hesen went through the duties of her day. Though she tried to stay calm, the squabblings of her sisters over dinner were finally too much.

"Stop your eternal whining," she flared at them. "Go to your rooms and stay there."

Sherit and Neferu, their eyes large and frightened—she had never used that tone with them—fell immediately silent. Penre, who had just taken her first bite of duck, her favorite dish, was less inclined to be pliant. "No, Hesen," she resisted. "I haven't finished!"

"Do you dare raise your voice!" Even the sound of their careful chewing raked her patience raw. "Take them away. No morning meal either; nothing at all until they learn restraint."

The three of them burst into loud wails Hesen could hear all along the route to their quarters until they were finally herded inside. She would make it up to them tomorrow: Could she not for one minute permit herself human emotion? Regretting having banished them, and aware that, fearful of her next outburst, the servants were surrounding her with careful silence, she felt burdened by guilt, only part of which was her sisters. In fact, at its center was Pharaoh's fearful state—and the knowledge, not completely conscious yet, that it was up to her to change this. His sanity was in her charge.

She didn't disrobe that evening but sat in her apartment, dressed and expectant. When the entire court had settled into sleep, the silence was abused by the whisper of Sephy's slippers on the tiled floor and the soft rustle of her gown.

"Senedjm wishes to speak with you."

At Hesen's nod, he materialized at her side. "Pharaoh is very agitated, my lady. He calls for the queen."

She turned to Sephy. Though her consciousness was surprised, she had been waiting for this summons; she knew what she had to do. "Bring me my mother's blue crown." The words were issued in a low tone reminiscent of the queen's. With Pharaoh's very soul endangered by Nefertiti's absence, Hesen, his daughter, must restore his wife.

Sephy wrung her hands. "Foolishness, my lady."

Hesen's eyes flashed. "Get it immediately and be still."

Hesen hardly was aware that time had passed until with trembling fingers, Sephy was sweeping up her hair and lowering the crown on her forehead. It was heavier than Hesen had expected and forced her chin higher than she normally held it. From the shock of surprise on Sephy's face, she knew the crown had changed her. Tonight she would be Nefertiti. Without waiting for makeup, she rose and left the room, keeping her eyes ahead to avoid meeting Sephy's troubled stare. She walked through the corridors, neither hurrying nor hesitating—and read her intention on the stunned face of every guard along the way to the king's chambers.

That surprised her: It was nothing new in Egypt's past for Pharaoh to take his daughter as wife. Why, back no further than Amenophis III, Pharaoh had lain with Sit-Amon, his daughter, and from that union had come Smenkhare, who now sat on the throne, and Tutu, next in line. It was not until the sentry outside Pharaoh's room fell to his knees at her approach, murmuring "Highness," that she realized they did not recognize her—they thought Nefertiti had returned. She took a deep breath and entered her father's chamber.

"Leave us," she ordered the servants attending him. She waited until they hurried to obey before turning to Pharaoh. Then quickly she covered the length of the huge room, her sandals clicking on the mosaic floor. In this brief but expanded moment she was surrealistically aware of the intricate pattern of the floor, its dark-blue surface broken by the brilliant orange and yellow of the representation of Aten. The god's hands radiated to all corners of the room.

> *Help me, O Lord*
> *Who bindest me by Thy love:*
> *Though Thou art on high,*
> *Thy footprints are the day,*
> *The warmth of thy fingers are my strength. . . .*

She stood at Pharaoh's side. Thrashing and twisting on the carved wooden bed, he was tangled in the thin covers, sweat glistening on his naked body.

Hesen stood beside him, composed. "Dearest, what is this?"

His head whipped around. "Neferu," he breathed tremulously, a grateful prayer.

"Wait, my dearest." With his eyes drinking in the sight of her, she untied her gown and let it fall. His fingers touched her breast, his thumb pressing the hardening nipple. He closed his eyes, his body trembled with expectancy. "Beloved." His voice was stronger than it had been for days.

Breasts tingling from his touch, all her being committed to saving him, Hesen eased her slim body onto the bed next to his, touched his length with her cool, firm flesh.

Pharaoh's breathing quickened. Turning on his side, he pressed his mouth against her neck, her breast, her stomach. His hands stroked her thighs, his fingers covering her curling pubic hair, pushing deeper to the warm moistness within.

Hesen's body shivered with what she hoped simulated passion. Blood of his blood, bone of his bone, she returned freely to her beginnings, of her own will gave him back what he had fashioned.

His body was alive now as he pulled her closer; his hands were demanding, his mouth insistent on her breast. Her hands dug into his arm, guided him on top of her. She spread her legs as his weight pressed on her, his bulk overflowing her body until she was almost smothered under its spreading flesh.

She reached between his legs to guide his sex to her entrance—plunged through his coarse, sparse hair—and could find no bud of manhood.

Heart thudding painfully, she rolled him unprotesting on his back, working her mouth over his in the way Senumet—in the way she had learned. Hands stroking him, she moved her lips along his body, searching, in the flickering light of the alabaster lamps, for his hardened manhood.

When she found his penis, it shocked her—small, soft and flaccid, jerked upward in weak, unsuccessful movements. Her eyes filled with tears.

With a skill born of desperation, she straddled his body, took his limp sex into her mouth and nourished it, her tongue licking it, her lips closing, willing her own vitality to give it life. It swelled in her mouth. When it was firm, guiding it between her legs, hot now and pulsing, she lowered herself to thrust it into her entrance.

Both hands on Pharaoh's chest, she pumped her hips. And while her father's eyes closed and he moaned at the pleasure of her warm, sweet body, she loved him, prayed for him . . . yet felt like a spectator, watching as she moved on top of him, pressed her mouth against his, stroked his legs. Looking at his passion in the lamplight, she saw the firm, strong thighs of someone else, held the muscled arms of another man. And when Pharaoh came inside her with explosive force and shuddered into deep unbroken sleep, it was another man she comforted in her arms . . . and the bittersweet tears that fell on Pharaoh's shoulder were for someone else.

She must have drifted, finally, into exhausted unconsciousness. When she opened her eyes, Aten had made the room a golden dazzle and Pharaoh, dressed and smiling, watched her with clear, unclouded eyes.

"Father, you're back!" she cried, making no attempt to cover her nakedness.

"Yes, my daughter, sister, wife—for you are all those to me now—I am myself. And I shall proclaim today, to all of Akhet-Aten, what you have in fact become to me."

He sent her servants to her in the king's quarters—but they already had foreknowledge of her presence there. Sephy dressed her with meticulous care, encircling her arms with the glittering shine of gold bracelets, slipping a cobra ring of power on her third finger, hooping gold and lapis through her ears. When she came to Hesen's hair, she merely brushed it so that it shone resplendent with its own blue-black lights—then Sephy waited.

"The queen's crown," Hesen ordered. The words were bitten off in a sharp intake of breath then Hesen summoned exoneration: Nefertiti should not have taken it off—with that act she had relinquished her right to it.

Still Sephy hesitated. "You are certain, my lady?"

Hesen looked at her steadily. "Dare you question my command?"

Dressed as a queen, she rode, Pharaoh at her side, to the Temple of Aten. The people of Akhet-Aten stared as they passed and she read on their faces first confusion as to her identity, then recognition. Some, sharper than their neighbors, bowed to her, some called her Highness.

Meire, chief priest to Aten, waited for them in the courtyard of the temple—the gold symbol of the god blazing on his forehead, his priests in parallel lines behind him, their robes rippling in the morning breeze. Beyond them, Hesen could see the sparkling Nile. As she allowed Pharaoh to help her alight, her heart was filled with equal portions of love and fear. What if this peace he had found was too fragile to last?

"I wish to announce a new queen," he proclaimed to the waiting priests. "Ankhesenpaaten—the king's daughter, of my body, whom I love—I now name great royal wife. My beloved, mistress of the Two Lands, Ankhesenpaaten—living and flourishing forever and ever."

His hand at her waist, he led her to the priest. Meire fell to his knees and raised her hand to his lips declaring his loyalty. The line of priests followed suit.

They were standing beneath the second stela. As Hesen watched, her hand on her father's arm, an acolyte was sent scampering up its face. Taking a chisel with him, the boy struck out Nefertiti's name. Each hammer blow echoed in Hesen's heart. When the name of her mother had been obliterated from the stone—to be replaced later with her own—so was Nefertiti erased from her daughter's heart.

As of this hour, Hesen was queen.

Ankhesenpaaten. The king's daughter. His wife.

# XIX

From the balcony of the palace at Zoan, Ay stared at the pieces of gleaming pink sandstone.

This morning, when servants entered the palace garden, they had found the monumental statue of Akhenaten smashed and scattered over flower beds of blue lotuses and buttercups. Pharaoh's face, serene and beneficent, his inlaid, shining eyes radiating wisdom, his hands clasped on his chest in knowing acceptance of the crook and flail of power. Crushed! The inlaid eyes gouged out; the nose hacked off. Pharaoh's ka symbolically blinded; the very air stopped from his nostrils; his power as diffused as his arms, each hurled to opposite ends of the garden, and the crook and flail broken off.

Ay had been called when the damage was discovered. Returning now, he experienced the same shock. To have felt such outrage that they would hack Pharaoh's body to fragments—and in such a way as to *damn him forever!*

This destruction of Pharaoh's hallowed image, however, was Ay's triumph. More than shock, he felt gratification.

"Yes?" he said to the servant who approached.

"A boat has docked from Thebes. The headman sent me to inform you."

When he reached the dock and saw who disembarked, Ay tensed with surprise. Tushratta! If Tushratta could be spared from Thebes, order must have been restored there. Had Nacht broken—had the garrison acted to police the workers and rioters? Was his strategy of disruption, Ay wondered, beginning to go askew?

Ay drew himself up to his full height and greeted his ally ceremonially, observing with urgent curiosity that the old priest's robes were rich linen, his girdle a fine gold mesh. Over his shoulders was the leopard robe of priestly office, in his hand the staff of Amon as in the days of Amon's reign. How—why did the old priest dare? The dockworkers were falling to their knees, a crowd was gathering to wonder and worship. Ay led the old man from the wharf to a garden path, secluded and lightly trafficked.

"You wear your tidings. Explain them," Ay demanded.

"Of such import, I had to be the one to bear them."

"For the love of Amon, speak!"

"Smenkhare and Meritaten are come to Thebes—"

"That is of no great moment." Only extreme self-discipline kept Ay from striking Tushratta.

"Smenkhare comes as co-Pharaoh and Meritaten as queen." The old priest's voice quavered to its highest pitch. "And Amon-Ra has come again!"

"And what of Akhenaten?"

"Akhenaten himself decreed the coregency and will permit the true gods to be worshiped again. The Aten will reign only in his city."

Ay considered and with grudging admiration admitted, "Always I underestimate Akhenaten. Damned hermaphrodite's craftier than I ever gave him credit for. But this time his move comes too late. If he plans to placate the people temporarily and then spring Aten on them again, he has miscalculated. Aten is permanently vanquished."

Tushratta stroked the symbol-of-Amon ring he wore again on his finger. "The first thing we did was reopen the temple. Now we're bringing back its treasures. Nofret is preparing to leave."

"Smenkhare is very like his father," Ay reflected. "He'll be easily controlled."

"Already he has turned to us. He begged me to end the work stoppage: I did, of course. He is appropriately grateful."

"And Meritaten is a biddable girl. . . ."

Tushratta's head trembled with his effort to control his excitement. "At Akhet-Aten, Nefertiti has been banished to the north palace. She is no longer queen."

Shock flickered over Ay's face, but he recovered quickly. "Oh, come now, Tushratta. Whose message bearer have you become? What kind of a fool do they suppose me?"

Tushratta's smile widened. He delivered his last piece of news: "Like you, I was stunned. But it's all quite true. You see, he has a new queen now—his daughter, Ankhesenpaaten."

"Hesen!" Ay exploded, and had sudden kaleidoscopic visions of a slight girl clasped to the breast of her bloated grandfather, a sunlit young woman clad in gold on the royal barge docked at Thebes, and a mourning princess sitting beside him on a funereal boat only a few years ago, explaining how she could hold both gods in her heart. A ripe, beautiful copy of her mother, Nefertiti's equal in royal bearing, but more clear-eyed, more pragmatic, more willing to compromise. . . . Hesen, indeed!

Oh, much better this way! Better to spare Egypt the agonies of revolution: better to return gradually to the old ways—to have a brief respite before he made his final bid for power. In the glorious resurrection of Amon, Thebes would be strong and prominent and solidly under his control. There would be time now for his plans to ripen gradually in the course of events.

On the fourth day after Tushratta's arrival, the barge from Gaza, carrying the survivors of Byblos, was sighted. At the call, waiting crowds of nobles and peasants who had come from the expanse of Egypt rushed to the landing. With infinite slowness, the shape of the barge took on definition, grew larger, and entered the harbor. The crowds cheered as the crewmen threw heavy mooring ropes to the dockmen, who secured the lines. Hundreds of hands helping, the landing ramp was soon in place.

First the commander of the rescue vessel appeared, his face wreathed in smiles. Then the first Egyptian guard stood at the head of the ramp, one side of his face swollen and discolored from a massive bruise.

Ay sprinted up the ramp and flung his arms around the man, who was gaunt from suffering. "Horemheb!" Ay's voice choked. "Never did I think to see you again."

"Nor I Egypt." Horemheb returned Ay's embrace. "But look, there are six more, as well as a corpse to be prepared for a burial of honor—Hapu died on our way home."

One by one the survivors appeared to thunderous cheering. Four of them were capable of marching down the ramp, although three limped badly. The last two were carried on litters, and one of these had his entire right side bandaged and his arm strapped to his body.

His eyes dark slits, skeletally thin, his skin chalk, this last survivor was conscious but so weak he could hardly exert himself to force a cracked smile.

"Senumet!" Ay cried, appalled, and clasped his protégé's good hand.

The six were taken to Usherhet's estates to rest and regain strength. In the evening, Ay met privately with Horemheb. He did not interrupt often, though parts of the story confused him. He realized Horemheb would need time before he could speak calmly of the events he had lived through. What was clear from the painful omissions and disjointed narrative was that Horemheb (indeed, all of them) had seen horrors that would follow them all their days.

Ay could see Horemheb suffered from recurrent attacks of blinding pain. Periodically he would stop speaking and grip his head, shuddering until the seizure passed. Finally, he concluded, "To the end Senumet was a brother to me. Twice we saved each other's lives. I am grateful the gods spared him to return with us."

"What injuries has he sustained?"

"His shoulder was crushed, his arm badly slashed. I fear he'll never use his right hand again. A small price, for survival!"

Ay pressed his shoulder. "What you did rivals the courage even of Menes, who united Egypt. Perhaps it will lighten your own suffering to know you will be granted Supreme Commander of the Army."

Threateningly, Horemheb leaned forward. "I renounce it. I will not serve Pharaoh any longer. I cannot serve a man who refuses to protect his dependents from such barbarism. Supreme general, bah!"

"Listen well, Horemheb. Much has happened since you left. You may still wish to serve Egypt."

Gradually, as Ay recounted the recent events, Horemheb's expression changed. "You will send me to Thebes, then, to serve under Smenkhare?"

"Yes." Ay suppressed a smile. He had wanted for many years to sever Horemheb from Akhenaten. He had him now, not yet ready to lift a sword against Pharaoh, but no longer staunch in his support. "When you are fully recovered, you will go to Thebes and assume your command there."

"Thank you, my lord."

"I must talk with Senumet, too. You will inform me when he is sufficiently strong."

"Yes, my lord."

While Senumet recovered slowly, Ay had other matters to attend to. First, he must stem the tide of fury unleashed by the sight and stories of the half-starved, maimed survivors. He and Tushratta delivered glorious harangues, promising the populace that Smenkhare, now co-Pharaoh, was a man in his father's mold, a veritable lion who would soon avenge Egypt's losses. Their promises, along with the reopening of the temple of Amon-Ra and of Geb, the local god, diffused the first burst of rage. The remaining discontent the priests channeled into honoring the survivors, heaping them with the traditional gold collars, carving their exploits on stone pillars. As Ay had intended, anger turned to pride.

Initially, they told Senumet nothing of recent events, and he asked nothing. Lying on scented sheets in a quiet room in Usherhet's house, he was filled with gladness that he was alive, that he was home. Too weak even to feed himself, he didn't yet wonder about his shoulder or notice that he couldn't move his arm. That his immediate physical needs were attended to was all that mattered. When he was strong enough to sit up and to try a few faltering steps, Senumet began to ask questions. A team of physicians visited him regularly. His arm was unwrapped and studied, his shoulder and elbow palpatated gently, his fingers pricked with a thin needle. Twice daily the arm was thoroughly massaged, anointed with holy oils and strung with amulets. The remainder of the time, splints, made of the rod of Nektanebos, immobilized it.

"You are fortunate to have survived the massacre," the senior doctor, Khufu, responded evasively.

"So having my life spared is boon enough for the loss of function in my arm. I take it from your expression that loss will be permanent."

Khufu smiled gently. "Because your arm was not set immediately, it healed improperly. You have lost all function—yes, I will not lie to you—but we have done what we could. Now we can only watch—and I think we can hope for some restoration."

"Thank you for your efforts," Senumet tried. "But for a scribe to hear of loss of his right hand—" He bit off the words. How did he dare think only of his selfish concerns when so many . . . "Happily"—he was recovered now—"a diplomat needs only the use of his tongue, which has always been the more potent tool."

"Senumet will yet make his greatest mark," Khufu offered graciously, before leaving.

His arm becoming less painful, his strength returning, his mind active again, Senumet grew restless. He lived for Horemheb's daily visits, yet when he questioned his friend about the royal family and the state of Egypt, only his long training as a diplomat kept him from revealing how shocked he was at the answers. Amon above him, so many changes! Hearing that his Hesen was queen to a dying city and a lost Pharaoh—for that was how Horemheb described Akhenaten—Senumet knew he must not reveal his true feelings until he determined Horemheb's position.

"What shall you do?" he asked.

"I'll serve Smenkhare at Thebes."

Senumet could understand it. Horemheb's inability to serve under Akhenaten was implicit in everything that had happened.

"And you?" Horemheb asked.

Whose loyalties will never change, Senumet thought desperately, knowing he must get to Akhet-Aten as quickly as he could and see her, help her. "I'd like to consult Ay," he said levelly. "I want to return to whatever duties I may still perform."

"Amon works in unfathomable ways. The old beliefs are stronger than ever and freely followed again. I've been meeting with Ay, too. He has great need of ambassadors he can trust to inform him about the empire and, even more important, about the happenings at Akhet-Aten." Horemheb said the words casually enough, but Senumet realized suddenly that as he himself was offering only half-truths, Horemheb was testing him. Ay and the priests must be sure that, if he had once felt love for the queen, the emotion had not survived the destructiveness of Aten, his own sufferings, the fate of hundreds of dead comrades.

"It would be very hard for me to see Akhenaten again. I'm not sure I could do it." Senumet paused for effect, playing Horemheb's emotions skillfully, regretting that nothing could bind them together as before in this world where it was impossible to be totally candid, even to a brother. Whether or not Horemheb was conscious of being used, he was, in fact, a spy, sent by Ay to question his scribe brother, certain Senumet would bare his true feelings. So be it. But they must never know he had but one loyalty, which transcended every other human emotion.

Later when he met with Ay, his interview proceeded so easily that Senumet knew Horemheb must have spoken with him first; and after a show of appropriate reluctance—deeply felt silences, hesitant objections, choked responses—Senumet permitted himself to be recruited in Ay's service. Ay felt confident enough to hint that Senumet might use his long-standing friendship with the new queen—if, of course, he could bring himself to do so—to further the great cause.

Senumet, barely able to control his pounding heart, promised only that he would do his best. After seeing so much horror, and all of it Pharaoh's doing, he might not be able to deal with the royal family. Was Ay sure he should be the delegate to Ahket-Aten?

Each demurral increased Ay's certainty—as Senumet knew it must. In the end, Ay was so eager to learn of the intrigues at Akhet-Aten that a boat to bear Senumet on his way was readied with unprecedented haste. In two days' time—sooner, actually, than was wise, given his incomplete physical recovery—Senumet set sail. An emotional farewell with Horemheb the night before had further drained his strength. They had been through so much together, had so come to rely on each other that it was hard to part, particularly when Senumet knew their goals no longer coincided. He had always taken pleasure from standing at the rail and watching the city recede, but as the barge pulled into the river, he lay on his pallet, dizzy with emotions he couldn't name. And though he wished for journey's end above all else, he forced himself to be patient. He knew he must have time to strengthen himself emotionally, physically, even spiritually, for seeing her again. He husbanded his depleted resources, rested more than he normally would, consumed healthful meals, made himself exercise regularly. Even so, his first glimpse of Akhet-Aten almost completely unnerved him.

From a distance, it glowed as it always had, the sun dancing on its bright buildings; but as the ship drew closer, it quickly became apparent that the once-splendid city had been drained of vitality and life. The dock, once jammed with ships, was largely empty. On his way to the palace, Senumet's was the only chariot in the streets, and the handful of passersby stared at him curiously. The markets were almost all closed; the few shops still open were sparsely stocked —and that merchandise more than enough to meet the needs of the remaining customers. The Maru-Aten was empty, a thin layer of sand covering its pavements and green scum lying in ugly patches on once-sparkling lakes. Yet the temples were still tended, the Kings-Way gleamed as he remembered it; and the gates to the royal palace swung open with military precision to admit his chariot. As he entered, he suddenly realized he irrationally hoped that Hesen would welcome him personally—and felt a ridiculously fierce disappointment when she wasn't there.

Bek was delighted to see him, as were the other scribes, the remaining guards and bureaucrats. Hailing him as a hero, plying him with hyperbolic praise, they carefully avoided questions about his arm—although he knew they all were glancing at it surreptitiously. The evening meal was to be a banquet in his honor. Celebrations being rare at Akhet-Aten, the entire court was almost childishly eager for the occasion. As Senumet finished dressing for it, Senedjm came to his room.

"Their Majesties wish to see you."

There were no words he wanted more to hear, yet as he followed the servant, his steps dragged with his reluctance to know her new role had changed her. He was brought to the south garden; that surprised him—he would have thought audiences were granted in the throne room. The king and queen were sitting together on a simple bench, Pharaoh intent on studying the river. Grateful for the opportunity, he stared unabashedly at Hesen. Oh, Isis, blessed mother, no goddess could be lovelier! Even the sadness on her face had graced her features with a special charm; and as today's joy transformed her, her delicate golden crown of twisted flower stems was no brighter than her eyes. She rose in a graceful flowing motion. He fell to the soft ground at her feet, and trembling as he knelt before her, pressed cold lips against the living warmth of a hand he had never hoped to touch again.

"Highness," he managed, "all who see you, great and small, must honor you. You are queen; there is none beside you."

Her fingers moved under his until their hands clasped.

"When Byblos fell, I mourned you as dead. To see you is . . . as if the gods had freshly created you." She turned to Pharaoh, her voice soft and low. "Look, beloved, here is your loyal ambassador returned to Akhet-Aten. You must greet Senumet, your friend."

Pharaoh's head swiveled obsequiously at her summons, and suddenly Senumet understood: Akhenaten was not sane! Wiped clean of concern, of strain, of even the characteristic deep lines of suffering, his face was as smooth and as blank as a fresh papyrus roll.

"Welcome to Akhet-Aten, Senumet," he said as bid, and turned to Hesen with a bright, expectant smile.

"Very good, dearest." She pressed his hand. He sighed contentedly before turning back to his absorption with the empty river.

To Senumet she said levelly, "Unfortunately, we will not be able to attend your banquet, but we wanted to welcome you personally and convey our gladness that you are safely returned. All Egypt commends your heroism."

"Thank you, Highness." He bowed, took his leave. Of course they'd be unable to come to court. It was incredible that she had managed to maintain even this semblance of normalcy—and all alone. Oh, his brave, gallant love!

In outward form the banquet was like the feasts of the past. Differences were trivial. Talk was a bit louder, drunkenness started a bit earlier, jokes were a bit more cruel. But taken in sum, the effect was unsettling, as if the missing center, which everyone tried to avoid, was the focus of attention.

For several hours of torturous gaiety, Senumet managed to appear cheerful, applaud when appropriate, laugh at the ribald jests. He even nuzzled the naked slaves as was expected of a warrior who had endured a long, painful abstinence. But his endurance was limited. Finally, using his injury as excuse, he made an early departure.

Telling himself he needed to walk alone, refusing to admit the hope in his heart, he slipped unobserved along the familiar path that skirted the line of tall sycamores to her Sun-Shade. He paused outside the door, irresolute. She was the queen. She could not be there. Almost involuntarily his hand reached out to slide open the door; he pulled it back. Why prove that it was locked? His mouth a tight line, he reached out again. Blessed Amon! It moved freely and easily under his hand.

Hesen had been waiting so long, staring so intently at the door, her eyes were glazed. As in a dream Senumet was suddenly standing in front of her.

Neither spoke. Motionless, they drank in the sight of each other. Hesen felt tears rise in her throat; she choked them back. He was so thin! In the flickering light of the oil lamp, deep shadows hollowed out his cheeks. He was half turned away from her, his right side obscured. Her heart began to hammer in her chest: in their first meeting, with its mixture of private magic and public ceremony, she had not thought to assess the extent of his injury.

"Let me see your arm." These were not the first words she had planned when she dreamed of this reunion.

Obediently he turned. His arm hung limp and useless; his fingers, through which the gods had spoken, curved inward toward the palm; bound to stillness. He closed his eyes.

"Beloved." His pain revived her. He must not doubt her love.

"So you are queen." His voice seemed to come from a great distance.

But it was Senumet's voice. Suddenly it didn't matter to Hesen what words he chose—or how clumsy she sounded in her turn. Joy made her tremble. Incredibly, he was here—alive.

"Queen to a dying city and a dying king," she said. She would let him know at once she understood her position.

"But not alone any longer." He took a step toward her.

"Are you to stay?" She had not dared hope he might remain.

"I am ordered here to spy on you. By Ay, of all people." He laughed aloud, and was shocked at the sound. Moving toward him until their bodies almost touched, Hesen placed a soft finger on his lips. They moved, savoring the shock of her touch. "I haven't tasted mirth in weeks."

Gently at first she brushed her lips to his, then more insistently, expertly working their tongues together. His good hand moved, lovingly encircled her as he drank in her sweet breath, felt her shuddering sigh.

They slid to the tile floor.

"We are not careless lovers anymore," he cautioned.

Inwardly she smiled at his fear that they would not find the same rapture together. It was true that she was not the same, but not all changes were detrimental. She had learned many arts in his absence. They would know even greater delight. Her eyes bright with tears, she moved a hand to his groin . . . to press and warm and caress in ways she had not tried to please him with before.

And Senumet understood. He felt his sex harden, let her ease him onto his back and raise herself above him. As she guided his penis between her thighs, every part of his body seemed to awake to the joy of that warm, lithe length on top of him. He had never cherished or honored her more than he did now . . . his love who had offered her own sweet gift to another man—to Pharaoh, who had such need of her—and offered it with that reckless generosity which was as much a part of her as her extraordinary beauty and her bright, courageous spirit. And before he was engulfed by passion and became unable to think coherently, he knew that even though it would last only until poor mad Akhenaten was destroyed, they would know happiness.

# XX

Three days after Senumet's return to Akhet-Aten, Tiya, the Great Wife of Amenophis III, slipped away painlessly, almost willingly, preferring death to what her world had become.

After seventy days of preparation, her body was carried to its final resting place in the hills above Pharaoh's city. The queen's tomb was a glorious tribute to Aten. Surrounded by walls depicting the founding of the city, Tiya's body lay in its open alabaster sarcophagus. On the ceiling glittered the golden Aten, his hands reaching down to bless His daughter lovingly.

At Meire's side as he began the last rites, Hesen mourned only that there were so few to mark the queen's passing. Akhenaten was not there; he could not grasp who had died, and Hesen was afraid the funeral would shatter his fragile peace. Nefertiti declined to emerge from the north palace, and refused to allow Tutu to attend without her.

Meire held up a curled and twisted rod, the adze that would symbolically open the queen's mouth, so that, when her ka united with her body, she would have the power of speech. Meire touched the rod to the lips of the gold face-mask, molded in Tiya's image, that covered her mummy's bound head. Except for the gold, and despite the mummy's protective amulets and their own potent prayers, the linen-wrapped form seemed small and slight, almost negligible.

"The servants of Aten purify Tiya." Meire's voice echoed in the caverns:

> *"We bathe her and dry her,*
> *We recite for her the spell of the right way*
> *We recite for her the spell of the ascent*
> *We open her mouth and give her speech.*
> *Tiya, our daughter, ascends to heaven:*
> *She embarks in the boat of Aten;*
> *She will emerge at the eastern side of heaven*
> *In peace, in peace."*

Hesen stood dry-eyed as the alabaster lid was sealed forever over the body of her grandmother, who had ruled for so long, who had loved and hated and felt pain and plotted badly and well. Tears would be superfluous; the old queen's life had been full and rich, and she had called for her own death.

While Hesen had been overseeing the works for the entombment of Tiya, Senumet took it upon himself to rescue Tutu from the oppressiveness of the north palace. Nefertiti granted him permission to visit, and when he was announced for the first time, Tutu dashed down the corridors to meet him, his dogs racing with him and barking joyously.

"Senumet!" Impetuously Tutu threw his arms around his old friend, then cried in remorse, "Oh, your arm—did I hurt you?"

Senumet gripped Tutu's hard, velvet waist with his good arm. "No, you didn't hurt me. That arm has almost no feeling. And it's a joy seeing you again."

"I honor you for your wound," Tutu burst out.

"Thank you, my Prince. I was honored—as you would have been—to serve Egypt. I have something for you that Horemheb and I thought you'd like to possess."

"I wish he had come to Akhet-Aten, too. I so would like to see him."

"Come," Senumet suggested, anxious to escape the somber palace, "let's drive along the beach in your chariot. There I'll give you your gift."

Tutu handled the reins with dangerous flamboyance, recklessly expending his pent-up restless energy, and he careened the vehicle to a halt in great swirls of sand that almost obscured the whole chariot and filled Senumet's face with grit. Tutu led his old tutor to a rocky precipice overlooking the Nile.

"Hesen and I walked along here every day, watching for your boat and praying for you," Tutu confided, as they sat down together.

"We were protected by your prayers, I know. When we escaped, Horemheb took a Hittite ax as a precaution against enemies. We both want you to have it now."

Watching Tutu unwrap the bulky package, Senumet felt his own mouth curve. Though he was growing to young manhood in a complex, political court, Tutu had no duplicity in him. All his earnest and generous feelings were written clearly on his face. How in the name of Amon, Senumet wondered, not for the first time, had lecherous, corrupt old Amenophis spawned this warm, loving boy?

Layer by layer Tutu peeled back the wrappings of woven hemp until he exposed the Hittite ax, wickedly gleaming.

"Aten protect us!" he gasped. On the head a warlike vulture had been painted; blood dripped from its twisted claws, and its beak was sharp and aggressive. "What is this?"

"That's Mithras, their fierce and terrible god."

Tutu placed the weapon across his knees. "I know only that Byblos was overthrown. I don't know the story at all. Would you tell me, please?"

Patiently, he recreated the battle of Byblos—the valor, the glory, the waste. Knowing how the boy loved Horemheb, he gave that soldier central place.

The story concluded, they sat silently for a few minutes, Tutu turning the ax in his hands. "So Horemheb will stay at Thebes," he said at last.

"Yes."

"It's very lonely here. Of course, this is an important post for a soldier. The queen needs me."

"There are not many," Senumet offered, "who could serve with the same grace."

"You really think so."

"I know it." Senumet paused. "As you know, I can be a scribe no longer, I must make new plans. Would you like to study with me?" The boy needed something to occupy him.

"Above all else!"

Senumet smiled in spite of himself. Tutu's answer was a measure of his boredom: that he should welcome the idea of being a student!

"Shall I ask the queen, then?"

Tutu's face hardened. "No need. She only cares that I pray."

With the daily lessons and tending to Pharaoh, Senumet and Hesen's days slipped into comfortable, gloriously placid patterns, interrupted only by the event of Tiya's funeral. And Hesen found herself again consumed by an overwhelming passion . . .

Since Senumet's return, she had gently discouraged Pharaoh's need of her body. Although they shared the same bed, she gratefully discovered Akhenaten was content merely to feel her cool limbs next to his, to rest his head on her breasts, to breathe her mother's name. Justifying her one selfishness, she told herself, yes, she could have aroused him, but, as she had seen, taking his seed into her body did not restore him to the world. And could never restore his world to him. She comforted him, held him, loved him. But the child she would bear would be Senumet's.

She watched for the early signs of pregnancy with longing. Even before she could expect the absence of monthly bleeding, she noticed darkening and broadening in the areola surrounding her nipples. She felt a flutter of hope.

The menstrual time came and went, and there was no bleeding. This time Sephy did not frown or scold. Her hands were gentle and loving.

During their meetings, Senumet traced the veins that grew prominent on her breasts and cupped their increasing fullness with speculative eyes. But he said nothing. He would never suspect she had discarded the shield she used with him.

The time of the second bleeding passed, and she decided she must tell him before the court buzzed with the news.

She chose the moment after the messages from Thebes were received, and they walked together in the garden. He had been translating from hieratic into polished speech. "To Akhenaten, Pharaoh of Egypt, Lord of the Two Lands, from his brother, King of Egypt, Smenkhare of Thebes. The country is restored to order. The temples flourish. Amon-Ra is again bright and Nehkbet spreads her wings over us all. Our wife and daughter, Meritaten, Queen of the Two Lands, will soon birth the first claimant to the throne. Blessed be Akhenaten, son of Aten: may he flourish forever."

Hesen's mouth tightened. "How poetically Ka-Aper has rendered Smenkhare's grunts!"

Senumet laughed.

"I have news too," she plunged ahead, "but only, now, for your ears. There will be another royal child—though not, I thank Aten, first claimant to the throne."

His forehead creased. "Does Pharaoh know?"

"My love. Is that all you can say to me?"

"I know you want a child. I cannot be glad." He stood rigid fighting for control. "Forgive me, beloved. It seems a bad time. . . . politically."

Hesen knew he lied, understood that though he had accepted the fact that Pharaoh was her husband, he couldn't bear that she might nourish any man's seed but his own. "We cannot always choose our time," she said reasonably—while her heart sang: for she *had* chosen her time. *Now* was her time, and she had chosen him.

"I take it our meetings in the temple must stop now."

"Nonsense! We may continue to meet for some months yet."

At another time he might have protested; she understood he was not yet able to limit their time together. Their daily trysts continued, though he was gentler with her and very tender. Soon she noticed her waist thickening and gloried in the small mound her belly was becoming.

Noticing the change, the court responded with the warm interest breeding always created. Even Pharaoh smiled at the news, slept at night with his hand curled on her belly. Once, he put his head on its soft swelling and she felt his tears.

At first she had chafed at the hours lost sitting with Pharaoh. Now it exactly suited her—the sun warm on her back, the hum of small insects, the perfume of the flowers. Drowsing, her arm linked through her father's, she would drift in and out of easy slumber, hugging the blissful knowledge of the child thriving and growing inside her.

This afternoon she had slipped into a dream: They sat by the river, the child playing at Pharaoh's feet. Drawn to the child's antics, Pharaoh smiled. . . .

Suddenly spasms in Pharaoh's arm awakened her. His hand shaking uncontrollably, he pointed to the river. Approaching the harbor, a black-draped ship sliced through the sparkling waters, the bright feluccas hastily clearing a path.

"No, no, Father," she soothed. "Truly. It's nothing." She clapped her hands sharply for Senedjm, and as he led Pharaoh away, she shivered with flashes of fear. *Aten, dear Father, who now?*

For a moment she watched the ship. When she rose, she saw Senumet striding toward her, his face a stern mask.

"It's Meritaten," he said without preamble.

"In childbirth?" Somehow she got out the words, her hands crossed over her abdomen.

"The child lives. A girl."

She could hardly hear him, there was such a roaring in her head. Only his eyes, alive and burning with love, kept her upright. Obedient, compliant Meritaten, who had longed so for Thebes, would never leave it now, would sleep forever in those stark hills. Hesen moaned, a little sound of pure pain.

"Highness!" Senumet couldn't touch her, surrounded by servants as they were, but she steadied at his voice. "Listen to me, Hesen!" He saw how she cradled her abdomen: he knew her fear. "Meritaten's daughter *lives*. Tey will nurse her. The infant is already betrothed. Think! You remember that Tashray, Ay's concubine, had a child, *a boy*. Your sister's babe is already betrothed to Bata, Ay's son. The succession is assured. *Your child is safe*."

Gradually the stiffness left Hesen's body. "Thank you, Senumet." Her voice was a whisper, but she was in control again. "I must go to my temple, now, to pray for Meritaten."

"Yes, Highness." Senumet bowed as she moved past him. Counting minutes, he waited for an interval. Then he took a circuitous route to her Sun-Shade.

As soon as he was inside, she flung herself on his chest and fell into a wild fit of weeping. He didn't try to stop her, just held her and stroked her, his brave, lost love—who had shouldered great burdens, but who finally could bear no more. At last the sobs lessened.

"Listen, beloved—" he began.

"No, Senumet. Listen to me. All I can think about is my child. You must promise me one thing."

Her fingernails dug into his arm with more strength than seemed possible: she had drawn blood. "What, my dearest?" he asked, keeping his voice calm.

"Don't treat me like a demented child you must quiet! Promise me you'll do whatever I ask. Promise!" Her voice rose hysterically.

"I promise," he said quickly, although he had no idea what she referred to.

"If you fail me, you shall dwell in the darkness of the west," she recited out of her childhood prayers. "With no door, no window, no light to illuminate it, no north wind to refresh the heart."

"If I betray you, I will live there gladly." He couldn't tell whether she had even heard him.

Her eyes, burning with a fierce blue-black light, stared through him at some lonely, terrifying vision. "The sun will not rise there. You will live all your days in fearful darkness."

"All that I accept."

She drew a deep, shuddering breath.

"What do you want of me, my love?" he asked gently.

"If I should die—"

"You won't." He cut her off.

"If I should die," she went on relentlessly, "you must promise me one thing. You are to see to my child. *You and you alone.* My child must not fall into Ay's hands."

He was appalled. "How can that be? It will be a royal child."

"I don't care how. If you must steal the child and hide it, if you must be an outcast and a criminal all your life, so be it. Who, besides you, could my child turn to—poor mad Pharaoh . . . Smenkhare . . . Nefertiti? Senumet, *Ay must not get his hands on my child.*"

"I am yours." He gripped her hands. "I will never abandon your child, I swear it, beloved, in the name of our love."

"Pledged, I see"—she smiled shakily, touching the red welt on his arm—"with your own blood."

"You were more forceful than perhaps was necessary," he tried, anxious to lighten her mood—but her eyes filled with tears and he saw she was still threatened by that wild, dark storm.

"I am with you, my darling," he said softly, "and we can stay here awhile yet: we have time."

In the past, dark possibilities could always be dispelled by the power of their love, the mating of their bodies. Now he could give her only the firm, undemanding pressure of his hand on hers, his only hope to reassure her of his promise: his total commitment to her and to her child.

# XXI

Out of horror and despair, Hesen found herself awakening into the sunshine of total joy. As her body swelled, so did her delight. Even the dark brown line stretching from her navel and disappearing finally in her curling pubic hair pleased her; she willingly accepted the waves of nausea at the odor of spicy foods, endured the leg cramps that sometimes knotted her calf muscles so tightly she limped for days. Four months into the gestation, at the morning meal, she suddenly set down her wine goblet and sat absolutely still, her eyes radiating an intense blue light.

"Sephy," she breathed in wonder.

"Yes, my darling." The servant was at her side in an instant.

Hesen gripped her arm. "I felt it move!" And she burst into tears.

Now she would not lie even with Senumet; she would do nothing to endanger that child. Still, they spent much time in each other's company, and Hesen, who had never really had a friend, discovered the pleasure in platonic intimacy. She told him everything, described each miraculous change, each unpleasant symptom.

"Feel it, Senumet," she demanded one afternoon when they were alone in the garden. "He will be a soldier, so hard he pounds me."

Senumet placed his hand where she indicated. "Maybe a princess, who will run even faster than her mother."

"No!" Hesen snapped. "A boy who can do and be—and will never have to wait and wait and be told nothing."

"A boy, then," he easily agreed.

And while she was certain that perfect honesty existed between them, Senumet knew that it was an illusion. There was something she must never know: he hated that child, her body's invader, distending her stomach in grotesque ways with the claims of another man's seed. He would support her and comfort her, be anything she needed, but he would not, could not, love that child who had taken her from him.

Finally, she grew so big that her legs swelled and walking was hard for her.

"How too bad of me!" she complained disgustedly to Senumet. "I had in mind to stop one afternoon, have the child and continue my duties."

He burst out laughing. "Do you think yourself a peasant, then?"

"I would prefer it," she declared, leaning heavily on his arm. "I would bake your bread and till your fields."

"And wear a water jug on your head instead of a crown."

"It would have more real use."

"But less real value."

"That, I think, is truly open to question." She stiffened suddenly "Oh, Senumet—"

"Yes, beloved?"

Before answering, she took a few deep breaths. "I think," she whispered, "we'd better return to the palace."

Supporting her tightly with his good arm he hurried her through the garden. Servants raced to meet him, but he wouldn't relinquish his precious burden. Helping her all the way to her room, he eased her to her bed. Then, and only then, he permitted himself to be escorted out.

Sephy placed her hands on Hesen's abdomen, waited until she felt for herself the increasing tightness of the uterine muscles and their subsequent relaxing, then nodded. "It begins," and having made Hesen comfortable, she hurried to summon Meire, the high priest, and Reddjetet, the midwife.

Hesen lay on her bed, her fingers pressed to her abdomen, feeling the regular, steady rhythm of contraction and relaxation.

"Soon . . . soon, my darling," she whispered at each involuntary motion. She almost regretted, when the room filled with priests and servants, that she was no longer alone with her child in their private, cooperative labor of birth.

Reddjetet, plump and bustling, arrived with three men who hauled the brick birthing seat. Hesen waved away the women who would help her to the chair. "I can manage!"

She took two steps. A contraction knifed through her. She doubled over and would have fallen if two servants had not gripped her arms and supported her the rest of the way. Lengths of heavy padding softened the seat's hard contours. She was placed on it in a semireclining position, with her knees drawn up. "Well!" She smiled at Sephy. "This is nothing at all."

"This is all there is," Sephy crooned. "It just takes a little time."

They bathed her forehead in cool rose water; held her hand at each contraction until the shadows lengthened on the tile floor. But as the water clock dripped away the afternoon, she discovered she was tiring. Each contraction was stronger and lasted longer than the last, holding its peak until she felt she must scream before it finally subsided. Would she be able to endure the next one as a queen must? *Please Aten, dear Father*, she prayed silently, *lend me your strength.*

She felt the slow beginning of another contraction. *Oh, blessed Father! So soon! Please*, she begged. Tighter—tighter—harder—stronger: the center of her knotted with incredible agony, consuming her entire body. The world swam in front of her. *Please*, she cried silently. *Please!* She had forgotten what she was begging for, could not remember where she was, could not feel the hands she was gripping. The only certainty was that she must keep her lips clamped together, not utter a sound. The pain subsided briefly. She was aware of a bitter taste in her mouth.

"It's all right, my darling." Sephy's white, anxious face bent over hers; she dabbed gently at the blood on Hesen's mouth: The queen had bitten through her tongue. "Soon, my darling—it's coming soon."

"Oh, Sephy!" Hesen dug her fingers into the servant's arm. "Again. Another!"

Sephy's hand was warm and knowing on the great mound of her belly. "No, Highness!" Her voice was joyous. "Now! It's coming now!"

Hesen gasped. Elation surged through her. Though her body was in the grip of a powerful force, it was utterly different. Even before Sephy said, "Push, now!" Hesen was bearing down with every ounce of strength in her, her face almost purple with the strain. The contraction ebbed.

"My child!" she cried. "Is it born yet?"

"Oh, no, Highness." Sephy laughed gently. "You have more work ahead of you."

Again and again her body demanded all her efforts. Her muscles worked together, bearing down with more energy than she had ever expended, with more strength than she had known she possessed.

"Dear Aten," she panted during one of her brief respites, "does this child come full-grown?"

At a signal from Reddjetet, there was a quickening of attention in the room. Incense was lit in hanging censers, sistrums sent up a silvery welcome; priests stood expectantly.

The pressure on her abdomen was incredible; her thighs trembled with effort. Bathed in sweat, she clutched at her servants—as if to borrow their strength.

"The head crowns," Reddjetet cried.

Suddenly Hesen felt a tremendous surge. She pushed with abandon. Clearly, her body would split in two. She did not care. In a watery, bloody gush, something wedged out between her legs, and she felt an enormous relief.

As the servants sighed, Reddjetet exulted, "The head is out!"

There was another tremendous contraction. Hands pushed downward on her abdomen, helping her. She expelled a huge weight. With it came an utterly new sound, a high-pitched wail of protest.

"Aten be praised!" she murmured and tried to rise. They held her back, and she was too weak and tired to resist. "Let me see!" Though she had uttered a command, the words were only a whisper through her parched lips.

Reddjetet was still busy between her legs, where she could feel a warm liquid. In the air was a pungent, not unpleasant scent of blood and oil, sweat and perfume. Priests, handmaidens, ministers, servants gathered around her as, triumphantly, Reddjetet held up a small, perfect infant, its tiny fists waving in the air, its mouth wide, its face red with wailing.

"A girl!" she announced. "A strong, healthy girl!"

Hesen held out her arms: They gave her the child. She stared in wonder at the delicate, perfect body. Suddenly the child stopped crying and seemed to look straight at her mother out of her huge dark-blue eyes with golden lights. Hesen's heart melted. She was consumed with adoration for this tiny living proof of her love. Bending her head, she touched her lips to the downy forehead—and felt such joy that never, not even in her wildest imaginings, could she have envisioned it.

The sistrums, vigorously shaken, flashed with silver lights. Waving a small golden censer whose powdery incense sweetened the air, Meire stepped to her side.

> *"Blessed be Aten, who created this child,*
> *Who made Pharaoh's seed,*
> *Who placed life in the Queen's womb!*
> *And blessed be this royal child*
> *On this day of her birth;*
> *Fill her with Your grace;*
> *Accept her as Your daughter!"*

Conscious of the child lying warm and sweet next to her, Hesen motioned to Sephy, drowsily. She was so tired, she could barely whisper—which was as well. This was not something she could shout. Sephy's ear almost touched lips. "Tell Senumet," Hesen breathed. Her eyelids fluttered closed even before she had completed saying his name.

A royal birth—even to a Pharaoh repudiated by so many of his people—was a significant event; and in the morning Senumet was summoned to Hesen's apartments to discuss the announcements that must be sent to Thebes and to all the other nomes.

As Senumet hurried to the queen, he was uncertain how he would find her. It had not been an easy birth, he knew, and Hesen hated anything other than robust good health; he also knew she had wanted a boy. But when he saw her, the civilities of protocol, so well ingrained, entirely deserted him: There was a radiance about her that almost blinded him.

She was suckling the child, holding that tiny form to a milky breast. He was transfixed by the tenderness and love on her face. She looked up, smiled; held out a slender arm.

"Senumet! Come see my daughter."

He walked the length of the room, her eyes welcoming him, waiting expectantly for his praise—as if the babe were in fact their own.

He stood by the side of her couch: In truth, he could only see *her*. The plucked chicken at her breast had no reality for him. For once, diplomacy failed him. "She's very . . . pretty," he said, stiffly.

"Look how perfect she is," Hesen directed, placing the child's hand in her palm. "See how tiny her fingers are—and each rosy nail!"

Sensing something was expected of him, Senumet tentatively poked the little hand. Incredibly the fist opened; small fingers curled warmly around his giant one.

"Mother Isis!" he murmured.

Replete now, the infant let her mouth fall away from her mother's breast, and Senumet saw for the first time the delicate shape of her lips. Before she lapsed into noisy sleep, he caught a look at her eyes, almond-shaped like the queen's, with flashing golden lights.

"She's beautiful!" he breathed.

"A miracle!" Hesen admitted.

With expert ease, Sephy scooped up the infant and bore her away.

Hesen waited until her breasts were cleaned and oiled before speaking with Senumet, and he realized—without jealousy now—that she was void of desire or passion or personal need. She was thinking only of serving her child. As his lips touched her ring, she unobtrusively stroked his cheek. He felt a leap of gladness: She hadn't forgotten him. "All Akhet-Aten rejoices with you—and I am happiest of all."

"There is someone else who should share my joy."

He assumed she meant Pharaoh. "The king will know her." He made himself sound certain of it.

"I mean my mother."

She would always surprise him.

"I want you and Sephy to bring the child to her. Now that I know what it means to carry and bear an infant, what love one feels for it, I can forgive my mother. How strong her beliefs must be, if for them she must abandon the flesh of her flesh, birthed out of her pain. I want her to see my child and to bless her."

"Yes, Highness." That bitterness had been washed from Hesen's heart made him suddenly glad. And realizing that the babe had already begun to make the world over, he wondered what other changes might be expected from this sleepy and helpless but already significant new life.

Nefertiti was expecting visitors. Having received the message that Senumet requested an audience, she had told herself she was finished with that life and should refuse, but she did not. In fact, she still cared very much to hear whether Hesen was well.

She waited for him in the small south garden, having chosen the outdoors because she needed the daily reassurance of Aten's presence, unvariable and steady, blessing the observable world. She was dressed simply, in the black she always wore now, without jewelry or makeup. No longer did she study her face or the shape of her body; she had passed beyond personal vanity, beyond anguish and bitterness. For her there was no future, no past. Memories of her former life dared not be recalled, and the coming years would be spent in total service to her god.

Her one pain, unexpected and not suppressable, had been Hesen's rejection of her. Nefertiti was glad that her daughter had taken her own place at Akhenaten's side; only Hesen could help him bear the burdens he must shoulder unsupported by her own love, which he had needed so much. She had also been happy for Hesen when she heard about the child. But that there had been no message from Hesen herself . . . no word of comfort at Meritaten's death . . . no personal announcement of the girl-child's birth! Hesen had a loving heart—was there nothing left for Nefertiti?

She rose when Senumet was announced. Long ago she had hardened herself against the shock waves, only partially masked, on the faces of those who remembered her as reigning queen.

Taking her hand in his left one, he smiled ruefully but made no reference to his disability.

"How is Hesen?" Nefertiti inquired.

"She does well. Sephy has come with me. She waits in the palace."

Nefertiti's eyebrow rose.

"And the child."

She fairly ran back to the throne room, Senumet at her heels. Before he could see the exchange, the infant had been passed from Sephy's arms to Nefertiti's. The queen mother bent her head over that small form, memorizing each feature. Finally she looked up, heedless that her face was wet with tears.

"The queen wanted you to share her joy," Senumet said gently.

"She has forgiven me, then."

"She respects you and loves you and craves your blessing for her child."

Nefertiti shut her eyes. Tears of forgiving and of being forgiven flooded beneath her closed lids. She must somehow return Hesen's gift. She waited a few minutes until she was in control of herself.

"I want my daughter to know how I honor her strength and her loyalty. Tell her my wish is that Tutu shall return to the court. That I am confident, in Hesen's care, his faith will grow and flower."

Though he accepted Nefertiti's decision with iron composure, as a soldier should, Tutankhaten was almost beside himself with delight.

Senumet was awed in the presence of the happiness the child had brought to that small threatened outpost. Heaven—if it had real boundaries—could offer no more.

Hesen bloomed: Her face, its outline softer, glowed with a light not entirely of this world. Her cheeks were flushed with the rosy tint of perfect health. Her eyes blazed clear and untroubled. Her body's curves had deepened. She was a woman: She carried herself with the majesty of fulfillment.

She adored the child shamelessly, suckling her for so long that even an indulgent court laughed about it. Let them laugh, she thought. For as long as she could, she would maintain that special closeness. The one blemish to her happiness was that Senumet still was indifferent to the child. She exposed them to each other as often as she dared, certain he could not long resist those small charms, but the only result was that her daughter adored him . . . in that, very much like her mother.

"Oo-met" was her first word. To Senumet she aimed with her first, faltering steps, holding out plump, rosy arms for support and comfort. "Oo-met!" she cried eagerly. Watching for signs as she always did, Hesen saw that small body, sweet-smelling and warm, burrow into his chest and knew just how those loving, trusting arms would feel around his neck. Aten be praised, he was charmed. Her delight was mirrored in his eyes. He couldn't understand the unexpected surge of emotion—she knew that. And in a sense it was unfair: she was manipulating him; but she was pleased at the same time that he was growing to love the child even before he knew it was his own.

Even Pharaoh responded to his queen's daughter—he had always loved children—and it was he who named her. Though Hesen planned to call her Ah-Hotpe, Akhenaten referred to her only as Hesen, and so it remained: she was Ankhesenpaaten the Younger. As she began to confuse herself with her mother, Hesen would frown, but the court was enchanted when she extended her small hand to be kissed or answered to "Highness" when her mother was addressed.

She was Sherit and Neferu's pet and Penre's special charge. Some observers at court remarked that she didn't look at all like them; which was surprising, considering her parents' relationship. She was much taller than they had been, and her eyes darkened to the deep purple of midnight, though they retained those golden lights. Her hands were different, too. Though they were slim and delicate, as were the hands of all royalty, this child's fingers were long and supple, almost an artisan's; and when she stole into Bek's workrooms and painted on his walls, her first efforts not only earned her a reputation for willfulness, but surprised them all with their raw skill and freshness. The servants also had to smile at her pert explanation, babyish, but quite logical, for why she had broken the rules. Clearly, here was a little one who was learning to use her tongue to bend others to her own way of thinking.

As the months stretched into a year and then two, Senumet came to feel that they might live out their lives here, forgotten by the rest of the world. They were out of the succession here, entirely separated from any power struggle. He had become so relaxed that when he was given a message that a ship from Thebes was docking, he didn't even feel the anxious lurch that had always accompanied such news in the past. He strolled easily down to the dock and greeted his old scribe friend Narni with unfeigned pleasure—without thinking to wonder why he was here.

Senumet's arm affectionately around Narni's shoulder, they walked along the Kings-Way, Senumet enthusiastically pointing out its restored beauties, hardly noticing the man's reluctant responses. Finally Narni put his hand on Senumet's arm.

"Listen, my friend. I am sent here by Horemheb."

"Yes?"

"There is news, not yet made public, that Horemheb thinks you should know."

Coldness gripped him. Though their paths had diverged, Horemheb was a friend. "Yes?"

"Meritaten's child is dead."

Suddenly the day lost its luster. Narni would have spoken further, but Senumet waved him silent. On a sleek ship it had come unsuspected—ironically welcomed—from the lips of a friend: the end of the world. It was his to tell now. Dreading his duty, Senumet knew he must hurry to her.

*Meritaten's child was dead!*

Let Aten protect them all:

Ankhesenpaaten the Younger was heiress to the throne.

# XXII

"Give me some time," Hesen stated tonelessly after he had told her of the heiress's death. "I need to think."

He would have left her alone, but she needed him there in her Sun-Shade while her mind whirled with desperate plans.

Finally she looked at him squarely. Hands clenched, she almost spat out the words: "I can't bear—"

"There is no time for that," he said sharply. "Let's not review the implications. We both know them. We have plans to make."

"Plans! The only way out, I think, is for my daughter to die too."

"Exactly my thought!"

She was shocked out of incipient hysteria. "What—"

He pulled her next to him. "I haven't forgotten my pledge. There's only one way. Unless Ay thinks Ankhesenpaaten the Younger is dead, she'll center in his every plan, every action, every thought. Don't forget, his son still lives."

"But how can we say the child . . . died . . . here, when she is watched constantly?"

In her heart, Senumet knew, she could not yet accept even the fiction of her child's death. Her mind, usually so agile, refused to lead her to the only logic available to them. He didn't know if she had the strength for the renunciation she must make. They'd go slowly toward it, step by bitter step. He held her hand.

"She is the undisputed heiress. To capture the throne for his son, he needs her. At Akhet-Aten there's no strength politically or militarily, not even spiritually, to prevent him from working his will."

She closed her eyes. "I have known all this time that we have lived here on his sufferance."

Having come this far, he must carry her to the next enormous acceptance. "Then, he can pluck her up and place her anywhere he wants whenever he chooses. And you are powerless to prevent him."

Her fingers moved in his hand—she would protest verbally if she could only prove him wrong—then stopped their futile movements. "So. He must think her dead."

"And to accomplish that, she will have to leave Akhet-Aten." Relieved that it was said, he ignored the pallor of her face. "But if you move quickly and courageously *you* will control her future, not Ay."

There was no more to say. He must wait while she struggled with accepting her dreadful loss. Ankhesenpaaten the Younger must be removed from court, must be separated from her mother, and there could be only the slightest possibility of ultimate reunion. He watched the denial on her face . . . her anger at him, at Ay, the world . . . her stubborn refusal even to consider the option . . . and finally, her sorrowful acknowledgement that she had no choice.

"Have you a plan?" she asked bitterly. "Have you worked out the means of this torture?"

"I thought you would want the child to go to Sephy's family, if at all feasible."

"Ay will agree to that, of course!" After all this dreadful pain, was he to come up with only a preposterous plan, doomed to failure?

"My darling, Ay will never think to suspect Sephy. At my suggestion, Ay will agree the child must be raised away from exposure to Aten's contamination. He will then select an appropriate noble to raise her. Unfortunately, transporting her, there will be an accident. A child's body will be returned to you and will be buried with honor as befits a royal princess. Under cover of which, Ankhesenpaaten will be taken to live in Zehut, her identity hidden, her person safe."

"Will you be able to persuade Ay?" Her voice trembled with doubt, with urgency, with the beginning of pain.

"She'll be safe," he promised. "She'll grow as your daughter must, surrounded by affection and friendship, properly schooled, to glowing womanhood."

"And who knows?" Hesen choked. "We may—we may—meet—" She pulled away to stand with her back to him, rigid as stone. He dared not touch her. He could only hope his presence, his support, his commitment would somehow give her the strength to make the terrible decision.

He decided to return to Thebes immediately on the boat that had brought Narni: He must persuade Ay to accept his plan for the princess before the grand vizier had time to implement one of his own —one which Senumet would be unable to control. Sephy, taken into his confidence, was already working on her part. He was half-relieved not to have to watch Hesen's last days with her child, her pinched, hurt look, the desperate intensity of love.

At Thebes, the docks were again bustling; the streets were crowded and noisy, the Temple of Amon shone with all its former glory. What shocked him was Smenkhare so corpulent and dissipated that he could almost have been Amenophis returned. Women were scarce in this new court: slim boys and well-muscled young men, Smenkhare's catamites, surrounded Pharaoh with blazing collars and sparkling eyes and skillful hands. How this was received by the Thebans, Senumet could not tell, but clearly Ay was not displeased with Smenkhare's entourage of submissive male bodies. Sitting with Senumet at the evening meal he remarked, "At least there will be no new queen to contend with."

And no new heiress: though the grand vizier left the words unsaid, his meaning was clear. Senumet nodded agreement as their glance exchanged levels of understanding. He had been a little surprised that Ay had accepted his unexpected appearance in Thebes with smiles and kind words and without questions. Ay was biding his time; Senumet would hear the new strategy when Ay was ready to divulge it. Awaiting the summons, he slipped easily into old, familiar routines and passed the time in friendly conversations. And while he was greeted affectionately by Ka-Aper and with real warmth by Horemheb, both followed Ay's lead and asked him nothing.

Not so Smenkhare. Pharaoh summoned Senumet for an audience the day after his arrival. Senumet entered the throne room with distaste, remembering Meritaten and thinking that Hesen's poor sister had known less joy than she deserved. It did not require firsthand knowledge of their relationship; her humiliation was implicit in what Smenkhare had become. Lounging, now, on his gilded throne, surrounded by naked boys, who sprawled on pillows or waved ostrich-feather fans, Smenkhare stroked the muscled thighs of a Minoan as the young man rested his crimped head against Pharaoh's arm. For Pharaoh's amusement, a young man with the physique of a god—

perhaps he was a soldier of Pharaoh's garrison—foreplayed and caressed a handsome boy, whose body had yet to grow hair.

Smenkhare watched Senumet advance out of half-closed, glittering eyes. "Welcome, old tutor." He held out his hand. As Senumet bent to kiss his ring, Smenkhare turned it palm up, so that Senumet's lips pressed into soft flesh. Masking his repugnance, Senumet stood respectfully still. He repressed a shudder as Pharaoh stroked his neck.

"Tactful as ever, I see," the king observed, rapping a long, painted nail along Senumet's cheek. "Why are you come here?"

"To express, formally and personally, the grief of Akhet-Aten's royal family at your daughter's death."

"I'm sure they grieved excessively." Smenkhare's voice took on a dangerous, silken tone—"And how does the queen's daughter do?"

"Very well, Your Highness."

"I expect there'll be a passel of royal children before the game is all played out."

"I see no reason to doubt it."

Smenkhare drew the Minoan onto his lap, allowing one hand to stroke the boy's head while the other crept up under his kilt. "I mean *my* children."

"My thought as well," Senumet smiled warmly. "May Amon grant you long and joyous years."

Smenkhare's tongue flipped wetly across his lips. "Tell the queen to expect another royal wedding and other claimants to the throne."

Offering diplomatic good wishes, Senumet's mind raced: Could Smenkhare hold his inclinations in check to achieve the power he wanted? Was it possible that Hesen might be spared? Should Senumet wait before making his proposal to Ay? But though Senumet probed delicately in a score of directions, he could hear of no negotiations afoot for a royal marriage. Had Smenkhare been lying? Were there secret plans? He needed time to find out, and he didn't have it. On the fourth morning of his visit, so early that he knew the pretense of civility was ended, he was summoned to Ay's rooms.

The grand vizier was still in bed when Senumet was ushered in. Slaves had just brushed his sparse gray hair and wiped his hands with scented towels. As Ay swung his feet over the side of the bed, two servants rushed to his side, each with one gilded sandal.

"As I grow older," Ay sighed ostentatiously, "I become more dependent on small comforts. Join me here, Senumet, for the morning meal."

He indicated a small wooden table inlaid with ivory and gilt, spread with hot biscuits and colored glass goblets filled with milk. Senumet remembered that Ay didn't like wine.

"Thank you." He took a seat on one of the wooden chairs, another luxury in this tree-scarce land.

As they ate, birds fluttered to the terrace and Ay scattered crumbs for them in what was obviously an established morning ceremony. Pointing out a young redstart that had snatched a morsel from a larger bird, he said without changing focus, "And why have you come, unsummoned, to Thebes, Senumet?"

With his next sentence, either the maneuver began or it did not. Looking directly into Ay's eyes, Senumet couldn't doubt the grand vizier's power. Hadn't he seen it blatantly demonstrated even in the few days he had been at Thebes? If the headmen and priests and nobles and bureaucrats bowed to Smenkhare, when they listened, it was to Ay. The words they spoke to the king were polite and meaningless; the tablets, the papyruses, the tributes went to Ay. Senumet took a deep breath. He could only proceed as planned.

"I could never dissemble to you, my lord. I heard of the heiress's death."

"A dreadful loss."

Senumet felt his palms grow wet. It had been years. He had almost forgotten the parrying and innuendo, the lightning shafts of Ay's tongue that aimed at keeping him off balance so that Ay could get at his real purpose. Senumet's mind desperately reestablished pathways that had rusted at Akhet-Aten: he was back in the real world now. "I begin to think I may have acted in an excess of zeal. Forgive me. Away from Thebes I forgot my place. I'll return with your leave, on the next boat." He stopped to break open his bun and pour honey on it from a glazed blue pitcher. "That is," he added stiffly (Let Ay think he had grown officious!), "if my reports have been satisfactory."

The grand vizier's eyes crinkled. "You have grown too sensitive, my son. Of course I wish to know your thoughts: You are closest to the feelings at Akhet-Aten."

Senumet kept his voice deferential. "It was only that I see the new heiress all the time. I couldn't help remembering your son. And the connection is not unique to me, I think."

Ay looked at him shrewdly. "No doubt the connection has occurred to many. If that were all, your journey here would be superfluous."

"The queen felt it was a matter of some urgency. As I have reported, the Aten is still strong in Pharaoh's city. I thought it a shame that the child be tainted by it. The rest of Egypt will not soon forget that it was her father's faith that almost destroyed the country."

"True." Ay's face was impassive.

"When I put the matter to the queen, she was quick to perceive the political realities of the situation." Senumet caught the merest flicker in Ay's eyes. "Ankhesenpaaten would like her daughter to rule Egypt."

Senumet had considered that point carefully: Blinded and driven by his own ambition, Ay would never doubt its echo in another's heart.

"So!" Ay's derisive accent proved Senumet right. "Our little Hesen has discovered the joys of even a partial queenship."

"She thought you would be more agreeable to a betrothal between your son and her daughter if you could have the raising of the child. At the end, Tiya regretted she had not given Akhenaten to his father earlier."

Ay spread his hands on the table. His fingers were gnarled and old. "I considered taking her by force," Ay admitted, and Senumet knew he had not come a moment too soon. "How much more suitable this way . . . And I do not minimize your efforts in this, Senumet. You will be rewarded."

"Thank you, my lord—although my only purpose has been to serve you."

Ay nodded reflectively. "So you've had enough of banishment in a backwater."

Senumet looked ruefully. Inwardly his nerves were tuned to a note of high-pitched tension. How long could he continue to lead Ay by the nose?

"I'm sorry, my boy, but for now I'm afraid you'll have to be patient. You must return to Akhet-Aten again. There's still work for you."

This was the critical maneuver. Delicately Senumet must channel Ay's thinking. He permitted an ingenuous note in his voice. It must seem so logical Ay would not question his motives.

"You want the child brought here!"

"Not to Thebes," Ay frowned. "I want no hint of coercion on my part, particularly since the queen is compliant. To a family in Heliopolis, I think."

"Where you were chief priest . . ."

Ay nodded. "As safe as Thebes. I'll work out the details in the next few days. The child likes you?"

"Very much." Had it not been true, he would have answered in exactly the same way.

"I suspected that," Ay laughed. "Your appeal extends to all ages, I see. In that case, your mission will be easier. I want you to escort the child to her new home . . . and there must be no trouble from her."

"With pleasure, my lord." He kept his voice steady though his body trembled with relief.

"That's settled, then." Ay clapped his hands. A servant bearing a tall pitcher glided into the room and refilled the glass with the bubbling white liquid.

Though Senumet had won, he could not permit himself to relax. Yet he was convinced when he bowed his way out of Ay's chambers, remembering to look reluctant, that the grand vizier suspected nothing.

His real mission accomplished, Senumet moved mechanically through the activities at Thebes, all his thoughts concentrated on what must take place at his return to Akhet-Aten. In a few days Ay again met with him privately, this time to give him details of the princess's move. When he sailed, he took with him Ay's assurance that, once the assignment was completed, he would return to Thebes as Ay's chief minister. Senumet did not rebel, even in his heart he thanked Ay. The day that Narni delivered his message, Senumet had accepted that his idyll had ended. . . . Whatever had meaning in his life was finished. He had only to perform his last service for her.

As his ship pulled into the dock at Akhet-Aten, on the hill to the north of the landing area he saw the flash of the royal chariot's abrupt spin as the queen wheeled sharply away. Hesen was cold and distant when he reported to her publicly and did not come to her temple later that day or the next. Though his heart ached for her and he could understand her fierce need for denial, still he grew angry: Delay could only increase the risk, and to incur Ay's displeasure was perhaps to force his hand.

In the afternoon of the second day Sephy met him as he walked on the beach with Tutu.

"Where is she?" Senumet demanded. "We must move quickly."

"She knows that," Sephy's voice was low. "This is terribly hard for her! She adores that child."

"Let her wait a little longer, and she'll have no say in her daughter's future."

"She'll be there tonight. I have made arrangements too. My brother's wife has died. He'll bring Ankhesenpaaten the Younger to my family at Zehut to raise as his child. She'll be called Mut-Nodjne, an old family name."

With his finger, Senumet traced their route in the sand. "They must hide their boat in the marshes at Letopolis. On the fifth night after the rising of the Decan star, we will arrive with the child, her nurse and two boatmen. You must come too, Sephy. I'll need your help."

Sephy nodded. "You may count on me."

Senumet erased the map he had drawn. "The queen has a loyal and wonderful friend in you, Sephy."

"And in you," the servant admitted grudgingly, her eyes suddenly moist. Waving her hand in impotent despair, she turned abruptly and hurried away.

Senumet waited until countless stars merged into a milky-white avenue through the blackness of the night's expanse. Hearing the soft scrape of a door, he realized she was there, the moon haloing her hair with silver. He moved forward to light the oil lamp: She stopped him. He realized she didn't want him to see her face, ravaged by grief as it was.

"When will she be taken?"

"As soon as you permit. Accept it, Hesen. Trust me!"

She was a shape without eyes in the darkness. "Senumet, I had not planned that you should know, but you must! Ankhesenpaaten is *your* daughter. You have a double responsibility for her—not just to me . . . to yourself!"

Senumet felt such a rage storm through him he was barely able to speak. "Do I need your lies to buy my service? If our love means nothing, why did you not bring me a gold collar?"

"Surely you have seen it—your seed created her."

"Your sense of timing is impeccable," he said drily. "At this particular moment, I could not possibly believe you, even if it were true."

"You do not question me?"

"Hesen, calm yourself. We are children no longer. You and I both know what you might have done as princess, you would never attempt as queen."

"Indeed. What makes you so sure?"

"You would have told me!" Though Senumet spoke in the same

firm voice, he had to strain to mask an edge of uncertainty.

"Oh, yes, of course I would have told you . . . let you revel in your fatherhood . . . let you plan for her future! Aten above us, why do you try me so? With a single word from Ay, you could be separated from us forever. Did you need that additional pain—a new burden of responsibilty, one that you could not control?"

"She might be Akhenaten's child. My seed and his have mingled in your womb."

"I did not lay with Akhenaten for many weeks before becoming pregnant."

"I cannot accept it!" But Senumet was no longer angry. "What if someday—unlikely though that might seem now—she should become queen. I cannot believe that *you*, descended as you are from a long line of mighty rulers, would have the child of a . . . peasant . . . on the throne."

He caught a glint of tears in Hesen's eyes. "To me, Senumet, you are royal. I could wish for nothing more than for the queen to have your wisdom and your strength and your fineness. To me, you are fit to rule the world."

"Hesen!" he reached for her.

She shook her head. "Just look at her in the next few days, Senumet. Study her closely—and deny it if you can. She is your seed." She spun on her heel and fled back to the palace, her gown a billowing white wake swallowed up by the dark path, her muffled sobs in his ears long after she disappeared from sight. Senumet waited until he could assume his usual demeanor before leaving the Sun-Shade. But later, as he tossed fitfully in his bed, images of the young princess flashed across his mind . . .

The boat was waiting at the dock the next morning. He must see to its preparation. It took only two days—they were not going far. The night before departure, Senumet slipped aboard unobserved. Climbing below deck, he took out a chisel, carefully loosened the bung, and oiled it so that later it could be easily removed. Having wrapped a papyrus sheet around it before reinserting it, he was ready.

The procession to the boat was a merry one. The child's favorite dancers cavorted; jugglers tossed bright balls; musicians played lilting melodies. Joining in the revelry, Tutu and the young princesses laughed and sang. Senumet's heart lurched. Unsummoned, memory flooded him: In another time, an untried, hopeful boy and a beautiful, innocent girl had laughed so.

Unet, the child's nurse, boarded, with Sephy at her heels. Sephy's eyes were onyx-hard, merciless. The two boatmen took their places next. Meruka greeted Senumet affectionately, calling him brother.

"We've not been together since Byblos," Senumet responded warmly; not a flicker betrayed him. Then he saw her at the top of the hill, walking slowly, holding her child's hand. The little girl, excited by the coming adventure, chafed at the restraint. As they neared the boarding ramp, she pulled away, racing joyously to the other children and the dancers.

"Ankhesenpaaten," Hesen's voice, quiet and hard, was distinct above the noise of the crowd. Dutifully the child returned to her mother, where, scooped up, she was given a fierce hug and covered with kisses. Senumet turned away. That white, bereft face hurt him more even than had the littered, silent field at Byblos.

When finally she put down the child, Ankhesenpaaten the Younger fairly danced on board.

Senumet gave the signal. The ship pulled into the river. He didn't look back until he knew Akhet-Aten would be only a blur in the distance. He didn't want to see her stricken face.

Purposely forcing consciousness of the coming event from his mind, Senumet spent much of each day with the princess. Perhaps not strangely, he found he enjoyed her company more than ever before.

And he couldn't help it—as he began to listen for her observations, as sharp and as fresh as her mother's must have been when she was a babe; and as he watched a gamut of expressions play across her enchanting face, he searched for a resemblance. Those golden eyes, could they be his mother's, only faintly remembered from his boyhood. Were those skillful fingers the heritage that had been passed down from scribe-father to child these six generations? No doubt this leap of joy he felt at her soft good-night kiss was no more than he would feel for any pretty youngster—it need not be the love of a father for his child. . . .

Along the riverbanks the landscape was changing. The cliffs became rolling hills, then disappeared entirely in the thick marsh reeds of the delta. Finally the day arrived. One brief glance at Sephy was enough to know that she could read the message of the shoreline as well as he. In the afternoon, when everyone else was occupied, he sprinkled the pink powder of crushed poppies in the wine jug and, considering, added more. After all, he had only one usable arm, and the boatmen had been soldiers.

He and Sephy drank nothing at dinner, though he refilled glass after glass for the others with cold-blooded generosity. Drowsiness caught them almost without warning. Unet and one oarsman staggered off to find a bed; Meruka slept where he was, falling forward with his head in his arms. The moon had traversed only one quarter of its nightly arc when their stentorian snores began to drown out even the buzz of the rich marsh nightlife.

Frightened when her nurse wouldn't rouse, Ankhesenpaaten started to cry. Sephy gathered the child in her arms. As she rocked the babe, Senumet stared into the darkness. Could there have been a mistake, an accident? *Where were Sephy's kinsmen?*

Light flashed, was quickly blotted out, flashed again and yet again.

Amon be praised. Senumet held up the small lantern he had prepared. After five long seconds, he signaled Sephy, who threw a dark cover over it. He waited again, nodded again. Sephy whipped the cover off. The light glowed for five seconds more. It was done.

Senumet took a deep, resolute breath: grim work ahead. All his instincts rebelled against what he must do. All his study and breeding and life here in Egypt deplored needless violence. Yet there must be no living witness to the princess's transfer. With everything in him, he wished he could draw out these last moments, but inevitably the small boat bearing Sephy's kinsmen drew alongside. With Ankhesenpaaten whimpering in Sephy's arms, the two of them were transferred to the other ship. Unmoving, he waited until both were hidden in the launch's covered cabin: the little princess must not see, even by chance, the events of the night.

Hurrying below deck, Senumet reached for the loop of the bung. As he removed it, water covered his hand and began its slow steady rise. It would not take long before the ship was flooded: Hurrying to the wooden chest that held his possessions, he reached into the furthest recess and pulled out the heavy club he had hidden there—and was ready. Blanking from his mind everything but action and efficiency, he swung himself above deck. He bent first over the sleeping form of the nurse. The ship lurched in its death struggle. He raised the club . . . and smashed it down mercilessly on that sleeping, innocent head. Her body jerked once, then was still. Keeping a firm grip on the club, he rolled the limp form of the nurse to the edge of the ship, then over the side.

When he had registered its soft splash, he hurried to the oarsman, who slept unsuspecting, one hand curled easily under his chin. Thud! The spastic jerk of death. The almost-effortless disposal of the remains.

The ship was listing. He had very little time for the final, hardest murder. His comrade, his brother, Meruka, who had survived the slaughter of the Hittite barbarians only to meet his death from the hands of a friend.

That soldier still slumped in his chair, his head on the table, snoring loudly. Grateful to be spared the sight of his friend's face, Senumet raised the club. The ship rolled. Meruka slipped off the chair and crashed on the deck. His eyes opened. Confused, he took in Senumet's stance over him and clumsily lurched to his feet. "Senumet," he mumbled in disbelief.

Off balance himself on the listing deck, Senumet staggered and fell against him. The club flew from his hand. Of a height with the burly soldier, his good arm locked around Meruka's neck. That was his only chance—to end it quickly before the other man could shake off the effects of the drug. Careless where he stepped, Senumet's foot trod on empty air—the passage to lower deck. He plunged below deck, pulling Meruka with him into water that had risen to waist level.

The shock of the cold river revived the boatman and he threw a heavy blow at Senumet's head. Senumet crashed backward into the water and Meruka was on top of him, his fists driving the air from Senumet's lungs. Senumet brought his knee sharply into the man's groin and twisted quickly away as Meruka howled with pain and loosened his hold. He flailed to his feet, avoiding a heavy wooden box, one of many that had been lifted by the water and was floating freely in the confined space. Clawing at the nearest box, Senumet put all his power into one final thrust and lunged at Meruka, the box a battering ram. It caught the soldier in the chest and shoved him backward, his head hitting the ladder with a loud crack. Meruka now was prone. Before he recovered, Senumet maneuvered the box on top of him and levered his weight on it so that it pinned down the other man and immobilized his arms. Senumet's hand plunged into the cold water, twined into Meruka's hair and forced his head as far back as he could. The man's eyes flew open and he thrashed his legs wildly. He could not dislodge the weight on his chest. His eyes bulged—his mouth opened in a silent scream.

"*Amon judge me,*" Senumet prayed silently, his hand unyielding on that struggling head, "*it is too much. Why hast thou given me light to watch his life bubble away?*"

Blinded by tears, he held Meruka long after his comrade had stopped his struggles. When the waters swirled dangerously high on

Senumet's own chin, two of Sephy's kinsmen splashed down after him. Dragged up onto deck, he watched, exhausted, as they dumped Meruka's limp body into the river.

For the rest of the long night he and Sephy must cling, sodden and helpless, to a plank of the doomed ship. They would raise an alarm only after they could be sure the princess was well under way. As he half-drowsed, waiting for sunrise, Senumet knew that a dead body, dressed in Ankhesenpaaten's clothes (he had never asked where they had gotten the dead child) was thrown into the river to be counted with the rest. Throughout the hours of darkness, long after her kinsmen's boat had vanished from sight, he heard echoes of the princess's terrified cry when she realized she was being taken away. "Oo-met, Oo-met!" It seemed he would hear it always.

Clinging to that narrow plank, he knew that his heart, one day, would weigh heavier on the scales than the feather of truth, that for his actions this night, his ka must sink to the Underworld . . . and that he would not will it otherwise. From life he asked nothing but to fulfill his pledge to her. He welcomed eternal damnation.

# XXIII

Although his features remained as rigidly inscrutable as stone, Ay received the reports from Akhet-Aten with stunned disbelief: *It could not be!*

He questioned the priest of Aten who served as royal messenger until he was certain the man could tell him nothing more—then dismissed him.

The fact of the tragedy was that the boat had sunk. But in the sluggish waters of the wide-channeled, well-charted Nile, boats did not generally sink. That a barge bearing royalty should have met with such an accident was even more unlikely. That the boat bearing the Princess Ankhesenpaaten had settled into the silt at the bottom of the Nile bed meant, in all probability, the boat had been *deliberately* opened to the invasion of water.

The question became then, which of his enemies so desired the death of the child that he had dared to act?

Smenkhare? Eventually he had much to lose from an heiress who was personally unaligned to him. Or perhaps, with an unusual spark of insight, Smenkhare had seen that Ay might use the princess to advance the royal succession and depose him now before he produced an heir from his own loins. Both intelligence and natural appetites, however, were unlikely in Smenkhare. Ay doubted that the king could spare sufficient time from the pursuit of his perverted and insatiable lust to plot so rationally.

Besides, others had sufficient motivation. Ay could envisage them even among his allies. Perhaps Nabamon, the anointed successor of Tushratta as High Priest of Amon, would envy and fear Ay's power, were Ay the regent aligned to *Aten*. Perhaps behind the solemn mask of Nabamon's devotion coiled treachery. . . .

Ay brought his fist smashing down on the table, scattering food from platters in all directions. Fearful servants waited uncertainly at attention, reluctant to attend the table until his anger had abated.

Or could the culprits be the priests of Aten?—desperate to prevent any marital link with Thebes that would strengthen the legitimacy of the co-Pharaoh's reign. Would the fear of Amon drive them to violate the basic tenet of their faith? Ay's features twisted briefly into a grimace as he considered. . . . Where power and wealth were concerned, men compromised their faith quickly enough—or faith died altogether. Ay had seen that principle demonstrated time after time. After all, was his own life not the prime example?

And in that respect, even the palace at Akhet-Aten could be involved. Could Pharaoh have accomplished the death of his own flesh to thwart Ay and Amon? If so, Ay could not rule out of question the queen's complicity, even though she was the child's mother. Taken simply at face value without probing further into dark conceits, Ay's calculations tipped the scales in favor of Akhet-Aten as the enemies with the most to lose should the small princess have been betrothed to Ay's son. In that light, one thing was certain: Senumet had failed Ay. Even if Senumet had grown sloppy and careless in the lassitude of days at Akhet-Aten's wasted city, he should have ferreted out a plot of such magnitude. Ay frowned. He had put to death underlings for lesser omissions. Yet no one was closer to the queen. He might well have need to call on Senumet's services again at some point in the future. As punishment for his negligence, then, let him temporarily rot in Akhet-Aten! Senumet would not return to Thebes.

*If, indeed, it was negligence*, Ay speculated grimly. By Amon, he could trust no one. In that moment, Ay knew he had already decided to journey to Akhet-Aten to see the child's body with his own eyes, gauge Pharaoh and the queen's grief firsthand, judge for himself Akhenaten's capacity to direct events, and determine Senumet's reliability. He would go in proper estate. He ordered the barge of Amon prepared.

He was at ease during the days of the voyage upriver, and arriving at the city of his enemies, what he saw pleased him. No longer a seat of glory, the city was rotting. The remaining citizens went mechanically through joyless burdens of living, while in the palace Hesen was almost prostrated by grief, moving despondently by rote.

When he caught her thinking herself unobserved, he saw her features sag with ineffable sadness and watched her rouse herself with enormous effort. Similarly, Akhenaten was no threat. He responded only to Hesen, and then with little more than the formal patina of royal habits designed to mask the essential man. Pharaoh was no more than a ceremonial shell.

Ay examined the child's body, which was being mummified. After he observed its bloated, disintegrating flesh (the body had not been recovered for three days), he realized he had half-suspected they would attempt to bury a pig or a goat. And yet the child was unrecognizable—the tiny carcass might not be the princess after all. Then what had he proved? Nothing. For all his efforts, he had gained no certainties. And always his suspicions clustered about one person—Senumet. How could he determine the truth? Over the years Senumet had evolved from merely a talented scribe into a consummate diplomat who, Ay feared, might even be sufficiently skilled as to mislead Ay himself. Casting about for a tactic, Ay decided to meet Senumet's dispassionate rationality with a hailstorm of fury, and it was not hard for Ay to work himself up into a rage that rivaled the elements at their worst.

His face red and choleric, Ay swept like a ravaging wind into the scribes' bureau and found Senumet tutoring the son of the noble Mena. The boy and the other scribes scattered on swift feet, leaving Senumet alone with Ay. "You are not careless!" Ay thundered. "What blinded your meticulous ears and eyes?"

"I was not expecting treachery." Senumet did not pretend to misunderstand. "I too was drugged. It must have been the wine—I drank less than the others. I have been able to take very little wine since Byblos."

"But who put it in the wine? All are dead . . . except you and Sephy."

"I questioned Sephy carefully. She is still suffering from the effects of the drug. It was only by the merest chance that I found her—her hair had twisted around a plank, and she was able to keep her head above water. It was as I sent you reports."

Ay's gaze informed Senumet that he acknowledged Sephy's sickness, having dispatched physicians to examine her. Senumet thanked Amon he had overruled Sephy's protests, forced her to swallow some of the powder afterward. She would never have convincingly simulated the symptoms of numbness in her limbs, blurred vision and memory, and difficulty of breath.

"I regret I did not see reason to be alert to danger," Senumet concluded.

Ay regarded him narrowly. "It centers on your dulled faculties."

"I feel my fault keenly. My failure in my duty to you is inexcusable."

"But to whom *did* you fulfill your duty, Senumet? In whose pay are you now, you who were once loyal to me? Do you take your gold from Smenkhare? Meire? Tushratta? Nabamon?" Ay paused significantly before adding, "Or the queen?" With each name, his eyes drilled Senumet, searching for some clue.

Senumet kept his face impassive, his hands loose and relaxed on the low scribe's table at which he sat, and concealed a surge of triumph. The grand vizier knew nothing; the very length of his list betrayed his doubts.

"As always, my lord, I am *your* servant," Senumet avowed.

"Let mold stop and cover that smooth tongue of yours," Ay cursed finally, "as it will cover the rest of this corpse of a city!" In a swirl of rich robes, he swept from the bureau as he had entered, with a difference that his rage was now unassumed.

At his return to Thebes Ay met with Tushratta, now so fragile that, walking, he must be supported, and with Nabamon.

The three men sat together in the priests' residence adjoining the temple and overlooking the sacred lake. Tushratta haltingly explained the latest developments, in the slurred speech characteristic of him now.

"You had just left," he began, "when Smenkhare came to us. He wouldn't have dared, were you still here." Tears welled up in his eyes. Ay's jaw set with impatience at the sign of weakness: The old man was increasingly unable to control his emotions.

"We suspect he was goaded to it by Nunit, his current favorite," said Nabamon.

Ay recalled that young man: a nubile, clever Cretan with the muscled body of the athlete he had been and the flattering tongue of the grasping sycophant he had become. "Very likely. Nunit's greed knows no limits."

Nabamon's hands clenched into tight fists. The priests of Ra had been out of power too long to be sanguine about threats to their prerogative. "Smenkhare wants his tribute increased."

Ay raised his brows. That was easily dealt with. But as he started to speak, Nabamon waved him silent. "Smenkhare has sent a delegation to Nubia to negotiate a marriage with Belet, the first princess."

In the company of those with whom his interest exactly coincided, Ay did not attempt to conceal his shock. "So he is not, after all, quite depraved enough. And of course with his coffers swelled by the gold of his dowry, he will no longer have to answer to us."

Tushratta's head bobbed with his agitation.

Surprisingly, Ay felt calmer than he had in years. The sign was clear, the waiting ended. "Enough," he said steadily. "We have compromised too long. Ra will not live again in obscurity or acquiesce in the loss of influence. Smenkhare is dead!"

Tushratta's eyes shifted fearfully from Nabamon to Ay. "And what then?"

"Then," Ay declared, "we will overrun Akhet-Aten as you wanted to do some time ago, my friend. You showed remarkable prescience. We should have listened to you. It will be done now."

Nabamon's smile revealed his strong, straight teeth. Ay regarded him with satisfaction as the younger man made an almost imperceptible signal. Responding to the command, acolyte priests brought flagons of wine. It seemed the deed was already done with their first sip. And furthermore, Ay's suspicions of Nabamon and Tushratta were put to rest. In the next few days, Ay kept his sharp eyes fixed on the affairs at court and was rewarded by the discovery of Mehi, a courtier whose smoldering, envious expression implied a dissatisfaction that could surely be exploited. Ay remembered vaguely and made inquiries. Yes, a likely prospect. Mehi had been Pharaoh's favorite before Nunit. Unwilling to accept Smenkhare's rejection, Mehi had continued to offer himself to Pharaoh, even when he was repeatedly spurned, until his volatile hurt and anger erupted into embarrassing incidents before the throne. Finally, Smenkhare had ordered him back to his village.

Ay arranged to meet with Mehi before he was to depart and had the boy brought to his villa, a three-story dwelling of sparkling white bricks set in a grove of sycamores. Within the high walls of his estate, with its garden oases—one around a pool lined with masonry coping and filled with bright fish, the other upon the roof of the main house—Ay felt the least risk of discovery.

When Mehi arrived—not at the main entrance with its imposing brick pylon, but at the tradesmen's entrance—a slave led him past the grain silos, the stables, the quarters for slaves and minor servants, and the well to the outside stairway ascending to the roof. Mehi climbed the stairs alone. The swaggering steps with which he normally moved slowed as he took in Ay's figure, powerful even in repose, reclining on a couch shaded by the foliage of the rooftop arbor.

"I have heard," Ay began without preliminaries, "that you are no longer to remain in Thebes. I find it a pity. The luster of the court shall dim without you." He patted the cushion of his couch. "Refresh yourself with wine, and come, do sit by me."

Mehi raised his head and absorbed the glint of passion, accepting it, as Ay intended, as genuine. He had never considered an appeal to the grand vizier, had never thought Ay might be inclined to appreciate his dark good looks and his one talent. He did not conceal his surprise nor his eagerness to surrender his body if Ay so wished. He did not take wine. He went directly to Ay's couch.

*The whore is stupid, too,* Ay thought with satisfaction as he warmly pressed the boy's thigh and stroked the inner muscles. The boy responded with a carefully tended hand on Ay's shoulder.

"I would be pleased to serve you," the young man offered, his voice deep in his throat.

"And I should be pleased with your service. I hear you are highly skilled in certain arts."

The boy smiled, cruelty in the sensuality of his lips. Ay's informants said Mehi was adept in the pleasure of pain, which only made the young man's temperament more malleable to Ay's use.

"My rewards are generous," Ay promised, "but the tasks I demand are sometimes dangerous. Your courage might be tested. Do you have courage, Mehi?"

"My lord, for you I am ready." The boy laid his hand over Ay's and moved his fingers with expertise. He let the fringe of his lashes touch the smooth skin above his freshly shaven cheeks. "Your favor is all I ask."

"You would devote yourself to me."

"Yes, my lord."

"You have reason to feel mistreated by Pharaoh."

"I have, my lord! I did nothing for him to deny me his chambers."

The young man would have continued, but Ay quieted him with an upraised hand. No need for the recital of lovers' squabbles and jealousies. "I know all," Ay said. "A shame, when the gods have gifted you more handsomely than Nunit." Ay's fingers stroked firm muscle again.

"Nunit is a swine," Mehi hissed.

"Pharaoh has estranged many, not only you, my friend. He has trespassed against men of importance. His excesses have not gone unnoticed by even the priests of Amon. He has given sufficient cause for many to believe Egypt would best be served if Pharaoh slept in the Valley of the Kings."

Mehi's caressing fingers stilled.

"The man who sends Pharaoh on his final journey would be a hero." Ay took from linen wrappings a gold collar, spectacularly bejeweled, and laid it across the boy's knee. "And he would receive a purse of gold and the revenues from Philae."

Mehi's breath whistled faintly. "Indeed, those are rich rewards."

Ay delved the dark pools of Mehi's eyes. "And he would have the fulfillment of *his* vengeance as well . . . and the solace of my affections."

"Entrust this to me, my lord."

Ay feigned hesitation, then he raised Mehi's wrist to his lips. "Hunting," Ay said, "can be dangerous sport. I am amazed so few accidents occur."

A royal hunting party had been scheduled for the last week of the month. Pharaoh, wearing the new tight kilt that accentuated the bulge of his manhood, held up the blunt-edged spear and gave the signal. Ten boats veered from the channel of the Nile to cut quietly through the reeds.

Mehi stood in the boat of Renit, a noble whose desire for him he had spurned until it provided the means by which he could be included in the hunt. Twenty hunters, eyes sharp, began the search for game.

Pharaoh must be first, of course. His scout pointed to a darting shape, a sparkle of moving sunlight in the water. Pharaoh hurled the spear in a golden flash, held up a bright silver fish in victory. The hunt was on.

They were all absorbed in the discovery of prey, their slim green boats, curved like the lotus, gliding easily through the quiet waters eddying near the bank. Spears sliced the air, game was neatly stacked, decoy herons were held aloft. Eyes followed ripples for the snout and ridged back of the prized crocodile.

Unobserved, Mehi slipped off the blunted edge of his spear. As Renit's boat drew abreast of Pharaoh's, Smenkhare's smooth and straining back was directly before him. His eyes locking his target, Mehi took aim. His spear, cast with such force no eye could perceive it in flight, bit deep into flesh and held. Pharaoh jerked upright.

Bright red streamed down his back, his knees gave way, and he sagged to the bottom of the skiff.

In the subsequent pandemonium, Mehi recovered his second spear from the boat.

"To the palace!" someone shouted, and, given direction, the boats headed for shore. Pharaoh was placed, stomach down, on a hastily contrived litter, the spear still upright. His face was gray, eyes open, staring, tongue lolling.

Pharaoh was dead.

Mehi slipped to the copse where he had been instructed to wait. The acolyte was there. Smiling, Mehi held out his arm for the purse. With his left hand the acolyte reached into his robe and brought out a small pouch. Mehi bowed as he took it. The priest smashed the brick he held in his right hand on Mehi's unsuspecting head. Retrieving the purse, the acolyte dragged the body to the river and shoved it into the water. It sank into the mud among the reeds. When discovered, the body would not attract much attention. Jealousy, rage, remorse, were a not-uncommon pattern in Mehi's kind, and suicide a not-uncommon end.

Bending with Tushratta and Nabamon over Smenkhare's body in the temple courtyard, Ay saw his messenger's return. Unobtrusively the acolyte took his place in the chanting ranks of priests. Intoning the blessing, Ay lowered his eyes to conceal the triumph he felt.

> "Blessed be Amon,
> Great of spirit, great of strength
> To whom we consign his son.
> Receive Pharaoh with honor,
> Receive him in thy sign,
> That he may arise in thy glory."

When the news of Smenkhare's death reached Akhet-Aten, Senumet wasted no time in speculation. Of course the official version was false. Without question Ay was behind it, and its meaning for Akhet-Aten was clear. The time they had dreaded was upon them. Unless Senumet could somehow alter the chain of circumstances that had already been set into motion, the world as they had known it would end, possibly within a matter of days.

Dawn foretold the sunrise that would send the mourning boat on its journey back to Thebes. Senumet, walking along the beach, was surprised to see the captain hurrying toward him. "Is there any need of yours we have overlooked?"

"Not at all. It's merely that Horemheb directed me to speak with you privately."

"I hope my friend does well. . . ."

They were alone on the beach, yet the captain lowered his voice. "He wanted you to know Ay plans to seize Akhet-Aten. Though if it wouldn't be out of place for me to say it, my lord—in my opinion"—the sailor swept the city's dimensions with a practiced eye—"they'll have an easy job of it, in and out in time for their noon meal, strategy or no—if you know what I mean, my lord."

Apparently, thought Senumet, the captain believed he was delivering orders to weaken Akhet-Aten from within. Senumet knew, however, that with Horemheb's abhorrence of illegitimacy, though his friend might despise Akhenaten's beliefs and waverings, still Akhenaten was Pharaoh. In fact, by giving Senumet this warning, Horemheb was trying to assuage his considerable guilt for his part in the coming insurrection.

And instead of anger or fear, Senumet felt something akin to relief. The communication gave shape and outline to Ay's threat. As the captain took his leave and the boat shoved off for Thebes, he knew, as if the plan had sprung full-blown into his mind, what their response must be. Its logic was overwhelming. Hesen might prefer death to what he must propose. Whatever was truly her wish, he would perform for her: only let him not live on without her.

He requested an immediate audience with the queen; his news could not wait until evening when they would steal moments together within her Sun-Shade. She returned his scribe with a summons to her apartment. One glance at his grim face and she cleared the rooms of servants.

He made no attempt to ease the blow. "Horemheb has sent us word. Ay plans at last to seize Akhet-Aten."

She stood as if she had joined Pharaoh in his madness beyond the vale and did not hear him. Then she laughed bitterly. "The old gods will grant him his easiest victory."

"You'd welcome death, then?"

"I have seen too much of death not to have considered my own. I shall die at Pharaoh's side. As queen."

"Are you so certain Ay plans Pharaoh's death?"

Something moved in that pale mask. "What do you mean?"

"Ay will claim he has deposed Pharaoh for his crimes against Egypt. Criminals must be made to suffer public abasement for their crimes. Ay could well drag Pharaoh through the streets of Thebes in chains."

She had not thought of such an outrage. "Pharaoh is still the living god!"

"My darling, consider," he said quietly. "Ay must give Egypt some justification of his actions. Is there a better, more honed to his purpose?"

Her mouth twisted with pain, but she was alive again. "What do you want from me?"

He hesitated: now that it was upon them, he found he couldn't say it. His tongue was thick and dry in his mouth.

As if his thoughts passed to her unspoken, she understood. She did not lack courage—or vision either. And in truth, it was not his to pronounce but hers alone.

"Pharaoh must die," she said.

"More than that," he supplied softly.

"What else can you fear to tell me? That I, too, must die? Then it is done. The dream died years ago. Why should any of the dreamers survive it?" She enveloped him with her gaze in an embrace of love. "If I must renounce life, I have known fulfillment."

Her ability to stare unflinchingly at the coming cataclysm forced him to match her courage. "What I have to offer is harder. Death would require only the grand gesture of a single moment. I am asking you to consider *living* with the knowledge of sacrifice and sin."

"Tell me!"

"Ay's whole strategy rests on Akhenaten's removal. What if he were presented with a Pharaoh whose legitimacy he could not dispute?"

"Who?"

He paused. "Tutu."

For an instant she seemed frozen; then, trembling, she rose. "I see." She began to pace. "He's in the direct line of Thutmosis, Lion of Egypt; hard to dismiss. He's good-natured, tractable. He could command Horemheb's loyalty—and the Guards. Yes." She nodded. "It would be hard to depose Tutankhaten: Should Ay attempt it, he might ignite a revolution."

"And the double crown would rest even more securely upon his head," Senumet persisted, "if he married the heiress . . ." In that moment, Senumet committed himself to his own sacrifice.

She was standing where her feet led her, on the polished terra-cotta tiles of the terrace, beyond the delicate papyrus columns of her reception room, in the serrated shade of low-growing palms. Her eyes were downcast at a bed of blue lotus. She turned toward him, her features cast as hard as bronze. "There is no heiress," she declared metallically. "I thank Aten you forsaw the need of her death and *I will not resurrect her.*"

"Hesen, what is a widowed queen but the heiress?"

Like an unbreathing statue she regarded him, but he felt the silent screams of agony at the plight with which he confronted her. There was nothing he could do or say. Then he saw her raise her chin in an exact replication of Nefertiti's gesture of command, saw her face assume the same cold impassivity. She had accepted her role.

"If Pharaoh must die, I shall give him death."

"My love, that's too much to ask of you," Senumet whispered.

"Who shall better administer his judgment? He will go to his God with the love and honor and respect he deserves."

Blood enough on *his* hands. "By his friend, who would freely and willingly and sadly perform this last act for him."

"No!" It was a command. "No other hand is as fitting as mine."

He bowed to her will. "When?"

Delay would only make it harder. "Tonight," she intoned.

Pharaoh was clearer that day than he had been in weeks.

"I have learned, beloved," he said kindly, misinterpreting the despair in her eyes, "that loss is best assuaged by some hopeful plan. The child can never be replaced—that I know by bitter experience—but another can ease the emptiness a little."

It cost him a massive effort, she knew. He was forcing himself, for love of her, to acknowledge a world too painful for him daily to live in. She made herself respond, made herself offer him the gift of false hopefulness.

They took the evening meal at court for the first time in months. In the dining hall, Aten glittered across the ceiling; a youthful, vigorous Pharaoh and his queen strode across every wall. At the clash of cymbals, all heads turned to welcome the naked acrobats, oiled and gleaming, tumbling into the hall. It was then Hesen opened the silver vial Senumet had provided and tainted the sweetness of the wine. Hiding the vial beneath the cinch of her girdle, she felt it press into her flesh.

She poured his wine herself and urged him with loving smiles to drain the goblet. She knew the court was pleased that the queen seemed in higher spirits and Pharaoh was more himself. They were allowing themselves to hope a little: now that Akhenaten was sole king again, perhaps power and influence would return to their city.

Hesen prolonged the evening's entertainment as long as she could, summoning another troupe of acrobats and more dancers, demanding more songs from the harpist, until the nobles sank into drunken apathy, until even the jugglers' usually faultless timing began to miss, and bright, dancing balls were bouncing on the floor.

When Pharaoh's speech thickened and his face grew pale and his skin clammy, she knew it must end. At her word, Akhenaten tried to stand but could not. The servants who were summoned to help him to his chambers found that they must virtually carry him. They undressed him with unusual haste. Something was wrong. Pharaoh must sleep. But even after they had placed him in his bed, he was restless and agitated. His body thrashed, dripped with perspiration, his breathing grew heavy and labored. When servants tried to rouse him, his eyes rolled back in his head and he muttered sounds no mortal could understand.

"Summon the doctors . . . and the priests," Hesen commanded.

She stayed at his side all through the night, while incense clouded the room, while physicians dotted his body with amulets, while Meire and his priests chanted at his side. Steadily she bathed his head, straightened his garments, held his hand as if to heal him with her love . . . while praying for the poison to overcome his mighty heart, which even now, with all its losses, still fought on the side of life.

Finally, his struggle slackened, his muscles twitched and then relaxed. Each breath was a rasping effort, and the intervals between breaths became longer and less certain.

Hesen summoned Senedjm. Nefertiti should share his last moments. "Bring the queen!" she ordered. "And hurry."

The first light of dawn paled the night beyond the curtains. Gently Hesen wiped the saliva from Pharaoh's chin. As she bent over him, she noticed a foul odor and realized that, having lost control of his bodily functions, Pharaoh lay in his own excrement and urine.

"Cleanse him," she sobbed.

The chief physician gently drew her away from the bed, ordered a thin cover to shield Pharaoh's body from view. "Don't disturb him now," he said quietly. "It's almost over."

A slave announced Nefertiti. Hesen hadn't seen her mother in almost three years. The two women stared silently at each other, love and pain and loss etched on both their faces. Almost as if summoned, they moved to either side of Pharaoh's bed, each lifting one of his unresponsive hands.

Aten's light gradually increased, brightening every corner of the room. Finally the sun's rays bathed Pharaoh's face in golden warmth. With that touch, he drew a last shuddering breath and was still. It was over: the reign, the dream, the man.

Wordlessly, the two women approached each other, lingered in a mutual embrace, and, wordless still, drew apart. Nefertiti returned to the head of the bed. Bending over Pharaoh, she seemed to memorize his face. Then she knelt at his side and pressed her lips against his palm, still warm with his departing spirit. She rose unsteadily, resisting the servants who would have helped her, and stumbled from the chamber.

As Meire ordered everyone present to his knees, the priest's voice was thick with unshed tears. He extended his right hand toward the recumbent form of the king.

> *"While you endured on earth,*
> *You performed justice,*
> *You oppressed not your fellow man,*
> *You punished not unfairly.*
> *Stand fearless now before your father,*
> *O glorious King,*
> *And having reached eternity without wrongdoing,*
> *You shall arise yonder like a God,*
> *Striding freely with the Lords of eternity."*

Withdrawing his hand, the priest covered his face in sorrow.

*Forgive me*, Hesen prayed silently, *my father, husband, God—you were all those to me. So long as I have breath, you shall not be forgotten.*

She reapproached the bed and kissed her husband full on the lips. When she arose, she was steadfast, resolute. Her work had only begun. Her head high, her back straight, she turned to go, and did not look back.

# XXIV

There was no time to grieve or repent.

Senumet departed on horseback when the sun was high, and she found Tutu later that afternoon. When he turned at her approach, his eyes were red and swollen. He lowered his head to hide his unmanly tears.

"Don't be ashamed to weep, Tutu."

"I loved Pharaoh," he said simply.

"Tutu, Egypt has no Pharaoh."

"Egypt has a queen, still," he said after a moment.

"But Egypt must have a king. And that king must be a prince, the son of a great Pharaoh, descended from a mighty line."

The boy's face whitened and he scrambled to his feet. Hesen drew back to look up at him. He almost looked a king, silhouetted against a bright enamel sky, tall and slim. Aten's fingers crowned his head with a golden aurora while behind him the Nile sparkled in assent.

"No, I can't!" Tutu cried, breaking the spell.

But for that brief, glorious moment, she had glimpsed the god's vision: Could it be, after all, that Aten, blessed Father, had sent his daughter a sign? "Of course you can!" Her voice was warm with conviction.

"You'll help me?" He reached for her hand.

"I'll be your queen."

His smile, spontaneous and relieved, held something else too—a hint of command. Arms linked as their bodies soon would be, they made their way together, back to the palace.

While Akhenaten's corpse floated in its natron bath and the wrappings and offerings and prayers were still being readied, Senumet returned with the priest of Amon. If that holy man had demurred and faltered and hesitated, he was in control of himself now ... through the force of Senumet's will. In the very shadow of the funerary tent—in an action unprecedented in all Egypt's history and with every citizen of Akhet-Aten witnessing it—the priest proclaimed Tutankhaten Pharaoh and Hesen his queen.

That same day, a papyrus scroll was enscribed, proclaiming what had occurred. When it had been emblazoned with the new king's cartouche and the seal of a priest of Amon, Senumet took it in hand and set out to intercept Ay.

On the fourth day of his journey Senumet sighted a fleet of ten ships, ready for battle, long, low hulls and raised bulwarks, painted with the thrusting beak of Horus, the war god. The first ship, its stationary sail sparkling with Amon's golden sign, slowed and allowed Senumet to board from his small, swift barge.

Ay's head was shaved as befitted a high priest embarked on a holy war. The whole skin of the sacred leopard was draped over his body, the tail whipping with his angry stride across the deck. "What brings you, Senumet? This is no place for a useless scribe with a withered arm."

Although his demeanor was appropriately contrite, in his heart Senumet felt a bubble of mirth, an emotion long absent from his days. "Only the urgency of my message emboldened me to disobey you, My Lord Ay. I hope you will not find I have been lax and erred once more." Bowing low until he nearly scraped the oiled planks, he offered Ay the scroll. As he felt it removed from his hand, he heard the rhythmic slap of oars dipping into the Nile. The warship was again gaining momentum.

Straightening his back, Senumet saw Ay's brow darken with suspicion as he unrolled the papyrus. His eyes darting over the formal hieroglyphs, Ay absorbed their meaning. His face blanched a ghastly white as he lingered on the seal of the priest of Amon from the Temple of Eshmanon. Senumet breathed a silent prayer that the priest might meet a mercifully quick death.

Ay raised his gaze over the scroll to impale Senumet. Struggling to suppress his choleric temper, Ay rumbled, "Who stands to accept responsibility for this coronation? The Queen Ankhesenpaaten?"

"The deposed queen mother, Nefertiti, ordered the priest sent for, my lord," Senumet lied. It was a lie he had prearranged with Nefertiti; she would support him. He had won her by emphasizing that

Tutu held to his faith in the Aten and might one day reestablish the sway of the one true god over Egypt.

Cunning appraisal glowed in Ay's eyes. "And who was her messenger?"

"I, my lord. I offered my service to the queen mother for your benefit, to dissuade the priest."

"Yet here is his seal."

Senumet nodded.

"Strange that a priest of Amon would defer to a heretic over the argument of your silver tongue." Ay tried to read Senumet's soul, but he could not penetrate beyond the handsome features. "The day will come, Senumet, when we shall settle the question of your loyalty. Until the solar barque sets sail on that dawn, remember: The enemies of the great god Amon shall never triumph. They will fall—and fall miserably." Ay crushed the scroll in his hands.

"Yours is the wisdom," Senumet replied, "that inspires my every act."

The grand vizier turned angrily away. "Sound the trumpets!" he commanded.

The fanfares from seven brass throats shattered the air. Herons rose up from the reeds on both banks at the call, and on the decks of all ten warships, soldiers and crews assembled.

On the flagship, Horemheb led two brigades smartly at drumbeat into formation, infantry with spears and swords, charioteers and archers. From the stern Ay raised to his lips the brass horn that magnified his voice. "Akhenaten, Pharaoh of the Two Lands, is dead. Hail, Tutankhaten, son of the living Horus!"

From the decks of the warships, the cry was taken up: *Hail, Tutankhaten, Son of the Living Horus!"*

The grand vizier retreated to his pavilion and did not emerge until sunset. He ignored Senumet, for which Senumet was grateful. Nor did Senumet see Horemheb again, which was not to his liking. Horemheb needed to be reminded that the strength of Egypt lay in a country united under a Pharaoh descended of the legitimate line. To this tenet Horemheb had been as changeless as the North Star; yet Horemheb was no mental match for the wiles of Ay. Manipulating Horemheb's ferocious resentment of the Aten, Ay could still persuade the warrior to his side.

The braziers were lighted and cast the reflection of dancing flames on the rippling, darkening waters.

When the warships back-oared and glided along the wharves at the royal city of Aten, Senumet pondered. What would Ay do?

Once more Hesen and Tutu walked along the beach scanning the horizon for the first sight of sails, but with a visible difference. Tutu now wore the jeweled collars, rings and armbands of Pharaoh, and he wore the crown, though with boyish delight he picked a different one each day.

To Hesen it was important that he understand he was truly king. Soon he would be tested to extremes, and the greater his sense of his sovereignty, the better his chance for survival. Beginning with simple daily decisions, she deferred to him. He must choose the entertainment at the evening meal, the times he would receive suppliants in the throne room. Except at the quarter sun of morning and the quarter sun of afternoon—the times of the mourning prayers for Akhenaten—she saw that all deference and ceremony accrued to Tutu. In the night she lay with him, cuddling him with her warm closeness to assure him he was loved. There was no more she could do.

She had tried. After the hastily prepared feast on their first night as king and queen, nobles and priests had led Tutu to Pharaoh's bed with gently ribald wishes for joy and fecundity. Meire blessed the wedding bed, while the alabaster lanterns ignited an anticipatory sparkle in Tutu's eyes. No boy of eleven was unaware of the delight promised by the hardening and secretions of his young manhood and the soft curves and mounds of a woman's body. When he was ensconced royally in the huge bed, she came to him . . . his queen, seductively rouged and scented, her hair a shining mass down her back, her body shimmering beneath the diaphanous pleats of her gown. Servants discreetly faded away. She climbed into bed beside him. Although he was aroused, Hesen knew he was more than a little frightened. Terror paralyzed him; his eyes welled with tears. She comforted him with a soft kiss, while stroking his chest, still childishly narrow. Calmed, he curled against her with a contented sigh and fell instantly into a deep, relaxed sleep. If he had wanted a hot striving union with her body, she would have complied. Having always loved her young uncle, she would not have found it unpleasant, perhaps. But as he slept that first night and the nights that followed, she lay awake and apprehensive of Ay's arrival; and she thanked Aten that the awakening of Tutu's manhood was one urgency with which she did not have to contend.

\* \* \*

Akhet-Aten was a city distraught. All signs indicated a momentous evil about to befall. Against all hallowed tradition, the coronation of Tutankhaten had occurred six days after the death of Pharaoh—why had the seventy days of mourning for Akhenaten not been fulfilled before the crown was set upon the brow of the next living god? In all public appearances, the queen, although regally aloof, appeared tense and distracted. The royal guard patrolled the docks and stood sentinel throughout the night, while at the landing reserved for royal barges, a platform sheathed in beaten gold was being erected. What visitor was expected? Rumors spread wildly that the warships of Horus were under sail up the river from Thebes—was the end near? The last of the nobles at the court embarked with furniture, family and pets. On any departing vessel, men begged passage for wives and children, while other citizens packed what they could carry and headed for the dubious safety of the hills and desert. With each passing day, the city became less a city of people, more a city of ghosts. Among the citizens who remained, hunger gnawed, tempers flared, squabbles erupted, murder was committed. In the night, marauders looted what was left behind in the abandoned homes of merchants, craftsmen and nobles. For the first time in its brief history, the guard was called out against Akhet-Aten's citizens to enforce martial order.

On the eleventh day after Senumet had set out upon the Nile, a signal blared from the harbor. Trumpets throughout the city repeated the alarm. The last inhabitants of Akhet-Aten raced through the streets to the royal landing. There on the stone piers extending into the Nile they gathered in sparse clusters, anxiously awaiting the first sight of their fate approaching on the river. Instruments dangling from nervous fingers, musicians took their places in the large square, and dancers stood in readiness, the gold disks on their braids motionless on motionless bodies. Children clutched banners and baskets of petals they would strew. From the palace along the Kings-Way came the golden royal chariots bearing the three young princesses and the new Pharaoh and his queen.

Pearl-white ostrich plumes, long and luxuriant, were anchored to the horses' finely worked leather bridles. In time to the animals' precise trots, the plumes rippled back over their heads. Behind them marched the guard, double-time.

As the chariots rolled onto the granite of the landing, Hesen glanced up at the towering statues of Akhenaten that served as a gateway at the river to the city, but she gave no thought to her father: the part he played in Egypt's history was finished. She sent Tutu to wait on the golden, rose-festooned platform erected on the widest stone pier. "Stand tall, my darling," she commanded, "as we rehearsed. Let them see Pharaoh in all his resplendent divinity! Soon I will join you."

Under the supervision of their nurse, the princesses ascended the royal platform. The platform should also be occupied by the high priest, but Hesen had requested Meire to forgo his prerogative on this day. Tutu followed the princesses. He held himself erect, looking more like a small effigy of Pharaoh than a living boy. Hesen waited until his brave figure had ascended and his subjects had bent low to Pharaoh, then she strode purposefully among the musicians, dancers and children, tongue-flogging them into a frenzied artifice of festivity.

"Wave those flags!"

Almond eyes wide and frightened, children swished scraps of linen bearing Pharaoh's cartouche with graceless desperation.

"Play!" she barked.

Musicians raised their flutes and harps, bells and cymbals, and lilting tunes obscured the murmurs of the citizens.

Majestically bellicose, the ten warships loomed over the horizon and swallowed up the river with their menace. The eternal time of the gods seemed to enshroud the royal landing as the ships grew larger. The fierce eye of the war god, painted on every hull, bore down upon the landing, diminishing and overwhelming human forms. The musicians' notes trailed off in discordant plunks. Hesen flashed their leader a murderous look. After a false start, the playing resumed.

"Dance!" she almost snarled at the huddled corps of performers. Their mouths trembled, but the women jerked to life, whirled and leaped in automatic choreography, their gold disks flashing about their heads and bodies.

Satisfied with the charade of joyous pageantry, she mounted the steps to the platform and took her place at Tutu's side. She flashed him a reassuring smile, then stared intensely at the ships, gliding inexorably toward them. On the decks she saw masses of red, the color worn by the garrison at Thebes, and bronze glints of swords, spears and shields. There was no way she could discern if Senumet had been successful in diverting Ay from attack. In any case, there was nothing more she could do. To Egypt she and Tutu appeared confidently regal and invincible. As she had planned.

She heard Penre whimper, and from the corner of her eye saw Sherit comfort the youngest with a kiss before their nurse moved close to take charge.

The warships approached the landing, and blocking the sun that had risen less than a quarter into the sky, cast massive dark shadows on the dock and the celebrants. Hulls scraped stone with the sound of battle shouts. Ropes were tossed to hands on the piers that expertly lashed them to mooring posts and rings. Landing ramps slid from the decks and were secured into place.

The tension was too great. Again the musicians faltered and the dancers with them, and there was nothing Hesen could do to revive them.

On the flagship, the soldiers raised their spears and swords and a salute roared from their throats as a man, stoutly muscular, appeared at the top of the ramp. He wore the headband of command with Amon's sign in the center of his forehead. Horemheb. His boots thudded firmly on the wood as he descended to the landing, flanked by two of his generals.

Tutu broke into a delighted smile at the sight of his tutor and friend; his body quivered with excitement. Hesen touched his arm to remind him to sustain his royal posture, but so much more than the mask of regality shown on the boy's face. She scrutinized her old comrade. Was he here to seize them, or to bow?

At a signal from Horemheb's generals, soldiers poured from the ships; first from the flagship and then the others, phalanx after phalanx of troops marching double-time, shoving back the populace and the celebrants, crowding the landing with tramping feet, muscled bodies and flashing arms and bows.

Chariots pulled by war steeds stopped before the royal couple. A hush at last fell over the ships and the landing. Horemheb lifted his eyes to meet impersonally with Hesen's. His gaze was as hard as his blade. Her chest tightened painfully while her heart missed a beat. And then he bent his knee before them, and all of his army with him. Hesen's own knees nearly gave way. If Horemheb's homage was not a convolution in Ay's strategy to throw them off guard, then they had won.

*Father Aten, where was Senumet?*

She searched the flagship—and found him there at the railing above the eye of the war god, rigid and impassive, and she understood that he knew as little as she about what was to occur next.

A herald of trumpets. Ay disembarked. Behind him came a man bearing the staff of Amon. *Nabamon*, Hesen thought, although she had never before seen him. Proceeding after them came a dozen priests.

Ay's aspect was murderous, yet she took Horemheb's veneration as a good omen. She would be undaunted.

She raised her voice. "The Pharaoh Tutankhaten and his queen welcome you, Grand Vizier of Egypt, exalted High Priest of Amon, to Akhet-Aten at the beginning of Pharaoh's glorious reign, he, son of the Living God, who shall bless Egypt with fertility and prosperity for years to come."

Years before, on the landing at Thebes, her voice had rung in Ay's ears and thwarted his ambition. In the bitter twist of his face, she thought she could see the memory of that day.

"Hail, Tutankhaten, Pharaoh of Egypt!" Ay began stentoriously. "The great god Amon bestows his blessings upon thy head. Praise to Tutankhaten, son of Horus, he of the Living God. And to his queen. Amon will bless Pharaoh with a new coronation, to be held forthwith in this city, under the eye of the Great God." Then Ay bowed, as if the weight of the heavens forced him down.

Through the cheers of soldiers and the populace, triumph soared in Hesen's heart. A coronation under Ay's hand? What could be better? Tutu's throne would be securely established, the right of the dynasty extended.

*Father Aten, I praise you for this day and for the love of the man who has succored me and who, with Thy help, has brought this day to pass.*

# XXV

Preparations for the coronation began the next day. Soldiers, wielding brushes, scrapers and buckets, swarmed into the square below the palace. In just two days the buildings and shops lining the square glistened again with fresh paint. Pillars were scraped to blazing whiteness, their dulled signs sparkling with newly applied gilt. Broken foot-tiles were replaced, then polished to gleaming brightness.

Driven to the site in her chariot, Hesen responded with pleasure to its fresh, clean look. But as she rode back to the palace she perceived, by contrast, how dreadfully blighted the rest of the city actually was. One block past the newly decorated square, paint was peeling from buildings in ugly patches; weeds were encroaching on untended flower beds; shop signs were dangling grotesquely, their painted hieroglyphs flaking. She raised her eyes to the temple. That, too! she thought sadly, staring at dulled electrum doors and grimy pillars. Even the palace looked dingy.

During the next few days she tried to hold onto the moment of triumph when the guard, then Ay bowed to her and Tutu. But she became uneasy. Somehow she could not believe the auguries were truly promising. She had expected Ay to wait until the period of mourning was over and Akhenaten was entombed, but no—the coronation would take place before the month was out, he informed her. And then she found her freedom circumscribed. Subtly, without explanation or unpleasantness, soldiers from the garrison at Thebes replaced her guard. They escorted her everywhere with implacable eyes—to the funerary tent, along the corridors to the throne room, on strolls in the gardens, to her Sun-Shade . . . where, though they did not enter, they kept watch until she emerged. It was clear that if she dismissed them, they would not hear. She had no means to escape the vise in which Ay squeezed her. Was he merely demonstrating so soon that his was to be a regency of tyranny? Or did he harbor a more drastic intent?

She needed Senumet, but because of the guard, she was cut off from him completely. She feared for his safety. Was he still in Akhet-Aten? She had no way of knowing. Sephy's ears at last gathered word from the gossip of servants. Sephy had come to love Senumet as a son, and she fearfully whispered the news. Ay had assigned Senumet to quarters in the scribe's bureau, and a posted guard prevented him from leaving there. He was allowed no visitors. Furthermore, Ay had exiled him. To where Sephy didn't know, nor did she know when he was to depart from the city.

Hesen and Sephy together devised schemes to pass a message to him and receive his answer, but in despair Hesen abandoned them all. The risk was too great; the message that could be traced to her would incriminate Senumet further—for she well understood her uncle's temperament. His anger set off, he wouldn't hesitate to crush the helpless.

Her young husband, almost confirmed in his kingship, spent his time much as he pleased, and it pleased him to pass the days with Horemheb. Seeing them together by the lotus pool in the inner courtyard, Hesen was struck by the thought that Horemheb might be her avenue to Senumet. For the sake of their old friendships, hers with him, his with Senumet, would he secretly help her? Yet as she watched him teach Tutu to string a bow, she became wary of approaching him directly. Perhaps he spent the days with Tutu as Ay's spy. Was there no one she could trust except dear Sephy? Tutu! She decided to weave the boy into her intrigue.

That night in the bed they chastely shared, she questioned her husband closely about Horemheb, what they did together, what he said. With excited delight, Tutu told her how in the afternoon, they had taken a chariot into the hills and Horemheb had discovered the spoor of lion, surprisingly close to the city.

"I'm going to slay a lion one day," Tutu vowed, "all by myself. And I'll give the pelt to you, Hesen."

"And I'll have it cured and stretched proudly." She laughed and hugged him.

Dreamily Tutu spoke of his fondest wish, to fulfill his long-ago promise to name Horemheb Master of the Horse.

"How thoughtful you are," she agreed, "and loyal." And she was moved. What was more, however, she saw instantly that the idea had another advantage. It could serve to bind Horemheb to Tutu, in case Ay ever tried to move against the boy. "I'll speak of it to the grand vizier," she promised. Although Ay would see the possible disadvantage to himself, he could hardly refuse—especially if she caused the word to spread among the soldiers that their commander was to be honored. If Ay then declined or delayed, it would look as if he slighted Horemheb. Looking into Tutu's happy eyes, she felt a stab of envy. So innocent. While she had reached the point in her life where everything, even the wish of a boy to favor his friend, must be politically weighed and played.

Casually she said, "You know, I'm sure Senumet would like to see how well you handle the bow, now."

"Where is Senumet?" he asked with surprise. In the fullness of the past week, he hadn't noticed Senumet had dropped out of their lives.

"I don't know, but Horemheb must. If you command it, he'll take you to see Senumet." There. If Senumet could speak with Tutu, he could send her a message, concealed—if need be—in innocuous words she could interpret. And she doubted Horemheb would refuse an order from Pharaoh.

She found she was mistaken. Next day, Horemheb deflected Tutu's command. Senumet, he explained, was preparing for a new mission, a journey, and could not be disturbed. Horemheb had to be aware that Senumet was under guard, she thought, so it was impossible he completely believed what he said. How deeply had Ay managed to poison Horemheb against his comrade-in-arms at Byblos?

Stung by failure, Hesen nonetheless persisted. She entered Ay's apartments in the north wing of the palace and presented Tutu's desire for Horemheb's appointment. With every show of enthusiasm, Ay took the matter into his own hands, even ordering casks of wine for the soldiers of the garrison to celebrate the investiture.

"The Pharaoh Tutankhaten also wishes to say good-bye to Senumet before he leaves and bless his travels," Hesen said.

Ay stared at her shrewdly. "It is fitting."

"Where is he going?"

The grand vizier withheld an answer while a young scribe removed a papyrus roll from his hands and replaced it with another. She knew he used silence to toy with her, and it seemed the delicate lilies painted on the walls would brown and die before he said, "To Zoan. Userhat needs someone skilled in languages at his side."

As she stepped into the corridor and two of the Theban soldiers fell into step behind her, Hesen's heart was aching. Zoan. The port city he had been brought to when he returned from Byblos. Her eyes were blinded with tears that she refused to shed. She would see him when he approached the throne for Pharaoh's blessing, and then how many years must pass before they would bask again in each other's sight?

It was over. Witnessed by the court and Horemheb's generals, the ceremony elevating Horemheb had been performed by Ay with Tutu at his side. Senumet, too, was present, standing on the outside of the gathering near the colonnade that led into the palace courtyard. She had been careful not to notice him, but against her will, her eyes sought him out. Then Ay had summoned Senumet forward, saying he was to embark that very afternoon on a vessel bound for Gaza which would first land a cargo at Zoan. While she and Tutu had exchanged formal farewells with him, Senumet kept his face serene. She knew she had acted her part well; her serenity had matched his, although her mind had been filled with memories of his body against hers, his arms strongly embracing her, his flesh inside her.

Now musicians played. What would be more natural than for the queen to mingle with nobles and officials in the free manner established by her father? She left the double throne she shared with Tutu, once shared by her father and mother as equals, and with gracious comments to all she passed, she made her way to Senumet. Handsome beyond all other men, her always love.

She offered her hand, and he took it in his, warm and strong, and bent to kiss her ring. She knew that he was as aware as she that Ay's gaze skewered them from where he stood on the steps to the double throne, and Ay must see no hint of their intimacy.

"Beloved," he whispered.

"Will you be safe?"

"Unless, in that wet swamp, I am devoured by mosquitoes." He smiled. "I think assigning me to Zoan is precaution enough for your uncle. He won't send an assassin after me. It's your safety I'm worried about. Never relax your vigilance. *Never trust him.*"

"We can't stand talking like this," she said. Already she had given him more time than protocol dictated, and Nabamon, too, was looking in their direction. Yet how could she turn and walk away?

"I'll be with you in my thoughts every moment," he swore.

"May Aten light your way."

Bowing, he warned under his breath, "It isn't finished. Beware—the coronation."

Later she would remember his words, but now she saw only the thick black hair on his head and remembered the glossy feel of it. So many times her fingers had combed through his hair.

Their eyes locked for one last final instant. "There is a little one we both love," he dared softly. "I'll see to her." Then he left the throne room through the colonnade, passing into the brilliance of Aten's sun.

She turned to the next claimant for her attention and finished the day radiantly. At its end, she had to ask Sephy to bring her a tall goblet of wine and bathe her throbbing temples before she could dress for the evening meal. She did not see his ship cast off from the dock and seek the current of the Nile.

The coronation but five sunrises away, two uncompleted tasks gnawed at Hesen: Somehow she must circumvent her guard and see Meire, and somehow she must insure the safety of her mother. Meire and his priests were under a clear threat of the sword, and it appeared daily more ominous to Hesen that Ay made no mention of Nefertiti.

In the afternoon, she boldly called for her chariot. As one of Ay's Theban guards moved quickly to step up into the chariot behind her, she dextrously snapped the reins. The pair of matched whites broke into a fast, nervous trot. The guard shouted out in surprise as the chariot rolled away. Another snap of the reins and the horses sprinted, shod hooves pounding on the stone of the Kings-Way. Alone!—for the first time since Ay's arrival—she indulged herself. She drove to the beach and raced her team along the strand, the wind singing in her ears and flowing fresh and moist on her face. The beach stretched emptily behind her; she was not pursued.

She turned her horses onto a path that led upward to one of four small temples of Aten that had been erected like sentinels on the perimeter of the city. Here in the southern temple, Meire and his priests had taken up residence when Ay and the Theban garrison entered the city. At the clamor of hooves and wheels, Meire emerged from the god's place. She pulled the horses to a halt and accepted his hand as she alighted. She expected to enter the temple, but he led her instead to the garden. Allowing him to seat her on a bench worked from stone, she knew that if she raised her eyes she would see a stela with her name chiseled in the oval cartouche.

The priest's hand covered hers in sympathetic understanding. "I'm glad to see you and bless you. You are Aten's true daughter."

She read compassion and respect on his face and was deeply stirred. While she could confront arrogance and evil, the homage of this wise good man threatened to unnerve her. Her mouth trembled.

"You must flee," she said unsteadily. "The grand vizier will not long permit Aten's worship. You and all your priests must escape the city. You must save yourselves."

A slow smile began in his eyes. "That does not sound like Pharaoh's brave wife and daughter."

"I could not hear of your death. I cannot bear more blood on my soul—" She stopped, appalled. What had she admitted?

"There is no blood on your soul." Comprehension was stamped on his features and, incredibly, respect was there as well. "You are Aten's strength and Aten's glory."

"Thank you," she said simply, then: "But you cannot believe Aten wills your death and your priests'."

"My priests are gone. And I wish to share my king's fate."

"Meire, if you are dead, who will tell Pharaoh's story? Who will set down the history of Akhenaten and his great dream? If as your queen, I ordered it, would you obey?"

"I must."

"Then go!"

He nodded slow assent. "I bow to your command. But first, Highness, about your mother. . . ."

Meire had been in touch with the queen. It was more than she had hoped.

"Nefertiti wants you to know you need not be concerned for her. She has plans for herself."

"Plans? . . ."

"She refuses to discuss them, but she will make everything clear to you in her own time."

Hesen almost smiled—that sounded like the old stone-willed Nefertiti. "Very well, then." She rose and accepted Meire's final blessing.

He escorted her to her chariot. She left him there, standing before the three columns of the temple, golden in Aten's rays. Another good-bye, another severing of a cherished human bond. It was almost, she thought, as if she were preparing for death.

Brightly painted feluccas crowded the harbor disgorging nobles and courtiers from neighboring nomes. Long barges filled with tributes in ivory caskets or carved wooden chests were unloaded. Some of the treasure was symbolically hidden behind stiff parchment screens in the square, to be revealed at the coronation. The city's streets that had echoed hollowly just a few weeks ago reverberated with shouts and laughter and life.

And at the center of the restored square, the coronation platform took shape. Nine steps carved with bright ankhs and sheathed with gold leaf led to a high stage. Slim golden poles were raised on three sides and a green canopy, symbol of the Nile God, rested lightly on their polished tips. Nekhbet's powerful wings, stitched on the underside, spread protectively over the stage where Pharaoh would stand.

On the morning of the coronation, Sephy molded to Hesen's body a white sheath; below the hip the skirt consisted of strands of glass beads that would tinkle musically with every step. For her head Hesen had chosen a gold crown adorned with the cobra—uraeus of power. The snake's jasper eyes gleamed out of a black obsidian face above the coils of its body, striped with gold and cornelian and lapis.

She and Tutu were carried to the square on twin golden litters. Golden trumpets were raised as they were borne to the throne. As they approached the dais, Horemheb bowed to them from the waist. Her sisters formed a line of beaming princesses to their right. Hesen heard Penre giggle.

Side by side, in measured cadence, Hesen and Tutu climbed the nine steps to where Ay awaited. His shoulders were draped with the forelegs and talons of leopard skin, his eyes burned like twin suns. Behind him, with the staff of Amon, stood Nabamon, unadorned except for the golden pin that clasped his yellow robe over his left shoulder, and behind the priest of Karnak stood five of Amon's ordained. Around the dais itself in concentric semicircles stood nobles and officials of state, ready to bend their knees to Pharaoh.

A final clash of cymbals vibrated into silence. The square below was absolutely hushed, the only sound the soft flutter of Amon's banner lifting in the light breeze.

Hesen and the boy king bowed before Ay. He extended his broad hands over Tutu's head.

Ay's voice rolled over the square. "You shall rise like the sun, rejuvenate yourself like the moon, repeat justice and mercy and great deeds as the inundation each year repeats its gift to the land of Egypt."

A priest stepped forward with the pharonic beard which he attached to Tutu's chin by strapping it over the top of the boy's head. Then a second advanced, bearing on a golden tray the double crown of Egypt. Ay lifted the heavy red and white crown. He held it high and set it firmly on Tutu's head.

"You are Pharaoh, son of the living god. You renew that holy circle."

The crown slipped forward on Tutu's small head, but Tutu did not flinch.

"You rise with Ra. You will ascend with him in the great reed float. You will pay homage to the great god Amon."

"I am ready." Tutu's voice, sweet and high, rang with all the promise of his steadfast heart.

"You shall reign over this land to the end of the circuit of the sky with power . . ."

A second priest advanced with an alabaster tray. From it Tutu accepted the lapis-banded golden flail. He crossed his right arm over his chest to hold the symbol of power at the opposite shoulder. From the tray Tutu also accepted the flashing crook and held it to his right shoulder as Ay intoned, "and with wisdom."

"Pharaoh is god," Ay continued. "He enters into all trees and animates their branches. He raises heaven to furor and the sea to revolt, and they become peaceful again when he comes to peace. He brings the divine Nile to flood and the crops to harvest. He fills all our hearts, and we hail him."

Ay took the staff of Amon from Nabamon and raised it to the sky. "The tenth Pharaoh of the line of Ahmose, you shall answer with the name of the true god. You shall be called Tutankhamon."

Tutu looked to Hesen. With an almost imperceptible nod, she bade him yield.

"I accept it," the boy responded uncertainly.

"And your queen shall be called Ankhesenamon."

Ay's eyes fastened on hers as he relished her helpless servility. "I accept it," she granted, but her tongue was awkwardly recalcitrant in her mouth. What choice had she?

Then Ay proclaimed to the assembly in the square, "A regency shall be established in Amon's name while his son Tutankhamon applies himself to learning and grows to manhood. Amon-Ra, great Father, lord of us all, has instructed me through his blazing light. He has filled me with his guiding power. *I* am to be regent to Pharaoh and to Egypt."

She felt as if gigantic slabs of weight were crushing her body.

Usurper! she cursed Ay silently. Yes, she and Senumet had considered the possibility of Ay's regency, but she had not convinced herself that Ay would actually move to violate her dominion. She was the undisputed reigning monarch, the legitimate heiress—and *she* was no child! There was no precedent for a regency when a mature queen shared the throne with a boy-Pharaoh; by right, she should have reigned in her husband's stead until he came of age! Claiming the intervention of his god, Ay was wrenching from her hands the power of the throne. She shook with anger and fear. For too many interminable years, Tutu and she would be forced to live with no recourse under Ay's grinding thumb. But they would survive—she would nurture and somehow protect Tutu, and the day *would* come when Tutu assumed full power of Pharaoh. Then Ay would be vanquished. Forever!

Her voice was loud, hate inspiring its own strength. "On behalf of Pharaoh, I accept your regency!"

Ay smiled. "Amon has further decreed that Pharaoh and his queen must return to Thebes . . . where their faith in the great god Amon shall be nourished by the spirits of their ancestors, eternally resting in the shadows of the sacred cliffs."

The line of her neck, the line of her back were defiantly rigid. With the enforced return to Thebes where he was sure of his control, Ay had done his worst and she was not broken. "We accept it!"

Drums and trumpets boomed and blared approval, and if Ay had heard the challenge in her words, he ignored it. He guided Tutu to his throne and Hesen to the gilded chair adjacent to it. Drums and trumpets quieted with a crescendoing flourish. They sat. The multitude bent low in worship. The double crown on his head, the pharonic beard on his chin, his arms crossed and the symbols of strength and wisdom in his hands, Tutu embodied the might and majesty of Egypt even in his boyish form that seemed to take on manhood before Hesen's eyes. She was stung with pride of him. Her emotion was contagious. Pharaoh's subjects broke into spontaneous cheering.

Ay moved to the forward edge of the dais. He raised his right arm and scythed the air. The cheering fell away. For long moments, Ay's glance flicked over the crowd, singling out individuals, then passing on. Jubilation was replaced with nameless dread.

At last Ay thundered, "Citizens of Akhet-Aten! Hear me and understand your doom!"

Father Aten, *what now?* Hesen thought.

"Amon has decreed your death!"

There was a collective gasp as loud as a shout. Terrified eyes darted glances at the sound of stamping feet and found the garrison of Thebes, Ay's troops, encircling the square, their blades unsheathed for slaughter. Archers fell to one knee, pulled bow strings tight with arrows aimed into the crowd. Women screamed, children cried.

"The great father Amon has demanded your punishment for abandoning his truth for an heretical god!" Ay declared.

Pharaoh's subjects collapsed to their knees.

"Ra, great Ra!"

"Amon, we adore Thee, Amon-Ra!"

"Amon, hear us!"

"Amon be praised!"

"Mercy, mercy! Great Ra!"

Hesen rose to her feet. She would not, *could not* allow this! Her eyes sought out Horemheb before the platform, but his hard warrior's face rejected her appeal.

She found her sisters. Sherit, her newly rounded form offering comfort to a sobbing Penre, gripped Neferu's hand while her wide frightened eyes were riveted to Ay's back. Hesen's mind leaped to the golden ceremonial dagger hanging at Tutu's hip. Before she would watch blood run in the square, she would snatch the dagger and murder her uncle in full sight of all—or die trying.

Again Ay scythed the air and the babble ceased. "Do you renounce the false god Aten?"

"Yes, yes! We renounce him!" cried a thousand voices.

Darkness filmed before Hesen's eyes. Had the sun's light actually faded at the renunciation?

"Amon has heard you," Ay shouted. "With my own prayers, *I* have interceded. I have pleaded with Amon. And Amon has absolved you!"

Again the people cried out, this time in thanksgiving.

"Praise Lord Ay!"

"Thanks be to Amon!"

"Blessed be the priest most high!"

"May Amon reign forever!"

"Great priest of Amon-Ra!"

"The great god knows you have been unwittingly misled," Ay roared. "In his omniscience, he sees into your hearts and knows you are no criminals. He knows, however, who the criminal was, who wickedly led you astray and blinded your hearts for sake of his own evil! Accept Amon's judgment!"

Ay pointed a gnarled finger. Every head swiveled in that direction. The funerary tent!

"The despoiler of his heritage, the ruination of our empire, the Pharaoh who drove out the living god from his body and from the land, the traitor to his people and to Egypt!" Ay bellowed. "The criminal Akhenaten!"

It was more than one loyal, loving boy could bear. "No!" Tutu cried. "He was a great king!" Below the platform, Akhenaten's younger daughters wailed.

"Silence them!" Ay flashed a murderous glance first at the princesses' nurse and then at Hesen. "Control him!"

Horribly festive, the glass beads tinkled, swirling around her legs, as she turned toward Tutu. Her heart went out to her sisters, but Tutu was her first and most important charge. He, too, was now on his feet, and she embraced his waist. She willed his stiff, resisting body to relax against her. "Words," she whispered. "Be still, Tutu. Thank Aten, Ay can't touch him."

"The criminal Pharaoh thought to escape the terrible wrath of Amon," Ay stormed. "Through death he sought to save himself from Amon's fury! But Ra can reach beyond the tomb. Remove the screens!"

Soldiers thrust their spears through the stiff parchments, ripping the screens away. No hidden tributes, no glittering treasures were exposed. Hesen stared uncomprehending at a braced, high pile of faggots.

"Akhenaten's ka shall be eternally damned," Ay pronounced. "His ka, laden with guilt, shall wander lost and homeless through the corridors of all time. *Drag forth the blasphemer!*"

The silence surrounding the dais was so profound that the call of an ibis in flight tore through the square, a continuous excruciating scream. It echoed through Hesen as if it were the scream she strangled in her own throat. The world drained of color before her eyes, but she would not faint. Fiercely she pressed Tutu's face between her breasts—he was the only reality she could cling to. Aten grant she could shield his eyes from this atrocity.

In similar anticipation the nurse was holding Penre to her chest while Neferu and Sherit, at twelve and fourteen, must stand unaided and choke back the sobs that threatened to burst out of trembling lips.

Soldiers threw open the funerary tent, and two of them, their uniforms a blur of brown leather jerkins over red tunics, dragged the lifeless form of Akhenaten into the midst of the crowd. His white naked body bounced on the uneven stone. Citizens cleared a path, knocking down and trampling unheeded any behind them who barred their retreat.

The two soldiers reached the pyre. They gripped the shoulders and ankles of the dead king and swung the corpse, its arms flapping, its head wildly rolling, in widening arcs. Finally they flung it to the top of the wooden pile where it grotesquely sprawled. The neck, white and frail, was almost twisted off. Its deformities magnified by the process of mummification, its manhood lost between mammoth thighs, the body was cruelly exposed to the stares of the populace.

"The fire!" Ay commanded.

Striking tinders sent up a shower of sparks, ignited, and caught. Blue tongues of the first flames licked at the dried wood and grasses bound into bundles, blazed orange and red and climbed hungrily higher. Smoke ascended through the bundles, curling and wafting around Pharaoh's fleshy shell before it rose to heaven and thinly veiled the sun. Within moments the first crackling flames seared Pharaoh's foot.

Clearly over the snapping blaze, a high cry rent the air and tremoloed. "Hail, Aten! Aten is the true god!"

Heads whipped around. No one could discover the source. Shivering, they began to think it issued from the god.

"Aten is truth! The false Amon and his pantheon of old gods live only in the night of men's hearts, on men's deceitful tongues!"

Again the crowd jostled and shoved each other, fearfully hunting.

"There!"

"Look there!"

With shaking fingers, the few who had discovered Aten's oracle pointed to the temple. At first, those who followed the fingers focused on the electrum of the doors. Had the god emerged? But the doors remained closed.

Hesen spotted her. Nefertiti, on the temple's roof, as glorious as she must have looked as a bride. The fine white fabric of her gown billowed around her slender, still sensuously lovely body. Collars and rings and bracelets, forsworn these past years, glittered around her neck, wrists and arms. But her greatest glory was her face, its incredible structure and planes heightened by the kohl and cosmetic paints she had declined in her grieving, more dazzling than she had ever been, more magnificent than Bek, with all his skilled artistry, had or could ever fashion. Hers was the face of a goddess, a perfection which Nature would never again repeat.

*O Merciful Father*, Hesen thought, unable to draw a breath. Somehow the queen had foreseen the extent of Ay's vengeance and *this* was what she had planned for her future! Passing over the edge of horror, Hesen could not even weep. Tears would only diminish the magnitude of what was taking place.

Nefertiti raised her arms. "Aten *is* god of all men and all creation!" she cried, her voice magically amplified on the wind that swept through the square suddenly as if she had called it forth. "And Akhenaten is his true son. Know you, Ay, and all you cowardly lying priests who think to doom his ka, you cannot crush that noble spirit. He shall arise shining unto the hands of the Aten to sit at the Father's side. And I shall rise with him unto the Father!"

She *was* a goddess. Her daughter believed it. Even Ay was cowed by her power—until with a stabbing gesture he signaled to the archers, who prepared to release their shafts at her. But as every eye was upon her, transfixed, already she was moving to the edge of the roof. Penre cried, "Mother!" but no one paid notice. She stepped into the air. For one incredible instant, her body, luminescent and glowing, hung suspended in space, the wind ballooning her gown. Then in a flutter of white, she plummeted to the paving stone, a crumpled heap. In a widening pool, a dark scarlet stain soaked her gown, spreading . . .

"Eh-ss, Eh-ss." Tutu had struggled from Hesen's protective hold. Loosened, the pharonic beard had slipped from his chin to dangle at his chest. Straining, he could stammer only that one sound. "*Eh-ss!*" Hesen clutched him to her. But while she shut his eyes to the rest of the ghastly spectacle, she could not grant herself that escape.

Soldiers scooped up Nefertiti, exposing the smashed ruin of her face. They tossed the queen's body into the inferno to join her king.

Hesen stared into its fiery core until it consumed wood and flesh and bone. The pyre sank down upon itself, flames struggling to revive in sporadic bursts, finally expiring in a mound of gray ash.

And still Tutu leaned against her breasts.

Unexpectedly the afternoon breeze stirred the ash to swirling life. Flakes spiraled upward in the current and a stream of live sparks rained over the square. Screams pierced the air. "Aiee! The hand of Pharaoh!" In the din, the crowd was dispersing, savagely shoving each other to escape the immortal wrath. Among them, the nurse disappeared with the princesses. As the square cleared, soldiers lined up before the platform. Under their boots, the gray ash became dark smudges on the paving stone.

Hesen stared dully at the even, disciplined ranks of uniforms. Here, in the mindless, unquestioning stance, was true menace. Was this, she thought, the simple loyalty of which Horemheb was so proud?

Suddenly she realized the bodice of her dress was wet. She lifted Tutu's head and found he had not been crying. What had dampened her chest was not tears but saliva he could not swallow. Terrified, he pulled at his lips with his fingers and grunted that same awful, hissing sound. "Eh-ss. Ehesssss!"

Having nothing with which to wipe his mouth, she resorted to her jeweled fingers, cleaned it, and wiped them on her dress, which she would destroy rather than wear again. "My darling, don't worry. You were so utterly frightened. That's why you can't talk. Speech will come back." But was that true? Was there anything in this insane landscape left to hope for? She wished Ay would order her death. How could she live with the awful images of Akhenaten and her mother burning forever in her soul?

"Put aside your arms!" It was Horemheb, not Ay, barking at the garrison. "You have your orders. To it!"

As one, the soldiers stripped off their harnesses, jerkins and tunics, baring their bodies to loincloths. They fanned out in prearranged patterns. From heavy horse-drawn carts pulling into the square, they took clubs, sledgehammers and wedges. Teams of twelve wheeled battering rams from the streets where they had been concealed. The soldiers crushed the walls of brightly painted shops, smashed the colonnade that led to the airy throne room and the palace. Beautiful mosaics were destroyed. The soldiers' muscular arms and naked backs glistened with the sweat of their strenuous efforts. They attacked the temple, battering down the electrum doors and the facade. Clouds of dust from stone and brick filled the air and clogged Hesen's nostrils and throat. Her ears reverberated with the rhythmic blows and were deafened so that she could scarcely hear the chanted prayer to Amon taken up by Nabamon and his priests. Over the work of destruction, Ay gloated.

She and Tutu must go somewhere, Hesen realized—but where?

How could they return to a palace that was about to be reduced to rubble, brick by brick and stone by stone? And how long would Ay force them to stand on legs with little strength left, here on this detestable platform—until the entire ciy was razed?

A soldier marched to the platform, an object between his callused hands. He held it up: Bek's sculpted head of Nefertiti. Hesen wondered if it were the master artisan's original, taken from a pedestal in the north palace, or one of the numerous copies hidden away when Nefertiti defected from Akhenaten's side. She stared at that marvelous face; it blurred before her eyes.

"Smash it!" Ay demanded.

Obediently the soldier lowered it to the paving, then raised his club. One blow split and halved it. An inlaid eye popped out.

Tutu screamed a high primordial note of anguish and collapsed. Hesen bent to cradle him, but she had reached the end of her own endurance. Reality was slipping away . . .

"Take him to the ship." Ay's order jolted her. Tutu was extracted from her arms. "Go with him!" Numbly she followed Tutu's limp figure as it was carried down the nine steps by two soldiers who were careful not to dislodge the crown of Egypt. They laid him on his royal litter, carried on the shoulders of four soldiers more. "To the flagship," Ay directed.

The streets were empty. The powder of brick and stone already settled over everything, even the docks where the refugees of Akhet-Aten were stranded, with the few possessions they had managed to salvage. A cordon of soldiers kept them from the ships. On the river, Hesen saw the last of brightly colored and striped sails, the barges and feluccas that carried the nobles and headsmen of the nomes away from the coronation and Akhet-Aten for the last time.

On the flagship, she stayed by Tutu's unconscious form late into the night, no servants appearing, no one available to search for them. From the city came the sounds of battered thuds and cracks of bursting, falling stone. At last she passed into sleep, exhausted even of dreams.

A hand shook her shoulder. Her eyes flew open—Sephy! Oh, thank Aten. Wordlessly they embraced, and Hesen was fullhearted with a gratitude too overwhelming to express. Whispering, Sephy told her she had brought the princesses aboard. They were sleeping below deck, watched over by their nurse. Sephy's eyes were tearful as she knelt by the couch on which Tutu lay and brushed his hair away from his forehead. Now assured of his safety, Hesen knew she must go on deck.

Pushing through the curtain of the pavilion, she stumbled to the railing. Through the rest of the star-studded night under the cold light of Shu, past dawn and noon and sunset into the second night, she clutched at the railing, watching the reversal of the dream. She thought of Senumet's warning that Ay might dare to drag Akhenaten as a criminal through the streets, and to save her father from that fate, she had given him death to drink. And yet she had not, after all, saved him. Her mind fastened on Tutu's dagger. Oh, Aten, why hadn't she seized the moment, no matter what the consequences, to rid Egypt of Ay's vile life. Sephy brought her bread and wine. If she ate it, she had no memory of it.

Again Sephy approached her. "He's awake, my lady."

She followed Sephy into the pavilion. He was sitting up, unnaturally still, his eyes huge and wild. When he saw her, a slow trembling began in his limbs. "Eh-ss, Eh-ss."

Fear knotted Hesen's stomach, but she sat beside him and embraced him with a calm reassurance she was far from feeling.

"You'll be all right, Tutu . . . Your Majesty. It will be fine, you'll see . . . you'll see . . ."

Finally the stiffness left his body. He actually yawned, and she eased him gently back down onto the couch. Soon he was snoring lightly, and again she left him to Sephy's careful ministrations. For herself, she was compelled back to the rail.

Dawn revealed that the city had been thrown down and pounded to the waste of broken bricks and stones, returned as much as was within Ay's power to the bare circular plane it had been before her father's vision, Aten's miraculous gift to his son.

From the fifth warship, the soldiers rolled twenty huge barrels. She watched the soldiers on the dock as they ripped off the wooden slats of the first barrel. A fine white substance spilled out. Salt! The barrels were hauled off to different parts of the plain, as plows were carried from the ship. Methodically, as they had devastated the buildings, the soldiers poured the salt over the ruins, and where there was bare ground, soldiers hitched themselves to the plows like oxen and salt was furrowed deep into the earth. She had to credit Ay's thoroughness. Nothing would ever grow here again. Forever Akhet-Aten would stand barren and desolate, an eternal reminder of what had befallen a Pharaoh who thought to repudiate the ancient gods of his fathers.

That night, torches flaming at bow and stern, the warships eased into the depths of the Nile. Pleading and crying, the refugees, men, women, children and babes in arm, were left behind to starve. Ay had betrayed them. Amon had not forgiven them.

Hesen forced herself to remain upright at the rail: Ay sent no one to order her away. She listened to the cries of those abandoned on the docks until they no longer reached her ears. Shu had yet to rise, and the plain that had been Akhet-Aten was lost in blackness.

She had passed beyond shock, rage, and despair. Only one thing sustained her: her duty—to Tutu, to Egypt, to justice. She *was* Ankhesenamon, Queen of the Two Lands. Small-boned, slender, delicate, fierce, alone and unaided, she would assume Aten's mantle . . . would stand between Ay and the boy Pharaoh . . . would bear the burdens of her beloved country . . . would avenge her losses with Ay's blood. And when the history of these times was written, Ay would be recalled as the criminal and Akhenaten praised as Egypt's most glorious Pharaoh.

With her life, her body, her spirit, in the dust and ruin of Aten's city, she pledged it.

# BOOK III

# TRIUMPH OF THEBES: 1369-1358 B.C.

# XXVI

After Tutankhamon and his queen were reestablished at Thebes, a proclamation went forth to all of Egypt. Priests of Amon summoned the residents of each city and village to the square common to them all. The priests read Pharaoh's decree, composed by Ay.

"Egypt has been topsy-turvy with the rule of a false god. I, Tutankhamon, son of Amenophis, inheritor of the true faith, restore the old gods to their rightful worship. Amon is king. His shrines and the shrines of his family shall be venerated. Your estates shall be reendowed, your grievances addressed under the old law, prosperity shall return. Amon's power is in my hand and, with it, I place my seal. So speak I, Tutankhamon, son of the living god."

In the months that followed, Egypt gladly returned to the ways of the past. The sands closed over the few remains of the new style of architecture and naturalistic art introduced by Akhenaten. The bursts of unbridled creative energy that had characterized his reign were extinguished. Openness and intellectual freedom were again enshrouded by dark mysteries and ancient ritual. The beliefs that extended beyond memory, the always-were and always-would-be, were more devoutly followed than before. In the nomes, headsmen suspected of Akhenaten's taint were replaced with solid conservatives known to have been loyal to Amon. The few disgruntled who let slip a treasonous word were stripped of their possessions and lands, and enchained. All images of the Aten and Akhenaten were destroyed or defaced beyond recognition: All hieroglyphs inscribing their names were painted over or chiseled away. In Amon's name, Ay clenched Egypt in his fist.

From Zoan, Senumet observed the transition to the old ways, knowing it would make for a resurgence of a strong Egypt but suffering for Hesen. He had been appalled at the reports of Ay's vengeance enacted at the coronation, and he had experienced the horror of her ordeal almost as if he had been at her side. That he had not been with her was his burden. He rose each morning knowing the day would be blighted by his guilt; he lay down on his mat each night knowing sleep would not refresh him, the morrow would bring no peace. His guilt was rooted irrationally in his love of her, for he couldn't have stayed in Akhet-Aten. As punishment and a test, Ay had ordered him to Zoan, and to protect her he had had no choice. Suspecting Ay would use the coronation to denounce Akhenaten—but not to that awful extent—he had tried his best to warn her. There was nothing more he could have done.

What tore at him most was that he had no way to relieve her pain.

The principal thing was they had been spared, Tutu, himself, and Hesen . . . and a little princess disguised as a peasant.

He threw himself into his work. Almost single-handedly he settled the confused accounts of the Delta and efficiently greased the flow of trade and tribute with his multilingual tongue and diplomacy. He knew his praises were sung to Ay. Yet, when the regent's business brought him to the Delta, Ay did not bother to see Senumet. Three full years passed before Ay, in appreciation of a job well done, rescinded the ban on Senumet's travels and ordered him south to villages and towns in Egypt's upper quadrant to review accounts and make sure that Pharaoh and the temples of Amon had received their proper tithes. Senumet gladly prepared for the Nile voyage, not only because confinement to Zoan was boringly constricting, but also because the trip would take him close to Zehut.

He would see the princess. She was almost six now. He wondered if she would know him.

Zehut was a poor village and Sephy's family little more than illiterate peasants, their rough existence rendered somewhat easier by the help that Sephy was able to send.

Senumet's arrival at the rude dock caused a stir. He had dressed simply; still the fineness of his garments, the richness of his jewelry, were not often seen by the inhabitants of this provincial backwater. He was trailed by swarms of naked, unkempt children, shouting, laughing, pulling at his kilt. Was she among them? he wondered unhappily as he searched each dirt-streaked face. He could not tell. He climbed to the higher fields, near the shadfu with which the fields were watered. Sephy's kinsmen were entrusted with the care of those well-sweeps, he had been told. The well-sweeps were filled with clear water, clean of algae, and the channels through which the water would course were uncluttered by weeds. The counterweight, by which the hide bucket was hoisted and emptied, was a large stone, and that had been smoothed and secured firmly to the pole. Sephy's kinsmen were good workers, reliable and diligent.

The mud-brick homes of the peasants bordered the desert. The thick-walled dwellings were crowded together, with high, slit windows.

He was directed to a house somewhat more spacious than the others. Sephy's nephew and his wife awaited him outside; word of the affluent stranger had carried quickly, and they knew his visit must relate to the princess. He addressed the man first.

"Mena of Zehut, I bring good wishes from your kinswoman. She has charged me to stop here on my journey."

"Please enter our house. You must be in need of refreshment."

Before he entered the dim interior, Senumet observed a trace of an anxious frown above the woman Yuti's eyes.

On the tightly packed sand floor stood four undecorated chairs and stands for three water jugs. Sephy's gifts, bright, adorned bowls and faience dishes, were proudly hung over the oven. Unused, Senumet thought, for fear of breaking. He noticed two smaller rooms leading from the main one, and he could discern the outline of simple beds. He felt relief. He had entertained visions of the princess sleeping on a straw pallet.

Courteously he sipped the homemade beer Yuti poured for him and ate the hot flat bread she removed from the oven. Finally he judged the time had come to begin.

"As you have no doubt surmised, I have come in the hope of seeing your charge."

Yuti's hands twisted in her lap. "I have come to love her as my own," she declared. "You will see. She's a wonderful girl. And we have kept her things safe."

Mena padded on bare feet into one of the other rooms and returned with the inlaid ivory chest Hesen had packed. He held it by two gilded handles and placed it, seal foremost, at Senumet's feet. Senumet stared at the clay with which they had covered the keyhole. He had not needed to see it to know Sephy's kinsmen would never betray the queen's trust.

"She knows she is not ours," Yuti said, and added a little defiantly, "though she loves us as her kin."

"We have told her she is her parents' eldest daughter," Mena explained with simple dignity, "that this is her inheritance, which one day she may open."

"I will be visiting regularly now, on the half year, if not more frequently." Unexpectedly, Yuti's frown dissolved into a smile. Not having intended to take the child from them, he had not realized that this was the source of their fears. "I'm sure you are like parents to her, and that she loves you deeply," he said. "I should like to see her now."

They stepped into the bright day. A stray urchin was dispatched to fetch the girl. Senumet watched for her form to detach itself from the scrambling, shouting herd. A slim figure advanced. Before he could distinguish her features, he recognized a familiar light, swaying step. She noticed him and hesitated, her body taut—then she ran the rest of the way. Yet once she reached them, she hung her head shyly. He could see only a crown of shining black tangle.

"Muta," the woman scolded, "look at you!"

Grasping the child's hand and casting an apologetic look at Senumet, Yuti escorted the child into the house. A few minutes later they returned, the child's face rosy from scrubbing, her body hidden beneath a rude but clean cotton shirt tied at the neck, her feet bound in woven sandals.

"Don't think she runs wild each day," Yuti exclaimed, but Senumet cut her short.

"All children go naked," he said kindly. "Muta and I will become acquainted now." He took the child's hand and led her past the clustered houses.

Amon guide him, he breathed, as he felt the warm soft hand in his, the wrist so delicate he was afraid too tight a clasp might snap it. He stopped when the village had vanished from sight and they were alone on a sandy strand by the Nile, peacefully flowing.

He raised her chin with his finger. A lovely child. Her heritage was her mother's: those deep violet eyes flecked with golden lights in that exotic almond shape he knew so well, and a long aquiline nose with gentle, flaring nostrils, and her mouth full and lush . . .

He had intended to reassure her, but he saw at once it was unnecessary. Her gaze met his gravely and calmly.

"I knew your parents," he began.

"I know you," she said in a wondering voice. "The time is far away, but . . ."

He felt a sudden thrill of pleasure. "Do you know my name?" Silently she searched into herself. She shook her head. She couldn't, of course. She had been too young. "But I do know you!" she told him finally.

"I am Senumet of Thebes. You called me Oo-met then."

"I remember a lady too, with a wonderful smell and beautiful beads . . ." Her voice sank to a low whisper. "And soft arms."

Senumet realized with dismay that in their preoccupation with Hesen's grief and the arrangements for the princess's safety, they had not once considered what effect the severance would have on the child's emotions. Hesen had loved her so consumingly, so tenderly. The child must have ached at the loss.

"That was your mother. Do you think of her often, Muta?" As they were bringing her up a peasant, they had given her an ungraceful name.

"No . . . only sometimes I dream of her."

Clearly she was a child who would never whine or complain. Her seriousness was heart-wrenching in such a small child. He wanted to lighten her mood but could think of nothing hopeful to tell her.

"Why don't you take off your sandals?" he improvised. "I remember how I hated wearing them when I was a boy."

Her face lifted. "They hurt my toes," she confided. Sitting down, she quickly untied them, jumped up and dangled them from one finger.

They strolled past the dock of stone and mud. It was clear now. After the excitement of his vessel's arrival, the villagers had returned to their tasks. Two of the men from his crew were lazily swimming in the river. Tutu's cartouche was emblazoned on a hull of his barge; it gleamed at them.

"That's Pharaoh's name," he explained, suddenly aware that the royal princess would not be able to read.

"I know," she asserted: "Tutankhamon. I know the queen's name too. It's Ankhesenamon."

"How clever of you." He smiled.

"And I can write their names."

"You can?" He was surprised. "Is there a school you go to?"

Her eyes darkened. "I don't know that word," she admitted.

He controlled a chuckle. Her lip had curled in Hesen's pout. "I'd like to see how you write," he said, and he searched for a thin stick, smoothed a patch of sand. Growing intensely aware how like Hesen she was, he knew she'd be delighted to demonstrate her skill, and with deep concentration, she traced a careful cartouche. She outlined a bird and placed two semicircles in the right and left of its body. The TUT. This done, she drew an ANKH, ending with the feather and wave. The AMON. Watching her fingers, supple and long, he was unable to crush the pride that coursed through him. And then he didn't try. He let himself revel in the fierce, unexpected love he felt for this wonderful child. His child—with his thirst for knowledge, his restless curiosity, his grave study of the world. And *Hesen's child*—with her grace, her matchless spirit, her enthusiasms and, he suspected, her pleasure in being admired. "That's wonderful," he told her and was rewarded with a bright smile. "How did you learn to do it?"

"From our temple's pillars," she said with a toss of her head. "Those were the only words in the squashed circle, so I knew one must mean the king and the other the queen. And two parts of their names are alike. Look!" More confident, now, she drew another cartouche, placing the ANKH and the AMON carefully in its oval and adding the crook and wave that completed Hesen's name. "I noticed the bird sign painted on the boats that take away our harvest. I figured that was Pharaoh, because he's more important, you know." The words ran together in her eagerness to share what no one else in her village could understand, and he was dazzled at the way her eyes glowed when she was happy.

"Muta . . . shall I bring you a stylus and some ink on my next visit? And when I come again, shall I teach you more beautiful signs?"

"Oh, would you? Did you notice, I made the bird a hoopoe? Because I love his crest. Was that wrong?"

"It's a beautiful hoopoe." As indeed it was. For the first time in three years, Senumet felt the beginnings of warmth and simple pleasure.

When he told her he must go, the joy faded from her as she politely wished him a safe journey. He watched her small, slender figure on the dock, watching, waving, until she was no larger than a mote of dust. The princess had nourished his heart as water revives the starved earth.

*Worth it, all of it,* he thought, *to have saved her.*

In the next few months, fate took one of its fortunate turns. Ay assigned Senumet to Gebet, two days' journey from Zehut. Miraculously, the headsman owned a stallion which he put at Senumet's disposal.

Yet Senumet didn't visit the child too often, for her sake as well as his own. He must not breed in her too great a dissatisfaction with her life, nor could he allow his feelings for her to grow too strong. Thus he traveled to Zehut but every three months, and it was these trips that sustained him through his bleak days.

She was an apt pupil. Quickness of mind he had expected. But the princess had more, a quality even her mother had never acquired: a love of learning for its own sake, coupled with a precocious talent in controlling the stylus. He taught her gladly, guiltily, rationalizing: Should her identity be revealed one day, he could not have kept her an illiterate peasant. On the other hand, given his teaching, how was she to exist if she were never to be elevated by heritage? Already she had begun to separate herself from her rough youthful companions. Could she ever marry one among them? And if not, what might her future be? Her unique talent not withstanding, she could never be a scribe. The only professions open to women were dancing, temple singing, mourning or midwifery—none suitable. And barmaids were invariably prostitutes. Unthinkable.

And what of Senumet himself? How long could he tolerate this loneliness? The sun passed six more times on its yearly cycle; he began to feel that the pattern of his life was fixed at last. Perhaps hope was an illusion, an amusement. If so, he felt tired of the sport. He began to think of taking a companion.

Every few weeks, when the demands of his body required release, he would visit a neighboring village and frequent a tavern. He chose one of the painted whores, relieved himself quickly, revulsion souring even that animal pleasure. Lately, on the mornings after the whores, he had begun to think of the plump and good-natured widow whom he had come to know. She had been married to a sickly older man who had died a scant five years after they were wed. He had left her a comfortable house, a large land allotment, ten oxen and an unwakened body. She had not passed the age of breeding, and Senumet was thinking of the continuance of his name and his father's, the only immortality in which he could believe. She was compliant and admiring. She would make him an excellent wife.

Before he would decide, he paid another visit to Mut-Nodjne. Almost twelve now, she was tall and lovely, with the sweet curves that hinted at approaching womanhood and a sensuous fullness to her lower lip that wrenched his entrails. Another woman danced from her golden eyes, hopeful, expectant, not yet touched by life. He could not visit Muta more often—it took him days to recover from the intermingled joy and pain. At his chariot's approach she ran to meet him, delight sparking her bright eyes.

He handed her the papyrus scroll on which, laboriously, he had detailed "The Story of the Doomed Prince" with the left hand that years of tedious, painful practice had rendered legible.

And though she had waited impatiently for his visit and had stored up, as always, so much to tell him, she couldn't resist peeking at the scroll to read a little of it.

"If you wait until I leave," he laughed, "you will extend your pleasure."

She colored faintly, a light blush high on her cheeks.

"I have something for you too," she hurried on. "A poem I have written myself."

She handed him a slate tablet. She must have bargained for it with one of the vagabond traders who visited every village. He wondered what she had exchanged for it. His shrewd glance studied her: he noticed red burns on her arm. Perhaps she had bartered fresh-baked bread. Where could she have gotten the flour for that? From Yuti's store, he decided, and if not, he did not want to know.

She was watching him closely. "Is it bad?"

Hastily he scanned the lines. Pain, intense and sharp for being totally unexpected, coursed through him. All unknowing, she had pierced the toughened exterior he had thought impenetrable. "No," he managed in a thickened voice. "It's wonderful. Not a single error!"

"But the *sense* of it," she demanded, an edge of young Hesen's impatience sharpening her tone. "Do you approve that?"

"Beautiful and true." His words were oddly spaced, spoken through the mist of commingled visions from his past, her past, the queen's. "Read it aloud."

"Sweet of love is the daughter of the king," she began in her softly husky tone.

> *"Black are her tresses as the blackness of the night*
> *Black as the wine grape are the clusters of her hair.*
> *The hearts of the women turn toward her with delight*
> *Gazing on her beauty with which none can compare.*
>
> *Sweet of love is the daughter of the king!*
> *Rosy are her cheeks as the jasper's ruddy hue*
> *Rosy as the henna which stains her slender hands*
> *The heart of the King is filled with love anew*
> *When in all her beauty before his throne she stands."*

He hung on every inflection, glorying in the cultivated accents she had acquired from him, disregarding the anguish her words evoked. Pain was, after all, nothing new, he had lived with it for so long; now his initial shock was over, he could respond to her with his usual undemanding affection and easy style.

"This is now one of my treasures." He smiled. "I'll read it whenever I need to feel close to Muta during our times apart."

They walked in companionable silence for a time. Finally Muta faced him and said a little breathlessly, "Don't be angry. I've been thinking about this since the day you first came to me. I have to know. Are you my father?"

His heart lurched. He understood the courage it had cost her to ask and he saw hope brighten her face. He understood something else too. When she had said, "Father," he had been filled with such a sense of well-being, of everything in its proper place—such a calm certainty—that he suddenly knew he had planned all along to acknowledge her. But that could never be: He must renounce all claim. If the day should ever come when her mother would be made known to her, Ankhesenpaaten the Younger must be unquestionably of royal blood.

"No, Muta, I am not your father," he answered gently, his mouth dry.

She turned her face away. He saw in her neck's rigid line that she fought her grievous disappointment. When she faced him again she managed a small smile but it was tight with bitterness.

"Really, I thought not. If you were my father, *you* would never have left me."

"Your parents loved you very much, Muta. Your father is dead, that I can tell you. Your mother almost died, too, with sorrow when you were taken away. You must believe me. You have been dearly loved."

"I remember flashes of things," Muta said slowly, a puzzled note in her voice. "Blue eyes? A golden chariot? Pools with gold fish?" In her sparse young life, void of beauty, he thought, these must seem strange visions indeed.

"You must not discuss these thoughts with anyone, not even with Mena and Yuti," he cautioned. "But you should know; your memories are true."

She nodded with that sweet seriousness that long ago had melted barriers between them. "I like that, even if I understand only imperfectly."

"What do you like, sweet girl?"

"Why," she replied solemnly, "that there are secrets only you and I can share."

As Senumet reined his horse across the trackless sands toward Gebet, he hardened the decision he had made during the night while seeking sleep on a pallet in the main room of Mena and Yuti's mud house. He would detach himself from the promise of the widow's honeyed comforts. He could no more belong to her, with her homey possessiveness, than years before he could have belonged to Nephrus. He was Hesen's. There was little left for anyone else, and what was left of him by right must belong to their daughter. Mut-Nodjne had reminded him of that.

Under the golden ascending orb of Amon, Senumet accepted his lot.

# XXVII

Hesen concentrated on the polished oval surface Sephy held up before her. At the corner of her mouth, was that a crease? "There, Sephy." The servant dusted the offending shadow with a light powder.

With each passing year, the daily ritual of makeup had grown more lengthy. Hesen was thirty-one now. "Lord, what an age," she would complain. "My skin will soon be as dry and wrinkled as a mummy's." And Sephy would reassure her: "My lady, as the whole court avows, you are more beautiful than ever." In her heart of hearts, Hesen suspected it was true, that time had in fact lent a depth and richness to her spectacular appeal.

In the beginning, after the removal to Thebes, when she studied her image, it was not her own features she wanted to see. She had had Sephy paint her in Nefertiti's style and had searched desperately for her mother's perfection in the face formed in Nefertiti's womb. With increasing frequency, as time dulled her memory, she would catch a flash of the queen's spirit in the eyes reflected by the polished silver mirror and recall the queen in her glory, forgetting briefly the smashed ruin tossed into the burning pyre. She had hoped by seeing her mother in her own face, she would also find she was inspired with the strength of Nefertiti's will.

Within the last few years, however, the ritual of makeup had taken on another, more desperate purpose: She must so dazzle Pharaoh that, his fears forgotten, his manhood would rise and thrust his seed into the fertility of her living warmth. The line must not end! The end of the dynasty would be her ultimate failure, and Ay's triumph.

At first, she had believed that, like many boys of whom Sephy told her, maturity simply came late to Pharaoh. When he passed his fourteenth and fifteenth years without a quickening of manhood, she secretly consulted physicians and, with one pretext or another, persuaded Tutu to submit to examinations. His testicles had descended normally, she was told. Did he not pass the milk of life from his body sometimes in his sleep? He did, she admitted. The physicians recommended aphrodisiacs, such as oil of lotus or the raw eggs of the small whitebait, and when those produced no results, the physicians shook their heads. Then Hesen forced Sephy to brave the dark, dangerous streets of murderers, smugglers and whores near the docks. In the night, poor Sephy sneaked from tavern to tavern, paying for information that finally led her to an enclave of the black-skinned people from the south, Nubians skilled in magic. The spells and potions these magicians gave Sephy worked as well as the doctors' physic. And while she grasped at these extreme remedies, Hesen realized the problem lay not in Tutu's body but in his mind, and the fault of his impotency lay with Ay.

After nine years, Tutu was still beset by the horror of the day he was crowned. As his speech had not returned, so he had not gained the power of his manhood. Dwelling upon this, Hesen began to think that perhaps she was too closely linked in his mind with the terror of that day. Perhaps other women must first arouse him before he could turn to her, hard and strong. Again Sephy served her, searching out exotic foreign concubines from Crete and Babylonia, who first had to submit to the scrutiny of a physician to make sure they were free from disease before they were ushered to Pharaoh's bed. The harlots were handsomely paid and further encouraged with promises of rich reward should they succeed. But their arts failed.

Perhaps Tutu's arousal must begin with untried virgins, Hesen decided, and she dispatched messengers. The quarters in the palace which Amenophis and Pharaohs before him had filled with wives and concubines now filled again, and the court was overrun with ripe, eager girls vying with each other for the honor of exciting Pharaoh's first desire. Their high-pitched chatter and youthful giggles bored Hesen excessively—did she envy them? she wondered. But she urged them on and instructed them carefully. They must not mind Tutu's grunts—he understood everything they said to him. They must smile and entice, thinking only of his fine handsome body and his melting eyes, his powerful arms.

"Imagine his words," she told each new hopeful, "from his sweet smile and gentle touch. Love him." Endlessly, it seemed, she was repeating lists of orders, clasping gold collars on white necks or slipping jeweled bracelets on slim arms. And they tried, more out of love for her than for the king, but in vain.

With her, as during the first years they shared the marriage bed, he struggled to overcome his deficiency with such desperation that the very intensity of his efforts hindered fulfillment. She soothed him, as always, with the promise that one day soon his manhood would be his pride.

Meanwhile, she had cultivated enough confidants to know Ay's spies were spreading detailed accounts of Pharaoh's insufficiency. How she wanted to lash her uncle's smug, evil face! Instead she smiled prettily and demeaned herself before him like the most unctuous sycophant. She could not tell how much he actually believed of the reports brought to him, yet she wanted to give him no cause to suspect that she harbored rebellion in her heart and was other than absolutely compliant. If all else failed, if Tutu reached his majority still without strength in his groin, she would kill Ay. That was her firm constant promise to herself; fantasy of the deed had possessed her since she had thought to do it on the dais in Akhet-Aten. She imagined herself plunging a dagger into that vile heart, aiming the sharp point directly between his ribs so that the blade sank deep with little resistance, and laughing as the black liquid bubbled away his life. Were the truth to be told, she was not, she thought, entirely sane. That was only to be expected, she decided, accepting the fact. And perhaps it was because she, too, lived enclosed in the same darkness that so often overcame Tutu, she alone could understand him. She would gladly play senet with him all through the night, whenever he needed to push back the terror of those recurring dreams.

Only one thing that Tutu asked of her caused her intolerable pain: he wished her to offer friendship to Horemheb. Tutu loved Horemheb, was easy in his company, and there were too few others who could overlook Pharaoh's disability. She knew that if she were cold, Tutu would be hurt, but for her sake he'd renounce Horemheb. She would not add to his burdens. So the three of them—wild, uniquely beautiful, reckless of personal safety—careened through Thebes, racing chariots, rowing with abandon that at times had each of them sputtering in the Nile, venturing on lonely, dangerous lion hunts. Hesen knew why risk so enthralled both her and Tutu: they must increase the excitement, keep each sense so alert and involved that they could forget briefly the horrors that had made him king. She could never forget Horemheb directing his soldiers to the destruction of Akhet-Aten. Each sight of Horemheb's uniform brought to mind the uniforms of his men as they dragged her father's naked corpse from the funerary tent. With a glance at his thick, powerful soldier's fingers, she saw similiar fingers gripping clubs and hammers and smashing to rubble the brightness of Aten's city. She hoped, as she raced her horses downhill against his, that Horemheb felt the hot flames of the Underworld lick at his soles.

Or perhaps the Master of the Horse burned in another way. At times when he didn't expect her to notice him, she caught him staring at her as if he couldn't help himself. He had loved her once, she knew. Did he still burn with love for her? If so, he had made his own torment. She teased him with playful touches, alluring smiles and coy words. Let him know the tortures of a love absolutely forbidden! She had grown hard and unfeeling, Hesen realized, with unflinching honesty. She sometimes wondered if she loved even Tutu. There was no softness left in her . . . except what she had reserved for two whose names she dared not say.

"Sephy," she complained now, as the old woman moved the mirror to another angle, "how did you let that curl show gray? Take it down!" Impatiently she tugged at the combs and pins herself, pulling apart the elaborate hairdo.

Sephy picked up the brush and calmly stroked Hesen's hair with the slow, firm motion that always eased the queen's tension. Hesen realized she was trembling. How could she have destroyed what Sephy had taken hours to arrange? Those fingers, twisted now and painful, must do it all up again.

"No, Sephy!" she snapped as the servant began. She made her voice querulous—that old friend mustn't suspect she was being kind. "I want it loose, down my back in the old style. And I want to wear tonight the gold dress that I wore when I came to Thebes as emissary at Amenophis' death. Do I still have it?"

Sephy looked doubtful. "It is packed with rose petals, Highness, but I don't think—"

"You don't think I can wear it? Have I grown fat? Are my breasts not firm? We will see!"

Sephy brought it to her, holding it almost reverentially, the smell of roses clinging to its gilt-threaded fabric, still fresh and bright. Hesen realized suddenly she didn't want to put it on. It belonged to another time, when triumph had been real and victory possible; never again would winning be so unambivalently splendid. Nonetheless, because she had insisted, she let her servant slip it on. Sephy's mouth pursed in concentration as she arranged Hesen's jewels, gave a final dusting to her exposed bosom and, stepping back, regarded her critically, a pleased smile the result of that inspection.

"Better than before!" she exclaimed. "Now you're a queen."

Hesen understood that, in Sephy's restricted vision, so long as the queen was well and beautiful the world was in place. She waved aside the mirror Sephy again held up. She would not commingle the image of long ago with the reality of today.

Accompanied by a retinue of imported virgins, Hesen entered the royal dining hall. Pharaoh had preceded her and sat upon his throne. That he had been feeling anxiety at her absence was evident from the stiffness in the way he sat and his tense, abstracted look. He was never comfortable without her to interpret his wishes, and his pride restrained him from the labored stutters with which he must make his wants known.

As his glance found her, a warm smile ignited his eyes. He rose to greet her, and the lips that brushed her cheek were soft and tender. "Eh-ss," he blew in her ear. "Bu-bu-bu—" His face strained.

"So, beloved." She stroked his cheek. "You find me beautiful tonight." Each evening he complimented her. "Ah, my darling, while I am merely beautiful, you are the glorious Son of God. Must I remind you?"

He burst into a laugh, his expression wondrously lifting, the lines of worry that sadly etched his youthful face dissolving into the boyish glow she fondly cherished. His brighter mood carried into the meal. He fed her dates, teasing her as he used to as a child with confections, holding them at her lips and then snapping them away. And Hesen observed him closely. She sensed a change in him. Despite his animation, he was more relaxed and self-sure than she could remember seeing him in—how long, dear Aten? It was as if he felt himself a man . . . his responses reminding her of a man intent on seduction. A sense of accomplishment and hope warmed her cheeks, encouraging her to resort again to oft-tried tactics.

She rested against his shoulder. The pink tip of her tongue brushed his ear. Her fingers stroked his thigh. Her white teeth tore off a small piece of duck. All the while her eyes flashed a compelling message. She called for more wine. They must drink from one cup, she insisted, delighted that with their faces so close, her warm breath sent visible shivers down his arm. She saw to it that his hand brushed her breast, leaned into him so he could feel its soft fullness with a hard nipple thrusting against the gilt fabric as though begging to be caressed. She made sure he inhaled her scent, sweet and a little sharp, the way she fancied it. Before them, her virgins rose to dance at her signal, the wisps of sheer fabric twirling about their legs, highlighting the nude lovely bodies beneath those diaphanous folds and revealing the patches of private hair.

Suddenly Pharaoh clapped his hands and the court fell silent. He stood as two slaves brought forward the magnificent pelt of a male lion and, tottering under its weight, held it up. The glass eyes shone with the ferocity of life, the claws were polished, and the thick tawny fur had been combed to plush softness. Pharaoh gestured, and the slaves spread the skin at Hesen's feet, while Pharaoh leaned over her and whispered, "Ess . . . yu . . ."

So before her was the secret of his newfound confidence. This lion was his first. He had killed it himself on a hunt with Horemheb six weeks ago, and without her as his voice, he had arranged for the curing of the pelt and this presentation. She gestured for the skin to be brought forward. Stroking the regal mane, she found the underside of the skin had been lined with linen. "Thank you, my darling. I shall treasure it."

His eyes sparkled with happiness as she ordered the pelt carried to their apartments and took his hand. In return, he warmly enclosed both of hers.

Again the music, again the dancers, and more wine!

All through the sensuous dance, her hand was expert on his leg, her breath light on his neck, but so utterly without urgency that he forgot to grow anxious. Letting himself be overcome by the wine, the fragrances, the gentle loving, and her appreciation of his gift, his eyes half closed and his nostrils flared with a carefully suppressed yawn.

She stood. "It grows late and I am tired. Come, beloved."

Indicating that the court should remain, Hesen and Pharaoh made their way out, their arms around each other. Someone snickered. Hesen kept herself from stiffening with a tremendous act of will. Casting an anxious look at Tutu, she was relieved to see he was as relaxed and pleasantly excited as before. This time he hadn't heard. She hated this public retiring, dreaded the smirks behind his back.

Her sense of annoyance vanished as they entered their chamber. Of all the rooms in the palace, this was her favorite. Redecorating it for Tutu, she had designed it to remind them both of the best parts of their lives together, and in this room she was still able, from time to time, to hope. The chamber was, of course, dominated by the huge bed. Its footboard rose higher than the head. On it a graceful scene had been painted in vivid colors—so that Pharaoh's eyes on first waking would feast on beauty: the king and queen hunting, Tutu's body lean and bronze, his spear appearing to quiver with readiness, Hesen at his side, pointing to a flock of birds.

Around the bed, the expansive walls were covered with perfectly rendered reeds and flowers and other marsh plants in charming profusion, small birds and animals faintly discernible in their midst. The wall decorations, Hesen had insisted, must contain everything Tutu loved on this earth. And no gods . . . there were enough of them in temples.

Having left her husband to the ministrations of Senedjm, the queen retired to her dressing room. "Hurry, Sephy," she urged struggling to free her arm.

The alabaster lamps had already been muted when she stepped into the king's room. Was it their light that lent slyness to the soporific faces?

"The king sleeps," Senedjm whispered as she approached the bed.

"Thank you." For Senedjm her smile was sincere. "You may leave now," she said clearly to the five of them.

As the gray shapes of the servants glided off into the dark, she eased next to Pharaoh. He sighed in his sleep and curved his body to hers. After endless nights of failure, tonight Tutu would become a man—somehow she was sure of it.

He turned on his back, one hand across her stomach. Carefully, she moved his hand along her breast, pressed her lips gently to his neck, touched her mouth to his, softly, cherishing his lips until she felt them open beneath hers, heard a moan start in his throat. She slid her hands along the outside of his naked thighs, then slightly spreading them, traveled her hands up his inner thighs, tenderly, repeatedly. She stroked the muscle behind the sac—he shivered. Lifting his penis, she lowered her head and nuzzled the sac before and behind, lightly nipping, while her fingers stroked his sex in an unhurried rhythm. *Aten help me*, she prayed. As if the god answered, his sex moved in her hand.

She wet and laved the glans with her tongue, then played her tongue along the soft length. Weak at first, its movements slowly strengthening, it began to swell. Its head pushed against her teeth. This far she had managed so many nights before, hoping in his sleep she could call forth his manhood before his dark visions could interfere. But then, even if she had plied him with soporific of wine or a drug, he would wake. The terror that stunted him and imprisoned him forever in his eleven-year-old perceptions would return; his sex would shrink. Blessed Aten, let him not awaken tonight until she was ready—until she fixed him in her body where he would remain hard with her body's warm wetness and gentle spasms holding his manhood firm. Until he could see and take delight in what he had accomplished.

For the first time she saw Tutu's penis fully erect. A marvelous manly sight. She swallowed him deep in her throat, feasting upon him with the combined skill of her lips, her tongue, the roof of her mouth. He sighed and stirred, and she released him. A drop of sticky clearness gathered at the tip of him, and of itself the shaft strained upwards. He was ready. Her heart pounding, she straddled his sleeping form, slipped him inside her, and lowered herself slowly until she engulfed the length of him. Gently rocking, she revolved her hips. His eyes were still closed, but his mouth was open, his breathing deep and fast.

*Father Aten, however it came to be, consecrate this hour!*
Raising her hips, she lowered them again.
*Sweet comrade of my youth, how I want to pleasure you.*
His lashes fluttered against his cheek. Now it was time. She buried her face in his neck and caught flesh between her teeth.
His eyes flew open. "Ess—!"
"Take me, my darling! Hold me tightly."
His arms sprang up around her, pressing her body against his. In the dim light, she saw the brilliance of his eyes, suddenly aware.
Still locked together, they rolled over onto her back. Mounting her, he needed no further urging. His mouth demanded hers and clumsily sucked her lips. She almost laughed aloud with the joy of it!
The muscles in his thighs and calves bunched, his toes pressed against the bed, and he pumped into her with all the wildness of first-known pleasure and the force of his healthy young body. Were she a virgin, he would have ripped her apart. Too soon, with a shout as loud as a battle cry, he exploded inside her and crushed her to his chest, forcing the breath right out of her.
The sandaled feet of servants clattered on the tiled floor. At the sight of Pharaoh, they halted, stopping short in astonishment.
Tutu raised his head, gave them an insouciant grin. As hastily as they entered, the servants retreated.
Pharaoh took his queen twice more that night so joyously, with such boyish gratitude—that Hesen's tears, long suppressed, came

flooding. He wiped them away. "Tha- tha- tha—" Dismayed, he tried to comfort her.

"No, my husband. Thank *you* for the great pleasure you have brought to me. You are a wonderful lover." And in a sense, there *was* something of glory in it: the heart-felt joy that suffused his face was almost enough to live for.

The entire court was aware of what had happened. Hesen was pleased that Tutu was freely given the bantering acceptance he had always craved. Tempered as it must be by the respect that was due him as king, nonetheless the men's camaraderie was enough to bring a youthful swagger to Pharaoh's step and an assured, quite openly lecherous smile to his lips.

She would have, however, preferred that his aroused manhood had remained their secret. The news could only render their situation more precarious. She had little doubt that Ay intended to move against Tutu before he came of age, but so long as Ay believed Tutu impotent, they warily enjoyed a term of safety. Now Ay would be impelled to act. She was in no danger, for Ay needed her, but—how to protect Tutu? She must entrust his care to someone besides herself, and she had but one choice.

On a morning that soon followed, she awoke with the dawn, summoned Sephy to dress her, and left Tutu, still asleep, to the vigilance of Senedjm. She directed the driver of her chariot to the outskirts of the city, to the barracks of the garrison and the drill ground. There a thousand soldiers exercised, marched and sparred in the dust under the eyes of Horemheb and his generals every daybreak. She sent her driver to Horemheb with a message, but already from his place on the platform overlooking the drill ground, he had seen her and was coming to attend the queen.

"My lady, what has happened?" he shouted above the savage grunts of his troops, the resounding clanks of sword against sword, sword against shield, spear against spear. He offered her his hand, and she stepped down from the sunshade of her chariot.

"Pharaoh wishes you to join him at the morning meal," she invented.

"You might have sent a servant," Horemheb replied bluntly.

"But I needed to speak with you. I'm worried . . . about Pharaoh."

"I'm surprised that you say that . . . *now*." His eyes joked salaciously with his approximation of the evasive allusion of a courtier.

"He has always been reckless, wild. Now I'm afraid he'll feel invulnerable. He'll take dangerous risks. He's still too much a boy." In fact, she spoke the truth, and it was this truth that would sway Horemheb.

"It may be," he agreed.

"I can't be with him every moment, and even when I am, he is, after all, my husband and the king; he doesn't have to be subservient to me. But he is attentive to you." She removed from her voice the imploring note she heard. "I want you to stay with him, always at his side. Never let him out of your sight. Don't underestimate your influence over him. You are his father, his brother, his closest friend. And he loves you."

"But, Highness, my duties—"

"Your generals, your lieutenants, are competent, aren't they?"

"They are."

"Then your duty is to Pharaoh."

Horemheb bowed, recognizing a command. "For the sake of our friendship and my love for Pharaoh, I promise you. He will do nothing foolhardy. I will be with him."

She held out her hand for Horemheb to kiss. His lips touched her fingers with more than formality, and she let them linger longer than decorum allowed.

"Thank you," she said, with a softly exciting curl of her lips.

She did not join them for the morning meal.

With that seasoned, alert, skilled warrior at Tutu's side, what could Ay attempt? She had done all she could, she reasoned. Still she worried. Was it enough?

Now she must, quite simply, conceive a child as soon as possible. Fortunately, Tutu's energies were formidable; arriving late to manhood, he must compensate for delay by insatiable desire. There were times when Hesen, exhausted, thankfully produced her virgins.

Nevertheless, it took her longer to conceive this time. Perhaps age played a part; perhaps desperation was less fruitful than love. It took five months before life began in her womb. The court buzzed with the news and Tutu was overjoyed. She began to hope that, when he held his firstborn, his speech might return.

Hesen terminated her reckless escapades. Let Sephy cluck and hover over her to her heart's content, but she surrounded herself with people, gave Ay no chance near her. With that, and with Horemheb permanently stationed at Tutu's side, they were as protected as they could hope to be. Yet she ate or drank nothing without it being tasted by a slave. . . .

Although she had plotted and hoped for and planned for this child, the pregnancy was perfunctory. Instead of the emotions she had expected, she felt primarily loneliness, a sharp, recurring pang. She missed her sisters, who were long since gone from Egypt, married off just as soon as Hesen could arrange their weddings to foreign princes—out of harm's way. Penre had not wanted to leave, had stormed and begged to stay with her. She hoped that little sister had come to peace; she had not had word of her for months.

However, it was not her sisters she yearned for. She felt *his* absence as sharply as in the days when he left for Byblos, and another life had grown within her. Where was he now? Still in Zoan? What skies did he see when he raised his eyes?

If the malaise did not lift, it soon became secondary to her physical discomfort, which had begun to crowd out any other consideration. Sephy spent hours trying to ease Hesen's excruciating spinal pains, which often knifed through her so sharply that she bent double and was unable to straighten up again. Dizzy and nauseated, she could not retain food. A servant with a basin must always be near her, and she grew to dread meals. No matter how sparingly she ate, the ugly, retching spasms seemed the almost inevitable result.

Meanwhile her abdomen swelled normally with life. Unconscious of its inconvenience to its mother, the babe seemed to be doing well. Telling herself the misery would pass, Hesen tried to ignore it, and feeling the need to maintain some regular functions, she decided to visit the royal workshop at Thebes.

Ipuki, the foreman, was sitting on his wooden stool, waving a stiff parchment fan at the ubiquitous insects and keeping a sharp eye on his workmen when she entered. He rose; she waved him seated. The workers had frozen in respect for her; at her word, Ipuki commanded them to resume their tasks.

"Highness, they are working on the articles for the royal tombs." Of course she had known that all through the lives of Pharaoh and his queen mortuary equipment was being readied; nonetheless she felt an involuntary shiver pass through her. She regretted she had come. "There," Ipuki pointed, "they are weighing gold rings. Over here"—he indicated she should follow—"wood-carvers shape the *djed* and the *sa* . . . for stability and protection."

She had to get out of here. Sawdust and the smell of cleansing agents seemed suddenly suffocating, and terrible visions were flashing through her head. "That is truly—" She stopped abruptly. A warm fluid seemed to be coursing down her thighs. She swayed. Ipuki caught her ungracefully as she lost her balance.

"Run!" he shouted to a supervisor. "Get help!"

She felt light-headed, but when she laughed out loud at her drunkenness, she could hardly hear the sound of it. She moved her foot and slipped in a puddle. Did Ipuki, that funny little man, permit such sloppiness? From a great height she looked down—and screamed—and couldn't stop until she felt her lungs must burst. She was staring at her own blood, running out of her, pooling on the stone floor.

She opened her eyes. She had no idea where she was. Tutu's face, blurred at the edges, was white and drawn. She tried to smile reassurance but found she couldn't move her lips. Tutu faded away. When next she opened her eyes, strange men bent over her, dark, unknown shadows that came and went until, finally, Sephy was there, fixed in space, clear and sharp. Sephy looked distraught. What was wrong with her old friend? She struggled to speak.

"Here, my darling," Sephy crooned, silencing her efforts. "You must eat something."

If she argued, she would not prevail. Where Hesen's health was concerned, Sephy was fierce; she would stubbornly persist until Hesen had no resistance left. Hesen opened her mouth. Very slowly. Sephy spooned broth down her throat—why, she was starving! Greedily she accepted spoon after spoon until Sephy was satisfied.

Handing the bowl to a servant, Sephy brushed back her hair with a cool, loving hand.

Hesen felt tears gather in her eyes and run down the side of her nose. "I lost the child," she managed.

Sephy nodded. Hesen turned her face away. Suddenly resenting the servant's silent sympathy, she didn't want to see Sephy—or Tutu—or anyone. She just wanted to be alone.

As the days passed, though Hesen accepted most of the food Sephy pushed at her, she didn't seem to grow stronger; her spirit did not lift. She couldn't sleep. If she fell into a light doze, she would wake minutes later, heart pounding, stomach knotted with terror, cold sweat dampening her brow. Able to walk again, she paced, agitated and fearful, up and down the huge room, her servants watching her with deep, ineffectual concern.

She must rouse herself, must take charge! Specters of Ay surrounded and leered at her. He would move soon, before she conceived again. She told herself she must make an effort, must assume her rightful place, and she would order Sephy to dress her. Then, when Sephy held out the trays of bracelets, Hesen would stand before that glittering display, her hand trembling, unable to choose—and would burst into tears. Overwhelmed by uncontrollable storms of weeping, she spent the greater part of the day collapsed on her bed.

Strange new physical symptoms began to assault her. Sharp, stabbing chest pains made breathing difficult; often she held her breath as long as she could, reluctant to inhale, reluctant to subject herself to that slashing internal sword. So many things she had done automatically suddenly were hard for her. Tight bands around her thighs, her knees, her ankles, made walking practically impossible. She studied her legs: they looked the same, but something confined them. The royal physicians came often, examined her, reported hesitantly—they could find nothing. Tutu approached the bed, his eyes smudged with fatigue from the sleepless nights he had spent worrying about her.

"See," she tried, forcing a smile—she could not do this to him—"I'm well, my darling. I'll dine with you tonight." And such a look of relief flashed across his face that she knew no matter how hard it would be, she must be at court this evening.

She permitted her servants to dress her, endured the discomfort involved in preparation—the rings and bracelets cutting painfully into arms and fingers that felt as if they were thickened, tingling stumps —the sensation of knotted cords around her belly—sandals that were strapped over what must be heavy pads clamped to her bare soles.

She went supported by servants at both elbows into the great hall. As she took her place next to him, Ay bent over her hand, satisfaction in the cold black depths of his eyes. "So glad to see you've recovered, my child. I was saddened to hear of your loss, of Egypt's loss."

She wanted to scourge him with her tongue as he deserved, but she had no strength for invectives. "Thank you," she whispered, and even that brief response was so painfully costly that dark spots swirled in front of her eyes. She thought she might faint. A sense that the air was charged kept her conscious.

*Danger?* What had Ay said? So glad to see you've recovered—*recovered!* Aten! If he believed that— Where in God's name was Horemheb? She sat up straight, searched the crowd desperately. She couldn't discover him.

She needed something to steady her. She reached for the wineglass. Aten help her, she saw her fingers touch the glass, but she couldn't feel it. Panic surged through her. Her fingers had suddenly become dead lumps. She willed them to close around the glass, but they lay inert on the cloth. Horemheb forgotten, her anxiety consumed her. Nearly a half hour passed before the fingers began to tingle painfully, but at last they responded. She drank the wine in one gulp. The world clouded and disappeared.

She sat in the south garden the next morning. If she didn't move at all—if she kept her legs motionless on the footrest, made sure her fingers didn't touch each other, inhaled only light, shallow breaths—she could be moderately comfortable. The night behind her was lost to memory, she could not recall being brought to bed—or awaking this morning.

Tutu strode toward her, dressed for hunting. His kilt had been carefully pleated, and he wore his lucky sandals with the toe strap shaped like a lotus; the white crown was on his head. She masked her disabilities with a smile.

"Cu- cu-," he pleaded.

"No, beloved, I can't come hunting, not today. But you go, darling. Amon grant you good sport." God forbid he stay with her. Perhaps if she were completely alone all day, she might recover enough to endure the evening meal again tonight.

"Li-," he tried to persuade her.

Lion hunting! Oh, indeed, she might just manage that—if she could stand up! "I'll be able to join you soon . . . very soon now," she lied.

"Nor—ehli." He offered her the best hunting fields.

But she was aware only of the painful thickening of the hand he held, and the bands that tightened around her chest, forcing her to gasp for breath. She had to be rid of him now. She must order the steaming bath and the unguents, the only treatment that relieved her.

"Tomorrow, beloved." In another moment she would scream.

He bent disconsolately over her hand and kissed it gently. She watched him, for an eternity, until the garden was free of him.

A few minutes later, she lowered herself into the scalding water and let herself relax. Lying back, she watched her fingers float to the surface, felt her legs drift over the tiled bottom and be lifted by the water. Gentle currents made the lotus and papyrus patterned on the bottom of the glazed floor sway. The water clock dripped away the morning.

Suddenly she pulled herself to an upright position as if she had seen a cobra in her bath. "Sephy!" she screeched. "Sephy—Sephy!"

Bearing towels, the servant hurried to her side. "What troubles you, Highness?"

"Where is Horemheb?" Hesen demanded, fear churning within her. Aten forgive her for a whining, mindless fool! She had just remembered: She hadn't found Horemheb at the table last night.

Sephy looked puzzled. "He has been gone from Thebes these two days, Your Majesty. You were told he was leaving on a tour of inspection, to the borders. Why, he told you himself, my lady."

*Merciful Aten, what had she done?*

How could she have sent Tutu off alone? How could she have been so—careless! While she was still locked in this strange malady was the perfect time—for Ay! She had no doubt—Ay had decided an inspection of the border was prudent—now.

"Get Senedjm—Senedjm!" she hissed.

She scrambled out of the bath, was dressed within moments. Her discomfort forgotten, she was pacing the length of the room, her face a white mask. When Senedjm rushed in, she clawed at his arm like a leopard and shoved him back out the door. "Go after Pharaoh! Hurry—bring him back. Now!"

"Of course, Highness but"—he pleaded—"where is he?"

"What do you mean? Hunting! He's hunting! Get him!"

"But Highness," Senedjm persisted, "I don't know where he went."

"Sephy!" she cried. "You were here! Where was Pharaoh going?"

Sephy wrung her hands. "Forgive me, Highness, I—can't understand him. Only you know what he says."

"But I didn't listen!" Consumed by panic, she ran wildly out of the room. Where was she running? Outside . . . anywhere . . . She must think. In the garden, striding in impotent desperation back and forth, she struggled to remember what he had said, tried to push away the fearful vision that crowded out all other thoughts.

Suddenly a trumpet shrieked a strident note. She halted in a rigid, waiting posture. Other trumpets picked up the call, and others until their notes merged and it seemed that all of Thebes vibrated to the blaring, urgent summons. In motion again, Hesen raced into and through the palace to the main entrance where she stood in terror, not even daring to pray. From the short ramp that sloped to the garden, Hesen's glance tunneled down the line of sycamores on either side of the tiled avenue that led from the gold and lapis papyrus gates to the palace itself. Past their carved feathery splendor, the citizens of Thebes gathered in small, anxious groups.

Over the blasts of the last trumpets, wails pierced the air. The gathering grew, swelling to such a mob that it seemed every inhabitant of Thebes must be there. Then, starting at the back, the huge crowd fanned out, until Hesen could distinguish guards in red kilts, splintering the weeping masses . . . and in the center, two soldiers bearing a litter.

The gilded gates swung open to admit them. An arm touched hers. She spun around. She had assumed she was waiting alone. Confused, she took them in—the entire court, respectfully behind her, glittering and painted in their usual style. Who had touched her? Ay! It was Ay! As grand vizier, he had taken his place at her side.

Hesen's eyes returned to the litter. Though she knew what it must contain, still she hoped— *Please, Aten, dear Father, let it not be fatal, let it be merely a glancing blow, a knife that missed its mark. O Aten, dear Father, let him live!* She would be so alert, so careful, so attentive, from now on. . . .

Tutu's prone form lay at full length on the litter, an arm dangling, swaying in unconscious motion with the stride of the bearers, its fingers dragging insensate through the dirt. She couldn't see his face at all; in its place was a mask of blood, dry now, and caked.

The bearers stopped twenty paces away, and one of the two guards who had flanked the litter stepped out in front. "His chariot overturned and he fell," the spokesman announced in ringing tones. "The beast trampled his head. The beast has been destroyed."

"Take his body to the temple," Ay commanded.

Did Ay think he was already Pharaoh? "No!" Hesen objected loudly, and half-believing in the power of her words, proclaimed, "Pharaoh is not dead! Take him to his chambers."

She was queen! They must obey her. She took her place behind the litter and followed it into the palace. When she stumbled at the threshold, Ay's hand steadied her. She wrenched it away. But as she walked along the familiar, winding corridors, she became confused. Events collided in timelessness about her . . . she had been through this before . . . replayed her role many times—the incense, the chanting prayers, the priests, the doctors. . . . Whose body was she following? And why did not the queen take charge? Which queen? So many queens . . .

Her mind cleared as the little procession fanned outward into the light, airy space of the bedchamber. Watching the servants wash and arrange her husband's limbs, she thought, *Not so many queens . . . only one . . . one queen.*

*Without a king . . .*

Dully she knelt by the bed in a pretense of hopeful prayer, not even struggling against her disbelief: It simply could not have happened. One careless moment! Could she not have one inattentive moment without disaster?

She knew absolutely, even though she had not yet touched his body, that Tutu was dead—and that everything she had lived for had died with him. How could she face another sunrise after this night's vigil?

What had been the cause, she wondered now, of her earlier, childish despair? What matter one simple miscarriage? She stared unseeing at the tile floor.

She had no concern now, no hope, for the first time in her life.

The game was truly played out.

Ay had finally won.

# XXVIII

Ay had directed all of his life to this point. It had been so, he thought, since as a child he had seen the glorious family of the god riding through the streets and chaffed at the capricious fortune that had cast his lot not to have been a son of the god. Now the golden prize glittered in his hand.

The murder had been well done. Horemheb, never lax, had assigned a favorite lieutenant to guard Pharaoh in his stead, but that avid young soldier had been deflected through countermanding orders subtly placed in the mouth of an unwitting general. The charioteer who had struck the death blow with the blunt side of an axe was now himself lion's food. Egypt would grieve for seventy days and then Ay, at last, would have it all.

Pharaoh's body would be prepared according to tradition and buried with honor—indeed, with more pomp and ritual than the halfwit's short, unexemplary reign warranted. The treasures in his tomb would rival those of the great Sesostris. In the intricacies of the game, the irony of this—which he alone could appreciate—pleased Ay.

In the years ahead, with Egypt prosperous and content and Hesen as his queen, he would found his own dynasty, which would stretch into eternity. He imagined the sons Hesen would bear him, handsome, feisty boys, with their mother's lively spirit and their sire's ruthless intelligence, born to do heroic deeds, expand Egypt again into an unchallenged empire, be chronicled in history as great Pharaohs. And after the succession was assured with sons, Ankhesenamon would join her ancestors in the Valley of the Kings and Tey would sit as his queen on the golden chair by the throne. That much his loyal helpmate deserved. And his son, Bata, grown now to robust manhood, training to be a priest of Amon at Heliopolis. To his son would go the temple at Thebes, and Ay would control the two arms of Egypt.

There was but one remaining impediment to the fulfillment of this grand design: Hesen herself. Coming so soon after her miscarriage, Tutu's death appeared to have been too severe a blow. Although she roused herself every few days to oversee preparations for the funeral, she kept to her bed. When he took it upon himself to visit her in her chambers, she refused to address him and intractably turned her face into her pillow. She was, he thought, too drawn, too frail, and there was a frightening wildness in her eyes.

It was feasible, of course, that the wasting sickness was a ruse, that by appearing ill and half-mad she hoped to deceive him into relaxing his guard. Then she could counter him a final time. But how? To whom could she turn for support? Surely she was without recourse. Except for death. It was also feasible that she sought to defeat him by willing herself to die, and he would not underestimate the strength of her will.

The death of Ankhesenamon . . . the possibility scared him. If she died, then her younger sister, Sherit, would become heiress, and Sherit's husband would become the son of the god. Then Ay could become Pharaoh only by seizing the throne with force, and who knew better than Ay Egypt's incomplete recovery from Akhenaten's mischief? Another irregular accession, and those muted revolutionary fires could easily be fanned again—this time to engulf Ay.

His final triumph depended solely upon Hesen. He must do something!

Ankhesenamon loathed him, she would never yield to him of her own will. Someone else must persuade her, a go-between.

The question of Senumet's true allegiance had never been resolved to Ay's satisfaction. Hesen's daughter had surely drowned in the waters of the Nile, it would seem, since no Ankhesenamon the Younger had been brought forward.

Yet after nine years, Ay's suspicions of Senumet smoldered. To recall him was a calculated risk. What if Senumet proved to be Hesen's ally? What could they do against him? Ay placed his trust in himself: this time he would be at hand to watch them. The potential benefit of recall outweighed whatever danger there might be.

His decision made, Ay speedily sent a priest as messenger to Gebet.

In five days, Senumet arrived in Thebes. Under the cover of darkness, he was taken to Nabamon's sacred residence. When Ay saw him late in the evening, he was startled by the change in the man.

Senumet wore no gold, no jewelry. His kilt was in the style of the Old Kingdom, unpleated, of opaque material, without an inner skirt, with no decorated border. His girdle was of undyed wool. The hair of his wig fell straight to his shoulders, the ends uncurled, and he wore no sandals. His body was still lean and fit, although he seemed to have lost weight, and he was as darkly tanned as a peasant. The piercing clarity of his eyes outshone the lamps and almost made Ay blink. But what struck Ay hardest was the serenity of the man's face. Here was a man who had renounced restless ambition and self-seeking. Ay was immediately wary. What leverage did he have with such a man?

"I have disrupted your life," Ay began.

"I am yours to command, my lord."

"You must wonder why."

"The world is of a shifting nature. I wonder at nothing."

Ay summoned Nabamon's personal slave to bring wine. He continued to talk while the slave poured. He had no fear that the slave would repeat what he heard; like Ay's own personal slaves, Nabamon's man had been relieved of his tongue.

"I have brought you to Thebes because the survival of Egypt is endangered."

"How is Egypt threatened?"

Ay thought he perceived a hint of interest in Senumet's expression. Could it be that the facade of serenity was but a pose? "The queen is impetuous and resourceful, that you know. She has become obsessed with delusions and cannot see the welfare of Egypt. I don't know what she plans. I want to know."

"I think you may have chosen wrongly, my lord," Senumet replied evenly. "Years have passed. The queen and I have both changed. She must have confidants in the court . . . more able and eager to do my lord's bidding."

"I have called you from Gebet. Let that be your answer."

"What you wish, then, is not simply a gossip but an ambassador . . . to coax the queen from her delusions, to make her *see* what is best for Egypt."

The words were music to Ay's ears. Senumet hadn't lost the edge of his wit. He comprehended perfectly. Ay nodded, while noticing Senumet hadn't touched his goblet of wine.

"May I presume, My Lord Ay, that I am in the presence of Egypt's welfare?"

"Do not presume. Be certain of it or return to Gebet."

Senumet inclined his head in a slight bow. "Gebet can do without me for a while, my lord."

"I am to take the morning meal with her. I shall tell her you are here. Then go to her."

"As always," Senumet said, "I am honored to serve."

Ay was shown to the south garden. Not to betray his impatience, he stared at the flowering papyrus. He turned at her light step. She was beautiful as ever, but he could sense tension in the careful arrangement of her face. He kissed her forehead. "My child, I'm glad to see you so improved."

"Thank you, Uncle." Her voice was low and firm. He felt a slow anger. Before he was through with her, she would beg for release. "This time for mourning draws soon to a close," he said a little too quickly.

"There are fifty days left."

Rather than reply to her precision, he gestured her to the table that had been set with shat-cakes and beer. Over the light meal they parried back and forth with neither the clear victor. He had wounded her once, he knew, when he told her Sephy must go home to Zehut; he had seen, for a moment, undisguised fear.

"Come now, Hesen, let's not disagree any longer." He had saved his coup long enough. "While I may have removed Sephy, I won't leave you friendless. We share an affection for one person we both trust, who has just returned to Thebes. See Senumet as often as you wish."

She lowered her eyes, but not before he caught the blaze of joy in their depths, and he was satisfied that his scheme was set in motion. He was also enraged. Despite her awareness that she was a prisoner in his power, she still acted the queen with the insult implied that he was merely *an underling*! He was tempted to strike her, to shatter her. And there was another emotion mixed into the caldron of his rage. Her fathomless beauty goaded his lust. Her joy at Senumet's name ignited jealousy.

"You may continue your preparations for the funeral," he said.

Ay strode from the garden.

Senumet's steps, without his will, had taken him to the magic place. He found himself clearing the tile floor of accumulated debris —the rotted leaves, vines grown up between the tiles, chunks of fallen rock—then spreading sweet-smelling reeds on its surface.

He was oddly torn. As fiercely as his blood responded to the knowledge of her nearness, yet he felt an unexpected reluctance. To unleash those passions again—he didn't know if he possessed the strength. Bitterly and painfully, he had fought for his peace. Yet his fight had been for her sake, and his peace was false. Once before he had renounced eternity for her. He could not now renounce *her*. He willed his thoughts to be silent, and he went in search of her.

He found her in the sculptor's complex, her back to him, posing stiffly while the sculptor's hand lingered over her wooden likeness. And as he drank in her slim form—known, loved, yearned for— the years slipped away, together with the hard-won acceptances. His world had one sun only; the rest was darkness. Away from her, he had not lived at all.

The sculptor was attempting to mask his rapt worship. "There's a feeling missing—a certain tension. I want to capture you at the moment before movement begins."

"I don't know what you're talking about!"

Once, Senumet would have burst out laughing at her characteristic impatience; now her voice left him trembling. He would speak while her back was still to him, give her a chance to prepare. "Really, My Lady Hesen, how you've changed. You always knew everyone's heart."

Later, they walked through the palace garden, side by side, not touching. Senumet felt her soul teetered above a dark abyss. He was even fearful of taking her to the magic place, uncertain she would be able to bear joy. But she stepped eagerly enough into the ruin. The dappled light danced on her face; her eyes glistened. He could see the pulse pounding in her throat.

"Senumet, you were here. You made it ready."

His fingers shook as he lowered her to the tiled floor and they lay on sweet-smelling reeds. His hands relearned the feel of her body, slowly and thoroughly, and her face swam in front of his eyes.

"Beloved," she whispered. Her arms reached for him, trembling at first, then surer—stronger. Fierce. She took his head in her hands and urged him between her legs. Like date wine she tasted, he had once told her. His tongue, warm and tender, was probing that one burning place and waves of unbearable pleasure coursed through her.

He was no longer able to wait. And she, too. Her thighs opened and she took him easily and smoothly into the pulsing warmth of moist velvet. He came with explosive force as their juices mingled and their bodies strained to encompass each other. The years melted. They were newly joined. They were almost whole.

They had two months' time.

He would do anything to dispel her despair. Yet what she asked of him was harder than any service he had yet performed.

"In the kingdom of the Hittites, Shubbiluliuma rules. Ask him to send me his son for my husband, and Shubbiluliuma's son shall rule over Egypt."

She could not know what she asked. One of the marauding horde to be King of the Red and Black Earth? But if she needed a Hittite prince to restore hope, he would drag that prince to her feet and force Egypt to accept a barbarian king.

The first necessity was a courier to the Hittites. He sought out Narni in the scribes' barracks. Narni, who had ever hoped for preferment and riches and was always bypassed by Bek, Ka-Aper, and fortune. Senumet's magic tongue offered blandishments that so bribed Narni that the scribe begged to ride to the enemy stronghold of Hattusas, pleaded to make the arduous journey across the triangular peninsula, the wasteland of Gaza, up and around the curve of the Great Green to the Anatolian plain, where the city of Hattusas was guarded by rudely carved stone lions at its gates. And there deliver, for his own political advantage, a treasonous tablet into the hands of Shubbiluliuma.

Narni departed. They must wait.

Meanwhile the pace of preparations for Tutu's funeral quickened. The four outer shrines of gilded wood—each meticulously crafted to fit one inside the other, the innermost to hold the inlaid coffins—were removed to the valley. The ceremonial bows and arrows which would lie between the third and fourth shrines had been completed.

Large, resplendent flabella had been crafted of ebony overlaid with sheet-gold. Encrusted with turquoise, carnelian and translucent calcite, each fan bore forty-two plumes, and the great white and brown feathers waved in the soft breeze above the procession of workers loading the barges.

And there was no word.

Days passed and the magnificent yellow quartzite sarcophagus was hauled to the dock and rowed across the Nile.

Still they waited.

The three coffins were almost finished. Daily Hesen examined their progress. The outermost one, gold-sheathed wood carved in his likeness, depicted Tutankhamon in his young manhood. The portrait was faithful, even to the pain and suffering which life had stenciled in the creases of his mouth. His garments were encrusted with precious stones, his hands, crossed over his chest, held the lapis-banded crook and flail of power, he was enfolded by the loving, golden wings of protective goddesses.

Upon the second coffin he was the young Pharaoh newly crowned, bright and boyish and expectant.

The last coffin, of solid undecorated gold, would hold his bound, mummified form. In this likeness, his features were perfectly rendered, but in the smoothness of the metal, passion and sorrow were wiped away. Pharaoh accepted his death. Pharaoh was at peace.

They waited no longer. Narni returned.

Alone. He had failed.

"It is over then," Hesen managed woodenly. Color drained from her face.

"No, not yet," Senumet's voice was low and fierce. "*I* will see this Hittite king. *I* will persuade him."

Even as she protested, he saw hope animate her expression. That was all he needed.

"No," she cried. "Ay will know you act for me."

"He should always have known that."

"You won't be able to return."

"I shall bring your prince."

"Senumet . . ." she began.

"Pray for me," he directed and, without touching her, strode away with his firm, strong step.

Desperately, now, Hesen cast about for an excuse to explain Senumet's absence. For five days she did not appear at court and rumors of scandal abounded: the queen was spending an illicit interlude with the scribe Senumet. Fortunately, Senumet's mission coincided with the arrival of tributes, and Ay, involved with receiving headmen, overseeing the distribution of tributes, also avoided the court. But at last when he attended to Tey's report of the queen's behavior, he was furious. At the same time, when he turned it over in his mind, he wondered if this scandal were not too heralded for a queen who had always been, if not virtuous, discreetly circumspect. He suspected treachery.

*Time has run out*, Hesen thought, when she received Ay's summons to join the court for the evening meal.

The royal hall fell silent as she walked with measured steps to her gilded chair. She wore only a single golden bracelet and a transparent chemise, the linen woven as fine as cobwebs, as if she had dressed in haste to come to him. Arising from his table, Ay crossed the hall to greet her.

"I hope you are well, Highness."

"As ever, Uncle," she replied icily.

"I understand the court has been darkened by your absence."

"I do not willingly absent myself from this company. I have been indisposed." She heard her tones quavering to the far corners of the lamplit hall. Too much was at stake; her guilt was too profound. "A woman has her time, Uncle," she said softly.

Ay's voice gathered resonance. "Strange, is it not? During your indisposition, the scribe Senumet has been missed as well."

"Isn't Senumet among us tonight?"

"He is not."

"Indeed. I was not aware . . ."

A servant, approaching and bowing low, whispered to Ay and abjectly retreated. "And Senumet is not in your chambers," Ay announced.

So Ay had ordered her chambers searched the instant she abandoned them. How dare he! And he was interrogating her like a wayward child before her court. She flared at the humiliation of it, and anger quelled her fear. "If Senumet were in my chambers, *I* would have known it, Uncle."

"But you do know where Senumet is," Ay accused.

He was fully aware of a plot now, Hesen realized, and was hunting for the kill. "I beg your pardon. I do not!"

"How can that be? When every tongue proclaims you and Senumet have been together for fully five days . . . *alone!*"

A sound like a gasp hovered in the hall. The entire court held its breath as Hesen clearly saw Ay's gambit. Later, when he married her, he would declare her innocent, but now he would openly shame her, accusing her of licentious behavior to force her into a posture of self-defense and divulge the knowledge she held close. But in the face of Senumet's courage, her shame was nothing.

"In the stead of your husband, the glorious son of the god whose time upon the soil of Egypt was tragically cut short, Niece, I name your sin!" Ay towered righteously.

"I'm afraid you have been misled."

"Exactly!" Ay thundered with a fierce irony Hesen understood but the court could not share. *"Where is Senumet?"*

"Your Excellency, I regret I must repeat myself. *I do not know.*"

Ay's rage bloated his face. Hesen expected to see him kick over her table and send glazed duck, honeyed rolls and creamed onions flying among alabaster goblets. Surprisingly, however, Ay controlled his fury and pronounced. "Then you stand convicted of your sin."

"I am unjustly defiled, Uncle."

Ay stared at her, his eyes hardening with respect for a worthy adversary, the same petrified stare he had bestowed upon her when she arrived in Thebes in place of Akhenaten, when he arrived at Akhet-Aten to acknowledge Tutu as Pharaoh. It reminded Hesen once more that Ay would never show her mercy.

As if his back would break, Ay bowed. "Forgive me, Highness. I apologize for having troubled you. The court rejoices that you are among us again." He gestured for his wine goblet to be brought to him. "To the health of the queen," he called. In unison the court raised goblets and drank. Ay returned to his place. Musicians played, conversation began again.

Hesen knew she had gained but a small victory in the scheme of things, but it was a victory all the same. An even greater victory now would be forcing down morsels of food.

She raised her eyes to gaze at Ay's place.

But Ay was gone.

Having bought passage on a barge emptied of its tribute and returning to the Delta, Narni felt himself well out of Thebes.

Buried among his things in a trunk, Senumet's generous payment of gold gave him some comfort, although he would have preferred to be chief scribe, as Senumet had promised if his mission had succeeded. He smarted at the thought that his strenuous journey to Hattusas, capital of the Hittites, had come to nothing and he feared he would someday be found by the hand of Ay if his journey and its purpose were discovered. Senumet had promised more gold in the future. Narni considered assuming a false name.

Someday came more rapidly than Narni feared.

The voyage up the Nile was leisurely; the captain wanted to acquire goods from towns and villages along the banks to barter in the Delta's ports. On the eighth day from Thebes, the barge was overtaken by a sleek scull with Amon's symbol painted on the hull. A yellow-robed priest of Amon demanded the scribe called Narni of Thebes reveal himself. Cringing, Narni kept silent, but the captain pointed out his passenger. Two burly soldiers leaped from the scull onto the deck of the barge and bound Narni with thick ropes.

Two and a half days later, Narni was dragged to the feet of Ay.

In the dim and dusty cell deep within Amon's temple, once used to sleep young novitiates, the yellow-robed priest beamed at Ay. He had been threatened with forfeiture of his life if the scribe were not found.

"You were seen in earnest conversation with Senumet in a tavern and in the scribes' barracks. Where is Senumet now?" Ay demanded.

"I don't know," Narni replied truthfully—although he could guess. A soldier twisted his arm behind his back. He howled in agony.

"You told Bek you were sent south by Senumet."

"Yes," Narni managed. "Senumet—directed me—to transact the business his attendance at court prevented him from completing. In Gebet, my lord."

"But you did not go to Gebet. *Where* did you go?"

In terror, Narni's mind blanked. He couldn't tell the truth; he could think of no lie. Impatiently Ay gestured a soldier forward. His short knife drawn, the soldier held Narni's face in the vise of his left hand, while his companion restrained Narni's body by clamping both of the scribe's hands between his shoulder blades. Narni's eyes bulged and crossed as he followed the tip of the knife to one nostril. He felt the sharp bronze delicately placed inside his nose. Then the blade slashed through the soft flesh. Blood gushed.

"Free him," Ay ordered.

The soldiers stepped back. Clasping his hands to his ruined face, Narni was unable to stem the heavy flow of blood. It dripped

*339*

through his fingers, ran into his mouth, over his chin, and splattered on the floor. He gagged. Mingling with the blood, vomit poured out of him. His knees rested in the foul mess. Inwardly he cursed Senumet.

Ay's eyes were lifeless holes. "Now. Where did you go, you piece of dung?"

Narni's mind refused to function. The two soldiers stepped forward, and Narni screamed.

"Crush his right hand."

"I went to—went to—" Narni cried. But already the soldiers had grasped his wrists, pulling his hands from his face. His left arm was again cruelly twisted up his spine, while his right was stretched forward, his fingers splayed on the stone floor. The soldier who held his right wrist raised a mallet with a head of stone.

"No o o!" Narni screeched. "I went—to Shubbiluliuma!"

"To Hattusas?"

Narni nodded vigorously, slinging drops of blood.

"For what purpose?"

Tears streaked the blood smeared on Narni's cheeks. A spasm of coughing prevented speech, and the soldier with the mallet prodded Narni with a kick in the ribs.

"To bring back—a prince," the scribe spat out, utterly wretched.

"To marry Queen Ankhesenamon." Ay's words dropped into a silence so profound that the scraping and clicks of beetles in the cell could be heard like rhythm sticks. The silence stretched into long moments, and at last Narni could stand it no longer. He dared to raise his head to peer up at Ay, to try to determine what his fate would be. The sight of Ay's face sapped the last of his strength. In Ay's face he saw death. Having deduced the rest, Ay needed no more from him.

Suddenly in motion, Ay passed from the room with a rustle of robes and the soles of his sandals slapping stone.

Narni twisted his head. "My lord!" he pitifully implored. He saw only the yellow robe of the priest who followed Ay.

The soldier who had held the mallet stepped before Narni. The mallet having disappeared, he stretched a knotted cord between his hands. He whipped the cord around Narni's neck.

The man's strength was massive. The time was short until Narni's rasping gurgles could no longer be heard.

# XXIX

She dreamed that she was being held like a babe in Sephy's arms and Sephy was crooning a lullaby . . .

Then she opened her eyes to the morning and lay still, savoring the sense of warm well-being that remained from the dream. She yearned to look upon that loving face she had known since her earliest memories. If only Sephy were here.

The last warmth of the dream faded as she heard padding footsteps. It was Senedjm.

"Forgive me, Highness, but I bring news."

"What news?"

"Of Horemheb."

She had seen Horemheb only once since his return from the frontier, when he sought an audience to express his grief over Tutu's death. His grief had run nearly as deep as her own, and although he justified leaving Tutu in his lieutenant's care, he blamed himself. She had absolved him of that blame. He vowed to discipline the lieutenant severely. He agreed to lighten the man's punishment for her sake, but he wouldn't commute it entirely as she requested.

"Tell me," she said to Senedjm.

"He led fifty of the guard from Thebes before daybreak. They were on horseback, fully armed for battle."

"To where?"

"No one knows, Highness."

But she knew. Ay had found out. Horemheb went after Senumet. She thanked Senedjm, and he retreated.

In the afternoon she forced herself to leave her bed and dress.

Word had been brought from the embalmers that the wrapping of the corpse was to begin. While it was not required of her, for love of Tutu, for her penance, she would go.

When Hesen entered the embalmers' tent, four morticians in their strange white robes with the single left sleeve stood ready to begin. A priest of Amon was present to intone the prayers. She sat in a chair of ivory, ebony and gold, and the morticians began their work.

Tutankhamon lay before her on a long table of cedar. His body, shorter somehow than she remembered it, had been rendered almost fleshless by the long immersion in natron. His mouth had been stretched back over his white, well-formed teeth, ready to be wrapped. First, bracelets that he had worn in life and loved were placed on his desiccated arms, seven on the right, six on the left: scarab bracelets, bracelets with flexible bands, golden bracelets encrusted with turquoise and lapis. Over his chest and closest to where his heart had pumped life's blood—that organ, like the others, having been removed, embalmed with bitumen and placed in the Canopic jars under the protection of the four sons of Horus—was laid the vulture pectoral with the hieroglyphs of his name upon it.

The priest reverently raised his voice to invoke the protection of the fine strips of linen:

> "Hail Tait . . .
> Bind together the bones of Tutankhamon
> So they do not fall apart."

The bandaging began. Each toe was separately wrapped. Then his legs disappeared under the strips of linen. His sex, a frail stump now like a child's, was wrapped in the erect, stiffened posture it had so briefly mastered. The morticians wrapped Pharaoh's abdomen and chest, which had been filled with spices and bitumen; bandaging the arms, they carefully strapped them across Pharaoh's chest.

> "Hail Tait . . .
> Protect the head of Tutankhamon,
> That it becomes not detached."

After the neck, they wrapped the chin, and then with bands of fine cloth closed forever the mouth that had curved in ecstatic triumph when he first expelled his seed against her womb, the nose that had breathed her perfumed flesh, the open eyes that would never again follow the redstart's flight or the flash of the ibex.

Hesen's nails cut into her palms. The interior of the tent blurred, but as no eyes were upon her, she did not force back her tears. From a table of his belongings, she picked up Tutu's golden dagger, the very one with which she had thought to murder Ay, and hiding it in the folds of her blue mantle, she tested its keenness. Easily, with no sting, it sliced into the meat of her forefinger. Ay's guard was outside the tent; the embalmers could not stop her. Now it could be done. Like her mother, she could follow her sweet king into eternity.

But unlike Tutu, who would rise like a falcon to join the true god Aten, she would be damned. In the Hall of Two Truths, her heart would testify against her and unbalance the scales of *maat*. But she had no fear of eternal darkness. Let her ka wander blindly down corridors of endless time. She wanted no reanimated consciousness, for emerging again from darkness to awareness would only bring back the bitterness of her life and the burdens of her sins. And what better moment to do it than now? With Horemheb and his Imperial Guard headed for the kingdom of the Hittites, her wild, improbable attempt to thwart Ay was doomed to failure. How could it succeed? Horemheb would not allow Senumet and the prince to reach Thebes. If there was no queen at stake—was it possible that Senumet might be spared?

She shivered. No, she must not. She could not profane the dagger's purity. When Tutu, blameless and noble, woke again in his body, everything he needed must be at hand, and his dagger must not be stained with bloody sins and selfish love. She couldn't grant herself the indulgence of death. She must live until Tutu's eternal comfort was assured. She must live until she knew Senumet's fate.

Unseen, she replaced the dagger on the funerary table.

Each dawn for the next three days, she went to the embalmers' tent.

After the first layer of linen wrappings, his bound body was anointed with unguents, spices, and resin.

> *"Death stands before him*
> *Like the fragrance of myrrh. . . ."*

Eighteen more times the process of wrapping was repeated. Eighteen more times he was anointed so that the bindings of linen would paste together. Eighteen more layers of amulets and jewelry adorned the linen strips, and eighteen more times were prayers and hymns raised to the god that had been Pharaoh and the gods of Egypt to protect his ka in his terrible spiritual journey before, like Osiris, he rose again in his body.

For each of these three days, Hesen didn't leave the embalmers' tent until the sun cast long dark shadows and the work stopped. It was a brutal, punishing ordeal she imposed on herself, seemingly interminable. Her guilt at her failed guardianship of his life demanded she guard him in death. She had heard tales of workers' carelessness, of dried fingers and arms broken off and discarded, dooming kas to wander forever maimed and prey to fierce demons, unable to defend themselves against the snapping crocodile. She vowed Tutu would meet his fate whole, equipped with all the power, magic and might Egypt could fashion.

Finally the golden mask of Pharaoh's likeness was laid over his face, and the body was lowered into the first coffin, and the eight men, straining and grunting with the enormous weight, placed the solid-gold coffin within the second one. Having carried with her the pectoral garland she had plaited, Hesen put it gently on his sculpted breast, its blue water-lilies, willows and sprigs of wild celery spreading their fragrance even after the second coffin was closed and the entire massive structure was lowered into the third coffin. From its lid, Tutu's face stared at her placidly, his obsidian eyes shining with visions of everlasting glory.

Tutankhamon was ready for his final journey to the Valley of Kings.

On the morning of the burial, she arose and thought, *The sun will not rise on the day after this.*

She insisted Tey bring her the dress she had worn the night his manhood had been born.

"This is a dress of celebration," Tey objected. Her lips pursed, she molded the gilt-threaded dress to the queen's body, while Hesen thought: *Today he enters eternal peace. What greater happiness for a lost, suffering boy.*

Hesen herself painted away the stress lines stamped on her face, applying the paint and then the kohl for the last time in the mode of Nefertiti. Tey lowered onto her head a long, curled wig and covered this with a gold-threaded net interspersed with beaded rosettes. Then Tey raised the golden vulture headdress, worn for centuries by Egypt's queens.

Hesen waved it away. "Bring to me the stag circlet."

Tey's eyebrows arched, folding the wrinkles of her forehead. "Majesty, do you relinquish your power?"

Hesen twisted on her stool to face the sarcastic creature. "He loved animals and flowers. When his eyes are opened, he shall not remember failed promises and *brutal murder!*"

Tey's eyes flashed and she stalked away. Had she gone mad, Hesen wondered, to say such a thing to Ay's wife? But she felt glad it was said.

Tey returned and placed the electrum band on Hesen's wig. The four small gazelles alternated with octofoil rosettes. In the center was the large stag head, its ornamented antlers sweeping back in a splendid curve. Hesen stared at herself in the mirror of polished silver and approved.

"They await you," Tey informed her. Hesen turned her back on that hateful countenance.

Regally erect, she walked out of the palace, her ministers and the nobility falling into procession behind her. Heavy, sonorous drumbeats heralded their coming. Crowds of weeping Thebans parted to let them pass as they made their way to the docks.

Already Tutu's coffins, placed in a golden boat-shrine, waited on the sledge in the first barge. The ten other barges were laden with treasures to be ported to the tomb.

At the ramp to the second barge, Nabamon awaited her. For five years since the death of Tushratta, he had enjoyed the position of Chief Priest of Amon in Thebes, the stronghold of the great god. She feared him almost as she feared Ay. He led her aboard and there she saw Ay, his shaven head gleaming with oil, his black bestial eyes stalking her. He was seated on a stool by her throne.

"Move my throne to Pharaoh's barge!" she commanded Nabamon.

Nabamon looked to Ay, expecting him to override the queen. But Ay nodded assent. Two of the regiment of soldiers that accompanied the funeral party carried the throne in the blazing heat and placed it on the lead barque next to Pharaoh's bier.

Oars dipped into water, and the eleven barges, draped with black streamers, eased into the river.

Wails from those crowding the shore almost drowned the booming drums. As the keening faded into the distance Hesen kept her eyes fixed on Tutu's coffin until his likeness, wrapped in Nekhbet's loving arms, merged into the golden dazzle of morning, became one with the sparkling waters and blazing sun.

She was barely aware the boats had docked on the west bank. As the funeral party disembarked, twelve soldiers heaved the sledge onto the bleached white stones of the shore. Four white oxen were harnessed to the sledge; six stony-faced soldiers, Amon's sign flashing on their chests, lined up on either side of the sledge; and the march began.

Hesen walked directly behind the bier, treading in the dust she had raised with her sandals once before, in the procession behind the sledge bearing Amenophis. Above the stark cliffs, the sky was again (or was it *still?*) bleached white, and a white pall seemed to fade even the soldiers' bright spears and flashing pectorals. The drums were muffled; the oxen's heavy feet seemed padded as they plodded carefully on the small stones. Behind her in their leopard skins came the priests, Ay foremost; next Pharaoh's ministers followed; then his servants bearing golden shrines, inlaid boxes, small godlike statues of the king, bright jewels. The procession was led and flanked by soldiers; twelve more brought up the rear, striking the drumheads in a slow steady rhythm. Straggling behind them like a ragged train were the professional mourners—forty women who wailed unceasingly, ripped their clothes, tore at their streaming hair, poured dust on their heads.

Finally they reached the sloping hills and wound their tortuous way over piles of loose skree toward the cliffs. In the white silent world of death, the drumbeats were hurled back at them in eerie, distorted echoes. They passed sealed doorways—entrances to other tombs of other kings—and the hills seemed alive with hovering, departed spirits of gods and their kin.

They stopped before a freshly cut stairway: They had arrived. The waiting muu dancers, wearing the traditional crown of reeds, spiraled toward them. Affixed to their fingers were small copper plates, struck to the rhythm of their frenzied leaps and kicks.

Removed from its sledge, the coffin was held in an upright position by the soldiers while the muu dancers prostrated themselves before Pharaoh's image. Tutu's golden face, his obsidian eyes fixed on eternity, looked past Hesen as if he already knew secrets he would not share.

Touching the adze to the eyes, nose, mouth, of the coffin mask, Ay began:

> "*Heaven was pregnant with thee,*
> *The morning bore thee, together with Orion,*
> *Who lived by the order of the gods.*
> *Thou shalt live.*
> *Thou shalt rise with Orion in the eastern part of heaven.*

*Thou shalt set with Orion in the western part of heaven.
Your companion is the Dog Star.
She will guide you in the pure places
Which are in Heaven, in the Field of Rushes."*

The coffin was hoisted to the shoulders of twelve soldiers and carried slowly down the twelve steps that led to the tomb. When the door was opened, they proceeded down the thirty-foot passageway. The door at the bottom opened into the antechamber.

The larger treasures were already there. Two life-size ebony statues of Tutu, both hands grasping spears, stood as sentinels at the far end of the chamber. Passing over the three great couches headed by animals (cow goddess, lion, river beast that melded hippopotamus and crocodile), Hesen's glance lingered on his throne, for the last time seeing the Aten whose hands blessed the king and queen sculpted on its back. There were four chariots, covered with gold, bearing inlaid designs in colored glass and stones.

Servants stepped forward and interspersed the smaller treasures: the alabaster cup, the lotus chalice, the copper and bronze trumpets, the wooden chest containing the king's mantles and robes, the small golden shrine embossed with loving scenes of the two of them walking in a garden, hunting, anointing each other. She watched calmly until they brought in his folding stool and child's chair on which he had struggled to master writing under Senumet's tutelage. Then tears spontaneously threatened again.

The smaller treasures in place, they passed through the doorway flanked by the sentry statues into the burial chamber, where the massive quartzite sarcophagus gaped. Wall paintings depicted Ay performing the ceremony of the Opening of the Mouth with the adze so that Pharaoh might see, hear, speak and eat when he awoke. That ceremony Ay had performed outside before the coffins were carried down into the sepulcher chambers. Hesen added it to her tablet of grievances against Ay that he had had his own representations rendered larger than Tutu's.

While the nobles and priests lined themselves about the walls, she stepped aside into the Treasury to make sure the inventory was complete. The gold-and-black-lacquered statue of Anubis, jackal god, permitted her entry. Identical copies of the Selket whose beauty had been molded after Hesen's own, Isis, Nephthys and Neith, raised slim arms in magical protection of the Canopic chest that held Tutu's internal organs. In beautiful inlaid boxes, his jewelry awaited his resurrection, as did his writing implements, bows and arrows, his headrests, royal scepter, the lion jar, the ibex vase, all guarded by statues of Ptah and the cobra god, Neith. Once again tears flowed when she looked upon his gaming board on which they had played senet through so many long nights. She could stand no more and turned back into the burial chamber.

The coffins were positioned over the sarcophagus, and at her return, Ay began the prayers, leading the chanting priests. Their voices resounded in the room hewn from stone.

> *"He flieth as a bird*
> *And he settleth as a beetle*
> *On an empty seat that is in the ship of Amon-Ra.*
> *He roweth in the sky in thy ship, O Ra,*
> *And he cometh to the land in thy ship, O Ra."*

Carefully the coffins were lowered into the sarcophagus, the darkness within consuming the outer coffin until Hesen could scarcely see the glint of Tutu's golden features.

> *"Thou art one with Osiris.*
> *With Osiris thou shalt arise.*
> *Thy bones, O Osiris, are the bones of Tutankhamon.*
> *If thou walkest, he walkest."*

Her time came. Stepping forward, she looked down into the sarcophagus and studied for the last time the image of his face, carved into the wood and covered with gold. So young, so sadly mistreated by life. She placed on his chest the collarette of blue beads and berries of the woody nightshade, the one she had been stringing when Senumet brought her Shubbiluliuma's message. Resting her fingertips upon his breathless golden lips, she uttered her final farewell in the soft, sweet voice that had calmed his terrors.

> *"To whom can I speak today?*
> *The gentle man has perished.*
> *To whom can I speak today?*
> *There are no righteous men.*
> *To whom can I speak today?*
> *I will speak to Thee, My Lord,*
> *Who art yonder, forever a Living God,*
> *And thine image, my Sun, will shine in my heart*
> *As thy life brightened my days."*

Looking up, she found Ay staring at her with naked antipathy. In an instant, the tender love that had flowed as freely as the Nile for Tutu became a torrent of hatred. Over the open sarcophagus they dueled with hatred until, startled by the virulence of Hesen's loathing, Ay glanced away.

Four priests, their muscles bulging, lifted the quartzite cover into place and permanently sealed Tutankhamon into eternity. Ay began the final prayer:

> *"Thou shalt sail on the waters of the flood,*
> *Thy life shall start afresh.*
> *Thy Ba shall not depart from thy corpse*
> *And thy Ba shall become divine*
> *With the blessed dead . . ."*

Suddenly the heat of life emanating from the bodies pressing near her was unendurable. Sweat dripped down her back. Thick with incense, the air was suffocatingly stagnant. The walls with their paintings were closing in to crush her and all those with her. In the dancing light of lamps, her vision swam, focusing steadily only on Ay's gleaming head. And Ay was—changing. His ears were growing large and pointed like the ears of the fennec-fox, his moving jaws elongating into a narrow canine snout with terrible sharp teeth. What was he—who was he? But she knew. He was the storm god, the god of darkness, the slayer, the author of murder, the Evil One, Seth! And as his head and that animal snout revolved toward her, she saw it glistened wetly with scarlet—Tutu's blood—and her own!

She choked out a cry and ran from the burial chamber, through the antechamber and passages, up and out into the sun and fresh air. Before the entrance to the tomb, the professional mourners were still wailing, and their howls tore at her ears until she left them behind. At last her feet slowed on the hot sands and white pebbles of the floor of the valley and she stood motionless in the blinding sun.

She could breathe. The vision passed. Inside the burial chamber, she knew, the doors of the three shrines around the sarcophagus, painted with scenes and incantations from the Book of the Dead, were being closed; the bolts were being slid into place as easily as Tutu's life had been snuffed out.

Soon the others would be emerging from the tomb and regrouping for the processional return to the funeral barges.

She waited for them where she stood. Hot gusts filled her eyes and mouth with sand.

\* \* \*

Whenever he could trade for or buy a fresh mount, Senumet had changed horses and had ridden each mount to the limits of its endurance. Late on the ninth day after departing from Thebes, he had entered the land of Hatti on the Anatolian plain. He urged his wheezing mount along the cobbled streets between the squat mud-brick and wooden structures that were the stronghold of the Hittites.

Hattusas was as squalid as a peasants' village. Even the temples of Tarhum, the weather god, and of Arinnitti, the sun goddess, built of rough blocks of stone, were devoid of grace and beauty. He was surrounded by surly louts as he led his sweat-soaked horse to the water in the trough before the very palace doors. He sent word to the king that Senumet of Thebes wished an immediate audience. Before hostile, curious eyes, he stripped off the filthy mantle and tunic in which he had traveled, took fresh attire from the bags over his horse's rump and rinsed the grime from his body. Having shaved with a small mirror and razor, he wrapped the inner and outer skirts of a fine linen kilt around his waist, adorned himself with armbands, a collar set with lapis and glass, and a wig of human hair. When word was returned that he was to come to the hall of the king, he looked the part of Egypt's ambassador.

Brutishness he had expected, but the lack of cleanliness in Shubbiluliuma's hall profoundly offended his Egyptian senses and repelled him. The air reeked from the dung of the animals that ran freely in the hall, the rotting scraps of food tossed or fallen unheeded to the floor, the rancid oil that fueled the lamps and blackened the walls and ceiling with its smoke, the unwashed bodies and the sweat that soaked thickly woven, tasseled woolen robes. The hall was filled with men—scarred muscled arms, tangled, greasy beards and heavy, pointed boots that filled his nightmares of the sacking of Byblos. He couldn't distinguish the king from his chieftains and warriors until he was led to a long wooden table and a man as squat and rude as his buildings stood to greet him.

The king's grin, in a face nearly covered with black hair, exposed chipped and missing teeth. "So another Egyptian takes his life in his hands to come among us, so soon on the heels of the first!" Shubbiluliuma roared. "But this Egyptian we have heard of. Years ago he traveled the lands as a spy for Pharaoh! His sword took the lives of our brave warriors! You know we should kill you—and yet you come?"

Haltingly—for his knowledge of the Hittite tongue had served until now only for reading and writing—Senumet answered, "We met in fair battle. I carry a permanent reminder of that conflict and can no longer swing a sword. Because of your honor, I place myself with confidence in your hands."

The black eyes glittered with amusement. "Well said!" Food was shoved aside, wine overturned as men pushed each other to clear a place for Senumet beside their king. A goblet was thumped down on the table before Senumet and sloshed to the brim with wine.

"Do you ride in advance of your caravan?" Shubbiluliuma asked, drinking deep of his wine.

"I ride with no caravan. I come alone."

"How then do you expect to bring to the King of Hatti, conqueror of Mesopotamia and all the earth unto Egypt, the gifts he deserves?"

"I bring no gifts. Save one."

"The same as the fool before you?"

"The greatest gift Egypt can bestow."

"Egypt herself."

"Egypt and Egypt's queen."

Around them spread silence like rings of ripples from a stone dropped in a still pool. The king swirled another mouthful of wine over his gums and spat it upon the floor. "Tell your queen this: The Hittite king is a mighty soldier who thirsts for the blood of the dying, the Hittite king is strong in his body and in the smell of his skin . . . but the Hittite king is not soft in the head! When the Hittite king wants Egypt, Egypt will be devoured by his hordes like lambs by wolves. Egypt shall *not* steal back by trickery the empire Egypt couldn't defend in battle! Tell your queen *that!*—so she may hide her face in fear and all of Egypt may tremble with her."

And all of the king's chieftains and warriors in the hall approved Shubbiluliuma with the ululating war cry that chilled Senumet with blood-curdling memories of death.

Raising his goblet, Senumet filled his mouth, swished vinegary wine from cheek to cheek in the ritual cleansing, and spat it onto the straw-covered stone at his feet. Senumet spoke loudly enough to reach throngs in the Theban square. "The Queen of Egypt would have the King of Hatti know that Egypt fears neither him nor his hordes. At Byblos, did not a handful of Egyptians surprise as many Hittites as there are birds in the air, and did not those Hittites turn their backsides and fly into the hills?" Senumet saw the king's face harden; Shubbiluliuma remembered well. "Egypt's queen has no need of trickery. But the queen does have need of a husband. He who was her lord, her uncle, and her king is dead. She knows of the mettle and the strength of the sons of thunder. She offers an alliance that would make the world shake before the might of two crowns, of Egypt and of Hatti! This from the mouth of Senumet, whose words are the Queen of Egypt's."

Shubbiluliuma struck the base of his goblet on the arm of his chair, which was carved into the head of a dragon. "Already the world quakes and moans like a sick old woman before the King of Hatti and his warriors!"

Again his men hailed him, sounding as if they charged into battle. Triumphantly the king sank back into his chair, and the men returned again to jests and coarse laughter among themselves. At last Shubbiluliuma turned to Senumet and sallied, "I hear Egypt fills the tombs of her god-kings with gold, never to shine again before the eyes of men. This is true?"

Senumet bowed slightly.

"If the seers divine that the god favors a union of Egypt and Hatti, I say a son of my seed is worth three of your kings."

"You think the crown of Pharaoh is made of gold, my king?"

"Three tombs' worth."

"And if the queen agreed a prince of Hatti was worth so much?"

"Then it bears thought," said Shubbiluliuma, "but thought is never wise on an empty stomach."

The king gestured. To tumultuous shouts, three servants staggered into the hall under the weight of a huge wooden board on which was a monstrous roasted boar. They placed it on the table before the king. Shubbiluliuma rose, and brandishing a battle axe, he mightily swung. The crash shook the table and shattered the boar's skull. The Hittites crowded around the king's table, jostling each other and shoving Senumet to a place directly behind the king's five sons. In turn, after their father, each son dipped his hand into the cavity, drawing forth oozing brain which he gobbled with relish. Senumet's gorge rose as he followed suit. He found the taste was surprisingly delicate, much like eggs, and his success was rewarded with bone-bruising slaps on the back. Knives were drawn, and the Hittites carved away great hunks of meat from the carcass. The piece the king cut for Senumet took both of his hands to hold.

As he gnawed at the rib and wiped his greasy fingers on his beard, Shubbiluliuma slyly glanced toward Senumet. "I am told the Queen of Egypt is delicate and frail. Her womb takes not to man's seed, and she has brought but one child to term. Why should a son of mine plough barren ground?"

"Her lord was only a boy. Bedded with a man, her womb will bear sons a dozen times over."

"Are there no *men* in Egypt?"

"As you must know, her lord was the last of the line of the great Amenophis III. There are contenders for her bed, but the queen prefers a prince of royal blood."

Senumet knew the king was considering what went unsaid—that the Queen of Egypt was involved in a struggle for the power of her throne. If he helped her, Egypt would owe him much more than gold. "This must be done in haste," Shubbiluliuma judged.

"With or without a prince of Hatti beside me, I must ride for Egypt before the next sun is high."

Shubbiluliuma grunted. He tossed his bone to the dogs behind his chair. "I am told the beauty of the queen is such a man must be drunk to part her thighs."

"The eyes of men who utter such lies should be gouged out, for their eyes are blind and useless. Her face surpasses even that of her mother, Nefertiti, whose perfection is legend."

"Gold brightens any bed and makes any face beautiful."

"Egypt shall make payment, my lord."

"Three tombs' worth?"

"As Pharaoh, I'm certain your son will see to it."

The king absorbed himself in eating and drinking as though he had lost interest. Suddenly, the king shouted, "What say you, Zennanza? Will you have Egypt?"

At the other end of the table, Shubbiluliuma's son leaped drunkenly to his feet and thrust his hips forward obscenely. "And the queen with it!" he slurred. Ribald cheers assailed him.

Senumet knew the prince to be the king's third son. While he was young enough that his beard was still sparse, his muscles were equal to those of the strongest men Senumet had ever seen. From his keen observation of the king's sons since his arrival, Senumet had decided that of the older sons, Zennanza was least favored by his father. The ox of a boy appeared to be not exceptionally quick of mind. Of course Shubbiluliuma would not send his oldest, the heir. The second, Shabeka, had a gleam of intelligent cunning in his eye. Of the princes, it was he Senumet would have preferred. Still not trusting Egypt, however, the king would not risk his best.

Shubbiluliuma leered. "Zennanza ruts like a he-goat. His sword of love is large and mighty. Women of our enemies have died of it."

Braying loudly, the boy continued to mimic a copulating donkey.

Shubbiluliuma roared with laughter, while Senumet was revolted at the thought that this vulgar dolt might wear the double crown of Egypt, outraged at the vision of those fleshy lips hungrily bruising Hesen's mouth, those stocky hips hammering between her fine white thighs.

"I will send with him twenty men only," the king declared. "I will waste no more than that. And I charge you, Senumet of Thebes, with his life. If Zennanza dies, I will carry your head upon my spear!"

Huge stone jars of wine were rolled into the hall. Jeweled goblets of gold were substituted for the clumsy clay ones, and Senumet had no need to look at the symbol of Astarte to recognize the finely wrought artistry. The goblets were booty from Byblos. As his fingers curled about the stem, he heard the horrible screams of Elyssa as the babe was crushed from her huge womb by Hittite boots.

"To the bridegroom, Egypt's next king!" Shubbiluliuma shouted. He pitched his chalice high and it flashed a golden arc toward the rough-hewn rafters.

Cocks crowed to raise the sun, and the small cavalry of twenty, feeling the retribution for a night of debauched celebration, headed out of Hattusas onto the dusty, sunbaked plain. Led by Senumet and the prince, they rode through the Empire of the Hittites, then southward through the lands of the Hapiru tribes, at last on the fifth day crossing the wasteland of Gaza.

At night, resting for a few hours underneath the stars, Senumet was left shaking by waves of anxiety. Chances were Ay would never hit upon Hattusas as his destination or guess the object of his mission. Senumet would bribe a minor priest of Amon to sanctify the wedding ceremony. But once the wedding was consecrated, *then what?* Given Horemheb's rabid hatred of the Hittites, how was the loyalty of the army to be secured? How were the priests of Amon, under Ay's sway, to be persuaded to accept the prince as Pharaoh? His mind revolted against the image of Egypt in open rebellion against the palace. His hope—and Hesen's—depended on Egypt's determination to accept *what was* as the decree of the gods. He felt that hope was slim. What he and Hesen were doing *was* mad!

On the dawn of the sixth day, the unbroken wilderness of the triangular peninsula lay before them. The sun was directly overhead when a pair of Hittite eyes first spotted the disturbance of dust on the horizon.

"Riders," alerted Zennanza's man.

Like the prince, Senumet reined in his horse. Cold fear gripped his entrails.

"A band of cutthroats," the prince declared, eager for battle to enliven the boring journey. "How many?"

His man squinted. "Half a hundred. They punish their mounts."

"Too many for brigands," the prince observed.

"Egyptians," Senumet said. In his heart he knew it was true.

"Friend or foe?" barked the Hittite who commanded the prince's escort.

"They will take the prince captive," Senumet said, his voice as leaden as his heart. "Or kill him."

In the center of the dust storm, glints of bronze refracted sunlight. They could hear the hoofbeats of the approaching force.

"Egyptian swine!" spat the prince. "As my father warned, you have tricked us!" Snarling, he whipped his ax from his hip and his mightly arm swung it at Senumet. Senumet's knees moved on his horse, turning the beast as he drew back, and the blade of the ax found a home in his steed's neck. The animal crashed to the sand, pinning Senumet beneath it. Its legs kicked wildly in its death throes. Giving the Hittite war cry, Zennanza and his twenty warriors raced to meet the Egyptians, and Senumet tasted the dirt the pounding hooves kicked into his face.

Struggling from beneath his dead mount, he stood and tested his right leg; the pain was intense, but the leg was unbroken.

With cries clamoring to heaven, the Egyptians ringed the prince and his comrades. It would be a merciless slaughter, Senumet knew, when he caught a flash of hieroglyphs, the insignia of rank, painted on a broad chest, and recognized the Supreme Commander of Egypt's army. Horemheb hacked and slashed as if he possessed ten arms and ten swords.

As Hittites fell, Horemheb forced aside two of his own men to attack the prince. With a cut of his sword not to be withstood, Horemheb disarmed the prince, then besieged his shield. His horse rearing, Zennanza rolled over its rump into the dust, and Horemheb leaped from his mount to straddle him. Horemheb's bellow, "Hittite dog!" reached Senumet's ears. Closing his eyes, Senumet could almost feel Horemheb's blade cleave his own throat to the bone. Strangely, sorrow welled up in his breast for the prince of Hatti. He opened his eyes.

He saw with horror a scene he would never have imagined; Egyptians, more bloodthirsty for carnage than the Hittites, mutilating the dead. Two soldiers were stripping Zennanza's body. After hacking off his limbs, they unmanned the prince with a blow from a Hittite ax.

Horemheb, ripping his leather helmet from his head, was striding toward him. "Senumet!" Horemheb rasped. He stopped ten paces away. Tears coursed down his cheeks. "How could you do this?"

Senumet gestured helplessly. And then one last spark of hope rose from the ashes. Was it possible Horemheb could be made to understand? "My old friend, would you have Ay on the throne of Egypt?"

"Yes, Ay! Better a hundred Ays than this prince who bathed in the blood of Byblos and of Egypt."

"This prince was but a toddling babe then," Senumet gently corrected.

"But he *is* Hittite!" Horemheb shouted.

"And I ask you, who is the more barbarous? The civilized man who wrongs his conscience and acts the barbarian, or he who was raised a barbarian and acts courageously, believing himself to bring honor to himself and his gods?"

"Say plainly what you mean."

"Ay is more savage than any Hittite. He had Smenkhare murdered, he would have murdered Akhenaten, and his mouth ordered the death of Tutu."

"Where is your proof?"

"Look into your heart. You know the truth." In Horemheb's eyes, Senumet saw him admit to himself what before he had vaguely suspected.

"But Ay is an Egyptian!" Horemheb defended angrily. "He would not crush Egypt."

"He would, if in Egypt were not the power he seeks."

"Do you forget Byblos?"

Senumet drew a shuddering breath. "You, of all men, can you ask me that?"

"Then how could you plot to exalt a Hittite bastard?"

"I have told you," Senumet said tonelessly. It was unfair, what he was about to say, reminding Horemheb of his hopeless love, but Senumet was beyond fairness. "My one allegiance is forged harder than metal," he nearly whispered. "You feel the same loyalty."

Horemheb's lip curled in disgust. "But I would not destroy Egypt for a woman!"

"Ay will kill her, when he has sons. I would keep power from a murderer."

"From an Egyptian!" Horemheb repeated, adamant.

It had been futile to hope. Horemheb was like a war-horse fitted with blinders in battle. "Remember how we fought together," Senumet adjured him. "Now give me my death."

"I won't take your life," Horemheb declared.

"But you are ordered . . ."

"Yes."

"You cannot disobey. There are too many witnesses."

"My men have trusted me with their lives. I trust them with mine. Go, Senumet! May Amon keep you forever from my sight."

He watched Horemheb stride back to his men, who were loading their horses with trophies and the twelve Egyptian dead who must be carried back to Egypt. Horemheb did not glance back as the Egyptians rode toward the horizon, leaving behind them the remains of the Hittites, food for vultures and jackals. And Senumet.

With his bare hands, Senumet dug a grave for the dismembered limbs and torso of Zennanza. The sand scraped away skin until his hands bled. Then he mounted the horse Horemheb had left him.

Like Horemheb and his soldiers, Senumet rode westward, to Egypt.

# XXX

No one spoke to her. Since Tey had observed Senedjm's faithfulness and he had, like Sephy, been removed, there were days she did not even hear the sound of her own voice.

Hours drifted by; she lost track of their passage. She waited for her release, whether the end came by marriage or by death. Yet should she decide now to take her life, she could not have done so. Watched every moment, she was attended even in her large, lonely bed where Ay's servants sat close by, wakeful and scrupulously alert.

Unsure of how much time had elapsed since Senumet rode to the Hittites, she was also unsure exactly when she understood he must be dead. With the certainty she would never see him again, she died in her heart. Nothing mattered. She withdrew further within.

She became aware that a bevy of servants coaxed and scolded her to arise. At last, under Tey's eyes, she was roughly pulled from her bed. Tey's hands were merciless on her body as she was oiled. She was poked, manipulated and painted. Kohl hid the lines around her eyes, rouge lent a youthful blush to pale cheeks, tinted powder gave her face and breasts a glow meant to resemble health.

Servants fluttered about her at Tey's direction, dressing her in a linen gown with embroidered borders of twined lotuses. Over it was draped the transparent outer garment woven with golden thread. She had no recollection of this dress—where had it come from? Her fingers were being weighted with rings. The uraeus was being slipped over her wig.

It must be today, she realized dully, the day when Ay's victory would be complete, when the double crown of Pharaoh would be set upon his head. And Ay could do with her what he willed.

Suddenly she heard the swelling booms of drums, the military notes of trumpets, horses hooves on paving. Horemheb!

She shoved aside necklaces held up for her approval, knocked over the jewelry tray, and kicking through the spilled glitter, she tore out of the room. Startled sentries sprinted at her heels.

Into the courtyard she raced, stopping at the sight of soldiers dismounting and Horemheb bowing to Ay while a soldier displayed a trophy: a severed hand, a signet ring of royalty on its middle finger.

"The hand of the slain Hittite prince, my lord," Horemheb reported. "The prince and his party are dead. We intercepted them on their way to Egypt, south of Rhinocolura. We did not see Senumet, my lord. If he was with them, he escaped. We searched for him, but with no luck."

He lived! Somewhere under the vast expanse of sky, Senumet breathed. Never would she see him again, but she had not caused his death. That knowledge enabled her to get through the day.

She was led into the darkness of Amon's temple where Nabamon wed her to Ay, and then into the great square of Thebes and onto the platform before the temple erected for the coronation. From where she was forced to stand by Ay's side, she looked down at Horemheb. His face was as hard as granite; she found no sympathy there. Nabamon placed the crook and flail in Ay's hands. He lowered the crown on Ay's head. Throngs prostrated themselves before Pharaoh, and the Sun Disk was carried on its ark from the temple to bless Pharaoh and his queen.

They returned to the palace. In the throne room, Ay received homage from an endless procession of investing priests, sly-eyed nobles, unctuous officials, foreign ambassadors, who lauded the tributes they laid before him. Seated on the golden chair by the throne, again she searched out Horemheb, willing him to be drawn to her. But he averted his eyes and did not approach.

The feast and revels in the great hall coursed into the late hours. At Ay's command, she rose numbly and followed her escort to the royal apartments where Ay would lie with her in Tutu's bed. Her black eyes inscrutable, Tey supervised the preparations. Unguents were rubbed into Hesen's breasts, on her neck, between her thighs, and her body was perfumed. A diaphanous white gown was carefully arranged on her body and she was led to the canopied bed. She stared at it stupidly, until a firm nudge from Tey ended the brief, mindless peace. She climbed onto the bed and stretched out her slim form. Tey arranged her limbs and smoothed her gown over her body.

The water clock continued its slow, steady drip. She began to forget for what she waited . . . there was such a pounding behind her eyes . . . perhaps if she closed them . . .

The bed tilted. Her eyes flew open. An old man reached for her with cold, gnarled hands.

*Who?*

"Father!" she cried. No, that was wrong! Akhenaten had scarcely reached half the age of this old man before her hand served him—death! And never had his sinews stood out beneath a leathery skin like ropes twisted over bone. The lamplight shadowed the lines of age in his face, making of them deep gashes. He sneered.

*What was this nightmare?* She struggled to clear her head, trying to penetrate the murkiness swirling about her. *Aten, dear Father, help me!*

His face was almost on top of hers, light gleaming on the curve on his smoothly shaven skull. She stared into black pits where there should have been eyes. And then she recognized him—from the tomb—the Evil One. *It was Ay!*

A scream constricted her throat. She opened her mouth to release it, but the hot cavity of his mouth covered it, his teeth grinding on hers. The scream, pushed back into her lungs, spread internally, filling every organ and fiber of her body.

With his sharp knee he pushed at her thighs. Frantically she locked her legs together. Raising his head, he barked an order, and two priests of Amon hurried to the bedside. With brute force they untwisted her legs and pulled them widely apart, their fingers digging into her ankles.

She tried to thrash, but Ay grabbed her hands and pinned them under his body, resting his weight on the arm that crossed her collar bone and nearly cut off her breath.

"Open for me!" he demanded, breathing heavily. Shifting his weight, he clawed his fingers into her chin and turned her head to face him. She shut her eyes. His hand smashed against her cheek. Her teeth clashed together with a pain that stunned her.

"Open, bitch!"

With a desperate twist, she wrenched one hand free of his grip. Forcing all of her strength into her arm, she flung her fist onto his face. At the impact of her knuckles, she felt his head snap back and heard his shout of enraged surprise. Again he bent his face over her, and she was helpless now, her resistance exhausted. She saw a rivulet of blood running from his left nostril to his chin, seeping waywardly into the valley between his chiseled lips.

*Blood on the lips of Seth the Slayer.*

Ay shoved his hand into her private hair. Quickly he found her opening. He entered now. Although her channel must have felt like rough parchment to him, and his face showed no pleasure, he determinedly rammed into her until he was done.

She did not know when he left her. As she lay in a miserable heap of throbbing bruises and such shame as she had never known, one message took form clearly: she must clean herself. Weakly she managed to sit herself upright.

"What do you want?" Tey harshly croaked from the chair beside her bed.

Wordlessly she slumped back onto her bed. There was no comfort. She would die of this. Ay couldn't deny her that. And the peace of that knowledge eased her down the steep slope into the darkness of sleep.

In the spring of the first year of the reign of Kheperkheprure Itnute-Ay, Pharaoh of the Upper and Lower Kingdoms, the god Hapi held back the flood waters of the Nile. Stone obelisks that annually marked the depth of the flood sat in parched earth beyond the reach of the waters. In the past there had been low inundations, and the fearful memories of hunger had been passed from generation to generation, but never before had the god of the Nile been so ungenerous.

Still, Pharaoh's ship sailed the waters of the flood to collect the promises of tribute that the people of the Black Earth pledged to Pharaoh in thanksgiving for the flood. This spring the headmen and their people received Pharaoh with joyless ceremony. The headmen knew that when the listless, meager waters settled back into their channel, the deposit of rich, alluvial soil would be thin, and as the boundaries were redrawn, frantic haggling would erupt over the few good plots of fertile soil. The more that could be snatched from friend or brother, the more food for oneself, and the more pledged to Pharaoh, the less there would be for the stomachs of the people. The headmen forsaw that at harvest, if they tried to collect Pharaoh's tribute, the nomes could well turn against Pharaoh—and against them, who governed in Pharaoh's name. Already the people muttered against the throne, for as all of Egypt gazed upon the low flood waters and began to moan before the specter of starvation, Egypt questioned: Why was Hapi angry? What—or who—had offended the god? Did he rage at . . . Pharaoh? There had been too many Pharaohs these past years, too many luckless deaths in the royal family, and this new Pharaoh was not of the royal line. Dark things were spoken that would have lain dormant had the flood been high. Egypt began to whisper of bloody crimes . . .

And yet another fear swept through Egypt: fear of the Hittites. From the Delta along the length of the Nile, rumors spread that the Hittite hordes were preparing to cross the vast desert wasteland of Gaza and the triangular peninsula which before had rendered Egypt impregnable. Egypt shuddered at the threat of death and destruction that had toppled Byblos and Mitanni and kingdom after kingdom before them. Then in the square at Bubastis, a dead ibis was discovered. At dawn, sweepers arriving to polish the tiles found the bird sprawled cold and stiff nearly at the center of the square. With screams and wails, they dropped their reed sweeps and scattered to alert the city. Messengers hurried from Bubastis with the news of the terrible omen: Nekhbet, the protectress, had cast a sacred ibis out of the sky. Her children no longer would sleep under her gracious wing. The god would not save them from the Hittites. What could have sparked her rage? . . . Was it Pharaoh?

When the planting that would feed less than a third of Egypt began to sprout, the people found that Hapi and Nekhbet were not the only wrathful deities. The precious green shoots pushed through the earth to be nourished by the rays of the great god Amon, but Amon veiled his disk with a cover of clouds. Amon, too, was angry. Would there be no harvest at all? As each new dawn for fifteen long days failed to bring Amon from behind the clouds, flowers that were accustomed to steady, ready light shriveled and wasted. And rumors spread outward from Thebes that the queen wasted, too. . . .

The Queen Ankhesenamon was seen only infrequently at court, and when she did appear for the evening meal, she seemed but a shell, not even knowing where she was. Led to her golden chair, she failed to extend her hand for traditional homages. Pharaoh rebuked her with a brusqueness she showed no sign of hearing but which must offend the departed spirits of her royal ancestors, wakeful and uneasy in the valley beyond the west bank. The court had not forgotten Ay's humble birth and condemned his treatment of the queen as less than should be accorded the daughter and granddaughter and great-granddaughter of a line of mighty gods on earth who were one with Osiris. Was it Pharaoh's disrespect of the queen that had angered the gods?

And with each rare appearance, the queen appeared to grow more frail, weak and sallow. She became so thin that bracelets slipped off her skeletal hands and servants whispered that children's bracelets must be used to adorn her fleshless limbs. Above her hollow cheeks, her enormous eyes were expressionless. When she could be coaxed to speak, her words were jumbled and incoherent. She would fall asleep over her untouched food before the entire court and could not be roused, even by the call of flutes and the clash of cymbals. It was beyond dispute that the queen's health waned. Pharaoh's seed did not take in her womb—could it be Pharaoh's seed poisoned her?

The rumors grew louder and uglier. The queen was dying and Egypt was dying with her. The fault lay with Pharaoh.

As the time of the pitifully small harvest approached, Egypt teetered precariously over the abyss of revolt.

As for Ay, he wore the double crown with a bitterness that tasted like gall—that he should strive so relentlessly, so ruthlessly, aspiring to the crown, and now that he had it all, it should come to this!

Through his spies, Ay learned the headmen throughout the nomes had begun to meet secretly among themselves and complain of the tributes to Thebes. For the first time in Egypt's history, the headmen were diverting their loyalty from Pharaoh to their own people. It was Akhenaten's fault, truly, Ay railed. Before Akhenaten, the headmen had governed by right of their long established lines, but Akhenaten had dismissed headmen at his whim, just as he had banished the old gods. The headmen no longer trusted Pharaoh, for if one Pharaoh could suddenly rupture the ages-old order, it could happen again. The headmen had one clear priority: save themselves.

And Ay also understood the fear of the priests of Amon. Egypt grew ripe for plucking, and they were afraid that whoever seized power would not recognize the prerogatives of the priesthood. The priests of Amon had been stripped of wealth and power once by Akhenaten; they must see to it that it did not happen again.

Understanding, however, was no solace to Ay. In his own growing terror, he fastened all hopes of keeping what he had gained on Hesen. She *must* be fruitful. She *must* live and bear his child, proving to Egypt that the gods favored him. Daily he surrounded her with physicians. Nightly he crawled on top of her in their bed.

Since that first night after his coronation, she no longer resisted him. She lay utterly passive, letting him freely work his will. She didn't respond to his approach or to his touch, and neither his cajolings nor his curses and blows could arouse her. Often he was certain she didn't even know what he did. Her beauty, even as she faded, became his torture. Once, straining above her, sweat running down his brow, he looked into her face. Her eyes were open and staring, her lips fixed in a faint smile. The lamplight on her face drained it of all color, and he realized her body was cold. Had she expired so quietly under him?

Desire fled. His sex became limp and shrank, withdrawing from her of its own lack of will. He twisted from the bed and hurried from the chamber, leaving his sandals behind. He urgently sent a servant for Tey, who, after entering the bedchamber, reported to him, "She breathes, my husband."

The next night he returned, but before he approached the great bed, he ordered all the lamps extinguished.

He would stiffen himself with the manipulations of his own hands and enter her.

But he could not look at her face.

She had guessed it, Senumet told himself. She had guessed the truth of her identity. He wondered how long she had known, and he marveled at her cleverness and disciplined patience in keeping her knowledge concealed from him.

It was in the month Sothis, two months shy of a year since the Pharaoh Kheperkheprure Itnute-Ay first sat upon the throne of Egypt. Without the distinction of jewelry, wearing his own hair—prematurely graying at the temples—instead of a wig, and a peasant's kilt, Senumet rested on his haunches in the reeds by the river and watched Muta as she gathered straight, thin stems to cut into styluses as he had long ago shown her. She was nearly the age of Hesen, now, when he had first met her that fateful day he disembarked in Memphis, not much more than an inexperienced boy. She looked so like Hesen, moving and talking like Hesen, that if he half shut his eyes, the years rolled back and he was again among the reeds with the young girl who was already then his always love.

Again he thought, *She knows*. But he should have expected it. Although they had tried to be circumspect, there had been far too much concern over the queen during the ten months he had lived with Sephy's family at Zehut. The girl was sensitive and intelligent and must have felt herself swept up from the night of his arrival in the currents of their concern. With that and the mystery of her birth, her memories of gold and splendor, it was inevitable she would hit upon their secret. Perhaps that was why she allowed herself to be subjected to long days of his schooling—about the history of Egypt, the glorious living gods and their deeds, with what countries Egypt had fought, what Egypt's great cities were like, how power flowed from the throne and the temples. There was not enough time to prepare her completely, of course, but he had made a good beginning. He wished he could invade her mind and see what she thought of it all. Did she fear the moment when the truth must be exposed? That moment was approaching soon, for the cycles of heaven were about to come full circle.

Hearing a voice faintly calling his name, he stood so that the boy might see him over the reeds. Someone must have arrived for him. Another messenger from Meire.

On the day the Hittite prince was killed and Horemheb had unexpectedly spared Senumet's life, he had decided to ride to Zehut. He knew, with this last act of mercy, Horemheb in his own mind freed himself from whatever debt he believed owed to Senumet from Byblos. He could expect nothing more from his former comrade; indeed, he had not expected this much. And while he would be safe with Sephy's family, to have knowledge of Hesen and Thebes, he needed to enlist other eyes and ears. He set out for the village of Coptos. At Tanis, in the Delta, he assumed the guise of a servant about his master's business and bought passage to a false destination on a barge carrying wine to Lisht. He traveled with no urgency; there was no way to forestall what must be. On the twelfth day of the ponderous journey up the Nile against the current, distant trumpets announced the approach of Pharaoh's golden barque. Joining the pilot, his crew and a few other passengers on the port side of the vessel, he watched Pharaoh's ship glide by. Emblazoned upon its pennants, sail and hull was the cartouche of the new Pharaoh, and the mission of its journey was to proclaim the tidings of the coronation throughout the length of Egypt.

And so it is done, Senumet had thought grimly. He watched its sail until that despicable symbol of Ay's victory disappeared in the direction from which his barge had come.

Three days later the barge approached Coptos, and after nightfall Senumet slipped over the side, sliding quietly into the water, and swam to the west bank. When the village slept, he made his way to the abandoned temple of Aten without disturbing the village dogs. The fragrance of incense lingered within the stone walls. Someone still worshiped here. That someone he had come to see.

As the first light of dawn filtered into the temple, Senumet saw that this temple of Aten, if it had been desecrated like the others throughout Egypt, had been restored, and he looked upon the hands of the Aten blessing Pharaoh Akhenaten and his royal family as they were when Akhet-Aten was founded. He was staring at Hesen among her sisters when he heard shuffling footsteps, an old man arriving to sweep the temple before the morning ceremony to greet the rising sun.

"I wish to see him who worships here," Senumet said.

"I don't know who you mean," the old man stammered.

Senumet slipped off a gold ring and pressed it into the old man's trembling hand. "Senumet of Thebes waits for him."

Casting a frightened look over his shoulder, the sweep shuffled away, and Senumet waited. The sky was the color of pearl when a tall figure in a red robe stepped into the temple. He seemed not to have aged a day.

"Meire. By all that's wonderful."

"Senumet."

The men embraced, but pleasantries could wait. "What brings you here?" Meire asked, and Senumet quickly recounted the attempt to marry Hesen to the Hittite prince.

"The story that Ay gave out," Meire told him, "is that Horemheb came upon a party of Hittite scouts close to Egypt's border and that the prince happened to be among them. He has made no public proclamation against you, but the word has been quietly spread that you are a traitor and that you should be killed on sight, your head sent to Thebes. I hear he would kill you with his bare hands if he could."

Senumet explained his need.

"My sources are good. The Aten's truth still burns secretly in many hearts. I can arrange to keep you informed. Know that in my *History of Akhenaten*, the name of Senumet is a proud symbol of steadfast loyalty and courage."

"May the line of Akhenaten not end."

The two men regarded each other silently, each absorbed with bitter memories. At last, Meire said, "I know we do not pray to the same god, but if both of us entreat mercy, perhaps one of us will be heard. Don't punish yourself. We can but play our parts in the eternal design. Rest here for a few hours. I will have a horse groomed for you and saddlebags stocked. I hope we meet again."

"May Aten light your way." Senumet clasped the priest's arm in warm farewell.

"I am sorry the Aten was never your god, for you have served him with more honor and righteousness than many of his believers. A safe journey, Senumet."

The Sun Disk began to peer over the horizon, and stepping into the yard before the temple, Meire knelt and pressed his forehead to the earth. Golden sunlight touched him as he began the hymn to the Aten, and when he finished, he rose and departed into the village that was even smaller and poorer than Zehut. The old man appeared again with food, wine and the horse. Senumet ate and then set out. As he rode, already he began to work out the plan by which he would tear the power of the crown of Egypt—and Hesen—from Ay's grasp.

Darkness had fallen and no lamplight shone in the high slits of windows in the mud-brick houses when Senumet reached Zehut. He knocked on Mena and Yuti's door and soon heard scuffling feet. The door opening, he looked upon Mena's fearful face, and Yuti's, Sephy's and Muta's.

"I have come here," Senumet said, "because I have no place else to go."

Sephy moaned and rolled her head on her shoulders. "She has no one now!"

Embracing her, Senumet comforted, "All is not lost. While the queen lives."

Month succeeded month, and as reports from Meire chronicled Egypt's discontent and terror, fear and hope warred in Senumet. Yet with each of Meire's messages, he felt more alive. Day and night he honed the details of his plan until its logic and precision awaited only the signal to action. The timing must be perfect. He did not doubt that when the moment came, he would recognize it.

Now as he walked through the dust toward Mena's house and saw Meire's messenger waiting before the door, he somehow knew the moment had come, a time of incredible upheaval and great changes for them all. He prayed silently for Muta.

The messenger slipped a papyrus from inside his tunic.

Sending the messenger within for refreshment, Senumet walked around behind the house to stand in the sliver of shade the wall provided. Unrolling the papyrus, he began to read. In Memphis, an angry mob had thrown stones at Pharaoh's envoy as he attempted to disembark. Although Nabamon had sacrificed publicly to Amon for seven straight days, crops still failed. The harvest looked to be half of what had been expected, and five nomes had declared they would send no tribute to Pharaoh or to Amon. There were work stoppages at Naucritis and Memphis. The grand vizier had publicly decried Pharaoh for draining Egypt's wealth to placate the Hittites, while a division of Hittites laid seige to an Egyptian fortress at the northernmost edge of Gaza. Already stomachs rumbled with hunger, and angry farmers had burned an empty granary in Buto to the ground. Then, at the bottom of the scroll, a line of hieroglyphs fairly leaped at Senumet. "For ten days, the queen has not been seen at court. The physicians are no longer summoned—"

With shaking hands Senumet rerolled the papyrus. It was time for Senumet to set his plan in motion. It was time for him to make a king, time to summon the queen-to-be. He would set Egypt aright.

*If only Hesen lived.*

The sun had reached its zenith, sending down the full force of its scorching rays when he entered the house. The messenger had gone; Sephy and Yuti were weaving. Straight as a spear he stood before them, and at the sight of him, the women stirred with alarm. His command sliced through the soporific heat. "Bring forth Muta's trunk!"

Yuti covered her face. Sephy sprang to her feet and brought the inlaid box, which she placed at Senumet's feet. With the blade he ordered brought to him, he scraped off the unbroken clay seal covering the lock, then pried free a panel on the trunk's side and extracted a key. He inserted the key into the lock. It turned easily. He raised the lid, and took out folds of fine, shimmering fabric. "Make her a dress," he said to Sephy, "that will not shame her mother." Sephy nodded. Yuti raised her skirt to wipe her eyes.

Then both women became as still as stone, staring toward the sun-filled doorway. Senumet turned. On the threshold stood Muta, her eyes wide at the shimmering material that Sephy had spread over her knees.

"Come here," Senumet summoned her. Hesitatingly, she approached. He took from the trunk a gold ring and handed it to her. "This bears your mother's name." Eagerly she read the ring's inscription: Ankhesenpaaten. "Her name is now Ankhesenamon."

"The queen," Muta breathed with awe but no surprise, fears and unthinkable hopes in her eyes.

"You are her daughter. And I have cared for you and loved you all the more for her sake, sweet child." He reached for her hand and eased her down to kneel before the trunk.

First he showed her the tokens by which her mother owned her to the world. The papyrus scroll providing testimony to her royal birth witnessed by Meire, chief priest, and enclosed in a golden case emblazoned with the twin cartouche of both her parents under the sign of Aten. He placed in her hand the cobra ring of power fashioned with such incredible delicacy and detail it seemed as if only a god could have designed it. He watched her as she discovered the jewels, bracelets, rings, collars, and three circlet crowns that had been Hesen's own. As she lingered over the likeness of Hesen, painted on wood and framed in pink-gold filagree, he said, "You do not remember her, but each day I have been with her, she asked about you. Only with terrible sorrow did she give you up, and that because she had no choice. Powerful men would have benefited by your death. To keep you safe, your mother hid you here." Kneeling beside her, he took her lovely face between his hands. "You are young, but you must try to understand. Our world is fragile, and the queen is its center. The well-being of all of Egypt depends on her well-being. It is her life that is endangered now, and we must save her, you and I. We must ride the whirlwind and see to it the center holds."

Muta touched his cheek with her soft hand. "You love her," she whispered.

"With all my soul."

"Do I look like her?"

"You do."

"And you love me as much?"

"I do." He ached with the intensity of his love for her, that most important part of himself he must forever conceal and deny. "Does my love for you matter . . . so much?"

"Always," she said, and sounded a woman, not a child.

"Your father loved you, too," he managed. And he was surprised to find his eyes burning. Angrily he turned his head to blink away the sudden film of tears.

"Who was my father?"

"Akhenaten, Pharaoh of the Two Lands, son of the living Horus," he heard his lips pronounce. "You are the royal princess, Ankhesenpaaten the Younger, heiress to the throne of the golden house of Thebes."

"What is to be done?"

"We will journey to Thebes to claim your inheritance."

Muta stood gracefully in the seriousness of assumed adulthood. "If the queen is in danger, we must go to her right away. With Yuti and Sephy's help, I will pack our things so we may set out at sunset. Whatever else you have to explain to me, you can explain as we ride, Senumet."

Yuti had stopped her tears, but Sephy was weeping loudly. Both women embraced Muta, and at Sephy's turn, the old nurse pressed her wet cheek to Muta's. Then Muta disengaged herself and reminded them of their tasks, while Senumet gazed at her with prideful admiration. Had he truly worried about her strength and spirit? Already she was falling naturally into the role of her regal heritage.

"It will be as you wish," he said softly.

And added, "Your Highness."

# XXXI

Sephy beseeched Senumet to travel with them. Although her age and her bulk must necessarily slow their journey, Senumet could not refuse her, especially since he foresaw the advantages of her presence. She would steady Muta in the cataclysmic changes the girl must face; and having been Hesen's comfort since infancy, the good woman with her loving ministrations would speed Hesen's recovery from Ay's ravages.

As the sun touched the horizon—a red, setting disk that was Ra-Atum, the god as a wise old man—Mena appeared with a gray mare. Sephy hefted her weight onto the mare's back, and Senumet mounted the roan, lifting Muta up before him. They began their journey for Thebes.

Sephy jounced along, regaling Muta with tales of her mother as a little girl. How Hesen, who inordinately loved honey, had sneaked from the palace and found the keepers' hives, invaded a hive with her fist and received thirty stings from maddened bees before her screams summoned the keepers to her rescue. The poor child, Sephy laughed, was in agony as Sephy bathed her in vinegar; later puffed and miserable, she cried she was as ugly as a river horse, and wouldn't look at herself in a mirror until the swellings were all gone. How another time, Hesen had tried to catch a fish with her little fist in a pool in a palace courtyard and had tumbled headfirst into the water. If a servant hadn't seen the child's upturned bottom, her hairlock floating above the water and bubbles bursting on the surface, the poor thing would have drowned.

When they camped in the hottest hours of midday, Muta prepared their simple meals while Sephy brought forth the ivory cloth and worked with her needle, fashioning Muta's royal gown. Before she slept for a few hours, Muta stroked the luminous folds with reverent fingers as if the cloth were a talisman. With such a dress, Muta's eyes said, a girl *must* be queen.

Late on the tenth day, they sighted Thebes, and even at a distance Muta was dazzled by the city: the soaring obelisks, the great columns of the temple rising above roofs of polished tiles that gleamed like jewels. They pulled around them the robes Senumet had brought for them and drew up the hoods to look like Bedouins entering the city to trade. Making their way among the mud-brick houses of laborers on the outskirts, they came without incident to a street of two- and three-storied houses, and at the end of the street, the residence of a minor noble whose heart still clung faithfully to the Aten. It was this house that harbored Meire when the priest came to Thebes, and from his last message, Senumet knew Meire was here now.

Calling to the Nubian slave he saw in the courtyard, Senumet asked to speak with the master of the house.

"My master and his family are not here," the Nubian reported. "They are in Memphis."

"Then tell your master's guest the scribe has arrived and calls him forth," Senumet commanded.

Surprised, the slave hurried within. Quickly Meire appeared, dressed in the linen shirt and kilt of a tradesman. "Aten bless you, Senumet." Meire received and embraced him. He bade them enter the shade of the portico, where Senumet lowered Muta's hood with his own hands. For long moments the priest absorbed her. At last he said, "I need no tokens or parchment. Her face is the living proof. It is her mother's." He bowed to Muta. "Welcome, Princess Ankhesenpaaten. May the Aten protect and strengthen you through all your days, Your Highness."

Shyly she turned questioning eyes on Senumet. "Extend your hand," Senumet quietly instructed her. Taking it, Meire bowed low and touched his forehead to her fingers, and releasing it, he straightened and smiled with warm reassurance. "Don't be afraid. I am an old friend of your mother and your father. You may rest here and eat and refresh yourself." He clapped sharply, and once again the Nubian appeared to lead Sephy and Muta inside.

To Muta, Senumet said, "I will come for you when all is ready," and to Sephy, "See to it she is bathed and dressed as the daughter of her mother."

When Muta and Sephy were gone, Senumet asked, "Is there further news of the queen?"

"None but the same. She still has not appeared at court and her apartments are heavily guarded."

"Then let us act with all haste," Senumet responded tensely.

In the month Thoth, Senumet had traveled to Coptos and had taken Meire into his confidence. Having pledged assistance even unto his life, the priest knew his part. "Shall I, then, go to Horemheb for you at once?"

Senumet nodded. "Say that twice he saved the life of his brother, and his brother would now offer him in return far more than a scribe's life could ever be worth."

Senumet himself was bathed, oiled and dressed by the time Meire returned with the answer: "Horemheb will come to you as soon as darkness falls. He deplores the risk you take in coming to Thebes, but I have told him you know exactly what you are about."

Senumet awaited Horemheb beneath the sycamores in the walled garden to the rear of the house. Led in by the Nubian, Horemheb waited for the slave's retreat, then strode angrily to the bench where Senumet had been sitting and was now standing to greet him. His face grim in the flickering lamplight, he did not bother with formalities. "You are a fool," he spat. "And your envoy, that priest who should also be dead, is as witless a fool as you! Know that our friendship was severed the day you decided to put a Hittite on the throne. I agreed to meet you only because I was afraid you would attempt to seek me out in the garrison or the palace. If you are discovered, I can't help you again—nor would I desire to."

"I would not ask you a third time for my life," Senumet returned calmly. "If I am discovered before I achieve what I have set out to do, I expect to die."

Horemheb glared at him, and the muscles in his neck and jaw strained. "I thought you must have come on some mad mission. I won't be enlisted in your cause!"

"And this time, what do you assume my mission to be?"

"What else but the same as your flight to Hatti? To save the queen."

"Does the queen need saving?" Senumet prodded.

A brief expression of pain flitted across Horemheb's face, but whatever horrors he had heard or seen, he refused to be trapped into bearing witness of them to Senumet.

"I come also to save Egypt."

"I won't hear your plan," Horemheb swore.

"Are you then absolutely loyal to Ay?"

The soldier drew himself up rigidly and Senumet realized his memory of the intimidating power of the man's physique and his spirit was more than fully just. What a lion of a pharaoh he would be on Egypt's throne, and desperately Egypt needed him.

"Whatever his means," Horemheb ground out through his teeth, "Ay is Pharaoh! He has married Ankhesenamon, the last of the royal line. What would you have me do—murder Ay? I'll have no part of it."

With satisfaction, Senumet did not miss the tenor of forced vehemence in Horemheb's reaffirmation of his loyalties. As he had expected, his old friend already saw the necessity of removing Ay from the throne and must have given the matter consideration. Easily he had imagined how the need of it and the inability to effect it except by drastic, revolutionary means would torture Horemheb's conscience.

"Then you will merely weep for Egypt's dissolution?" Senumet sallied.

"Amon help me," Horemheb blazed, "I pray for Ay's death!"

"If the gods should hear you, tell me your choice of the man who should become the living god."

Saying nothing, Horemheb glanced away.

Senumet broke the silence. "I could tell you of a man so admired, so respected by Egypt that he would be welcomed as Pharaoh by priests and soldiers, nobles and peasants together. A man the gods would surely favor for his stalwart and true heart and his heroic deeds in battle. A man who could bind all the people to his will and give them the strength to endure and survive."

"And who might that man be?" Horemheb still looked away.

"You know him better than I, my brother. His name is yours."

The soldier whirled on Senumet. "So this is how you plan to use me! Tempting me with criminal allurements? The people would turn against me if I claimed the throne by force."

Senumet masked a triumphant smile. Horemheb was no fool, and he was well aware of the high esteem in which he was held, the tumultuous cheers he received in contrast to the unimpassioned salutes and leery stares that were Pharaoh's portion.

Senumet knew his next move would corner his quarry. "What if I told you that you no longer have to pray for Ay's death . . . that there is a way for you to become a son of the living Horus by the natural line of succession . . . that there is an heiress?"

"I would say I am disappointed you are no longer an honest man." But Horemheb gave his attention eagerly.

"Hesen's and Akhenaten's daughter did not die. I have hidden her all these years. The legitimate heiress is yours, Horemheb. When I sent Meire to you, it was she I offered you in return for my life. The Princess Ankhesenpaaten."

With the same resolute calm with which he led his men in battle, Horemheb said steadily, "You have proof."

"More than enough."

"Where is she?"

"Here. In this house."

"I would see her. And your proof."

"Only when you have agreed to one condition."

"I won't give my word until I have heard it."

"That you entrust the queen into my care. That you let us leave Egypt together."

In the time it took Horemheb to answer, Senumet felt as if his life's blood were seeping from his body.

"Think what you ask," Horemheb responded at last. "She *is* queen."

"And the queen, Horemheb, is Hesen; she has sacrificed herself to Egypt. Can't Egypt in return grant her a release from suffering?"

"She is royalty. She can't simply resign her heritage. It would not be right. No, she must remain in Thebes."

Senumet battled to hold his impatience in check, knowing his friend's stolid lack of vision was at the core of his virtues of honesty, fairness and righteous zeal that would make him a great—perhaps a legendary—Pharaoh. Slowly he said, "Do you fear a threat to your rule?"

"If she so values royal blood that she would have put a Hittite on the throne, someone might persuade her to challenge a peasant's right to the crown."

Senumet had reached the limits of his endurance. He burst out, "She sought a Hittite only because he had behind him the might to keep Ay from the throne! Tell me, was she wrong in believing the murderer would destroy Egypt? With you as Pharaoh, her enemy would be overthrown, Egypt secure, the royal succession assured! Amon curse your stubbornness—her daughter would be queen!"

"Her daughter!" Horemheb shook his head. "I just can't believe it. I remember when Ay received the message the child had died."

Senumet's hands closed into hard fists. He wanted to shake Horemheb. Never had that soldier's careful thoroughness so enraged him. "We created a false death for her the same year Akhenaten and Smenkhare died. To protect her from Ay."

"Hesen's daughter . . ." Horemheb kept returning to that incredible fact. "How old is she?"

"You can count for yourself," Senumet snapped. "Thirteen," he amended quickly. He dared not offend his only hope.

"Of child-bearing age," he said slowly, still absorbing the implications. "Will she agree to this marriage?"

"She will."

"You've already told her?"

"No, but she will make her vows to you if I ask it."

"So, she too is under your sway, I take it!"

Surprised by the accusation, Senumet flushed. "She comes to you untouched, a virgin," he said.

"I would be convinced she is her daughter."

His knees weak, Senumet entered the house where Meire awaited him with Muta's trunk. Wordlessly he took it and carried it to Horemheb in the garden. Extracting the key from behind the panel, he opened it and took out the parchment on which was inscribed Hesen's declaration in her own hand. He uncapped the golden cylinder that contained it and handed the parchment to Horemheb. Although Horemheb could scarcely read, he knew the soldier would recognize Hesen's cartouche, which was her daughter's as well. Then he turned the box so Horemheb could study the same cartouche wrought on the underside of the lid in gold and lapis.

Reaching into the box himself, Horemheb took up the familiar cobra ring of power, worn by every Pharaoh and queen, its jasper eyes gleaming with dark red lights. His own eyes shining with ambition undisguised, he gazed at the ring for long moments before he reluctantly returned it to the box.

"And you will recognize this," Senumet said, lifting from the jeweled collars and ornaments a serpent bracelet Hesen had loved as a child.

"Very well, Senumet," Horemheb yielded. "Hesen is yours to take where you will."

"We would have a boat, provided as befits a queen."

"I've given my word. I won't be niggardly in keeping it."

"Long life, Horemheb. May Egypt be restored and may you and the princess beget many sons in your image."

"I would see her now," Horemheb said.

\* \* \*

Sephy opened for Senumet the door to the bedchamber of the master of the house, given over by Meire to Muta. Glowing with pride, she stepped aside to let him see her charge.

Muta held a handled mirror, and her smile was bright with innocent wonder at her own transformation. As she turned toward him in want of his judgment, her smile grew uncertain.

The dress Sephy had fashioned was startlingly lovely in its simplicity. It was a sheath with a shawl that rose from between her young breasts to drape her shoulders as sleeves. Around her hips was a girdle that let fall, from above her virginal secret parts to the hem of her skirt, a golden tongue. A collar of gold-and-green feldspar surrounded her neck; golden cuffs enclasped her slender wrists. Her wig of shining black human hair fell to her shoulders, and it was crowned with a circlet of expandable golden chain. She was fresh and young and luminescent with beauty that would capture any man's heart. In a matter of days she had become more a princess than Hesen's poor sisters had ever been. And through her, Hesen beckoned to him.

"Exquisite," he whispered and taking her hands, found they were shaking.

She exhaled the breath she had been holding and answered with charming candor, "I thought so, but I'm only sure now that you say it."

"As queen, your beauty will do justice to your mother and your grandmother, Nefertiti."

"Queen?" she asked in alarm. "Is my mother dead?"

"Your mother lives." Let his words not be a lie, he prayed. "Still you, not she, will tomorrow be the queen of this city and all the cities and villages of the Two Lands." She drew back in fear, and he said, "Pharaoh will help you."

"What Pharaoh?" she asked, bewildered.

"The man who marries you and through you becomes the living god."

"Marry? I hadn't thought—I can't—who?"

"A soldier, a general, the Master of the Horse. A kind man, a decent man, a good friend to me and to your mother. Surely you have heard of Horemheb."

Her eyes widened and she nearly whimpered in awe. "He is a hero. Songs are sung of him, of his deeds at Byblos."

"Muta, *you* are the heiress."

"What if he doesn't like me?"

"He will love you."

Her eyes glistened with tears. "Must I do this, Senumet?"

"You must. You were born to it. Trust me, Muta."

She gripped his hands as she struggled to regain herself. "You will stay with me always," she cried.

"I promise," he lied. "Now let us go to him."

Followed by Sephy, they proceeded through the house. Senumet stepped into the garden and announced, "The Princess Ankhesenpaaten attends you."

She walked very straight, a half-smile admitting a dimple to the corner of her mouth, the mouth which was Hesen's and Nefertiti's. Her almond-shaped, violet eyes met Horemheb's with the confidence that generations of royal forebears had imparted to her. The ivory gown accentuated her slim figure, the soft young breasts beginning to thrust forward, the hips gently rounding.

With triumph approaching happiness, Senumet saw that the soldier's face had paled to white, for the soldier was staring at a dream he had cherished in his heart for twenty years, a forbidden dream, a dream which suddenly lived and breathed and was surrendering itself to him, contracting all the years into that moment. She stood before him, again wanting judgment. Horemheb's eyes were unnaturally bright and in his dry throat, his whisper was husky. "You are the queen!"

Her smile was tremulous. "And you are Horemheb of the flaming sword."

"Are you willing to marry me, Muta?"

She hesitated. "Senumet explained it. He said you will be Pharaoh . . ."

"Are you willing to marry me, Muta?" he repeated.

Gravely she studied the Pharaoh-to-be, and Senumet saw with gladness she did not cast down her gaze in confusion. Clear-eyed, she would make her own decision and live by her word.

Raising her voice, she said, "I will marry you, Horemheb."

"And I will marry you, my lady, my queen."

Impulsively she held out both her hands, and as he took them, his face was a splendor of delight.

Horemheb looked deeply into Muta's eyes. "It is permitted that Pharaoh have many wives from among the women of Egypt and foreign princesses, but I renounce that prerogative. You, Muta,

Ankhesenpaaten the Younger, shall be my sole wife. I will have no other."

Her smile grew radiant. "I am not queen yet, Horemheb, but I will learn to be. If you will love me, I will learn to love you too."

"Till death," he whispered.

"And Senumet? He will stay with us—to help us?"

Horemheb sought his friend's eyes. Almost imperceptibly, Senumet nodded.

"If the choice is mine, Senumet shall guide us always," he promised. Muta did not hear the equivocation.

"Then accept my guidance, now," Senumet said, "and conclude this interview. We have much to do, Horemheb, and if the gods favor our strategies, the next time you and Muta meet, it will be to sanctify your union."

Her tears of joy flooding unchecked, Sephy led Muta from the garden, and Horemheb and Senumet settled down to map maneuvers that would, in less than a day, seat Horemheb on Egypt's throne.

"It is not only your urgency that kindles me now," Horemheb confided. "Before coming here tonight, I received a messenger from Gaza. The northernmost fortress has fallen, the troops have been massacred, and the Hittites are on the move to the second and only other Gaza fortress near the Great Green. Certainly it, too, will fall, and then Shubbiluliuma will prepare to cross Gaza and the Sinai and attack the Delta. I'm hoping that word of *my* ascension to the throne will give him pause and give me time to ready the army for battle at our border."

"Or to initiate negotiations for peace from a position of strength," Senumet offered.

"Strength depends on food. An army can't fight on an empty stomach. The tribute from the five defiant nomes must be collected."

"The army will have food," Senumet prophesied. "Egypt will gladly suffer for a Pharaoh she loves."

The water clock had dripped away half the night when Horemheb and Senumet, carrying Muta's trunk, left the house of Nebet and made their way to the residence of Nabamon on an estate near the great temple. Nabamon received them in the sanctuary of Amon. Nabamon was quick to comprehend the enormous implications for Egypt and the prospects for increasing the power of the great god Amon and his priestly servants. It was clear that Egypt could stand little more of Ay, and even though Nabamon had ridden Ay's mantle during the grand vizier's rise, he had no intention of clinging to that same garment as it trailed its master's descent.

Nabamon carefully examined the parchment and tokens proclaiming the heiress. He was convinced. They must be married as soon as possible, he told Horemheb and Senumet, a show of reluctance masking his delight. He would perform the ceremony at daybreak, after the daily ritual of washing, dressing and feeding the god, and he would insure the presence of witnesses.

It was exactly as Senumet and Horemheb hoped. The priest would see to the rise of his own star—let Ay's fall where it may.

The sky was indigo still when Sephy, Muta and Senumet slipped from the house of Nebet. Consumed with worry for Hesen's life—and knowing if all went well, today he would hold her—Senumet had been unable to sleep. The final victory was so close at hand. They would triumph, and she would be his, he would be hers forever, never again to be separated. Never again would she be forced to endure the touch of another, and his years of interminable loneliness would be over. He would take her to Crete, and thousands of suns would rise, thousands of suns would set, millions of waves would crash upon the beach for them before they slept together for eternity. His heart pounded, his blood rushed, and urging the drops of the water clock to fall faster, he had found he could not even lie still upon his bedding. Like a frayed rope pulling blocks of building stone, he was strained to snapping.

And Muta, it seemed, had shed all of her grace during the night and was as skittish as an unbroken colt at the touch of the first bridle. He attempted to muster sympathy for her—poor terrified child, about to hand over her life to a formidable stranger, to shoulder earthshaking responsibilities—but all feeling for her was gone. He cared for her as little as if she were an alien waif, an imposter. She mattered only in that she was an instrument to unite him with her mother. Muta, Horemheb, Ay, Egypt receded into inconsequence beneath his overpowering sense of Hesen. She needed him. He should be with her *now!* Muta cried out at a sharp stone under her sandal, and he whirled on her. Only the stricken expression on her face, stark with fright, kept back the angry words from his lips.

He hurried them on. Each part of the plan *must* occur at the appointed time.

They turned out of the street of markets along the Nile and set off across the bare sandy stretch which led to the massive granite wall surrounding the temple complex. He heard Muta's intake of breath. Karnak was the most monumentally magnificent temple throughout the length of Egypt, overwhelming in its grandeur, and if his heart, hard-set by experience against belief in the gods, felt the tug of its awesome power, how must it appear to this child? Muta clung to his arm as they passed through the great gates.

The only entry to the temple complex itself was through the third pylon, and as they ascended the wide stone steps that led to it, they passed between the rows of ram-headed sphinxes on rectangular pedestals. The sculpted rams' heads watched them with stone-cold, inscrutably empty eyes. Senumet felt shivers pass through Muta. Involuntarily she hung back.

"Their eyes go through me," Muta whispered.

"Their sight cleanses your heart," Senumet encouraged.

He led them through the entry into a hall of massive red-granite pillars that drew vision upward to impossible heights. At the top, just beneath the roof, clerestory windows admitted the first gray light of dawn, silvering the columns' hieroglyphs and gilded gods and sparking the electrum tip of the obelisk of Thutmosis, half-hidden beyond the incredible girth of the pillars. Muta released his arm and turned, looking lost beyond retrieval.

"The light of Ra shines on the new Queen of the Two Lands," Senumet said gently. He took her hand and led her toward the main doors of the temple, luminous in the dawn with electrum brilliance.

"Come, Sephy," Senumet ordered, for the old servant had stopped in her tracks, petrified.

"I cannot," Sephy croaked, beginning to quake. Beyond those doors were forbidden mysteries.

"I command you," Senumet said sternly. "You have no choice! And we need not pass through those doors. We have been directed to another entrance. Now rouse yourself, woman! For Muta, for the queen!"

Sephy dragged her feet into motion again.

The side entry Nabamon had indicated was opened by a young priest, who ushered them into the darkened temple maze and led them into one of the many rooms. Nabamon awaited them, flanked by two elder priests, neither of whom Senumet recognized. Sephy removed Muta's Bedouin robe, the same that had enwrapped her when they entered the city, and the princess stood before the priests in the same gown she had worn to meet Horemheb—she had no other dress. But now, on her wig, she wore the uraeus of a queen, taken from her trunk, worn on many occasions of state by her mother. From the band of the simple gold circlet, the cobra spread its hood above her forehead, and the golden hood of the serpent was inlaid with lapis. The bride was ready.

As Nabamon had demanded, Senumet entrusted Muta's tokens and parchment to him. He displayed them to the elders, they were examined, then all three priests turned stern visages upon the princess. While Muta endured their stares without flinching, Sephy fell to her knees and covered her head.

"Highness!" Nabamon's voice rang out and echoed off the stone walls. "To what gods do you pay homage?"

Muta paled. "I worship—" But her whisper faded. She raised her chin and began once more. "I bow to Amon-Ra, to the mother Isis, to Horus, the sacred child, and to his great father, Osiris." Her voice was clear and sweet.

"Ra is gracious," Nabamon responded. Pausing, he began again. "I have been told and have read the name given you by your mother, but since it is suffixed by the name of a false god, I may not pronounce it. Nor may Egypt! We could call you by the name your mother now bears, but I see no need to match the daughter's name to the mother's, for your claim is genuine and requires no such petty congruity. It is preferable, I believe, that Egypt see the princess as she is and know her by the name she has been called since childhood. Mut-Nodjne. Would that please you?"

"If Amon wishes."

With the elders, Nabamon nodded approval. "So be it."

They followed Nabamon and the elder priests through halls, colonnades and anterooms until they came to a massive thick door of cedar. In the shadows near it waited a small group of men. First, Senumet recognized Horemheb, standing a head above the rest. Behind him, their pectorals gleaming, were two of his generals and two of his senior guard. Then there was Hotep, headman of Thebes; Pa-shed, the grand vizier who, like Nabamon, was not willing to sink with Ay; and three of Egypt's most important nobles, influential because of the size of the tribute that came from the lands they held in Pharaoh's name, who were in residence in Thebes to attend the court. These witnesses, by their attendance, had committed themselves before Nabamon to the recognition of Muta as heiress.

"At the behest of Amon," Nabamon announced, "this wedding shall be performed in the holy of holies. Never before have the eyes of unconsecrated mortals beheld the sanctuary of the great god. Never will they again."

One of the elder priests slid back the heavy bolt, and both pulled open the door. Nabamon led the wedding party into the cavernous sanctuary, where flickering light from golden torches played over granite statues of the god, jeweled stellas and the carved columns. They proceeded into the inner shrine, where the god himself towered over them. Solid gold except for obsidian eyes and horns of ivory, Amon-Ra stood on a black basalt pylon. In one hand he held the shen of eternity; in the other, the ankh of life. Between his horns was the electrum disk of the god, seen by the people when his barque was carried through the streets by the priests. Around him the walls were sheathed in silver.

At Nabamon's sign, the party knelt, Muta and Horemheb side by side. Nabamon placed his hands on their heads and intoned, "Horemheb, sentinel of strength and valor, dost thou honor the great god Amon-Ra?"

Horemheb's eyes were fixed above the chief priest, on the god. "I praise Amon at the horizon and in the sky, in the sands of the desert and in the field of reeds, and in the body of the princess royal, who was engendered in the body of the queen by the living god."

"Will you protect her in this life and, in the darkness of the afterlife, guide her through eternal night to Ra's side?"

Horemheb turned his gaze upon Muta, concentrating upon her all the single-minded, fervent devotion that had always animated his loyalty and his acts. In response, her back stiffened, her head lifted. From his vantage point, Senumet saw them become, in that moment, what they would be throughout their lives. Unexpectedly his eyes burned with tears.

"I will protect her," Horemheb answered, "with all the strength of my arm and my being, here and hereafter."

"And you," Nabamon directed his words to Muta, "princess of a mighty line, from Ahmose to Thutmosis to Amenophis, who unlocked the floodwaters and transformed the mighty desert, you will fill all places with your beauty. The earth lies before you. Unto the ends of the earth you will extend peace, justice and fertility as you extend the line of Ahmose. Together with this mighty soldier, this strong prince, this living god, in Amon's name you will insure the power that is Egypt, ruler over all the world."

Steadfastly Muta replied, "Today I am truly blessed, and I pledge myself to my husband and my god. I shall try all my life to be worthy. Amon shall guide my days."

Bursting over the horizon, the sun sent brilliant rays through the roof slit of the sanctuary. The rays touched Amon's disk. The electrum blazed, showering Horemheb and Muta's faces with light.

"Amon accepts your vows." So saying, Nabamon took Muta's hand and slipped onto the third finger Hesen's token of her daughter's legitimacy, the cobra ring of power. Then he placed a like ring on Horemheb's finger.

"Rise, Highness, rise, Majesty," Nabamon bade them. As they stood, Horemheb's powerful body seemed to fill the sanctuary and vie with the golden body of the great god for preeminence. Loudly Nabamon proclaimed, "Pharaoh and queen, mighty rulers, the chosen of the great god Amon-Ra, live forever, living gods."

From Senumet's throat, from Sephy's and from the throats of the priests, nobles and soldiers came the response:

*Live forever, living gods.*

At the sibilant rattle of snare drums along the Avenue of Pharaohs, slaves with water jars slowed and listened, farmers with carts of vegetables and animals for slaughter halted on their way to the marketplace, shop owners forgot the laying out of their wares, scrubbers of pavement tiles set down their sweeps and craned their necks, dockworkers followed one another from the wharves, women left their breakfast fires and dragged their children with them into the streets.

To the insistent rhythm, twelve pairs of Amon's acolytes strode down the center of the avenue, each beating his drum with zeal. Before them the crowd scurried back, bowing as they recognized Nabamon in the leopard skin of his office, flanked by two elder priests, the headman Hotep and a gaggle of nobles, the grand vizier—and Horemheb, the metal-mirror breastplates of the generals at his back. And behind the generals marched fifty of the guard, ten rows of five abreast.

As growing numbers of curious Thebans jostled for a place along the route of the procession, a spontaneous cheer sliced the air and rolled toward the palace. *"Hail, Horemheb, Strength of Egypt!"* On other days the cheering would have thundered until the shouts seemed likely to lift the sky, but this morning it cut off jaggedly, to be replaced by murmurs and whispers: Who was she at Horemheb's side—ivory-gowned, young and lovely in girlhood with her head graced by the royal cobra, with a face that so strongly resembled the queen's? Could it be? How could it be other than—*her daughter!*

As the procession passed, the crowd closed the space behind it, shoving to follow and be among the first to hear the tidings. The cheer arose a second time: *"Hail, Horemheb!"*

At the golden house, sentries swung the gates wide to admit the procession. Dutifully the crowd hung back as the gates were shut, then they closed in to peer through the bright bars shaped like curving stems of papyrus. They waited for the news.

On the ramp leading between the pylons to the palace, the procession encountered Seshonk, the priest of Amon who personally served Ay. Nabamon proceeded to the head of the procession to confront him. "Nabamon, chief priest to Amon in the temple of Karnak, requests the presence of the living god in the throne room."

Seshonk entered the palace. Within moments he returned with Ay's answer: "Pharaoh, Ruler of the Two Lands, will attend Nabamon in the throne room when he has finished his morning meal."

At the insult, Nabamon thundered, "The business of the Great God Amon will brook no delay. Pray tell Pharaoh that!"

Ay's second answer took longer, but was inevitable: "The Son of Horus, Ruler of Upper and Lower Egypt, will receive you."

As the chill of dawn became the searing heat of day, Seshonk led the procession, drums resuming, through the gardens of the courtyard to the great golden doors of the throne room. The blossoms of the garden were small and sparse, Senumet noticed, and leaves were spotted and edged with brown. The blight had penetrated even to Pharaoh's house. Then the sense of Hesen and her desperate need staggered him—he missed a step.

*Only a minute more, beloved . . .*

Like swiftly darting redstarts, gossip had flown within the palace, and courtiers, nobles and ambassadors had already gathered in the throne room. Through the golden doors the procession flowed into positions Horemheb and Nabamon had choreographed. The acolytes fanned out in a semicircle. Nabamon, with Horemheb and Senumet at either side, moved forward to stand at their center. Muta, directly behind Nabamon, was buttressed by the elder priests at her sides and the nobles who had witnessed the wedding at her back, and behind the nobles, Sephy scrunched down in the futile attempt to render her bulk totally inconspicuous. Around them all, the guard formed militaristic lines, three sides of a box open to the throne. The verticals of their spears were walls of strength. When the last guards had taken up their stances, legs astride, the company stood frozen into the permanence of reliefs on the golden walls and waited. For the throne was empty. Ay had not, after all, jumped at Amon's bidding.

The snare drums ceased; the silence grew painful. Senumet cursed Ay. In those long moments, Senumet throught Ay's most monstrous sin was this procrastination, prolonging the time until he could go to Hesen.

The blast of twin trumpets shattered the silence. The doors leading from within the palace swung open, and through them filed a double line of yellow-robed priests of Amon, led by Seshonk and Osochor, Ay's minister of state, second only to the grand vizier. Osochor was dressed in a long black kilt and a black mantle, and his golden staff tapped resoundingly on the tiles. Seshonk, Osochor and the priests took up positions on the dais around the throne. Crafty to the last, Ay had quickly assembled his own ceremonial performers.

The trumpets issued a more elaborate fanfare, and Osochor rapped the end of his staff on the dais. "Hail, Pharaoh, Kheperkheprure Itnute-Ay, blessed by Amon, Living God on Earth."

Dutifully, the court responded, "Hail, Pharaoh."

With unhurried magnificence, Ay emerged and seated himself on the throne. Determinedly he planted his feet on the heads of bound Nubians and Syrians, captives carved in ebony beneath the cushion of his footstool. Above his head, among papyrus capitals of columns, Nekhbet spread glorious mosaic wings.

After recognizing Nabamon and Horemheb, Ay said serenely, "I see the purpose of this envoy is to bring me the traitor Senumet. Congratulations on having apprehended him, Horemheb. This is an occasion, indeed." Ay's eyes transfixed Senumet. "Egypt shall show you no mercy, Senumet. You shall be dragged through the streets of Thebes and then whipped until you are dead. The execution of this sentence shall take place immediately. Guards! Strip him!"

But no guards stepped to obey his command, which settled into silence like the dying of a river breeze.

Horemheb moved forward. "The guard will not touch the scribe Senumet."

Ay's knuckles whitened over the lions' heads of the throne. "You astound me, Master of the Horse. But I would hear your reasons."

Then Nabamon stepped forward. "Horemheb speaks with the will of the Great God Amon, and Amon declares that the scribe Senumet deserves not chastisement, but acclamation and reward."

"I cannot believe," Ay barked, "that Amon was pleased by Senumet's attempt to deliver Egypt into the hands of the Hittites!"

"But Amon is pleased that Senumet has safeguarded and has brought to him the heiress of the House of Thebes, descended from the line of Ahmose, daughter of the Queen Ankhesenamon."

Ay gave Nabamon a mocking smile. "Did Senumet act the part of Osiris and bring the mummy of a babe to life? Does this heiress have a bloated face and distended extremities? The queen was fruitful only once, and her child was drowned in the Nile. Senumet himself was witness of it, and I have examined the corpse myself."

Senumet spoke up clearly. "The princess Mut-Nodjne is the true daughter of Ankhesenamon the Queen and her father, Pharaoh of Egypt."

"I have examined the document and the tokens given her by the queen to establish her claim," Nabamon affirmed. "Amon approves her legitimacy."

Ay's nostrils flared. His black eyes scathed them with contempt. "Well then, let us rejoice. Let us welcome this princess that Amon proclaims. Where is she?"

Nabamon stepped aside. "Her Highness. Descended from the sacred loins of Ahmose, Thutmose and Amenophis. Heiress of the double crown."

The acolytes ebulliently rolled their snare drums, and Muta stepped into the view of the entire court. Her head high, her gown shimmering, she was bathed in an aureole of innocence and purity. A sigh of awe filled the throne room. Recovering his poise, Ay stood. "Welcome, Daughter. For your welfare, I place you under the protection of the throne."

Nabamon's smooth tones overrode him. "Pharaoh's protection is unnecessary. The princess has wed."

"I nullify this marriage! The princess cannot wed without Pharaoh's consent!"

"Pharaoh cannot dissolve the bonds Amon has sanctified." Nabamon's hand swept around in the direction of the wedding party. "And before these witnesses, who ascribed to the legitimate claim of the heiress, under my hand, Amon has joined the Princess Mut-Nodjne to the Eagle of Egypt, the Protector of the Gods, Horemheb!"

Horemheb smilingly stepped to Muta's side. The throne room erupted in jubilant cheers, and as if the exuberant shouts had dealt him a blow Ay's knees buckled and he appeared to reel. Again, however, he steadied and cloaked himself with pharonic imperative. "Pharaoh who so honors Horemheb would have wished to bless this union. The ceremony shall be performed again in public, and Pharaoh shall declare to Egypt: Horemheb is his heir."

As he beheld Ay, Senumet could not restrain grudging admiration of the devil. Cornered, outmaneuvered, still Ay fought back with wily quick-wittedness, resorting to each gambit that Senumet had predicted to Nabamon and Horemheb. But now Nabamon would trap Ay at last, as the hunter of vipers pins the head of snakes with a forked stick, and Ay would not wiggle away.

"The heir to the double crown stands before you!" Nabamon intoned. "It is Amon's will that you declare him, here, now!"

Ay's jaw clenched and he gritted his teeth. His eyes blazed, but he had no choice. "Horemheb is heir to the double crown," he grimly pronounced.

"It is Amon's will that the reign of Horemheb and his queen begin before this sun has set. Amon declares Horemheb Pharaoh and co-ruler of the Black Earth. Accept it!"

Ay stared incredulously at the chief priest's impassive face. From the presentation of the princess, he had seen the end, and as if his silence could defeat them, he hesitated. Then haltingly, hollowly, he began, "Amon's will be done. Horemheb is Pharaoh." Suddenly he smiled thinly 'With powers to equal my own."

"You have displeased the Great God and all the gods of Egypt. In their wrath, they have withheld the Inundation from the black earth, have withered the crops and have strengthened the arms of Egypt's enemies. It is Amon's will you depart from Egypt and Horemheb rule alone, Pharaoh and Living God!"

Ay's lip curled. His tongue flipped out. He drew himself up to more than royal height and his voice thundered with scorn for the last time. "Chief priest of the great god, is Amon so fickle as to crown and uncrown his servant by the same hand? As high priest of Amon and Living God, I will never step down from this throne unless I rise to sail in the golden barque of Amon! Stab me with your spears—I am ready. And Egypt shall never forget that this throne was stained with blood by an ambitious soldier, the son of peasants, and a plotting priest!"

An ominous murmur rose in the throne room. Over it, Senumet

raised his voice. "*We* are not murderers of Pharaohs. But I charge you, Ay, with the murders of Smenkhare and Tutankhamon, sons of Amenophis! It is you who have stained Egypt's throne with blood."

The throne room shivered with a gasp.

"Horemheb rules alone," Nabamon declared again. "Accept it."

Ay's legs would no longer support him. Heavily he sat down upon the throne. They had stripped him of everything, and his mouth seemed filled with grit. His eyes saw darkness, and from it loomed the memory of Hesen's face, hard with hatred as he forced her to his will on the platform before a thousand celebrants at Akhet-Aten. Was the gall she tasted then as bitter as the gall he tasted now? He speared Senumet with his gaze—there was the man who had engineered his downfall, and he burned Senumet in the inferno of his wrath. This conquering scribe, an upstart peasant whom he had raised with his own hand! Why had he doubted his suspicions? Why had he not had him killed? And even more lacerating was the knowledge that the royal family of Akhenaten had, in the end, beaten him. If the gods did await him on the other side of death, he had damned himself for—nothing. His one satisfaction was that Hesen, unconscious for days on her deathbed, would never know her victory.

"Accept it!" Nabamon demanded once more.

They could stab him a thousand times, Ay thought, but he would never say those words.

"You will remain in Thebes until after the coronation of Horemheb and his queen. You will act and speak as instructed, and then the guard will see to it that Amon's will is done."

Four guardsmen approached the throne. Ay would not allow them to touch him. He managed to stand himself, but the guardsmen finally had to assist him from the throne room or his stumbling steps would have thrown him down.

Servants dashed to carry the news to the Thebans waiting at the gates, while nobles and courtiers broke into swirling and eddying motion, too long restrained, around Horemheb and his bride.

Horemheb signaled two of his lieutenants, who pushed their way through the excited assembly to Senumet's side. However heavily Ay kept Hesen guarded, Ay's sentries would not dare to countermand orders from the Supreme Commander.

As he raced through corridors, the lieutenants at his heels, Senumet heard thunder swell from beyond the palace gates. Thebes had heard the tidings.

Then her door was before him, and before it, four soldiers at attention, crossing their spears to bar his way. The lieutenants barked Horemheb's orders to admit him, and the doorway to his love was opened for Senumet. His heart leaped painfully in his chest. Beyond the entrance was a blackness that seemed impregnable. He rushed inside.

At first he could see nothing. All the brightness of the day had been shut from her chambers. Disoriented by the unnatural night, he gradually became aware of a moaning chant and a thick fog of incense that stung his eyes and throat. He began to discern misty figures, priests and physicians and shadow-servants.

Trembling, he approached her bed, unaware he was holding his breath until he heard hers. Weakness sickened him as he realized that the other sound he heard, rasping, irregular, was Hesen's struggle to breathe.

*At least she lives!* He allowed no other thought until he stood over her.

She lay on her back, her head elevated on a carved headrest. Her face was small and thin. Her open mouth seemed incapable of stretching the tight flesh of her cheeks sufficiently to close. In the glow of the censers, he caught a glitter of her eyes. They were open—she was awake. But her head did not turn when he called her name, and he saw that her eyes did not blink. Her hands, absolutely motionless, had been crossed over her breasts. An amulet rested on the still fingers.

"Hesen!" Loudly. He must make her hear him.

But she did not answer.

The chanting of the priests throbbed with new fervor. A physician laid a hand of caution on his shoulder. He flung it away. Knifed through by terror and rage, he grabbed up the amulet from her hands and hurled it across the chamber. She was not dead, but they had virtually entombed her. He would not let them ritualize her into death.

"Out!" he shouted furiously. "All of you—leave this room!"

The danger in his voice threatened their lives. Instantly they scattered, hundreds of them, it seemed.

"And the incense with you!" Grabbing a silver censer, he sent it crashing at their heels, spilling coals. Servants gathered up the remaining pots and scurried after the priests and physicians.

"Raise the screens!" he commanded.

A single servant was left, and her eyes darted wildly, searching for escape past Senumet who blocked her exit. Helplessly, she burst into tears.

"The screens!"

Blindly she found the ropes that raised one of the thickly woven reed barriers, and light streamed in. The servant ran. Senumet drew up the other screens himself, transforming the chamber into a room of the living. Then he approached Hesen's bed again.

A net of blue veins traced the whiteness of her emaciated hands. The skin of her face was almost translucent in its tautness. Her lips were dry and cruelly cracked, her eyes opaque like painted glass. A groan escaped him. But wait—had her head turned, ever so slightly, toward the sun?

Lifting her, he placed cushions behind her back and head to raise her, and her breathing eased. Relief dizzied him.

"Hesen," he said gently, "is this all the welcome I am to have from my beloved?" Gathering her hands in his, he stared into her eyes, imploring her to see him.

At the sound of weeping, Senumet turned to find Sephy, followed by a slave bearing rose water. Her face distorted by pain, Sephy wordlessly bathed her mistress's forehead until the unstoppable flow of her tears brought Senumet again to the point of rage. "Give me the rose water and begone!" he hissed.

"No!" Sephy cried.

"Then remain in another room. Only I shall touch her! Go—or I shall have the guard carry you away."

Understanding he would not be denied, the old woman retreated to the queen's sitting room rather than be forbidden Hesen's chamber. Still Senumet could hear her weeping.

When the natural darkness of night shadowed the room, he ordered lamps. "Enough to light a feast. I want the room as bright as day!" Servants brought thirty alabaster lamps, light to rival the sun, and departed.

Horemheb summoned him. He would not go.

Muta sent word she would visit her mother. He refused her request.

The night was two hours old when Hesen's body stiffened—and then her limbs were thrashing wildly and she was screaming out in continuous, piercing shrieks of pain and terror. Senumet gripped her like a vise to keep her from flinging herself to the floor. It was all he could do to hold her.

He called to Sephy, whose eyes bulged at the grotesque spectacle. "Find out what this means! Find out what that bastard has done to her!" At last her screaming subsided into terrible gasping breaths and her body relaxed again into torpor. More frightened than he had ever been, Senumet wiped her face and touched his lips to her forehead.

Sephy returned to repeat with distress the whispers she had heard of rape and abuse. Only when Sephy threw her thick arms around his waist and clung to him did he realize that, like a madman, he had been about to bolt to Ay's chambers and strangle the lizard's neck until life was extinguished.

Through that night and the next—and the next—Hesen alternated between stupor and convulsive fits of screaming. Senumet stroked her and called her name, reminding her of their love, hoping his presence would somehow reach through the dark veils that surrounded her. Sometimes she looked at him and he prayed . . . but the reality of him did not penetrate to where she was. Once he heard her mumble, words slurring, "My best dream . . ."

*It is delirium only*, he told himself, *but at least I am there in the shadows with her.*

Five days melted into each other. On the fifth, Senumet's mind was quicksand; scorpions crawled over his skin; voices babbled on the air. His mind and body would endure no more the sleepless punishment he exacted. Against his will, as he sat beside her, his eyes closed.

He slept.

# XXXII

The touch of her hand upon his awoke him.

Her head, on the headrest, was turned toward him, her blue eyes *seeing* him. "Beloved," she whispered on the lightest breath.

Moving from his chair to her bed, he pulled down the coverlet from her body. He slipped his arm around her and drew her up against him. Tenderly he cradled her, pressing her face to his chest. The warmth of her cheek permeated muscle and bone and enveloped his heart. She rested her hand lightly, like a delicate lily, on his shoulder. Although he could not see her face, he felt her smile.

He murmured her name into her hair.

Again he heard, sweetly and faintly, "Beloved."

He did not know he was crying until the lamplight blurred into bright shafts that were cruel to his eyes and he tasted salt on his lips. He knew he could not stop his tears. When they had ceased of their own will and his face had begun to dry, she had returned to sleep, resting limply in his arms.

Gently he laid her on her bed and covered her. He brushed his lips once against hers and then went to awaken Sephy.

*She knew him.*

He felt the necessity, at last, to have himself bathed, shaved and groomed.

In the water of his bath, his body felt buoyant. When he surrendered himself to the slave who would oil him, he watched the man's slick hands move over his muscled body, the body that belonged to her alone.

*She knew him. She would grow well. His body would be hers again.*

Exhaustion fled. His spirits soared.

In the morning, for the first time since he had come to her, she woke naturally to the sun. Again she knew him, and she also knew Sephy, who fed her honeyed broth and a little wine and brushed her hair while Senumet helped her sit. But in her recognition, there was no wonder at how they came to be with her; she asked no questions. She seemed to exist in a timeless place where they had always been by her side.

In the afternoon, she noticed the descent of the sun and called Senumet to her. Touching his cheek she whispered, "I'm sorry, beloved. I must take the evening meal with my sisters. Nefertiti has seen so little of them, and I must see that they behave. But I'll meet you in the Sun-Shade in the morning." She smiled. "Tomorrow we'll have for ourselves . . ."

So. She had returned to days at Akhet-Aten before the horrors had begun to accelerate. To help her regain the years she denied, he would, he decided, revive her memories carefully, suggesting gently, sparing the worst.

Through the following days, everything she said to him came from the past. "Senumet! Don't let Tutu climb that palm. He's so little—it's too tall!" The tree was not too tall, he assured her. "Father Aten! You've come back. They've reported all at Byblos were massacred." He swore never to leave her again. "Call for the chariot. Let's ride on the beach together. I don't care who sees us! Father—Mother—Meritaten—anybody!" He had, he said, already sent word to her driver, the golden chariot was being brought around to the courtyard. At other times he would watch her staring vacantly into space, and then she would turn her eyes to him, bewildered and fearful. Was it too much to hope that she was on the verge of seeing through the years into the present? He could not tell. She continued to dwell in the past, just as her body continued its refusal to gain strength. For one thing he was thankful, however: The dark fits of screaming did not return.

Each day Muta sent Senedjm to Senumet to inquire if today she could see her mother. It had been Sephy's efforts, gathering information from the servants, that had uncovered what had been done with Senedjm: Ay had sent him to work as a laborer in the marble quarries at Aswan in the mountains to the south. Brought back to Thebes, he had been installed by Muta as her majordomo, and Senumet was glad to see the faithful man rewarded for his years of service to the royal family. Each day, by Senedjm, he returned the message that the queen had still not recovered sufficiently. But the day would come soon when Muta would tolerate no more delays, and Senumet knew he must prepare Hesen for her visit. The girl's claim could no longer be swept aside.

After the morning meal, he carried Hesen to the canopy he had had erected on the terrace and laid her under it on a couch. She seemed totally at peace. Perhaps it was time.

"Hesen," he said. "Ankhesenpaaten has been asking for you. Muta wants to see her mother."

She didn't seem to hear him. Then her eyes clouded and her lips began to tremble. Surprisingly, her face became suffused with happiness. "Send Sephy for the nurse. I would have the child brought to me in the garden." Excitedly, she asked him, "Did I tell you what she did yesterday? She tried to draw a horse. Sweet babe! The nurse was shocked I let her have the stylus, but I tell you she tried to draw a horse."

Not knowing what to say, he said nothing, and her brightness faded into agitation. "Where is my daughter? I have some blue beads I want to give her. Find the nurse, Senumet! Father Aten, something has happened to Ankhesenpaaten!"

Embracing her, he assured her the child was safe and he would go for the nurse. Finally, she drifted into sleep.

That evening Senedjm announced that Horemheb awaited Senumet in the anteroom to the queen's apartments. Following the majordomo, he found not only Horemheb, but also Muta.

"Please," Muta begged him. "The coronation is tomorrow. Be there. I need you."

"Be there, Senumet," Horemheb echoed her, "so we may honor you."

Tomorrow. Having reduced his world to Hesen, he hadn't realized, and he almost smiled, for the coronation seemed to him an anticlimactic, trifling affair. As he absorbed Muta, whom he hadn't seen since the day of her wedding, he found she had become very much a queen, wearing her regality with unconscious grace.

"I look at you, Muta, and I have no worries for you," he said quietly. "And you should have none for yourself. As for honor, Horemheb, I would be more honored if you understand: I cannot leave her."

"Shall I see her soon?" Muta asked.

"Sincerely, I hope so," he replied, taking his leave.

At midmorning, drums boomed, cymbals crashed, trumpets blew

fanfares, and waves of cheers seemed to rise from the very stones of Thebes. The sounds of ceremony vibrated in the palace as they filled the city. There was no way for Senumet to mute them.

At the first thunderous timpani and blast of trumpets—for Horemheb and Muta, Senumet thought, emerging from the palace—Hesen stiffened. Her eyes widened. Her recumbent body on the bed became frozen with alarm. With a surge of unexpected strength, she hurled herself into a sitting position and gripped Senumet's arm, her fingers like talons. "Someone has died!" she screamed. "Who is dead?"

At her screams, Sephy came running, only to stand by helplessly while Senumet emphatically swore the trumpets did not announce a death.

"Tell me who!" Hesen cried. "Aten help me! It's *Tutu*!"

"No, Hesen. The drums and the trumpets are for a coronation."

"Tutu!—I have failed him!"

"A coronation!"

Suddenly she was as unmoving as stone. "What coronation?" she demanded. "Ay! Is Ay Pharaoh?"

Heaven help him, Senumet prayed. She was remembering. "Not Ay. You have no need to fear Ay, ever again."

Her fingers gripped his arm tighter still. "What queen?"

"The queen who will be known as Mut-Nodjne. Ankhesenpaaten the Younger, your daughter, beloved."

"What is she doing here? She must never come to Thebes. Ay will—"

"Ay is vanquished. He is imprisoned and surrounded by guards. He can do nothing. Ay cannot harm her. He can never again harm you."

Weakly she appealed to Sephy. "Is this true?"

"Yes, Highness!" Sephy cried out eagerly.

"My daughter . . ." Again she turned to Senumet. "Is she beautiful?"

"As beautiful as her mother. She wants to see you."

"No! *Ay must not know of her!*"

"I have told you. Ay is beaten. *You* have won, Hesen."

Her ragged, shallow breaths began to grow deeper. "You have never lied to me . . ."

"I do not lie now. And you must smile."

She began to relax until her mind fixed on something else. "What Pharaoh?" she rasped. "Ay—she marries Ay? He forces her!"

"Dearest—"

"I must kill him!" She thrashed in his arms.

Pinioning her wrists, he shouted, "Remember, Ay's time is done! Ay is broken."

Her eyes filled with tears, and she whimpered, "I keep forgetting. . . . Who is Pharaoh?"

"Horemheb."

Her mouth stretched wide, and then she burst into peals of hysterical laughter that became racking sobs.

Stroking and kissing her gently, he said, "Horemheb loves and cherishes her, Hesen. He has sworn to take no other wife. She could ask for no finer husband. It is right and good that Muta has wed Horemheb."

She huddled against him until she calmed, and he heard her whisper, "I want to see her."

"Tomorrow."

"No. Today."

"Wait."

"Today!" She pushed herself away from him. "I want to be dressed. Sephy, dress me."

Sephy looked to Senumet for guidance.

"Obey your queen," Senumet said.

She could never wear a sheath—all her clothes would hang on that skeletal form. Finally Sephy wrapped her in a loose blue robe threaded with gold.

"And my face," Hesen commanded. "My hair."

Sephy painted her lightly, for too bright a color would emphasize the pallor of her cheeks. Dissatisfied with Hesen's hair, she suggested a wig and Hesen quickly agreed.

"I want to sit in a chair for her," Hesen requested, and Senumet lifted her weight, which was a feather, onto a cushioned couch. She gripped its arms. She was ready. "Send for her."

Senumet sent a servant to the throne room where Horemheb and his queen were receiving homage. Muta came immediately. She stood in the doorway of the anteroom, her eyes fixed on Hesen. Wordlessly mother and daughter stared at each other, seeing themselves in each other's figure and face; and the floor of the chamber that separated them encompassed time and space, transforming Muta into Hesen, Hesen into Nefertiti.

"Mother," Muta breathed tremulously.

Not Hesen but Nefertiti held out her arms.

Not Muta, but Hesen, in that old, uncertain, impetuous way, rushed across the room and buried her head in her mother's lap, under the benediction of Sephy's gaze, Sephy the bridge of time.

Her hands shaking, Hesen stroked her daughter's hair and touched the uraeus, ran her fingers over the cobra's hood which she herself had once worn. "You are queen," Hesen pronounced.

"As long as I can remember, I dreamed of you," Muta cried.

Mother and daughter clung to each other as if no power on earth could ever separate them again. Their eyes glistened with tears.

Then Hesen's words echoed down the corridors of time. "Always, my daughter, walk with *maat*."

While Hesen slept the next day, Senumet left her apartments for the first time. He made his way through the western wing of the Golden House to a roof terrace which provided a view of the Theban docks, filled with midday bustle. From his vantage point, he waited until he caught sight of the procession for which he watched. Led by a senior guardsman and a yellow-robed priest of Amon, two lines of five soldiers flanked Ay and Tey. Behind them trod two porters carrying the single trunk of belongings Horemheb allowed them, and trailing the porters were two bearers with a litter on which lay the linen-wrapped corpse of Bata, Ay's son, hastily preserved in natron. Five days after Ay had been forced to name Horemheb co-Pharaoh, the priest at Heliopolis had taken sick and died, and Senumet assumed that it was Nabamon, allowing for no risks, who issued the order for poison to be administered to Ay's son. As Ay had dispensed death, so death had been dispensed unto his own.

The procession was unheralded, but still a crowd gathered as Ay was recognized, and Senumet could see, even over the low rooftops that divided him from the wharves, that the people scorned Ay with hostile faces. Some shook their fists at him. His shaven head uncrowned, Ay accepted Tey's arm as they were marched by the soldiers up the ramp onto a freight barge. On its deck, a simple pavilion with rude cotton hangings had been erected for Ay and Tey, and for Bata's body, which was to follow the progenitors of its flesh into exile. The barge would carry Ay and Tey to the Delta, from where they would be escorted across Sinai into the wasteland of Gaza. There, in an encampment of tents, under permanent guard, Ay and Tey would finish their days with bitter memories their only companions, for the guard was under orders not to speak with them or answer them if spoken to.

With long poles, dockworkers pushed the barge away from the wharf. Bata's body carried below deck, Tey in the pavilion, Ay stood alone at the front of the barge. His white-robed form appeared stiff with hopeless anger.

Senumet felt no triumph. There could be no retribution, not even death, to equal the enormous suffering Ay had caused. One man. How could it be that one man's evil vision could unloose so much destruction? That one man could so alter the world through his evil deeds.

Each time Hesen woke, her mind grew clearer. She was rapturously happy. She asked questions that Senumet answered until her translucent, blue-veined eyelids fluttered and sleep again came upon her. Although she struggled to hide her exhaustion, Senumet became more acutely aware of it. She sleeps too much, he worried, and still she grows no stronger. Even Muta's daily visits imparted no real vitality. She would grow stronger, he told himself, when they left Thebes, when they sailed from Egypt. He announced their departure to Horemheb and Muta.

To Hesen, he said, "We'll go where there will be only joyous moments. I'll make you strong."

And she replied, "Yes, beloved."

Horemheb sent to him the chief physician.

"You should not subject the queen to this journey. She cannot survive such a voyage," the physician advised.

"She will not survive here!"

"You risk her life!"

"I must! Once out of Egypt, *with me*, she will fight for her life. She has a brave heart."

And it was fear as much as hope that spurred Senumet to speed preparations for their voyage.

Muta appealed to him. "I've just found my mother—you can't take her away. And you promised you'd stay by me."

"You have Pharaoh." Senumet turned away.

Horemheb entreated: "Stay. Egypt needs you. Shubbiluliuma and his hordes have encamped on Sinai. I need an ambassador. Whom else can I trust?"

"She needs me," Senumet said. "You have no claim. You must keep your word."

And Sephy, too. "She loves Egypt! How can you take her away?"

"We go without you, Sephy. You remain here."

Senumet forced everyone to yield to his passionate will.

On the tenth day of the month Sobek, they would embark in the hour before dawn, when few curious eyes would be open, when they could avoid a formal leave-taking that would tire her and prayers for the beneficence of a god she abhorred.

That morning, on the ramp between the pylons of the Golden House, Horemheb and Muta waited with torchbearers to accompany them. Hesen was carried on a litter by which Sephy walked, holding her hand. Excitement sparkled in her eyes. As they made their way to the royal landing, the litter jarred, and Hesen blanched. Senumet snapped at the bearers.

It was a small barge Senumet had chosen, but it was royal. The oars were mounted in silver. The hull, at the bow, swept upward into the spreading petals of a golden papyrus flower. Although they did not display her cartouche, the sails were of royal purple. On the forward deck, a pavilion had been erected. Golden poles supported linen hangings fine as gossamer, into which jewels were sewn, sparkling in the light from alabaster lamps. The pallet on her couch was of down. Above her couch rose the parchment shade in an ebony holder, chosen by Senumet with care. On the underside the shade was painted with green reeds and small birds darting among them in the style of Akhenaten's court. Next to her couch were the golden chests containing her clothes and jewels. At the Delta, they would transfer to a seagoing vessel, already commissioned.

On the landing, Senumet signaled the bearers to halt. Muta moved forward for her final moment. "I want only to be like you," she whispered.

"I am dust," Hesen replied. "Bless you. I wish you gladness and health. May your reign be free of strife. May it be fruitful."

"I will never forget you, Mother." Muta held back tears.

To Horemheb, Hesen said, "You will be a fine king. You awakened me to Egypt. Egypt will thrive in your care, as will my daughter."

Horemheb dropped to one knee by her litter and kissed her hand. "A safe journey, Highness. Egypt's love goes with you."

Senumet could bear no more of the excessive demands these leave-takings made upon her small reserves of strength. He signaled the bearers to carry her on board, and he followed. Suddenly Sephy charged up the ramp after them, her breasts heaving, tears reddening her coarse features. "I will not leave her," she bellowed stubbornly.

Senumet took angry steps toward her, but Hesen forestalled him. "Beloved, I would speak with Sephy alone."

The bearers lifted Hesen from the litter onto the couch in her pavilion. Senumet himself adjusted the parchment shade over her head and arranged a linen coverlet around her. Then, reluctantly, he allowed Sephy to approach. He stepped from the pavilion but stayed close by, prepared to drag Sephy off the boat if she upset the queen.

Sephy knelt by Hesen's couch and rearranged the coverlet to suit herself. Taking the queen's hand, she implored, "Take me with you. Let me care for you as I have always done. You are my life."

Hesen felt a muscle pulsing in her cheek. Her whole body was sinking into the cushioned depths of her couch and the world was blurring. So tired. Every fiber in her seemed tired of life. But she forced herself to make the effort. She owed Sephy the truth.

"Listen to me," she commanded in a voice so low and in words so oddly measured that Sephy must draw her old face close to Hesen's to hear. "You have always been my dearest friend. You have been to me what no mother, no sister, no husband could ever be. You know I am dying. . . ."

"Highness!" Sephy whispered.

"*I* know I am dying. I have fought the dark jaws of the jackal, and I can fight no more." She stroked the old woman's hand.

"Then let me be with you. Only I can make you comfortable."

"You have a more important charge now. Muta. For my sake, you must stay with her."

"With you," Sephy pleaded. "Who else can brush your hair as I do, or rub you and bathe you? Certainly not *him*!"

"Unfair!" Hesen sighed. "Senumet has done everything for me. Because of him, Ay is exiled, my daughter queen. I would be with him for this short, golden time. Now kiss me, Sephy. Kiss me farewell."

The old nurse's trembling lips touched Hesen's mouth, and then Sephy collapsed into a sobbing heap next to the queen. Senumet summoned a torchbearer from the royal landing to help the old woman from the barge.

He gave the signal. Two crewmen released the ropes that spun off the mooring post in a scraping whine. They scrambled on board just before the ramp was slid away. The purple sails unfurled and billowed in the early morning breeze. The boat eased into the inky blackness over the river that would soon fade into dawn. From the landing, Horemheb, Muta and Sephy watched the lighted pavilion, its curtains of fine gauze softly rippling around the reclining queen, float away from them into the darkness.

Farther along the wharves were stacked high piles of animal skins that had been unloaded the previous day. A black-robed hooded figure melted into the deep shadows of the stacks of dried skins and moved as close to the river as possible without being observed. The corners of his mouth tight with pain, Meire saluted the frail figure of the queen, barely discernible on deck. His lips moved silently. "Blessed Daughter of Aten, whose loving heart and steadfast faith never faltered, farewell."

He had had to come. Seeing her, he knew her life burned low and only an indomitable will was keeping her alive. With her death would end forever the brief Reign of Light. Her daughter, fair and splendid as she was, could never restore it. Akhenaten and his queen might live through Muta but the glory of Aten was eternally lost. His eyes stung and he felt a wrenching loss and desolation. He thought of Senumet, clever and loyal and totally committed to the queen. Would he have the strength to endure when the center of his life was gone? Meire, at least, would spend the days left to him in service to the small band of men still loyal to Aten. He would serve them faithfully, but he would rejoice when his God finally called him. Soon, dear Father, he prayed. Soon.

From the deck, Senumet watched the receding figures in the torchlight on the landing. They dwindled. He raised his hand, even though they could not see his farewell. The first hint of light silhouetted the buildings of Thebes, the palace and the great temple dominating his field of vision, as Thebes grew smaller.

Hesen slept as she forever left Thebes behind her.

Aboard the barque were four crewmen and their pilot and two servant girls, young handmaidens for Hesen. The handmaidens would do for her what no man should. Senumet would do everything else.

He let Hesen sleep without rousing her whenever she would, for he wanted her to husband her strength. But when she woke, he pulled back the hangings of the pavilion so she could watch Egypt, on both sides of the sparkling Nile, unrolling before them.

And as she watched through the days, Hesen met ghosts of herself who had sailed the Nile so many times.

She saw the young girl sailing to Thebes with a chest of magnificent jewels under her bed, forced to act as emissary for Akhenaten, and beating Ay and all of them!

She saw a young princess on deck, watching Horemheb polish his shield and instructing a robust and petulant little Tutu in the use of the bow.

She saw a glorious Nefertiti sweeping into her daughter's pavilion on deck to remind a wayward princess that royalty carried grave responsibilities to which all else must be sacrificed.

"Mother," she whimpered. Senumet reached for her hand. Looking at him carefully and regarding the dark smudges of sleeplessness beneath his eyes, she said, "You are the one who looks ill."

"Dearest, when we get to Crete, we'll both be well."

But Hesen did not want to hear of a Crete she would never see.

On the riverbank, black-robed peasant women gracefully climbed from the river, water jugs on their heads.

"Here," she said to Senumet, "it was here on the river, when you sailed with the royal family from Memphis to Thebes, that you said you wouldn't be my teacher anymore." Because you loved me, she left unsaid.

He laughed. "Always you've had your way, no matter what I've said."

"And now, as always. My deepest wish was to see you again. And here we are. And on the Nile. There can be no greater joy."

With a gentle finger, the sun touched her face and lent her a glow of health she knew Senumet would mistake for improvement.

"You look like the princess I first met, stealing a day away from the court."

"With Tutu," she recalled and grew silent. There seemed to be nothing they could say to each other that wasn't fraught with bitter pain. "My sins sail with me, Senumet," she said at last, thinking of how miserably she had failed in her charge of Tutu.

"You created Muta. And she is more than worthy in her spirit and her loveliness."

She shook her head. "Whatever Muta is, you have made her."

"Not true."

She held up her hand to silence him. "My greatest sorrow is you, my dearest. I ruined your life."

"You have brought me incredible joy." He kissed her hand. "I ask only to be by your side for the rest of my days."

She turned her head away to hide the tears that stung her eyes. To have inspired such love in this man. Oh, she must have been worthy . . . once. Yes.

The villages of Egypt glided by, neat and tended, and men cut the meager harvest with sickles, while women and children gathered up the fallen heads of grain in cotton cloths. Egypt would survive the famine, and Egypt would stave off the Hittites—Horemheb would see to it. But he needed Senumet to help him. And then she knew what she must do, what last part she must play. She must convince Senumet that she accepted her life and her death so he would not spend the years ahead in useless grief.

*Her death.*

The screaming terror of it roared and howled within her. The black, snapping jaws of the jackal filled her with unutterable dread. So unimaginable that the days of her life would end, that she would step from sunlight into eternal darkness, leaving behind a wasted body, flesh to rot from the bone. Oh yes, in the past she had desired and dreamed of death. But not now . . . *not now*. And she could not even reach out to her always love to ease her terror, for it was her terror she must hide from him.

She grew steadily weaker. Death was near, she knew, for already she saw the world from a great distance and felt separated from it, no concern of hers. But her dimming sight could not mistake the stretch of river her barge approached: the high cliffs with their jagged peaks rising from the flowing waters. She knew where they were.

Senumet appeared—oh, even his face and voice receded from her—and said, "Let me draw the curtains of your pavilion, beloved, just for a while."

"I know this river as well as you," she managed, "and there's no need to spare me."

"Please."

"No. I must see it."

He sat beside her, and hand in hand they watched as the barge glided into the vast blue curve of the Nile.

"Remember," she whispered, "it was at this spot that Aten spoke to Pharaoh, and the wind died."

"I remember."

"And Akhenaten was glorious and godlike."

"Don't look now," he begged her.

But she struggled to sit for a better view. Senumet's strong arm supported her. He who had never denied her anything could not deny her this, although it ripped him apart.

It was a lonely and starkly barren site, now, the plain on which the city had stood. Once-golden sand was white and parched. A few stubs of columns remained, and there were some trees, pitifully twisted trunks that would bear neither leaf nor flower. Such a glorious and beautiful city of dreams Akhet-Aten had been—and she watched amazed as it materialized from the twilight and lived again in all of its glory. She felt the peace she had always felt at seeing Akhenaten's city of Aten from the river. His city was truly her home, and she was returning to it. And there she was! Walking along the beach with her sisters, racing with Tutu in his chariot, riding in her father's chariot by the side of the living god, Akhenaten. And there again, alone in her own chariot, its gold flashing—she could hear the hooves of her horses thudding on the beach and feel the breeze whipping her face. And still again, a solitary figure near the river's edge, watching endlessly for a sail that would bring Senumet to her . . .

She sighed deeply as the visions faded. The sterile plain had passed by, and the hills were closing in again, lavender shadows softening their harsh profiles.

She kissed his cheek. "Remember, my love, you brought me my every triumph."

"I have forgotten it already. You must remind me every day."

"The time has come for the truth," she said, as the dusk gathered around them. "You have been blind, beloved."

"To what truth have I been blind?"

"I left Thebes only so that we could have this little time together."

"We shall have all our lives."

"Mine is ending."

"No. I'll make you strong," he whispered.

"I thank Aten for this time. It has been a beautiful, wonderful gift."

He gripped her hands. "You will get well."

She stared into his face, drinking it in, but somehow her eyes looked beyond him. "I will die with my eyes filled with my true lord and my hands in his. And I will die content."

"You can't leave me!" It was a cry torn out of him.

"Return to Thebes, my dearest. Help Horemheb and our daughter." Suddenly she whispered in alarm, "You do believe she's our daughter?"

"I know it," he choked.

"Swear it to me."

"I swear it."

She reached her fingers up to his face and gently wiped his tears. "Don't cry for me, beloved. It is I who should cry for you." She smiled. "Please don't place me in a dark tomb. Immortality, I think, is a wishful illusion."

"No," he protested, for in this moment he must believe in a future reunion. "Your ka shall rise and mine as well. We will walk together through eternity."

She shook her head. "I have seen too much death, too many shriveled bodies. It all ends in oblivion. Promise me a shallow grave at Akhet-Aten, where the warmth of Aten can reach me."

"I promise," he rasped. He would promise anything to quiet her.

She sank back, more exhausted than she ever remembered. "Hold my hand." How strangely difficult it was to get out the words, but he must have heard; she felt the strength and warmth of his fingers enclosing hers. With tremendous effort, she said, "Beloved . . ." She wanted him to lean closer, for she couldn't see his face. The sun was behind him and its light seemed to glow with increasing intensity. Unusual, this sun, when night was falling, and brilliance blurred into radiance or darkness, she couldn't distinguish which. A lightness lifted her as if on a gentle wind. Yes, there was the sun. Its disk beckoned. She looked back and saw the barge . . . and her pavilion . . . and herself on her couch . . . and Senumet by her. . . . "I'm going," she wanted to tell him, "somewhere . . ." But her lips would not move and she could no longer feel the warmth of his hands. Fear opened an abyss. Terror howled.

*I go—I go to nothing! . . . Hold me . . . keep me with you, beloved!*

Color faded. She could no longer find Senumet—no longer see herself . . .

*Please—please . . . a few more moments—hours—a few more days. Not yet, not yet!*

*. . . Not.*

*. . . Yet.*

She sleeps, he thought gratefully.

He studied each glorious line of her face in repose, lingering on those pale, full lips he had tasted, the straight nose, the slender throat, the bosom that scarcely lifted with each shallow breath. She was so frail. The breeze molded her shawl to her breasts and tugged at the pleats of her sheer white skirt. He leaned closer to adjust the shawl, letting go of her hand. Her hand slipped, glanced off the edge of the couch and dangled over the side.

Cold fear engulfed him. Desperately he pressed his ear to her chest, straining to hear the intake of breath, the beating of her heart. He heard nothing.

She was not gone!

She couldn't be gone!

He embraced her and clutched her limp form to his so tightly they seemed one body. He would burn his life into her. Already she was chilled. He would bring warmth back to her. While he held her, she would not go.

But she was gone. Aten's eye had closed on the day, and she had gone with the sun.

There was nothing left for him. Nothing but her body in his arms.

The pilot ordered his steward to light the alabaster lamps and cedar torches. The flames sparked and cast a warm glow on the oiled thwarts, the golden pavilion and the jewels in its hangings, the purple sails taut with evening breezes.

The reign of night was half-spent when the pilot himself climbed to upper deck and entered the pavilion. He touched the man on the shoulder. Very gently he released the man's arms from around the woman, and the man, sensing something was needed from him, arranged the woman lovingly on her couch and drew her shawl around her. Then he stood looking down at her as the wind blew a long lock of black hair across her chest and the flickering light touched her face in a parody of life. The pilot tried to lead Senumet from the pavilion to rest below deck, but the man would not follow. Sinking to his knees, his eyes fixed on the queen, Senumet began a last, loving vigil. While he could, he would never leave her.

The torches and the lamps blazed throughout the night until their allotment of fuel was burned away.

The Aten rose again on the horizon.

Aten's first rays brightened the gold of the papyrus petals on the bow of the barge and the poles supporting the pavilion.

Aten's first rays burnished the gold of her couch.

And for the last time, Aten wrapped the Queen Ankhesenamon in his light.